That Night

GILLIAN MCALLISTER

PENGUIN BOOKS

PENGUIN BOOKS

UK | USA | Canada | Ireland | Australia
India | New Zealand | South Africa

Penguin Books is part of the Penguin Random House group of companies
whose addresses can be found at global.penguinrandomhouse.com.

First published 2021

007

Copyright © Gillian McAllister, 2021

The moral right of the author has been asserted

Set in 12.5/14.75 pt Garamond MT Std
Typeset by Jouve (UK), Milton Keynes
Printed and bound in Great Britain by Clays Ltd, Elcograf S.p.A.

The authorized representative in the EEA is Penguin Random House Ireland,
Morrison Chambers, 32 Nassau Street, Dublin D02 YH68

A CIP catalogue record for this book is available from the British Library

ISBN: 978-1-405-94244-7

www.greenpenguin.co.uk

PENGUIN BOOKS
That Night

Gillian McAllister has been writing for as long as she can remember. She graduated with an English degree before working as a lawyer. She lives in Birmingham, where she now writes full-time. She is the *Sunday Times* bestselling author of *Everything but the Truth*, *Anything You Do Say*, *No Further Questions*, *The Evidence Against You* and *How to Disappear*.

For Holly, who I would absolutely bury a body for

Prologue

'Help me, please help me,' I say into the phone.

'What?' My sister has panic in her voice, her usually muted tone immediately alert. 'What?' The second *what?* is resigned, a full, heartbroken glob of a word, like syrup falling off a spoon.

The line crackles as if paper is being brushed across the mouthpiece, the signal poor. 'Please help,' I say.

It's night-time, but there's still just a hint of lightness at the edge of the horizon where the sun set hours ago, like somebody has torn a seam in the sky, just at the edge there. Otherwise, it's completely black, the air scented with summer hay and the final embers of barbecues. 'Please come,' I add, though I know she will. This is what family means. This is what our family means anyway.

She doesn't say anything back, but that silence contains her agreement, I know it does.

I move my gaze away from the sky and stare downwards, lighting up the ground with a torch which illuminates dust motes dancing in the air.

I slowly run the torch over it. Over the body.

1.

Cathy

Cathy only answers the phone call that comes in the middle of the night because she is awake, working. Chasing up bloods for a Labrador that she's concerned about. The results are already late, and the unreliable holiday Wi-Fi keeps cutting off just as she tries to send the email.

Frannie. Slide to answer. Cathy's eyes flick to the top of the screen to check the time. It's 1.25 a.m. The room is completely dark around the blue bubble of light the phone creates. All she can see is her sister, calling her in the small hours. Calling Cathy because she knows Cathy will be alone, because Cathy is always alone, whether on holiday or at home.

She sits up in the bed and swipes to answer. The sheet falls away from her. She's wearing pyjamas even in the Italian heat. It seems somehow wrong to sleep naked. That particular luxury, for Cathy, is reserved for the future, she hopes, with some as yet unknown man.

'Help me, please help me,' Frannie shouts as soon as Cathy answers. Electricity shoots across Cathy's chest and down her arms.

'What? What?' Cathy says. Sweat forms on her upper lip and between her breasts.

'Please help me,' Frannie says.

'Where are you? Are you safe?'

'Please come. I'm on the road. Turn right off the track road and then left. Half a mile, tops,' Frannie garbles.

Cathy waits. For Frannie to start making sense.

'It's him. The man from the market,' Frannie says, and then rings off.

Him.

Shit.

Cathy gets out of bed and starts scrambling around for clothes to throw on. She finds a pair of pink shorts she bought in Verona a couple of days ago and pulls them on, the price tag scratching against her lower back.

Why didn't she stay on the line? Cathy tries to call back, but it rings out.

She rams her feet into her dusty flip-flops and grabs her bag. As she leaves the silent villa, not thinking to wake anyone, the closing of the large wooden door behind her sounds like a gunshot in the night.

The outskirts of Verona are completely black at this hour. Even after a week and a half, Cathy still isn't used to it. Struggling to see her own feet as she walks.

The only light comes from her bedroom window in the villa behind her. It projects a neat rectangle of light on to the patio. And then: nothing, like she might be at the edge of the world.

Frannie sounded so scared. She tries to call again, but this time it goes to voicemail. Maybe she is exaggerating. Cathy hopes so. She's always enjoyed the drama of Frannie's hyperbole, the way she tells a great story. She's the family dreamer. 'There were literally fifty dogs in the waiting room today,' she once said. She's the receptionist at their family veterinary practice. She had refused to concede when Cathy probed. 'Yeah, *actually* fifty,' she'd said, and Cathy had thrown her head back and laughed. 'You must have had to sit some behind the reception desk,' she had said, while Frannie nodded emphatically.

Cathy rushes, the long, tough grasses whipping and snapping around her ankles like snakes, muttering pointless prayers out loud. Please be okay. Please don't be hurt, or frightened. As she reaches the end of the drive, she turns and sees headlights in the distance.

It must be their hire car, the Land Rover none of them likes driving. 'It feels like a *bus*,' their brother Joe had said on the first day.

She breaks into a proper run down the road. Right and then left, just like Frannie said. *It's him. The man from the market.*

It's him.

Cathy's pace slows when she sees the silhouettes. She would know them anywhere: her siblings. Joe, standing by the Land Rover, his hands on his hips. And Frannie, kneeling down, her hair and long limbs illuminated by the headlights. She is so beautiful, has always been so. A wide nose. Cat eyes. A mane of dark, shiny hair.

Why is she on the floor? Cathy stares, then takes a breath, just one. She breathes it out as slowly as she can. This is ... she stares at the shadows and the lights. A sweep of fear covers her shoulders. She starts to go cold.

She knows, somehow, that if she walks forwards, something is going to happen.

Joe has evidently just arrived too, from his end of their large, shared villa, and he paces across the lights, in and out of shadow, like a flickering bulb. Cathy wraps her arms around her middle. A bad feeling settles over her, like she is being watched. A small, unsavoury part of her is disappointed that Frannie called Joe before her. Cathy would certainly not call Joe first in a crisis – she might not call him at all.

She turns on the torch from her phone and shines it along the pale, dusty ground in front of her. Around them are the smells of Verona: dry heat, parched grass. It's been the hottest July on record. They had to buy after-sun most days. They've been through bottles and bottles of it. All of Cathy's clothes are oily at their hems.

She can hear only the car's engine and the cicadas.

Cathy moves towards them and sweeps the torch slowly over Frannie, who is still kneeling. And that's when she sees it.

Frannie is leaning over, staring at the ground. Cathy stops walking but can't stop looking at Frannie. She has something – a t-shirt? – in her hands. As Frannie stands up, Cathy realizes, stunned, that she's taken off her top, that she's in just her bra.

In the glare of the headlights, Frannie lifts up her hands. Red drips run down her wrists. Her stomach is streaked with blood. It's dried, burgundy, the colour of red wine. She is a terrible tableau. Nausea rises up through Cathy. 'Fucking hell,' she whispers to nobody.

Joe is leaning over her now. Frannie extends her hands to Cathy and shouts: 'Help me.'

The headlights are a Venn diagram of light, a portrait of her sister, and a body lying at her feet.

2.

Joe

Joe – highly strung, totally mad, actually – has always had bad dreams, and this must surely be one of them.

What the fuck, what the fuck, what the fuck, he is thinking as he arrives in front of the car and stares at his sister. She is kneeling on the ground. He can see each knot of her spine, illuminated in the headlights in alternating patterns of shade and light. She's too skinny. Always has been. He used to make her snacks after school, cheese on toast, yoghurts with nuts and berries. Anything fattening. They called it her second lunch.

'What . . .' he says, but his sentence ends there, like a match that fails to strike. He shakes his head. He can't believe what he's seeing. A body. 'What the fuck!' he whispers. 'What the fuck!'

'Help me!' Frannie shouts over her shoulder to him. In the distance, he can see the pinprick of Cathy's torch. Thank God, he thinks. She'll know what to do. He doesn't. Joe is a panicking kid in a man's body, it sometimes feels like. Cathy may be shy, but she's cool in a crisis.

'I hit him,' Frannie screams to both of them. 'I hit him with the car.' Cathy's torch beam wavers as she runs towards them, leaving tracks in the night air like a sparkler. 'It's the man from the market.'

'What?' Joe says. He can't stop looking at the man lying

in front of her. His skin is both bloodied and waxy, smears of red against the grey.

Joe cautiously approaches Frannie, even though he doesn't want to. Tears have left clear tracks in the blood on her face. A smear of snot sits underneath her nose. He wants to turn away from it, run back to his villa, and to Lydia. Away from this – this grotesque chaos.

It feels like he's walking through water that won't part in front of him. He tries to step forward, but he can't. He forces himself to look at the person lying on the ground. Tall, slim – his hip bones are visible. Frannie's lifted up his shirt. His torso is bleeding. His glasses are cracked.

He's very obviously dead.

Most of the Plant family are vets, including Joe and Cathy, and death is obvious to vets.

There's so much blood. Pints and pints of it. He begins to panic. He's usually fine with blood, but not like this. He tries to slow his breathing. It's a panic attack, he tells himself. Not uncommon for him, but not quite like ones he's had before either.

He gets out his phone as Cathy has and shines his torch across the road. The blood shimmers back like petrol. There's so much of it. Joe tries not to gag. It smells fetid, both metallic and rotten, like just-turning food.

He turns to look at his sister, in a begging position in the road. 'What the fuck's gone on?' he says.

'Please help,' she says. 'Don't be –'

'Don't be what?'

'Just help me,' she says, through tears. Frannie hardly ever cries. She's sunny and messy and imaginative and loves buying too many clothes on eBay. She isn't a crier.

Something deep and familial rises up suddenly through him. He felt it when Frannie fell off a swing on to her back when she was three, and was winded for ten whole seconds, the longest of Joe's life. When she choked on a sweet and Joe thumped her hard between her shoulder blades and she coughed it right up. The first time Frannie went out as a teenager and Joe waited up for her, although even their mother had gone to bed. He still remembers it now: the ticking of the grandfather clock in their hallway, the hum of the fridge. And the relief as Frannie's key turned in the lock.

And, of course, it reminds him of Rosie.

'I hit him – I hit him.'

'I can't – *how*?' he says.

Joe kneels down next to the body. Cathy joins him, but she's just looking, silently. He wishes he had her cool head. He and Cathy recently operated together on a greyhound and she spent at least a minute, after they'd opened him up, just looking. Not rushing. Just gathering information, in that way that Cathy does.

'Frannie,' he says, the word exploding out of him like a cough.

'I hit him on his side,' she says, gesturing. 'It was my fault. It was my fault. It's the man from the market. If we try to stem the bleeding, we . . . we just need to stop the bleeding, then he'll be okay, he'll be okay,' she begs them.

Joe glances sharply at Cathy.

'Hold your t-shirt to the wound,' Cathy says. 'Tight as you can.' Her face is inscrutable.

She moves towards the body. Her long hair is piled on the top of her head. She is a less beautiful version of

Frannie. Thicker set. Features slightly distorted somehow, or perhaps they only look so compared to Frannie's. Joe feels guilty every time he thinks it, but it's true.

Cathy peers at the body. 'That's a glancing wound,' she says. 'He's bleeding a lot for something like that.' She reaches to take his pulse.

'He'll be okay, won't he?' Frannie says.

'How fast were you going?' Joe asks. He thinks he's going to be sick. Sweat has broken out across his forehead and his stomach is rolling over and over, like a rough ocean. His sister has hit somebody and there's blood everywhere. And now – now it is his problem too. He's got to help her.

'Barely,' Frannie says, but Joe's forgotten what he asked. God, he wants a cigarette, for the first time in months. An old vice of his, he's mostly quit, save for holidays, treats and times of stress, which amounts to, well – almost all of the time, actually.

'Have you called an ambulance?' Cathy says to Frannie, kneeling over the body.

'Has he got a pulse?' Frannie asks. 'It will be fine, won't it?'

'How have you not taken a pulse?' Joe says. He leans over, his hands on his thighs, breathing heavily. Stomach acid sloshes up his oesophagus. Get it together, he tells himself. 'Where's the ambulance?'

'There isn't one, okay?' Frannie shouts. 'I haven't called one.'

'Why?' Cathy says. She draws the word out in shock.

'I . . . I called you two, instead.'

'We're not doctors.' Joe raises his head as he says it.

'We're not fucking doctors, Fran,' he almost whispers, turning his head to the side and looking into the distance.

'We don't have anything,' Cathy says. 'Adrenaline, bags of blood . . . look – you need to –'

Frannie holds up a hand. 'Please just help,' she says. 'If we save him – if he's fine – then . . .'

Cathy starts CPR, though she must surely know it to be pointless, and Joe joins in. He takes the heart while she straightens the head, the way they have with animals before. The body is cool beneath his fingertips. He darts a look at Cathy, who doesn't meet his gaze. He stares back down at it in the gloom. A dead man.

He pumps at the man's chest, his fingers just a few inches from this stranger's heart.

Cathy checks and opens the man's airway, a quick finger swabbing around inside his mouth.

'How did you hit him?' Joe puffs.

'Turn the car engine off,' Cathy says to Joe. 'I can't hear myself think.'

It takes Joe two attempts. The world goes dark, pierced by a single upwards beam from Cathy's phone. Cathy puts her ear to the man's mouth in the silence. 'How long has he been here?' she asks Frannie.

'He was right in my path, I just turned without thinking –'

'How long ago?'

'Half an hour.'

A beat of silence.

'What? What've you been doing? In all that time?' Cathy says.

'Half a fucking hour!' Joe shouts, walking over to them and going back to the chest compressions.

Cathy puts her mouth over the man's. She spits, licks her lips, then resumes.

She takes off her own t-shirt. 'Use this one to stem the bleeding,' she says to Frannie. She passes her the t-shirt. 'Yours is saturated.'

He's not the right temperature, Joe thinks, as his hands pump at the man's chest. The Verona night air is warm, at least twenty degrees, and the skin against his hands is moist from it. But the man isn't hot. He is slightly cooler than he should be, like a doll.

Frannie reaches for the man's wrist with the other hand. 'I can feel a flickering,' she says hopefully, and Joe grabs his other arm.

'It's your own pulse,' he says, after a few seconds. 'In your fingertip. Because you're frightened. I'm sorry. There's no pulse.'

'Keep going, then,' Frannie says hysterically.

'I *am*.'

Joe is staring at the body as he pumps away. Even if he gets the heart going again, it would be useless. He will be brain dead. Half an hour.

It's futile.

He sits back on his heels, looking at Frannie. All three siblings' hands are covered in blood. The man's body is stamped with their red fingerprints.

Cathy breathes into the man's mouth, then listens again. After two more breaths, she must come to the same conclusion as Joe, because she stops too. 'I'm sorry,' she says. 'I'm so sorry.'

'No, no,' Frannie says. She sits cross-legged, just as she did when they were children, her head in her hands, one still holding the wrist of the body to her face like a comforter. Frannie, the baby of the family. 'No, please, Cathy – Joe. Please keep going,' she says.

'He's cold,' Cathy says quietly. 'He's lost a lot of blood. His heart isn't responding.'

Frannie is shaking and shaking her head, over and over. 'No,' she starts saying. 'No – don't say it, Cathy, keep going, keep going.'

'He's dead,' Cathy says. She looks to Joe for confirmation.

'I'm so sorry, Fran,' he says. He reaches for her, but she doesn't respond, her head still in her hands.

'I was on the wrong side of the road,' Frannie says. 'I forgot. I forgot they drive on the right here.' She drops her head towards the body like a condemned woman. Joe stares at her, aghast. Cathy closes her eyes. 'I'll go to prison,' Frannie says in a voice so quiet Joe has to strain to hear her.

He looks at Frannie. Then at the body.

He knows the man is dead. But what he hadn't quite pieced together is that this means his sister is a killer.

3.
Cathy

Cathy's whole body starts to tremble. She's gone cold, out here in the hot, suffocating night.

'We – I . . . the policeman saw us arguing with him at the market,' Frannie says. 'They'll assume . . . they'll think . . . please tell me what to do.'

'I can't,' Cathy says.

'If I call anyone now,' Frannie says. 'I mean – I'll go to prison, won't I? No – no. This can't be true. Is it?' she implores them.

Cathy's eyes become wet. She blinks.

Joe's still sitting, staring into the distance.

Frannie is wiping her nose on her forearm. Something about it is so raw, so primitive, from her usually glamorous sister, who only last month drove two hundred miles to fetch a vintage vase that she just had to have.

Cathy is thinking, suddenly, against her will, about DNA. Fingerprints. Hairs. Fibres. Skin cells. They're all over this body, this crime scene.

'Right,' Joe says softly. 'That policeman. The one who thought you were . . . giving him a hard time.' He looks at Frannie, then despondently down at the body. 'They're tough here.'

'The police?' Cathy says.

'Yeah,' Joe says, apparently not feeling the need to

explain. Cathy stares at him expectantly. She knows what happened with Frannie, obviously. But not Joe.

'There was a thing in a bar on the first night,' Joe says. 'This guy cracked on to Lydia.'

'So . . .'

'Well,' Joe says, and Cathy's sure she can detect a blush. 'You know.'

'You hit him?'

'Might have,' Joe says. He looks away from her. He's always been this way. Quick to anger, then embarrassed by it, cagey about things he's done. He would never hurt anybody he cared about, they have always told themselves.

The ground is warm underneath Cathy's legs. She stares at her sister. 'I have to call an ambulance,' Cathy says.

'No – no! We can't, we can't,' Frannie cries, her voice ragged, hoarse in places, phlegmy in others.

'What are you doing?' Cathy says in the quiet. She can barely make out her sister's features in the gloom, but she knows her so well. She knows all of her moods. Her sunny resignation when her latest relationship ended. 'Oh, sod it, I'll have a gin and forget about him,' she'd laughed, her nose wrinkling attractively, but how, later, she texted Cathy from the bath, asking if there was something wrong with her, if she'd ever find somebody, if maybe she'd be alone with Paul, her son, forever.

Now Cathy can imagine her expression, even though she can't see it – streaked eyeliner, red nose. Her holiday freckles are out.

But, for once, she doesn't know what to say.

'Will an ambulance be able to help him?' Frannie says. She comes down to Cathy's level, right on to the ground, like an animal.

'No,' Cathy says. 'Not now.'

'And if I do call one – what's going to happen to me?' Frannie's hands are twisting together. Her shoulders are hunched. Cathy is aware of some dim notion that she will remember this conversation for the rest of her life. 'What's going to happen to Paul?' she says.

Cathy stares at the car. At the body. Thinks of the policeman who witnessed Frannie arguing with this man earlier today. Thinks of Joe's encounter. The police will think they're trouble, the Plant family.

'I don't know,' Cathy says. 'I don't know.'

'I can't call one. I can't.'

'We could say it was me,' Cathy says desperately. Tears start to clog her throat.

'But you were at the market too. They'd infer . . . that it wasn't an accident.'

Cathy drops her head into her hands, massaging her forehead. She can't think in these circumstances. Her brain isn't working. 'We could say we found him,' she mumbles. 'By the roadside?'

'It's too late,' Frannie says. 'It's too fucking late. It's been too long. Our car – the hire car's dented. And it's *hired*. We can't just get rid of it. I'm fucked. I'm fucked.' She looks at Cathy and then at Joe, who has his red hands over his face. 'I'm so fucked. Please do something. Please help me. Please help Paul.'

Cathy's mind races. A few feet away, Joe is finally sick. A fountain of *vino rosso* adding to the blood, to the mess, on the dirt road. The smell drifts over to her – acidic, tart – and Cathy thinks she might throw up too.

'Paul's got *only* me,' Frannie says. 'I mean – we have to . . . to cover it up.'

They sit in silence for a few minutes.

'This is fucked,' Joe says eventually, wiping his mouth on his t-shirt. 'You cannot seriously be asking us to – to what? What're you saying, Fran?' His eyes swivel towards hers.

'I'm not saying anything,' Frannie cries. 'I'm saying if I – or you – call anyone now, I'm going to go to prison and leave Paul alone for a decade. Probably more.'

Cathy looks again at the body. Their fingerprints are all over it. On his skin. On his clothes. And inside the wound on his side. Their DNA mingling, binding them to this injury, this accident, forever. This man in front of her isn't only a body. He is a body of evidence too. Cathy's shoulders come out in goosebumps.

She begins to shake, despite the hot night. She meets Frannie's eyes. They're wide, like a panther's, only the whites visible in the dark night. 'What are you saying?' Cathy whispers.

A sad expression arranges itself across Frannie's brows.

'I can't do this,' Joe says. 'I can't do it.' He stands up and turns away from them. 'Not even for you,' he throws over his shoulder at Frannie.

'Oh, walk off, why don't you,' Frannie says. 'Go punch something? Will that help?' She glances back at Cathy, who avoids her gaze. It's not the right time to bring up Joe's temper.

'You've killed someone,' Joe screams. Cathy and

Frannie sit in shocked silence while his words echo around the Verona countryside.

Cathy looks at her, now that she is close enough to see her properly. She was wrong about the expression. There aren't any tears, no red nose.

Joe begins fussing with the car, shining his torch light on to it and rubbing at it.

'I want to go back,' Frannie says, closing her eyes and looking heavenwards. 'I want to go back to when it never happened.' The tears come now, leaking sideways out of each eye. 'Please let me go back.' She looks straight upwards, into the navy-blue sky, scattered with stars by God's careless hand.

'I can't,' Cathy says, her voice hoarse, thinking of little Paul, innocent Paul, who loves cheese sandwiches, Party Rings, and his mother.

They sit in silence for a few seconds.

'We have to bury his body,' Frannie says. She wipes at her cheek and leaves another bloodstain across it. It's crusted and dry. She meets Cathy's eyes in the gloom. 'We have to bury the body.'

4.

Now

Jason's Office, early February, 5.00 p.m.

It's the coldest February since records began, apparently. It's late afternoon, in Birmingham city centre. Corporation Street is a white-out, the air dense with a thick winter mist, the pavements frosted, scuffed in places with black footprints.

It's just before five. Paul will be at nursery until half past, then to Mum and Dad's, where he will be handed back to me without fanfare, without conversation, since they found it all out.

A tram goes by as I walk up Corporation Street. It's lined with trees that haven't had leaves on them for months. The tail end of winter that seems to drag on like a flatline.

I press the buzzer that perfectly fits the shape of my fingertip and soon I'm on the second floor and sitting opposite Jason, who has his legs crossed at the knee. He has made us both tea, which surprised me.

I cradle mine, even though it is burning my hands. Outside his cocooned room with his two electric heaters and his books, I can hear the muted conversation of a colleague of his, and I'm momentarily reminded that this isn't Jason's life: it's only his job, something he leaves in the evenings and doesn't think about until the next morning. Maybe.

'How's your week been?' he says to me. He has dark hair and a greying beard, like a wolf. He fiddles absent-mindedly with the earring he wears in his left ear. This is how Jason operates. Heavy, professional conversations dressed up casually. He doesn't believe much in convention. He chews gum in our sessions and makes too many drinks, leaving teaspoons scattered on the desk where his *illegal kettle*, as he calls it, lives. But his brain is lightning-fast. When I mention small details, his eyes narrow, and, a little while later, I find that we are discussing them again, going in at a new angle that he has orchestrated without my knowing.

'All right,' I say. He sips his mug of tea, not taking his eyes off me, not filling the silence. 'Tough, I suppose. Like every week,' I add, staring at his wall of books. The room smells of them. That old, papery, dusty smell. There seems to be no arrangement whatsoever. Some are back to front. Some lie on their sides along the tops of others. Letters and postcards and flyers are tucked in beside them.

'You?' I say, and Jason gives a little laugh out of the side of his mouth.

'Yeah, had better,' he says. He checks his watch discreetly. I always see him at five o'clock, and he always accompanies me out into the foyer and leaves with me, heading off in the opposite direction, at ten to six, no matter the weather, no matter how busy he is. I have no idea where he goes, but I do know that it isn't the train station. He once cryptically referred to it as a *long-standing appointment*.

'I have been thinking a lot about Verona,' I say. He reaches for the tea again, downs half of it in a gulp. It's funny the clues and signs you spot in a professional relationship. I have no idea if Jason has a partner, a child even, but I know the sound he makes when he gulps too-hot tea. I can tell that he only irons the parts of his shirt that will be on show.

I like this appointment slot at the moment, because the sun sets during it. I go in in the light and emerge into the darkness, which seems fitting somehow.

Jason raises his eyebrows at me. 'What element of it?' he asks, his expression open.

'I guess – if I could have stopped it,' I say quietly. 'I *should* have stopped it. I don't mean the crime. I mean – the cover-up. My siblings' cover-up.'

Jason looks beyond me, out of the window, and on to the busy city below. A bus hisses as it pulls away into the mist, disappearing almost completely. Two pigeons are on the windowsill, close enough for me to see their gnarled toes, despite the spikes built there to deter them. The sky is beginning to darken at the edges.

'We all know,' Jason says, fiddling with the handle of his mug, 'that looking backwards leads to sadness, and forwards to anxiety. All we've got is now.'

I feel my shoulders relax, and take a breath, the air pushing out my tense stomach. 'I just – I just don't know,' I say, ignoring his advice. He doesn't labour the point, merely sits there listening, as he is paid to do. 'There were so many forks in the road, and I don't know –'

'Talk me through one of them,' he says. 'Your thought process.'

'The piece of paper we found on Will. William.'

'Yes. But, Fr –'

'Nobody knew how significant it would become,' I interrupt. 'And I just keep thinking – over and over – about the could-have-beens. If only this, if only that . . .'

My voice catches as it trails off. 'Anything but – be here, really. We made so many mistakes.'

'I know,' Jason says quietly. 'I mean – of course you did. I'd be worried if you hadn't. Look,' he says, then stops, appearing to think. 'To stay in the present – could you – can you think of Paul?'

I close my eyes. Paul. He's looking more and more like Joe every day. 'Living up to his middle name,' Joe said to me, years and years ago. In another life. Before Verona. Sometimes, if I bring Paul very close to me, it is as though I am looking into my brother's smiling eyes. Brown, straight lashes that point downwards, heavy lids. I almost expect a wisecrack, a flash of quick irritation. Things that belong to Joe and only Joe.

A ginger-haired girl and a woman who is obviously her mother walk by on the street outside. I stare at them. She's maybe eight. Old to be holding her mother's hand. I wonder if Paul will hold my hand when he's eight. I can't imagine him at eight. He is still so little. Cheeks the colour and texture of fresh, warm peaches. Folds of fat around his elbows and wrists.

'I offload to you,' I say to Jason. 'I don't let Paul know about it. About why we're all estranged. About where everyone is. I don't think he will remember – you know. I don't think Paul will remember those days when we all worked together and lived in a row of three cottages.'

I close my eyes and can remember them immediately. Rendered white on the outside. Ivy around the windows. Beams above that creaked in the winter rain and winds. Vibrant gardens that smelt of florals.

'I know.' Jason reaches to straighten a paper on the table in front of us. 'But maybe that's for the best.' He smiles at me warmly, and the weather seems to thaw outside, just slightly.

5.

Then

Joe

Joe's mouth tastes acrid, like he's swallowed poison. His limbs are trembling.

'What else are we supposed to do?' Frannie says. Joe wishes she would stop asking him questions. He doesn't usually mind. Mostly, it's charming. 'So,' she had said right before their holiday, arriving in work wearing a kimono, 'how long until you send me home for wearing this?'

'Five minutes,' he'd said.

Frannie had thrown her head back and laughed. 'But I'll still do the job! And look *lovely*.'

God, she could make him laugh with her verve and her randomness. A fucking kimono.

But nobody is laughing tonight.

'I am not burying a body,' Joe says.

'Neither am I.' Cathy's voice is tight.

He runs a hand through his hair. It's still snarled from sleep. He doesn't know what they're supposed to do, but what he does know is that nobody is calling the police.

He has downplayed what happened in the bar on their first night here. He and Lydia had headed gallantly into Verona as soon as their flight landed. One of the many things he loves about Lydia – apart from the fact that she's fucking funny – is her willingness to embrace life, to squeeze experiences out of it like fresh orange juice. They'd stood on a terrace outside a restaurant, the smell

24

of garlic and candle wax on the breeze, the softly illuminated arches of the Verona Arena across the street from them. Lydia's legs were long and lean and bare, and she had on the perfume she only ever wore on holiday, suffusing him with good-time memories.

But then it had turned sour. A sleazy man, Vespa helmet under his arm, had brushed past Lydia. Joe had watched, eyes like saucers, as his hand cupped Lydia's bum, just like that, as though it was his to touch and hold however he liked. Joe was squaring up to him without a second's hesitation.

A weird kind of pleasure accompanies Joe's temper, though he'd never admit it to anybody. It's like popping a champagne cork. He felt complete relief as his shoulders thrust forwards, as his fist connected with the man's cheek. Just one punch, a pretty light one, a telling-off. Two animals would do the same. The man had invited him outside and Joe, still full of testosterone and that pleasure-pain, had followed. Somewhere in the dimness behind him, a blur of heady-smelling plants and fairy lights puncturing the night, he was aware of Lydia protesting, but that part of him, his sensible brain, wasn't in charge.

Two Polizia di Stato stood outside, smoking cigarettes and laughing. The man had led Joe to them, shown them the mark on his cheek. Joe had thought they'd brush it off when he explained, but they didn't. Instead, *they* squared up to *him*. Their threats weren't only physical, not only evident in their large chests, their huge hands. They said they could arrest him *easily*, their lilting English feeling sinister in the hot night. They offered to take him for a chat. One of them gestured to a nearby alleyway.

Joe had backed away, suddenly frightened. And, that night, the first night of what was supposed to be their relaxing holiday, he had drawn his knees to his chest while Lydia slept, and gritted his teeth at what a dickhead he was. Why couldn't he have left it? Why could he never take the moral high ground?

What is he going to tell Lydia? She is already still mad at him about that first night, even though it's been a week and a half since it happened. And now he's left her sleeping, unknowingly in charge of Paul.

'Tell me what else to do,' Frannie says desperately.

Joe tries to slow his breaths. Her voice. His sister's voice. It does something to him. He used to read to her, she on his lap, when they were both little. A child holding a child. She never wanted to read the same book twice. He made sure they had different ones out of the library each week, their plastic covers sticking to each other in the bag when he unpacked them. Their parents didn't care, let him get on with it, and he stepped willingly into the patriarchal role.

'Just let me think,' Cathy says. She cups her hands around her eyes, like blinkers, her elbows on her knees. 'Be quiet.'

Joe relaxes into himself for a minute. Cathy will figure it out. He stares at his flip-flops, put on unknowingly not even an hour ago, before this nightmare began. He wiggles his toes. He is here. He is grounded. Breathe in and out. In and out. They will sort it. Nobody will go to prison. A panic attack cannot last forever.

'If the police get hold of this body, we will be implicated,' Cathy says eventually, her hands still curled around the sides of her face, but now looking directly at him. A light breeze moves its way between them. He catches a whiff of sun-cream.

'Not necessarily,' he says, trying to be useful. What would his father have done? He tries to channel him as he used to be rather than as he is now. Authoritative Owen. Way more like Cathy than like Joe. 'If we all backed Frannie up. If we all said, I don't know – that he walked out in front of the car from nowhere . . .'

'What, tell it to the policeman who gave me a fucking warning?' Frannie says.

'You and me both,' Joe snaps.

Think. Think. Joe tries to remember everything he knows about DNA. Hardly anything. He rubs at his forehead. He's been doing routine operations for ten years, pigeonholed into it because of his steady hand. And his poor bedside manner, Frannie had once said with a smirk. But it's true that he is better off doing the cutting, the anaesthetics, spaying, removal of hairbands and underwear that Labradors have eaten. He drags a finger through the dust in front of him. The line he draws is perfectly straight.

'I'm pretty sure they will be able to tell what time he died,' Cathy says. 'And that you were here . . . did you touch him? The wound? Right after?'

'Yes,' Frannie says.

'It's something to do with how your DNA mingles with his blood, I can't remember, I don't know . . .' Cathy says.

Joe stares at the body. Its eyes are open. Mouth going from slack to stiff, like cooling candle wax. There's a perfect oval thumbprint on his naked torso. Cathy's or Frannie's or his own, he can't tell.

'You're right,' Joe says eventually. 'Plus the car is probably on some CCTV camera somewhere. Where were you going?' he says to Frannie.

'I wanted wine from that little all-night place, you know?' Frannie says quietly. It sounds so trivial next to the body. Fucking wine. His hands have begun to shake again. They're cold and clammy. He bunches them into fists. He needs some sugar and some sleep.

'Is he getting rigors?' Joe says. He directs this to Cathy.

She immediately reaches for his feet, clad in white trainers. A hand around his black socks, she moves his ankles from side to side, then shakes her head. 'Not yet.'

But he will. Soon. And then his blood will begin to settle in the parts of his body that sit the lowest – his back, his elbows, the backs of his knees. He will begin to smell. That sweet, rotten-egg smell Joe comes across very occasionally, when somebody brings in a long-dead animal. Panic spews up through him. He'll never be able to work again.

He gets out his phone. 'I'm calling the police,' he says. 'What's the number?'

'It's 112,' Cathy says quietly.

Frannie rounds on Cathy. 'How could you do this to me?' she says. 'Now is not the time to be good, Cathy!' Joe winces. Cathy won't like that, but it's true. She *is* good, and controlled, and remote, at times too. She's never had a relationship, to his knowledge.

He dials 112 on his keypad, and Frannie lunges for his phone, batting it out of his hand. 'What the fuck?' Joe shouts. The phone lies face down, the soil and the blood bleached to a thin sanitized stripe around it by its light.

'If you call the police, I will go to prison for decades,' Frannie shouts. She sits back down on the ground, puts her head in her hands and begins to sob.

'Stop it, Joe,' Cathy says.

'Who was I supposed to call?' Frannie says, looking up at him. 'If not you?'

The pleading sentence, her huge wet eyes. He cannot resist. He was there for her when she laboured, alone, with Paul. He brought her whatever she wanted – and that was a *lot*. Iced water, a popsicle, a box of crackers she ate between contractions, and then – afterwards – a flame-grilled Whopper from Burger King that took him a forty-minute round-trip to get. Nobody is there for Frannie like Joe is.

Cathy is biting the skin around her thumbnail, staring at Frannie, her eyes wide.

Frannie passes him the phone, above her head, not looking at him. 'But sure, do it.'

'I . . .' Joe says, hesitating, but he takes the phone. Cathy stares at the transaction, then at the lit-up rectangle in Joe's hands. He looks at Frannie, and his resolve to do the right thing splinters to nothing, like a pane of glass being shattered. His little sister, his three-legged-race running partner, his Happy Meal sharer, his sibling, his best friend, his history.

'I can't,' he says softly.

Cathy looks at him. 'You can't,' she echoes. A sheen across her eyes catches the moonlight.

It looks just like the night-time at home. He, Cathy and Frannie live in a row of three cottages with no other neighbours – a feat they can't believe they pulled off – and he almost always goes round to Frannie's for bath time, closing his farmhouse door behind him and pushing open Frannie's. Cathy's and Joe's used to be a shop and a post office respectively, with small rooms and low ceilings. Frannie's was originally a house – part funded by their parents, for her – built in 1850, and is larger and airier than the others.

He shoves his hands into his pockets. He could hand her in. Save himself. He'd be mad not to consider it, wouldn't he? But she looks up at him now, his baby sister, her head tilted back. No. That isn't an option. It began its life as Frannie's problem, but now it's shared.

'We need to bury it,' Frannie says. 'Him.'

Cathy waits a second, clearly thinking. After a moment, she says only one word: 'Where?'

6.

Joe

Joe's shoulders feel like they're made of metal, not bone and sinew. He rolls them, trying to relax. 'We need to think clearly.'

The man was a horrible bloke, according to Frannie. Besides, she didn't mean to hurt him. It was an accident. A terrible coincidence. This is the hand they've been dealt, and now they need to play the cards. 'We need to think about the evidence,' he says, staring at the ground. 'What gets rid of blood?'

'Fire,' Cathy says immediately.

'Fire,' Joe repeats, nodding slowly. 'Okay.' He looks left and right down the track road. It serves only their villa and two others. The site used to be a convent and was converted to villas in the fifties. The private road is supposed to be maintained by the three villas, though they don't do enough. The grass is scorched yellow, the road not even tarmacked, just hardened mud, cooked by the Italian sun. Joe's only ever seen cars come down it when they're lost. Joe briefly wonders why a stranger was walking down this road, alone, in the night . . .

'We need to deal with the body first,' Cathy says. She gets to her feet, hesitating just slightly, then walks on.

Their villa is surrounded by fields, with woods lying beyond. They bought it five years ago on – embarrassingly – a whim. Frannie had been *fantasy Rightmoving*, as she called it, and the villa had popped up. It was old, shabby and going cheap. What began as a joke became a full conversation, then a budget scribbled on the back of a receipt, then a loan, secured against their business. That first summer they came out here, they couldn't believe they'd done it. They had thirty bookings for the rest of the year, and they'd paid off twenty per cent of the mortgage already. When they got the statement, they opened a bottle of wine at Frannie's. She'd raised a glass and said, 'To not doing things like other people.'

'There are shovels in the outhouse,' Joe says quietly. They all pause for just a second in the darkness. They were in there earlier today, preparing for a barbecue. The sun on the backs of their necks. 'We could . . . use the woods.'

'We don't own the woods,' Cathy says. She pulls back her dark hair from her face, looking at him intently. She is trying to communicate something, he thinks, but isn't sure what.

'But they're deserted. And the soil is soft,' he says. Are they really having this conversation? Everything is upside down and unreal, like the sky is suddenly underneath them and the earth above. Joe shakes his head, trying to clear it. He thinks instead of Paul, who just yesterday over the dinner table very seriously handed him a speck of fluff so small Joe had to squint to see it. His resolve strengthens. Paul doesn't deserve this. He doesn't deserve to pay for his mother's mistake. He's so tiny, so innocent.

'Yeah,' Cathy says softly, moving away from him. They went walking in those woods yesterday to cool down. As they stumbled over exposed tree roots, holding on to branches for support, they had talked about how Lydia and Joe were trying – unsuccessfully – to get pregnant. Cathy had said not very much at all, which was exactly what Joe had wanted, why he had asked Cathy to go, and not Frannie. They'd returned relaxed and tired, and opened a bottle of red wine.

'Cathy and I need to dig,' Joe says. She's bigger than Frannie, but she's meticulous too. Frannie would rush it.

'It needs to be really deep,' Cathy says. In the darkness, her voice is disembodied. Joe moves the beam of his torch to her. Her expression is blank, totally blank, a woman in shock.

'You need to burn this blood,' Joe says to Frannie, gesturing around.

'How?'

'You need to light every bit of it and burn it. Nobody ever goes up that road. Ever. We'll just say we had a cook-out on the grass. Make it look like a big barbecue. A bonfire. Something like that,' Cathy says. Her words are matter of fact but her tone is kind, as it always is.

'Okay,' Frannie says in a small voice. 'But won't people wonder why we had a . . . I mean – next to the road?'

'I know,' Cathy says with a shrug. 'We'll have to deal with that question when it comes to it. Get the car close to the house and clean it up too. Hose it down. But prioritize the blood.' She swallows. She looks at Joe. 'The grave needs to be seven feet,' she says.

'I know.'

'Because of sniffer dogs,' she adds needlessly. Joe nods. Spaniels. German shepherds. He sees their noses quivering during his examinations of them. They can tell when their owner is due back from work by how much of them they can still smell in the air.

'And then?' Frannie stands opposite Joe, her bloody hands on her hips, leaving two perfect handprints against her bare skin in the torchlight.

Cathy doesn't answer her, just stands looking at the body for a few seconds more. She points to the feet of the body. Joe picks them up easily, like it – he, *he* – is a fallen soldier, and follows Cathy, holding the shoulders, into the gloom of the woods.

PART I

Preventing a Lawful Burial

7.
Joe

Joe is already out of breath by the time they reach the woods, his hands slipping on the body's rubbery ankles. He reaches to wipe sweat away from his forehead. His muscles are shaking. He is so unfit. Joe hates the gym, once spent a week going *before work* like other people seem to be able to do and was useless all day, dropping scalpels and mainlining Mars Bars to recover.

A little way in, Cathy stops, placing her end of the body on the ground, where it settles at an odd angle. 'Here?' Cathy says.

'I don't know,' Joe says listlessly. He sees Cathy's eyes flash in the light from his phone.

'He was British, you know? You remember, at the market – he had an English accent,' she says, looking down at the body. 'On holiday or an ex-pat, I don't know.'

Joe lays down the body's feet. 'Right,' he says.

She moves away some leaves with her foot, still in flip-flops. Her toes come away dirty. Joe turns off the torch, and leaves them in the blackness.

'Do you think we're doing the right thing?' he whispers. As his eyes adjust, she comes into view, like a slowly developing Polaroid. First the whites of her eyes, then her bare limbs.

She bites her lip and looks away. He's surprised to see

Cathy's vulnerability. She is one of those women who is always in the same mood. 'I just . . . yeah. I don't know.'

It's still the exact middle of the night. Hours until the sun comes up. Joe hopes they can do it.

'I feel like I'm in a nightmare,' he says.

'Me too.'

'So, do you?' He runs a hand through his hair, leaving grainy particles of soil behind which make him itch. 'Think we're doing the right thing?'

'Do *you*?' she replies and Joe almost laughs. Typical enigmatic Cathy.

'Can you just answer a fucking question?' he snaps.

Cathy says nothing, leaning on her spade.

'We don't have to do it,' he adds after a few seconds. He knows he's needling her to discuss Frannie with him, but he can't help it. This instinct he has, sometimes, to divide and conquer. It's something to do with needing to be secure, needing to be . . . what, sibling number one? God, he's an arse.

Cathy stares at him. For a second, she looks exactly like Frannie in that eerie way that sisters sometimes do. 'I know,' she says.

'We could stop now,' he adds uselessly. 'Call the police. End it.' They look at the body at their feet. 'Before it begins.' His throat seems to close up after he's said it. It's just bravado. Suggestions. He could never do it. To Frannie or to Paul.

'You don't mean that?' she says softly.

Joe shrugs. 'No.'

They stare at each other for a few seconds more. 'It's

forever.' Cathy stares down at the body, now blackened by dried blood. 'You know?'

'I know.'

'What would she get? Really?'

'She might get life, if they infer intent,' Joe says. Lydia is a secretary at a criminal law firm, and he's picked up bits over the years from the cases she tells him of that she should keep quiet. That, and television. 'If they don't believe it was an accident.'

'Right,' Cathy says faintly.

She meets his gaze again. 'We should check who he is,' she says softly.

'What?'

'His wallet. It's better to know this stuff, isn't it?'

'I guess.' Joe looks down at the body – at this person whose name they'll soon know, who was living and breathing until just a few hours ago – and thinks he might be sick again. Cathy begins poking at the ground with the spade, so he kneels down and reaches into the man's back pockets.

A set of keys. A wallet. And a ragged and torn piece of paper. It feels inhumane, to him, like he is a robber, a looter, but he goes through them nevertheless. 'Four keys, including one for a car,' Joe says. 'A few debit cards. ID,' he adds. 'I don't know what this is.' He gestures to the piece of paper, torn and fluffy. As he opens it up, it falls into four pieces. It's sodden with blood.

'God,' Cathy says. She comes over to him and scans it with the light of her phone. Both of their hands are shaking.

'It's illegible. Let's just bury them with him,' Joe says.

'No. If we take them, we might be able to . . . I don't know.' She shrugs in that way that she sometimes does. 'Help in some way. If there is a next of kin.'

'What – post them off?' Joe says incredulously. 'Dear sirs, we enclose –'

'No. But you never know. We might be able to help,' Cathy says. 'We might be able to – to mitigate some of it. Some day.' Joe watches her go back to the spades, her shoulders rounded and sad.

He stares down at the body. What are they doing? He kicks a nearby rock, which goes flying.

Cathy turns and looks at him. He watches her watching him, saying nothing, trying to calm himself down. 'It's for our family,' he says quietly. 'Isn't it? This is what family is.'

Cathy turns away from him again and begins digging. There are three hearts, here in the woods, but only two of them are beating.

They're five feet in, standing in the hole now, and it's – Joe checks his watch – just after four o'clock. For two hours, they have dug in near silence, talking only logistics and how best to cut through the many tree roots. Owls hoot in the trees, but otherwise there is nothing except silence and darkness.

Until now. A noise in the distance. 'What's that?' Joe says.

Cathy stops, leaning on the spade. Her hands are filthy. 'What?' she says.

Joe cocks his head, staring at her.

'A car,' she says.

'Shit.'

'Don't panic.' Cathy keeps digging, her shovel moving faster than before.

Joe is paralysed, just listening. For sirens. For the call from the Italian police. The car's engine gets louder as it approaches. It reaches a crescendo and then – thank God, thank God – begins to fade. Joe feels his shoulders drop in relief. Thank God it's not near where Frannie's fire will be.

'I'm so fucking tired,' he pants to Cathy. His hands are slick with sweat on the handle of his spade.

'I know.'

'What are we going to tell everyone? What should I tell Lydia?'

Cathy pauses. Her hair is everywhere, sticking to her neck. She looks mad, standing there in the grave. They both probably do. 'You can't tell her,' she says. 'Can you?'

'No. The fewer people who know, the better – right?' Joe says. 'Plants only.'

He always wanted to incorporate their surname into the veterinary practice, when his mother handed it over to him, Cathy and Frannie, but everybody said it didn't work, said it sounded like a garden centre. And so instead they named it the anodyne *Vets 24* – something so modern it makes his mother wince. Evan, the most senior vet who isn't in the family partnership, is currently running it while they're away, here, though Joe is sure they will hear all about that when they return. Evan thinks he is a real hero. Their retired mother, Maria, is helping out a couple of days a week too. Hopefully she will prop him up.

Cathy nods quickly. 'Yeah.' Their eyes meet again. 'Only us. Forever.'

It takes another hour to finish digging. The last foot is the hardest. The soil is cool and packed, the night sky above Joe quiet and dark. Worms veer out of the sides of the hole, almost as if they are leering at him as he digs.

Frannie's head pokes over the edge of the grave at five thirty. She's finished burning the blood on the road and the grass verges, and cleaned the car. She couldn't get the dent out of the fender, she says, but Joe has a plan for that. She helps them get out of the grave, three chain-linked siblings, their hands in each other's.

When Cathy emerges, the sky is beginning to lighten, black to grey, dawn in monochrome. It's still warm, the night heavily scented and close.

'Right,' Cathy says sadly. She picks up the wallet. 'You didn't check his name?' she asks.

'Didn't want to,' Joe says.

He watches her run her fingers over the embossed name on a credit card. 'Mr W. R. McGovern,' she says softly. She finds his driving licence. 'William. He's thirty-one.'

'Was,' Frannie says, casting a glance at Joe.

'Was,' Joe echoes.

Frannie leans back over William R. McGovern, aged thirty-one, as if blessing him. When she sits back, her forehead is anointed with blood. The grave dug, Cathy leans over and closes his eyes with the very tips of her fingers.

8.

Now

Jason's Office, mid February, 5.55 p.m.

Jason and I are standing outside his office in the cold. He is shifting from foot to foot, wanting to head off, I guess, to wherever it is that he goes. He rushed me out with him at ten to six, but seemed to want to keep talking, asking me questions in the lift on the way down and as we crossed the shabby foyer, trying to make the most of the time given.

'Before I go,' he says for the second time, lighting a cigarette wordlessly, without explanation or excuse, 'still no contact with the others?'

'No,' I say. 'Nothing.'

'Right,' he says, flicking the end of the cigarette, evidently thinking as he breathes out two columns of blue smoke from his nose. 'Interesting.'

'Yeah?'

'Well. Not what I expected,' he says with a brief shrug. 'Families – you know. They usually find it hard to sever the ties.' His eyes catch mine, the tip of the cigarette a small sun in the descending winter murkiness. 'No matter the circumstances,' he adds.

It's strange to be continuing our session out here, in the dark frost, but I like talking to Jason and his clear mind so much that I find I don't care. 'You walking that way?' I say, gesturing to the direction he always goes in.

'Yeah. I'm almost late,' he says, rotating his wrist to

check his watch. I nearly ask then but stop myself. The relationship is one way: must stay so, for it to work. I confide my secrets to him, but get nothing in return. He is objective and me subjective, upset and wounded by the loss of my family, my estrangement from Mum and Dad, even from Joe.

We fall into step beside each other. It's the wrong direction for me, but that doesn't matter. I have nowhere else to be, not really, not right now.

'You know, I'm actually not surprised they haven't been in touch,' I say, as we pass a pound shop just closing for the night, navy-blue shutters noisy and crass in the soft mist.

'No?' Jason prompts, not seeming to mind the overrun of our session.

'No. They just . . .' I think of Joe, in particular, and how everything fell apart. My role in it, his role in it, the way he looked at me the night it all unravelled. It was the night that everything got discovered, just not in the way we thought it would be. 'I think . . . probably . . .' I say hesitantly, 'I just think they actually only thought about themselves, in the end.'

Jason lets out a sad laugh into the winter air as we come to a set of traffic lights. He jabs the button with his index finger and the WAIT sign illuminates his hand orange for just a second. I look behind me, back to his building, and at the side-by-side set of footprints we've made in the frost.

'You know,' he says, throwing a sidelong glance at me, 'I have family who are just the same. It isn't you. It's them.'

'Thank you,' I say, not knowing quite how to convey

the meaning to him, my confidant. We cross the street in silence and Jason curves us around to the left, down an alleyway lined with rubbish bins and out into a small square.

'This is me.' He looks up at a sixties-style brown building. It has small square windows, wooden cladding, like an old high school or sports centre. It's unmarked, no sign telling me what it is. I look at it curiously and hope he takes the hint. 'Until next time,' he says, two fingers on his right hand touching briefly to his forehead, a semi-salute. He heads inside, pushing a dark-wood door with a letter-box across it, messenger bag slung across his body, and leaves me in the cold.

9.

Then

Cathy

Much like a return journey seems to take less time than an outgoing, putting the earth back over William is an easier task than it was digging it out. Cathy is amazed she is capable of thoughts like this, monstrous thoughts about the administration of killing, but the adrenaline has run out. The panic can't sustain itself. It is a firework with no gunpowder left. Her shoulders and arms scream with pain. Anxiety is Joe's Achilles heel, but Cathy's will be guilt. With each layer of soil that suffocates William McGovern, Cathy thinks of something else he is deprived of. A funeral. His family of knowledge. An ending, a proper ending, with respect, not this.

At seven thirty, Frannie says, 'Paul will be awake.'

'Lydia will sort him,' Joe says. 'Don't worry.'

'Go, if you want,' Cathy says to Frannie. 'Lydia will be wondering – well. It isn't fair.' She tucks a strand of hair back into her bun, where it pulls tight against her hairline.

'How are we going to get in without Lydia seeing us like this?' Frannie says hoarsely. She gestures to them, to their dirtied and bloodstained limbs. Cathy shrugs, trying to stay in the now.

'I think that looks undisturbed,' Joe says, standing and looking at the grave in the woods. Cathy stares at it. It is

46

impossible to tell. Like a hidden object, her eyes are drawn immediately to it.

Her younger sister stares too. Frannie, whom she's always known so well, who had a baby after a one-night stand and never bothered to look up the man again. Cathy's always known exactly who she is. Outwardly confident, sociable Frannie. But now . . . Cathy suddenly feels, there in the woods, like they don't know each other at all. A stranger stands next to her.

'I don't know,' Cathy says quickly to Joe. 'Do you think it looks okay?'

'It's fine. I think. We need to put the spades away.'

'Were they clean?'

Joe exhales. 'I can't remember.'

Frannie is silent, standing next to them. She's looking at her phone. Worried about Paul, Cathy guesses.

'They were clean,' Frannie says, glancing up.

'No – I don't think they were . . .' Joe says. 'Why would they be? They're for gardening.'

'Just run the hose over them,' Cathy says. 'Okay?'

'Okay.'

They walk away. Cathy tries not to think of William lying there, seven feet under, alone. The sun has come up. The sky is a perfect, delicate blue. If you threw up a ball, it would shatter.

After a few minutes, Joe stops still on a lattice of tree roots. 'What if he wasn't dead?' he says.

'What?' Frannie says, a harsh, loud exclamation in the early morning. 'Joe, honestly.'

'He was dead,' Cathy says reassuringly. Joe blushes.

Funny how anxiety manifests itself. Joe once became convinced he'd left a surgical instrument inside a great Dane. Cathy had been present at the operation – there was no way it could have happened – but, nevertheless, Joe had wanted to open her back up. In the end, they'd compromised on an X-ray, which had shown nothing, of course.

She sees Joe's chest rise and fall slowly. 'Okay,' he says slowly.

'Let me see that piece of paper,' Cathy says. Joe passes it to her. It's illegible. Some sort of form, all in Italian. She looks at Frannie, ready to explain why they took it and the wallet, but she is lost in her own world, wandering haphazardly, staring up at the sky, lost in thought, lost in guilt, probably. Hopefully. Hopefully not just daydreaming.

'We need to think,' Joe says, as they walk. 'We need to think.'

As the three of them step into the sunlight, Frannie reaches for Cathy's hand. They wind their fingers together. The shovels clink against each other in the silence.

The blood on their skin and clothes looks even worse in the daylight. 'We'll have to throw everything we're wearing away,' she says quietly.

Frannie nods. 'We can go in the back way,' she says.

Cathy can't wait to shower. To slough off the dirt and blood and the history of it from her skin, the steam warm and wet in her lungs as she breathes it in. And then she can't wait to work, to forget the world around her, to lose herself in admin.

But, first, they must make sure this is sorted, covered up. The clothes. The blood. The car. Alibis. CCTV. DNA.

Forensics. It seems so endless to Cathy, walking next to her siblings, their faces squinting into the sun.

She turns her mind to the first thing. Because this isn't over. It's actually just beginning. This is the first day, in a whole lifetime of lies.

10.

Lydia

Lydia has become crazy about – of all things – the precise meaning of first-morning urine. That is her first thought as Paul wakes her up. He does it in exactly the way Frannie said he would when she briefed her and Joe. 'More an angry, hungry shout than a cry,' she had said drily. It had been one time – of many – when Lydia had wanted to be like Frannie. A single mother, still seeming to enjoy parenthood. Still wry. Still groomed, glossy, the same as all of the Plants. Dark hair, skin that tans easily, unusually bright eyes.

It's 5.55 in the morning. So does this count as first-morning? Or is it still the night? What exactly is the idea behind first-morning urine anyway?

Lydia has been pleasantly surprised to find that – unlike the art of conception – looking after a two-year-old overnight has been quite simple. Paul hadn't woken up at all and now, as she looks at him standing indignantly upright in the cot, he's thoughtful, his face a perfect facsimile of Joe's. It would be so easy to pretend for a second that he is theirs, but Lydia doesn't want to. Doesn't want to muddy the future with fantasies.

Paul smiles to himself, as he often does, as if remembering something deep in the past that made him laugh. She has noticed this week that he has an actual formed personality, something she wasn't sure most toddlers had.

He pretends he is a dinosaur when he eats. Broccoli because brachiosauruses ate from trees. Fish fingers because spinosauruses ate fish. He knows a handful of words, and almost all of them are the names of dinosaurs. 'He can't say *yes* but he can say velociraptor,' Frannie said yesterday in a restaurant, while they all laughed.

Lydia picks him up and holds him to her hip, his soft bare feet dangling down and hitting her thighs. Hazy from sleep, she turns towards the bed, in the dimness from the heavy curtains, and squints. Where's Joe?

She changes Paul's nappy while he gazes up at her, completely trusting. His thighs are cold and cushiony, delightful, the texture of a blancmange. Lydia presses a finger into his calf, watching the perfectly smooth skin yield and release. One day she might have one of these, she finds herself thinking, as though he is an object or coveted possession. She hopes her baby is as nice as Paul.

And today's the day. First-morning urine.

She checks her phone, but there's nothing from Joe. He must have gone to breakfast earlier than usual. It is strange for him – he's the night owl, she the lark. But in some ways she isn't surprised. It is not possible, Lydia learns over and over again, for an in-law to be truly knitted into the fabric of the Plant family. They shoot the breeze together, share bottles of wine, but she isn't quite invited into the true intimacy: the sun-lounger confiding sessions she sometimes overhears between Frannie and Cathy. The spontaneous trips into Verona she's implicitly not invited to. The late-night swims.

Anyway. Lydia is now tasked with the juxtaposition of taking a pregnancy test and looking after a toddler. She sets Paul on the floor in the bedroom and unwraps the packet, scrutinizing the plastic stick.

Each test is £15.99, and Lydia's bought hundreds of them. Like, actual hundreds. Picked up casually, these days, with milk and bread. She tries not to visit the same checkout twice, in case she gets put on some sort of watch list.

The sky outside the window is lavender-coloured. Lydia stares at it as she wees on the stick, listening out for Paul.

'*Paul?*' Lydia had exclaimed when she had received the text from Joe on the labour ward. 'Come visit! Now!' he added.

Joe's verve, his vigour. That's what Lydia remembers thinking that night as she drove to the hospital. The world was out there for them, if they wanted it, and Joe was the one who could help her get it, even if the world on that day was just a hospital Costa, cuddles with a baby and an evening car ride. It all added up. She didn't even mind that he'd insisted on living near his sisters. Didn't mind that no private occasion, involving only Lydia and Joe, not even wedding anniversaries, were off-limits. That was family, Lydia figured.

So first-morning urine, then. Eighteen periods since they started trying. Nothing. Not even a weak positive, even once. No chemical pregnancy. No period a day late. Nothing. It's almost laughable.

But today. Day twenty-four. She stands up, flushes the toilet, leaves the stick on the windowsill and picks up Paul.

This would complete it. It would. She sends out a bargain to the universe. 'I know,' she says, 'that I have had so much good lately. So much sun. But haven't I sacrificed?'

Not a single drop of wine has crossed her lips in a week and a half. She's been meticulous with the sun-cream. No fish. Going way beyond the NHS's advice. Because, you know. Why not?

Lydia does know – she really does – that she shouldn't look at the test early. She knows too that, if there is a God, he won't be interested in bargaining with her about how much Italian wine she's turned down, citing tiredness, faked hangovers and antibiotics. Everybody probably thinks she's already pregnant, but the truth is that she's lost her mind.

Sod it. She will just look. The time is almost up. She jiggles her leg nervously.

Seriously, where is Joe? She opens the door to the bathroom. Paul reaches for the handle – he loves door handles. Anything he can pull. He also loves to remove the entire contents of a drawer and put it back again.

Lydia brought six pregnancy tests with her to Italy. This is the sort of thing she means: there is no situation that, in two weeks, would warrant six pregnancy tests, but here she is. The stick is on the windowsill, three distended globules of urine next to it, shining in the morning sun. She holds Paul against her hip and creeps towards the test, still bargaining, then peers at it.

Not pregnant.

The words are an offence to Lydia, who has tried so hard, who has been so patient, so stoic, even able to laugh at how insane it's driven her. But these words. They are as traumatic as *HR have requested a meeting* and *Your hospital test results are back.*

Her period is due tomorrow. It'll be right on time.

*

Joe isn't at breakfast. It's after eight. Lydia has texted him twice, called three times, texted Frannie, eventually too, though she felt like a pain. God, Frannie is such a flake: the texts are undelivered. One tick on WhatsApp.

She stands in line for breakfast, thinking. She's trying to pretend to Paul, who has his small, warm hand in hers, that she's not worried, but she is. She worries about Joe all the time. She knows that she can never detach his volatile core from all of the things she loves about him – his dedication to work, his loyalty to her – but, nevertheless, she wishes she could. If he is home late – or not at all, in this case – her first thought is that he is fighting. Joe has kicked lamp-posts in her presence, punched Italian men in bars, shouted at bouncers in clubs, told parking attendants to piss off. And he regrets it. He always regrets it. That's the weirdest thing. The stupidest thing.

The Plants own their villa, and they go to this nearby villa with a restaurant that serves a cooked breakfast some mornings. They have an unofficial agreement to meet here, around now, but last night Frannie said she would come to Lydia's at seven to collect Paul. But she didn't.

Lydia sighs, standing there in the hot, coffee-scented, sunlit room. The entire holiday had been leading up to this day, the day she found out she was pregnant. She knows it's absurd to have believed that eighteen months of failure wouldn't become nineteen, that she'd be able to cancel their referral to the fertility clinic. But she thought it might. Just maybe. Didn't everybody say to go on holiday? To relax? And Lydia has relaxed with *intent*.

For once, she hasn't minded the Plants' inside jokes, their private language, the natural order of Frannie's banter, Joe's protectiveness, Cathy's seriousness. Lydia has relaxed as though she's been prescribed it. Three hours on a sun-lounger, twice a day. One book read. One swim. Ten hours' sleep.

As she's choosing a topping for her pancakes and trying to distract Paul with the knobs on the serving cabinet, she sees two shadows at the door. Men in hats, weapons on their belts. She stops for just a second and looks at them, a dark cloak of dread drawing over her shoulders.

'Let's go and chat to those nice men,' she says to Paul, praying that these are not the men who cautioned Joe the other night, and praying too that they haven't come across him more recently.

'Nice?' he says, with a toothy grin, pointing to the exact centre of his chest.

'You're nice, yes,' she laughs.

'I nice!' The full sentence bursting free from him surprises her, and she feels something pleasurable bubble up through her.

'No one is as nice as you,' she says. She picks him up, breathes in the lavender biscuit smell of the folds of his neck, abandons the warm plate of pancakes, and approaches the police. 'Is everything okay?' she says, not even attempting Italian.

'Sorry?' one of the Carabinieri says to her. He has high cheekbones, large eyes, heavy lidded. Black hair under his hat. His face is expressionless. Not kind or unkind.

'I – I just wondered . . . why you are here,' she says, trying to enunciate. 'I can't find the people I'm staying with,' she says with a tiny laugh. 'I just wondered – that they're okay.'

'Their names?' the policeman says to her in perfect, almost accent-less English.

'Plant. My husband – Joe Plant.'

'Joe Plant,' the policeman says slowly.

Lydia fell in love with his name first. A simple name for a boy that was anything but. It was Easter, and she was sixteen. He was eighteen. He hung out only with his sisters on his lunch breaks at school. She once heard him say that all the other students were *twats*, that he wanted to be a vet because he liked animals and hated people, a stance Lydia could get on board with.

He enjoyed science and wore trainers even though the uniform code said shoes. One evening, she got her Nokia 3210 and went up to her bedroom and sat on the bed and texted him. He replied – about homework – in a perfunctory way, and she replied to him, and it had stopped there. Lydia had sat, cross-legged and disappointed, on the latest bed in the latest foster home, until he had sent another message. That is, Lydia believes, when she fell in love. When that strong, simple name flashed up on her phone unexpectedly. Joe Plant.

And so Lydia has loved Joe for more than half of her life. When he was twenty, and she was eighteen, he had finally asked her to go out for burgers with him. He'd been unable to hold back when the waitress asked if they'd like a table – *that was the idea, yeah* – but he was not caustic with Lydia. That was the day she entered the inner sanctum and discovered the real Joe. The Joe who falls in love with dying dogs, the Joe who can't resist sarcastic remarks but then calls himself an *arse* on the way home from parties, the Joe who sometimes drinks too much, the

Joe who gets angry at people who can't afford to pay for their pets' treatments and then operates anyway, for free.

'Anyone else?' the man says to Lydia now.

'Frannie, Joe, Cathy. All the Plants. I'm here with them – the whole family. Three siblings.'

'Okay. Thanks. Do not worry. I bet they are fine – I will check.' He leans over to the other policeman as she leaves, feeling relieved, and whispers something that she can't hear. She pauses for just a second before walking away.

11.

Joe

'Where have you been?' Lydia says to Joe when she arrives back in their room. She's holding Paul, obviously pissed off.

'Uh . . .' Joe towel dries his just-showered hair, stalling for time. He had got his story straight in his mind, but he's forgotten it. His brain feels fractured, his thoughts, feelings, chemicals put through a centrifuge and spun out into disparate pieces.

Lydia has croissant flakes down her t-shirt. Only two. They're minuscule. Joe's eyes keep straying to them. How many minuscule bits of evidence have they left down there? Something rises up through him. Some misguided, over-the-top urge to rush back to the scene of the crime and obscure it further so that nobody can ever get to the bottom of what happened there. To detonate a bomb, to set the entire forest alight. To make such a mess that theirs is eclipsed.

'Have you been fighting?'

'*No*,' Joe says testily, resenting the assumption. He almost tells her, right then. *It's Frannie you should be worried about, not me.* He rakes back his hair and looks at her. 'Sorry, I went earlier,' he says.

'To breakfast? Where's Frannie?'

'She went too. Yeah. I couldn't sleep. Didn't want to wake you.'

'Well – does she *want* Paul back or not?'

Joe looks at Lydia dumbly, thinking of the blood that Frannie is probably washing off her body.

'I'm sure she does. Look – I'll text her.' He brandishes his phone. It doesn't matter if Lydia's mad at him, he thinks. He's protecting her from knowledge she'd rather not have, if she could choose. Rather a cold husband than be privy to a killing.

'Right,' Lydia says faintly. She looks like the same Lydia he went to high school with, today, here in the Italian sun. She's hardly aged. She has a face he sometimes sees places – on the news, on friends of friends. Wide-set eyes. Full cheeks. A snub nose. The kind of face people think they know. That's how it felt to fall in love with Lydia: familiar, warm, like turning over in the sun. Each day at work, he looks forward to going home to her. She is always home before him, and always doing mad things. Potting loads of plants she bought on a whim, cooking wearing crazy pyjamas with feet. Just a few weeks ago, she had tried to do her own gel pedicure and had stuck her toes together. 'Okay, we have a situation,' she'd said, when he walked in from work. He'd used a spare scalpel to remove the hardened gel while they'd giggled.

He stares at his hands. He's showered off the dirt. It took over half an hour, but it's still there, in the grooves of his fingernails. There are dry, hairline fractures of mud running through them. Impossible to get out. He stuffs his hands into his shorts pockets. His dirty clothes are in a carrier bag in his suitcase. He intends to throw them, somehow, somewhere.

'Text her, then,' Lydia says.

He can't deal with this, being under the spotlight of Lydia's gaze. There's so much to think of. To work through.

'There were two police down at breakfast – not sure why. I was worried,' she adds.

Joe steadies himself on the bed, palms out. It's lower than he thought, and he stumbles slightly as he does it. 'What police?' he says, clearing his throat. He coughs. Lydia looks at him strangely. Why the fuck are the police out so soon? William hasn't even been dead for twelve hours. Has he been reported missing already? Or – worse – been found?

Joe wants to look at himself in the mirror. The paranoia stepped into the shower with him, and now it won't let him go. What if there's dried blood on his forehead? Just at the hairline? It would be easy to miss.

He goes into the bathroom. He'll wax his hair.

As his brown eyes meet his reflection's, he tells himself he hasn't done anything wrong. He's cleaned up somebody else's mess, that's all. He's helped his little sister. *He* hasn't killed anybody. He looks at himself. Hooked nose. Large eyes. Clean face. No blood. No soil. Nothing. He holds the blue metallic tin of wax in his hand.

Is he a hero or a villain? *Has* he protected his sister from harm, or has he orchestrated other crimes? He looks away from his own intense gaze. He doesn't know, can't decide. 'What police?' he says again to Lydia, his tone imbued with what he hopes is a curious casualness.

'The ones with the hats,' she says. 'The black hats and suits with the red stripe down their sides.'

'Oh, right,' Joe tries to say casually, rubbing wax into his hair. What if William had told somebody exactly where he was heading? It would be so easy to find the grave if you knew . . .

Lydia meets his eyes in the mirror. She has pale brown freckles across her nose, hardly noticeable unless you're very close. 'I said I wasn't sure where you were.'

'You what?' Joe says. He turns around to face her, the cold basin cutting into the backs of his thighs.

'I didn't know where you were,' Lydia says. She leans over and grabs some concealer, starts rubbing it underneath her eyes. 'I'm tired and old,' she moans. 'And I look it. An old crone. With old ovaries.'

Joe tries to steady his breathing. He's got to act normally. This is his life now. Filtering every action, every word. He gazes at the clean sink. The taps are gleaming. Lydia must have wiped them. She's so neat. He finds it comforting. She would never be involved in something as messy as killing. As messy as dead bodies.

What would he usually say to her? He would find her self-deprecation amusing. 'You're beautiful,' he says woodenly, knowing he has to say something. Lydia may take the piss out of herself, but she's got a hard edge too. He loves that also, but boy is he afraid of it sometimes.

With no warning, the smell of the memory overpowers him. The soil. The metallic, tart scent of the blood. The body, the skin, in the earliest stages of decomposition. He pushes Lydia gently out of the way and leans his hands on his thighs, heaving into the toilet bowl.

'Are you all right?'

'Must have had a bad sausage,' Joe says, though the only thing he is heaving up is stomach acid.

It comes to him a few minutes later, as he's brushing his teeth, the acidic smell of sick slowly disappearing. If they don't want the police to find the body, the police have got to think William is alive. But missing. A missing person's investigation. But false. Staged.

12.

Cathy

Cathy has decided to ask Frannie exactly what happened last night. She wants a minute-by-minute account from her elusive sister. To cover it up, they must understand it, Cathy believes.

They're in their kitchen, which is both rustic and basic. Copper pans hang over the top of the window, which has old-fashioned red gingham curtains covering it.

Joe is standing by the door like a guard, in case Lydia comes in. Cathy stares at the wall above him, where a bronze Jesus sits against a dark-wood cross.

The owners who converted it from the convent wouldn't throw away the crucifixes, wouldn't take them with them either. Said it was bad luck. They were left with them, having inherited both the crosses and the superstition. Frannie tried to take some of them off the walls, but Cathy always stopped her. 'Better to be safe than sorry,' she'd said. 'Yeah, because God will curse us,' Frannie laughed. If there is a God, Cathy finds herself thinking, they will never meet him now. Surely.

Cathy looks at Frannie. Her arms have gone from propping up her head to being stretched out along the table, her head lolling on top of them, like a student asleep during a class. Her pink fingernail polish has started to grow out, little crescent moons showing at her cuticles.

The lights are on in the cool, dim kitchen, the curtains

closed to the view of the pool, where Lydia sits. The bulbs above them flicker, as they have most nights of the holiday, out here in the Verona countryside, but this time it seems ominous, a sign from God. Cathy stares at the old-fashioned chandelier fittings. Each time they come over in July, they say they will renovate, but they never do, preferring to drink cocktails and read by the pool instead.

'We need to make a plan,' Joe says softly. Frannie doesn't even turn her head. 'Are you even awake?' Joe says drily, and Cathy's glad of it, for once.

'Of course I'm *awake*,' Frannie says. 'I haven't fucking slept since.'

Cathy blinks, surprised by her sister's irritability. She's usually so full of positivity. Dashing off after work to see one of her many friends. Deciding whether or not a t-shirt with a bow on the back was special enough to buy. 'It's a big decision, Cathy,' she'd said smilingly, her finger hovering on the *order* button. Frannie is both a bargain-hunter and a spender, always finding discounts that allow her to buy the things she wants on the salary she has.

'Join the club,' Joe says.

'The police were in the main villa this morning,' Frannie says.

'Is it too early for a drink?' Joe asks.

That's one of the things that they do together at home. Every single Friday, no matter what, they share a bottle of wine together, in Frannie's open-plan kitchen. Often at her large oak table but, more often, they fold back her bi-fold doors – even in the cold – and they sit there, on the doorstep, three siblings in a row, their legs stretched out in front of them on to the patio, and they drink and talk

64

together. They like Frannie's house because it's warm and smells like a home and is full of interesting things. She has two copper kettles, a weather vane that looks like a snow globe, a cuckoo clock that hoots on the hour. Cathy loves it there. 'How do you know?' Cathy says, noticing that Joe doesn't seem surprised.

'Lydia told me,' Joe says softly.

And you told Frannie? Cathy thinks. Something about it makes her pause. Her brother and sister are so close to each other. She's out in the cold, and she needs not to be. They need to stay tightknit to survive it.

Cathy looks at her brother. She can't say it. She'll sound mad, paranoid. 'Lydia doesn't know, I guess?' she asks instead. Lydia isn't a Plant. She wouldn't get it.

'No,' he says shortly. 'No, she doesn't know. And she isn't going to know. She's pissed off with how much she's had to have Paul.'

'Paul is no bother,' Frannie says defensively. Her face lights up, just for a second or two, as she speaks his name.

Joe is about to start planning. Cathy can tell. She knows all of the clues her brother's body gives away. Poised, somehow, like a runner on the starting blocks, holding an intake of breath, eyebrows raised, about to speak.

So many questions need to be asked before they can start to plan. 'Look,' Cathy says. She pulls out a wooden chair – still with the purple crochet cushion from the previous owners – and sits opposite Frannie. 'I think it would help to understand it properly,' she says. 'If we could just talk about – about exactly what happened?'

Cathy detects nothing in Frannie's reaction. No flinching, no tension. She cups her face in her hands and raises her gaze to Cathy. 'I pulled out on to the left, not the right,' Frannie says. Outside, the old clock that sits at the centre of the convent chimes, ten o'clock. They pause, as though undertaking a minute's silence, then Frannie resumes. 'I hit him before – before I could even tell I was in the wrong place,' she says. 'I turned – and there he was.'

'Why couldn't you – you said you couldn't stop?' Cathy says, trying not to sound like a police officer. Frannie might not notice what she is implying, but Joe will. It takes hardly anything for him to become her defender, for both to turn their backs on her.

'It isn't that I couldn't stop,' Frannie says, her expression open and earnest, a fingernail following a striation in the wood of the pine kitchen table. 'It's that I didn't know where he was.' She reaches a hand through the gingham, checking on Paul.

'William?'

Frannie nods. She reaches to untie her dark hair from the thick bundle on the top of her head. It falls around her shoulders like a shampoo advert. 'I couldn't stop immediately. Obviously. And, when I did, I had to find him. The impact –' She pauses for just a second. 'It moved him. And I couldn't work out how far I had travelled after the impact. It was so dark – you know what it's like here. It took ages. To find a – a person in the . . . to find him on the verge.'

Cathy says nothing, trying to think it through. It does make sense, in that real life is often more complicated than hypothetical situations. Cathy once ran into the back of a taxi and, in her panic to pull over, steered to the right instead of the left. Nobody would believe that if she said it in defence of herself, but it was true nevertheless.

Frannie's eyes are clear as Cathy's meet hers. Unwavering. Naturally sunny and unsuspicious, she is the alkaline to Joe's acid. *I couldn't stop immediately.* The words echo in Cathy's mind.

'And then,' she continues, dropping her gaze, her voice low, the exact same voice she uses when Paul is asleep and she doesn't want to wake him, 'I called you two because . . . I wanted you there. In my . . .' Cathy can tell she is trying to hold back tears. Gone is the chaos of last night, when they wrung out blood-soaked t-shirts and shouted. 'In – at a time when I felt scared and I needed you, I wanted you,' she says. 'I know it should have been an ambulance.'

'Yes,' Cathy whispers, looking at her sister. 'Yes.' She understands completely. Frannie is the youngest sibling and they have never quite forgotten that. Cathy makes Frannie's lunch most days and brings it into the practice. Not because Frannie can't, but because she's . . . well, she's babied.

She looks at Joe, whose eyes are on her, his expression drawn. He holds her gaze for a moment longer than he would usually.

He clears his throat, moves away from his position by the door and sits next to Frannie. He scoots his chair slightly closer to her.

'We need to do something to make the police think he is alive,' Joe says. 'We need to stage a missing person's investigation.'

Cathy pauses for a second, digesting this. 'False hope,' she says softly. She tucks her hair behind her ears, saying nothing, thinking. Thinking how they can't do this, how they're monsters. If Frannie is the baby of their family, then Cathy is the conscience. Isn't it up to her to stop this? 'That's – that's wicked,' she says quietly.

'What do you suggest, then? Hand her in?' Joe says, not gesturing to or looking at Frannie. 'It's done,' he adds. 'We can't take it back. We can only go forward.'

'To what?'

'We need to do it,' Frannie says.

Joe looks at Cathy. 'Do you still have his wallet?'

It is a sentence which, Cathy feels sure, is significant. The moment they cross from panic to planning. From an accident to behaving like killers. She shakes off that feeling, surely incorrect – how could she possibly tell the future? – and meets her brother's eyes.

'Yes,' she says. 'I do.'

13.

Now

Jason's Office, mid-to-late February, 5.00 p.m.

Jason has a plate of custard creams on his desk. 'Left over from a team meeting,' he says vaguely, gesturing to them as I walk across his office and sit down in the chair. 'Help yourself.'

I reach and take one.

'You are clearly reluctant to discuss what you did,' he says bluntly. He takes off the top of a custard cream, brings the cream side to his mouth, then seems to think better of it and eats it in one go. 'Right?'

'Right,' I say. 'I mean – wouldn't you be?'

Jason has his head in profile, studying the bookcase. I can't read his expression. 'Sure,' he says, and I think he means it. He doesn't think that I am a monster. 'Okay. Let me ask you this: can you pinpoint the moment that you knew you wouldn't get away with it?'

'Yes,' I say. 'Absolutely, definitely.'

'All right, then – why don't we start there, today?' He passes me the plate. I take another two biscuits. We eat them wordlessly, looking at each other. As he holds my gaze, he inclines his head to the left, like a bird listening out for noise.

'I was sitting on reception,' I say. 'It was late. Late-ish. We'd already closed up. It wasn't getting dark yet but it was that kind of gloomy day.'

'Okay,' Jason says. Still no pen and paper. Just the custard creams and his sharp mind. 'What were you doing?'

'I'd done some general filing . . . things like that.'

'Right. So this was – back in the UK.'

'Oh yeah – of course. Back to work. We were all trying to pretend everything was normal. Everything was fine.'

'How successfully, would you say?'

'Pretty unsuccessfully . . .' He throws me a wan smile that says, *clearly*. I look around me at his office. A place I never thought I'd be.

'So, next . . .' he prompts.

'I logged on to the computer.'

Jason keeps his body language casual, dunking a biscuit in his tea, but his gaze is as sharp as a needle, never leaving mine.

'And that was when I saw it. That was when I knew,' I say.

'Knew what?' he asks, looking directly at me.

I shrug. 'That we had no choice.'

14.

Then

Joe

The villa is full of signs. Little metal statutes of Jesus on the walls, tiny, palpable stigmata on his hands. A palm-sized ceramic sacred heart nailed to the top of the fireplace, a cross erupting from the top of it like a sword. Their presence has never felt significant, until now, when Joe feels watched and judged at every turn. He doesn't even believe in God. And yet.

He rubs at the back of his head. He's bone tired, the night of no sleep and physical activity beginning to catch up with him. He keeps thinking of the body, the blood slowly pooling in the crevices and creases of his palms, just outside, just over there. *You buried him.* This single fact keeps repeating on Joe, as though, if his brain tells him often enough and in different, more shocking ways, it might sink in, and he might accept it. *Your sister killed that man. You hacked through a tree root with your spade and huffed like it was merely an inconvenience, in order to bury him. Cathy closed his eyes for him.*

'Right. We don't know anything about him,' Joe says. 'Except that he was half British.'

'Exactly,' Frannie says.

'And was staying near here?'

'I guess so.'

'So it's quite likely – if he's staying around here, or lives around here – that the police will question us.'

'It is,' Cathy says.

'And if they find the body,' Joe says. 'Then they will find our DNA.'

'Yes,' says Frannie.

'So we need to destroy all the evidence we can,' Joe says. 'And make it seem like something else has happened. A different – narrative.'

He takes the pen and starts to write down the evidence on the back of an Italian pizzeria menu that he will burn later.

The hire car.

Their whereabouts.

The crime scene.

He clicks the top of the pen, on and off again, on and off again.

'This is madness,' Frannie says. 'This is actually mad.'

'We need to be meticulous.' Joe finds his jaw is tensed. He wishes she'd keep up with him. He's trying to undo her mess, after all.

'You sound like Mum,' Frannie says softly. Their mother would say that sort of thing, Joe concedes. She's never quite been able to relinquish control of the practice, regularly going over and over the books, interrupting operations.

'*Don't X-ray clients' pockets*,' Cathy says, their mother's number-one catchphrase.

Joe gives a wan smile. 'Treat each animal as you find them,' he finishes. 'Regardless of their owners' income.'

Cathy smiles across the table at him. 'I was just thinking that. You really do,' she says. 'Joseph, Catherine, Francesca – whoever you are!' she says, an exact imitation of their

72

father's chaotic inability to discern which of his children he's speaking to.

'God,' Frannie says, throwing her head back. 'We're mad to be laughing.'

'They're old jokes,' Joe says with a half-smile. 'Our mad parents.'

Their parents used to be similar, both fans of hard work and dedication. Owen, their father, grew up in a council estate in Birmingham. When he was twenty-five, he had been sweeping the floors of the factory where he had worked for a decade when it went into administration. According to Owen, he knew who worked hard, and who didn't, and where the systems did and didn't function well, and so he made the administrators an offer. They accepted it, he got a bank loan and went from cleaner to CEO. He now owns fourteen factories. But, where their mother has remained hard working, since Rosie, their father has retreated into himself, fallen into sullenness.

'I'll take that as a compliment,' Joe says lightly. And he does. Here, in crisis, he can be the patriarch, the rescuer he never was.

'Do,' Frannie says with a tiny laugh.

He makes a pot of coffee, faffing with the ignition on the gas hob. They drink old-fashioned coffee here in Italy, dripped slowly through the moka like a work of art. The nutty aroma fills the kitchen. 'I just need to check on Paul,' Frannie says.

When they're back around the table, Frannie creeps sideways, towards Joe. Cathy scoots her chair in. Together, they pore over the list, heads bent, dark hair mingling together. Something about their proximity, the coffee, the earlier joke about their father, a pause in the panic, relaxes Joe. He is glad to be here, safe, with his sisters. He'd do it again, he thinks, looking sideways at Frannie, his sister who can make him cry with laughter at impressions of their parents, gradually becoming more accurate over the years as their mother and father have become caricatures of themselves. The other option – Frannie arrested last night, beginning an indefinite stay in an Italian prison today, the call to their parents – is unthinkable.

'The car has got a massive dent in it,' Frannie says. She rakes back her hair from her smooth, tanned forehead, releasing smells of orange shampoo. 'I parked it in the usual spot, I thought . . . anything else would look suspicious.'

'I have a plan for the car,' Joe says. 'Leave it to me.'

'Okay,' Cathy says. She is used to placing her trust in Joe, and he in her. They do it all the time at work, on operations requiring two vets, when he calls her into a tricky consult he can't figure out.

'Right. Look. We can't report him missing. That would be even more suspicious. So we need to . . . we need to make it look like he is alive. I think we should use his debit card,' Joe says. Despite himself, as he puts forward his plan, he feels something rising up through him. Pride, maybe? A sort of male confidence, a protective animalistic instinct.

If Joe didn't know Cathy, he would think she hadn't heard him. Her gaze stays trained on her coffee cup, her body completely still. But then she raises her eyes to his. She doesn't want to do it, he can see that, but she also knows that she has to.

'You really mean that,' she says coolly.

'Don't you?' he says.

'I don't relish pretending a dead man is alive to his family.'

'Neither do I. Tell me if you think we have a second option,' he says tightly. 'Since you're not into resurrections.' He says it to elicit a reaction from Cathy. As ever, he doesn't get one. She turns away from him, whatever feelings she has buried deep, sealed off.

'We don't need your wisecracks, Joe,' Frannie says in a bored tone.

'What we need is a plan. A direction,' Joe says forcefully.

Cathy sighs, a long exhale that doesn't seem to end. 'Fine,' she says.

'Fine?'

'I'll sort the debit card,' Cathy says quietly, her face still turned to the side. 'You do the car.'

To Frannie, Joe says, 'You come up with a version of events for last night that we'll all stick to, in case we're questioned.'

Frannie nods. 'Okay,' she says in a small voice, the same voice she used when she found out she was pregnant, the same voice she used when she left veterinary school and decided she would just man the reception instead. Scared, but pretending not to be. 'Okay.'

15.

Cathy

Cathy is standing by the hire car. The sun is slowly cooking her skin. A relentless, dry, deep heat, like an oven door is open somewhere in the universe. Her heart is straining to pump because of the pressure in her chest. She wants to release it, to shout from a cliff-face, to grab a stranger's lapels and tell them: *We are killers!* Cathy often fantasizes about saying exactly how she feels sometimes – that she's pissed off with an owner who let their dog get ravaged by fleas, or that she feels so lonely she sometimes eats dinner in front of a mirror – but this is different. This is worse.

'It's pretty bad,' she says to Joe.

'I'm going to take it back early.'

Cathy runs a hand over the dented front bumper. Frannie's done a good clean-up job, which is surprising. Frannie is messy. The receptionist desk at work is always cluttered with her things – some of them good ideas, like the lamp they turn on if a euthanasia is taking place, so people know to be quiet. But most of it is clutter, sometimes her ASOS deliveries that she tries on in the staff room while Cathy gives her opinions.

'Won't that look more suspicious?' she says to Joe. 'It's not due back for two days.'

'Better than the police inspecting the car, isn't it?' Joe says. He shrugs, looking at Cathy.

'They won't look at the car,' Cathy says, but she's merely reassuring him. She thinks about her own behaviour at work, how she forensically goes through each possibility when an animal is sick, running down a list of less and less likely outcomes, never really intending to stop. Yes, if someone were missing, she'd check everyone's stories, everyone's cars, she thinks. She'd interview every pair of eyes in the vicinity. She shudders at the thought of it.

'Here it is,' Joe says, handing her the wallet. They're safe out here on the winding driveway, which meets the track road where it happened. Both are lined with scrubby weeds, the road untended, unvisited, thankfully. She takes it, feeling like a thief. The leather is warm against her fingers, soft as a worn cloth. It's a simple black wallet, holding only cards, three crude slashes on each side forming the pockets.

'Okay,' she says. Joe stands in front of her, his hands on his hips. The setting is too idyllic for the conversations they're having: the sky a wide blue dome up ahead, the grass a parched yellow, pretty weeds growing by the side of the track road.

'I think it should be in a shop,' he says to her. 'Use contactless. Choose one with no CCTV or – if you can't – a crowded one so you blend in. Buy something . . . a bottle of water, I don't know. Something mundane.'

Cathy nods quickly, following his logic. She stares up at him for a beat or two.

'What are you looking at?' he says curiously.

'No, nothing,' she says, turning slightly away from him. She puts the wallet in her handbag. 'I'll get the bus,' she says. 'We'll say I was sightseeing.'

'Unlikely you'd stop working long enough to sightsee.'

'Well, it's all unlikely.'

'Okay. I'll tell Frannie. She can add it to – to our thing.' Joe waves a hand, intended to be a substitute for words, and he looks so exhausted, suddenly, that Cathy wants to reach out to steady him.

'Yeah.' Cathy begins walking down the track road to the place where she waited for the bus the other day, back when she was a completely different person.

Parked just down from the bus stop is a news van. Excited Italian reporters gather, smoking, making phone calls, and typing on their mobiles. Cathy stares at her feet as she waits for the bus, wishing she weren't a blusher.

The bus is air conditioned, the temperature of a fridge, and Cathy can't help but wonder how William is faring. How cold is it seven feet under, in the middle of the day? She can't bear to think of it. Of him in that way, the healthy, alive man from the market.

Cathy had watched something develop from across the square. The man they now know to be William – wearing a denim jacket and holding a cigarette – had been standing too close to Frannie, who was gesturing with a pineapple she'd bought. Paul was on her hip.

Cathy heard her sister's voice over the hum of the market.

The owner of the stall offered up the chip-and-PIN machine to Cathy, who paid for a fountain pen she didn't need. She refused a receipt, said, 'My sister,' in English, though she knew he wouldn't understand her. She weaved her way across the market to Frannie, who was standing alone with Paul next to a towering pile of oranges.

'What's going on?' Cathy said.

'That man,' Frannie said, pointing across the market to the dark-haired man, still smoking, then ducking under the awning and leaving, 'lit up and breathed over – everything.' She gestured briefly to Paul. 'Over him.' She wasn't indignant, exactly. That wasn't Frannie's style. She was just bewildered. So shocked someone could be so rude.

'Oh,' Cathy said, nodding quickly. 'Okay – well –'

Frannie was holding a canvas bag that she'd filled with fruit. 'Paul breathed loads of it in, and these pears' – she pointed to the bag – 'now stink. I don't understand it. Why you'd . . .' She pushed a strand of her hair behind her ear, her hand shaking. Cathy's gaze lingered on it, on that small window into Frannie's vulnerability that only she would notice.

'Let's just go,' Cathy said, always keen to avoid conflict. 'I'm boiling.' She glanced sideways at her sister. 'Where's Joe?'

'Over there somewhere,' Frannie said, gesturing to a stand selling espressos. Frannie led Cathy away from the market and stood in the heat of the sun. Around them were the smells of Verona: garlic, dry heat, hot rubbish bins. There was no breeze at all. Cathy would almost be glad to go home, back to the mild British summer. Frannie stood next to Cathy, still looking for the smoking man, but they were too far away now. Frannie's back was red and sunburnt. Cathy instinctively wanted to reach a palm out to see how hot it was, to soothe her little sister. Something about her shoulders, the visible spine, made her wince.

Joe emerged, carrying a tiny paper cup filled with coffee. He was holding hands with Lydia.

'What are you doing?' he said.

'Since when do you drink espresso?' Frannie said with a laugh that sounded somehow forced. 'Who are you – a mob boss?'

'I'm on holiday,' Joe had said.

'We're done,' Cathy said.

'We left because some bloke blew cigarette smoke all over Paul,' Frannie said, tugging Paul's white sunhat down more tightly. He reached up unconsciously to adjust it.

'What?' Joe said sharply, still sipping the coffee, his shoulders tensed. Cathy glanced at him and a feeling of unease settled over her.

'Look – let's just –' Cathy said, reaching for Frannie's arm.

'You can't just smoke these days, all over food,' Frannie said. 'Even here.'

'*Frannie*,' Cathy said. She darted another look at Joe, who had puffed up, somehow bigger, his feet planted far apart, his shoulders rounded.

'It's not fucking on,' Joe said, his voice raised above the hum of the market.

'Joe,' Frannie shouted. 'Honestly – don't.'

'What?'

'Go off on one.'

'It's not *going off on one* to punch someone for smoking on my nephew,' Joe said. 'Where is he?'

'Don't,' Frannie said, reaching for him and tugging at his arm. He threw her off, spun around, looking for the man, then shouted, 'Come on, then!'

A passing policeman stopped, looking at them. 'Everything okay here?' he said.

He stood in the shadow of a doorway to a bank, wearing an all-black uniform. Red stripes down the sides of his trousers. She'd seen them around. His brown eyes caught the sunlight, turning them a strange bronze. His bottom half was still in shadow, almost invisible in the gloom.

'Yeah,' Cathy said hesitantly. 'No – it's fine. Thank you.' Her cheeks burned under his scrutiny. 'Sorry. My brother's just – you know. Just . . .' Her voice trailed off; she was unable to finish that sentence. How could she? My brother is just occasionally violent?

'Well – apart from people smoking. He's gone now,' Joe said.

The policeman inclined his head slightly, looking at Joe. 'Who?'

'This total twat who blew smoke over my sister.'

'He was a twat,' Frannie said with a laugh.

The policeman said nothing for a few seconds, looking into the distance, then back at Frannie. 'For sure, it is best not to cause any trouble while you're here,' he said softly. He had heavy-lidded eyes, cheekbones so defined it looked like somebody had taken out two great round scoops from beneath them. 'No shouting in the streets.'

'He smoked over my fucking baby,' Frannie said, uncharacteristically coarse. Cathy found the development of Frannie's maternal instinct fascinating. Previously passive, she became occasionally fierce. It presented itself in myriad ways, Cathy remembers; in the early days, Frannie was smilingly unable to concentrate on anything but Paul, her gaze constantly trained on him, laughing off nights of no sleep. That's love, Cathy assumes.

'It is not nice for a young woman like you to harass

men,' the policeman said. 'Or to swear at people when I only try . . . to help.' He puffed air out of the side of his mouth, a small, contemptuous laugh that seemed, to Cathy, to say: you have no idea how powerful I am.

That was the catalyst. The first domino. The innocuous, stupid market altercation that led them to where they are now.

Cathy stares down at her handbag, which sits at her feet on the grey floor of the empty bus. Afterwards, she is going to Juliet's Balcony. She comes each time they visit. She wanted to go, was saving it, but now she's got to go to cover up what she's really doing here. Covering up cover-ups.

She leans her head against the window as the bus pulls up near the old amphitheatre. As she steps off the bus, the sun runs warmth up her body, starting as her legs hit the sun, and moving upwards.

She thought she'd prefer some time by herself, but it feels like her heart is straining in her chest. She keeps thinking of William. His parents. A girlfriend? A child? The wallet seems to weigh down her bag more heavily than before.

Verona looks just the same as earlier in the week. Tourists out in the sun in the little alleyways, half in shade, half in light, drinking coffee, laughing, shading their eyes against the glare. Cathy walks into the main square, past the amphitheatre. She looks down one of the tunnels leading to the centre, sees blood-red carpets. All that history. Those sacrifices. Performances. Power. She turns away from it. She can't bear it.

She needs a newsagent off the main thoroughfare. She

walks up Via Carlo Cattaneo. Grey stone beneath her, azure above. Cathy is a dot in the universe.

She blinks slowly. They're going to try to make William's family – whoever they are – believe he is alive. She catches her reflection in a window. Shorts, a t-shirt. Sunglasses. She looks like a normal woman, but she is a monster. Must be. Is her own family worth so much more to her than another's? And why?

Pastel-coloured buildings crowd in. She feels like she's on a boat, like the floor is moving underneath her. She stops for a moment by a window with bars across it, like a cell, but then she has to keep moving again. Keep moving forward. Cover it up. Think about it after. Put as much distance between yourself and the crime. Deny, deny, deny, and Cathy is excellent at denying herself things. It's not such a stretch to deny that something happened too.

She walks past two mini piazzas, a posh bakery and a restaurant with Italian flags up outside it that flap in the wind, a row of Vespas.

She looks around her. CCTV is everywhere. Little round cameras, rectangular ones pointing down like birds homing in on their prey. She can't do it here. She needs a crowd. The second she uses his card, they will comb the CCTV.

She needs something as everyday as possible. Trying to look casual, she gets out her phone, then navigates across the city to Juliet's Balcony. She passes clean, bright, white piazzas with neat green topiary, polished marble floors, little alleyways, Italian chalkboards advertising things Cathy can't understand outside cafés. Shit, shit, shit. Where are the newsagents? Just as she starts to think she won't find any, she sees one. A green awning with white trim. More than a handful of people inside and out. She could blend in. She looks up, trying to look normal. No CCTV that she can see. This is it. This is their chance.

Inside, the shop is warm and dark. It smells of newspapers and sun-cream. Cathy edges behind somebody to get a bottle of water. Her entire body is covered in sweat, which evaporates off her as she opens the fridge, leaving her shivery. Her damp fingers leave impressions in the condensation on the bottle of Evian. Fingerprints. She stares at them. Her hands slip on the cold bottle. It's almost icy, a solid weight in her hands.

Just get to the till, she tells herself, walking mechanically forward.

She reaches into her handbag to touch William's wallet.

Anybody could see her here on the CCTV. Anybody could ask her, at the till, why she is using a card clearly not belonging to her. They could be old-fashioned, and ask for a signature. And then what? No. This is stupid. The skin on her chest heats up, becomes mottled.

She can't do it.

She won't do it. Cathy can't disentangle the fear from morality and logic. It is all a mess in her mind.

She pays for the water with her own card and gets out, breathing heavily, her hands two spikes of pins and needles.

She calls Joe.

'How'd it go?' he says, instead of greeting her.

'I couldn't do it, Joe,' she says softly.

'What?'

'I just couldn't do it.' She uncaps the water and sips from it, from this bottle that was supposed to – on some other immoral planet – have been purchased by a dead man.

Joe hesitates. 'You're too scared?' he asks. She casts about inside herself, wondering if it is fear, and maybe it is, partly. But she can't use a dead man's card, can't pretend to be him. Lead his family to false hope. She can't, she can't. She knows that makes no sense, given what they're trying to get away with. That, in refusing to proceed down the slippery slope, Cathy is refusing to help her sister. Her sister who is relying on her, who has always relied on her, whose hand Cathy held tightly as they crossed the busy road outside their school. And what is she doing now? Letting go. Casting her into the traffic. There is guilt whichever action she takes.

Her throat clogs with tears. She never cries. She stops them before they begin, and speaks clearly to Joe.

'I just – I feel like a criminal. It felt too risky.'

'Just come home,' he says, his voice neutral, a tone she can't read. 'Back to the villa. Okay?' he adds.

'Okay,' she says.

She decides to go to Juliet's Balcony before leaving. She needs to, to pretend that this is why she went into Verona in the first place. It's free to go and see the Balcony, if you don't mind the crowds. She runs a hand along the graffitied wall, covered in padlocks made by hundreds of lovers before her. She wishes she had somebody to tell about all this, somebody to confide in who isn't a family member, wishes too that she weren't a failure, evidently unable to grasp the most simple of intimacies. Finally, she reaches the Balcony. She gazes up at it, the small, cream-coloured box covered in ivy, and she thinks of the Capulets and the Montagues. All the sacrifices people before her have made for love. For their partners, for their lovers, for their families.

PART II
Criminal Damage

16.
Joe

Joe slides the gearstick into neutral unnaturally, using his right hand, as he approaches the hire-car place. Vans line the forecourt, reflecting bright shards of light that stay in his vision when he closes his eyes. He's signalling right. He's already done one loop, hoping nobody would notice. And now he's ready. He's worked out his target, and he's ready.

He passes through their entrance barrier, then lines the car up and presses down on the accelerator. The car propels forwards into a curved line of crash barriers, a satisfying scraping noise. He keeps going, driving the crash barriers into the car, embedding them completely. Then silence. Joe cannot help but think of Frannie and of William. Is this how it sounded? How it felt? How did it feel to be alone in the quiet, in the afterwards?

Joe waits for a few seconds, then gets out, looking mystified. Hopefully. Hopefully. Hopefully it will have dented the same spot. The sun heats the back of his neck as he leans down to look at it, as intense as a hot blade on his skin. Suddenly, in the warmth, he thinks of Lydia, smiling Lydia. who, last January said, 'Let's go to the beach for the day,' and they did. He will remember that day forever. Fish and chips from a shared polystyrene dish, wooden forks, hot salty breaths mingling into the cold foggy air. The sea disappearing in the early sunset, into the darkness. Not caring about the chill in their bones. Flasks of tea on the way home. She'd spilt hers everywhere, and he'd said, 'There's pissing hot tea on my thighs!' while trying to join the motorway slip-road. She has expanded their lives so much, and now he has risked that, their big, expansive life together, for this.

He inspects the car now. Yes. He's got it. He's covered up the dent, subsumed into a second accident, one with witnesses.

An Italian man comes out of the office, on to the pavement, right up to the barrier Joe hit. A frown crosses his face as he looks at Joe and the hire car. Joe steps into role. 'Sorry,' he says, moving towards the man. 'So sorry. I didn't see the barrier.'

'Oh,' the man says, a hand going to his dark hair. 'Right, it is okay.'

'I guess there'll be an excess,' Joe says.

'Yes – is scraped quite badly, no?' the man says, his eyes meeting Joe's. He flashes a smile. 'Oops, as you Brits would say.'

'But good for you,' Joe would usually have said back faux-cheerfully. But he must play ball today. 'Sorry,' he says sincerely. He's surprised to find his voice imbued with feeling. He doesn't want to be here, crashing cars and telling lies. And so it is easy to apologize genuinely. There is just something else he is apologizing for, is all. 'So, so sorry,' Joe says, his voice hoarse with it, with how sorry he is.

The car is taken to the side of the lot and Joe is left on the pavement in the sun. He seeks out a bench in the shade and wipes his forehead against the shoulder of his t-shirt.

At least he can look stressed. Everyone will just think he is worried about the car.

He watches a woman inspect it. She is dressed in a full suit with a scarf around her neck, like an air stewardess. She must be so hot, but there isn't a single droplet of sweat on her that Joe can see. Her hair is perfectly neat.

Joe sits, watching the woman, wondering where the minuscule droplets of blood are on the car that Frannie's definitely missed. When the police will come knocking. What his sister will say to the authorities, to a court. How she will sit that first night in the cell, all angular arms and legs, curled up alone.

He puts his sunglasses on so nobody can read his expression. The breeze smells hot and verdant, the dog days of July. He wonders if summers will always remind him of this, or if he will ever forget, if he will ever move on. He wonders when they will next come back to the villa. He wonders how they will ever sell it, knowing what lies beneath the land nearby.

The man pops out of the office, from behind Joe, making him jump.

'You are to sign here,' he says, passing him a sheet of Italian text with a pencil cross next to a signature box. He has smoker's fingers, stained sodium-yellow. Joe signs it without thinking, craving a cigarette. Whatever is written there in those T&Cs can't be as bad as what he is covering up. He passes back the pen, curling his dirty nails into his palms unnaturally, defensively.

After he's signed, the woman with the scarf arrives.

'*Grazie*,' Joe says deliberately.

'*Prego*,' the man murmurs immediately.

'I'll go now?' Joe stands up, hoping the finality of the gesture will cut through any more admin. He can't take it. His chest is aching with the effort of keeping everything inside, of managing everything.

This feeling is no stranger to Joe. Only recently, in May, he worked eighty hours in a week, not able to leave a retired – but not old – greyhound called Lucie, who had had extensive surgery. He did everything – the operations, the drug administrations, the aftercare. Double, triple shifts. Needlessly: he trusts the veterinary nurses. He trusts Evan, who was working on her with him. But he wasn't able to leave, spent any breaks he took applying nicotine patches and keeping watch through the windows. 'I won't relax at home anyway,' he'd said to anybody who would listen. And that is the truth, but, as in most things, there are multiple truths: Joe was also too anxious, too afraid of losing control, to leave. It was only when he had had a panic attack and Frannie sent him away with wine that he finally was able to relax, fell asleep on her sofa to the sound of her saying, 'I find being generally useless makes for a much happier life.' He'd drifted off, laughing softly.

'Wait, wait, wait,' the man says, an arm outstretched. Joe's heart pumps lightning around his body. 'We have to see the car is okay – yes? Other than your accident, for which you have agreed to pay this.' He taps the sheet.

The woman and the man leave to look at the car. He thought they'd already done that. He watches them from behind his sunglasses, observing their body language, their faces, as they approach the front bumper. How does she walk in those heels all day?

'This is yours?' the woman says, coming around with something burgundy in her hands. Joe's entire body jolts. But it's just Frannie's purse.

He stares at the bag in the woman's outstretched hand. It's fine. It's fine. That's not evidence. He was so busy fixing the outside of the car, he forgot to look inside. What else has he missed? Her eyebrows rise. He takes off his sunglasses. The pale pavement is blinding.

He hands over the keys, and the woman takes them. She stumbles slightly in her heels as she does so, a tiny chink in her perfect armour. 'Might want to try flats,' Joe says drily.

'Not allowed,' the woman says with a smile.

'Get him in heels too, then,' Joe says, raising his eyebrows in the direction of the man.

The woman laughs and turns away from him. The car is being taken away. He's done it. It'll be cleaned now, thoroughly, professionally, any microscopic evidence that remains wiped away.

Joe's body sags in relief as he dials the taxi number handwritten on a sign in the window. He presses *call* and feels a tap on his shoulder. 'Sorry – you miss one signature,' the woman says. Joe looks closely at her and sees three distinct beads of sweat along her upper lip. He feels sorry for her, suddenly, in that suit in this weather, like she is an overworked animal, a donkey on Blackpool beach.

Joe's always been this way. Sympathetic to all animals and only some people. He took in a stray cat when he was nine, a ginger tom that sneaked in through his bedroom window, his hips so bony, his fur matted. He fed it leftovers for a week before he told his parents. His mother wanted to put up a sign at the vets', but Joe wouldn't let her. He kept the cat, named it Peanut. He slept on Joe's pillow every night for a decade, his first pet. He looked at him one night, his spotty stomach more rounded, his fur glossy, and thought, I want to be a vet. Not because of his mother, but because of that little Peanut that slept in his bed.

'We need your consent to tow it away,' the Blackpool donkey says. She gestures down the road. A red tow truck is coming. Joe's shoulders drop. 'Not safe at all to drive,' she adds with a smile. He keeps watching. Behind the tow truck is a police car. He squints at the horizon, trying not to look guilty.

'There's nothing else?' he says.

The woman nods and he leans into the hot car, checking, checking again, but it's empty. He's just paranoid.

The woman taps the paper when he comes back. He signs his name again, this time with a shakier hand than before. He looks at the two signatures, patchy blue biro, side by side, panic inscribed within them, then pulls his gaze back to the police, who have pulled up outside the building. They're sitting in the car now, two dark-haired men, just watching the world. And watching him.

Joe heads back to the villa to retrieve the wallet from Cathy. Another thing to sort. He doesn't mind the sorting. Like Lucie the greyhound, he doesn't trust anybody else to do it. He's the head of this family now, really. It's up to him.

'I can't believe you crashed the car,' she says to him. They're in her room.

94

He laughs softly, a dark little laugh. 'What a great metaphor a car crash is,' he says, and Cathy smiles wanly.

'Now I need to do what you were supposed to,' he says, but he says it mildly. He can understand why she didn't use William's card. She places the wallet into his outstretched palm. Something about it reminds him of their childhood. Some transaction that once took place. A pact, a secret, the details of which are lost to the past.

'You're sure it's sensible?' she asks.

He pauses. 'I think so,' he says. 'We need to – we need to throw people off the scent.' He winces as he says it. Cathy's face is expressionless, but, as he walks down the stone corridor away from her room, he thinks he might be able to hear her heave a deep, sad sigh.

In Verona, Joe inches into a stuffy alleyway and stares at the wallet in his hands. On the underside, in a disused flap, he sees the distinctive curl of a piece of paper in there. He inches it out slowly. Written on it, in pen, are four digits:

8305.

A PIN.

Joe's shoulders sag in relief. He has a PIN. He'll go to a cashpoint, one without CCTV, and use it. Withdraw a hundred euros, to make it look like William was headed somewhere. Less risky. Less chance of a person asking him what he's doing. Less chance of getting caught out.

It has taken Joe half an hour, so far, to find a cashpoint without CCTV. He has bought an ice-cream and taken many crap photos, trying to look like a wandering tourist. He would never be this person in normal circumstances, has no interest in weird fucking nude monuments and ruins, not now that they have owned the villa for several years. He's done the touristy stuff.

He stands, now, scanning the bottom of the buildings. No cashpoints. A Jack Russell being pulled along too quickly by a dickhead owner catches his attention. He stares at it. It has a very obvious – to Joe – luxating patella. A tell-tale hind-limb skip, which makes it trot like it is a rabbit, not a dog. It probably needs an operation on its knee. Joe watches it for a few seconds more, thinking of saying something, but stops himself when he sees a cash-point in the distance without any CCTV around it and BANCOMAT written in blue above. It's time to focus, not to draw attention to himself.

He hurries over and inserts William's card into the machine with a satisfying plastic *zip*. The machine prompts in Italian for the PIN. 8305, he types dutifully, then waits.

PIN ERRATO, the machine says, with three horrifying beeps. Joe's shoulders are up by his ears immediately. His head drops. 'Fuck. Fuck, fuck, fuck, fuck, piss, *fuck*.'

The machine says something in Italian. He sees BANCO. Communicate, is that? Communicate with your bank?

Joe feels like his body is swarming with bees. His knees are buzzing. He can barely stand up straight. He staggers away from the cashpoint, past the luxating dog, and back to the bus stop, the wallet in his pocket feeling radioactive.

The PIN was probably for another card, or an old one. How could he be so stupid? Why did he assume it was for the debit card?

He's fucked it, he thinks. He is fucked. They can't afford to make mistakes, and yet he has. He flags down the bus, his arm feeling weak, and collapses into the air-conditioned seat, his head in his hands. After a few seconds, he stops himself. He's got to look normal. He straightens up, looking around him, then sees the CCTV, an unblinking eye at the front of the bus, trained exactly on him. For a moment – just one – he is certain he will see this footage. Exhibited, somewhere, as evidence, at Frannie's trial.

17.

Now

Jason's Office, late February, 5.00 p.m.

Another Tuesday in endless February.

I am waiting to see Jason. Five o'clock in his anteroom. Both heaters are on, pumping stinging hot air on to my knees. I'm glad of it. Even out here, I can smell his room. Old books, coffee.

I'm checking Facebook for updates from my family. I don't do it too often – it's a kind of masochism, I guess – but I can't resist it today. It's been so long since I have seen any of them: since I have been permitted to see any of them.

As I wait, I turn up the heaters, put my feet clad in tights on them – Jason won't mind – and browse.

To Joe, first. He never puts much on there, and especially not lately, but there are a few nuggets here and there for me to find. He signed a petition about Guide Dogs a while ago, which has remained on his profile since the last time I checked. Still the same profile photo, taken a few weeks before the holiday. The same sunglasses he wore the day after the cover-up. I bet he's thrown them out now. He has taken Vets 24 off his current occupation, he's just listed as a vet, location unknown.

Paul has stopped asking for him. He used to, all the time, in that nonsensical way children do. The same way he asks often if it is his birthday. Paul is an information-hoarder. One day, after everything happened, he said, note perfect, 'Joe won't want to see us for a long time,' an exact imitation of me.

Jason greets me, notepad in hand, half a Mars Bar in the other. 'Good week?' he says, as he always does. He doesn't have on any shoes today. I glance down, distracted by his pink socks. 'Sorry,' he says with a short laugh. 'Shoes got wet in this pissing weather. Hope you don't mind.'

He sits down and crosses his legs in that way that he does, and looks at me, one pink foot bobbing up and down. 'Why don't we begin to talk about it, instead of around it?' he says, his eyes directly on me.

'Verona?' I say.

'Of course.' He holds my gaze for two seconds, three, four, then gives a deliberate, disarming shrug.

'Okay.' I breathe deeply. I knew this would happen. Some of our meetings have been led by me, about emotions, things I wanted to talk about. But now I guess it is time to grasp the stinging nettle.

Jason clicks the top of his pen, poised, finally, to jot anything down. Of course. The notepad. He intended that we discuss it formally today.

I don't speak for several minutes, and he lets the silence stretch on. A road gritter moves along in the rain on the street below.

I close my eyes. It's got to happen. It is happening. And I have to be ready to talk about it. Properly. Jason, the lawyer, must take my statement. He has been so patient, until now – once told me he has given me so much more time than other clients because he felt sorry for me, but here we are.

'It was eighteen months ago,' I start falteringly. Eighteen months since my family changed, and over a year since I last saw them. 'It began on holiday.'

18.

Then

Lydia

'I can't do this,' Lydia says tearfully to Joe in their bedroom the second he walks in. He's been taking back the hire car, to save money, which irritated Lydia. Holidays are not for saving money on. Holidays are for not really knowing what fifty euros is, exactly, in pounds, and spending it anyway.

'What?' Joe says, stopping dead, like he's heard a gunshot.

'Another negative test.' She kicks her feet against the bed. 'That's all,' she adds in a small voice, his overreaction making her infertility seem trivial, though she knows that's irrational. She hates that this is ruining her holiday. That she's letting it.

Her infertility. That is how Lydia has begun to think of it. In the early months, she would tell herself that it would happen soon. That, if not, they would access fertility tests, IVF, even. She kept a note of all of this on her phone: a list of all of the reasons why things will be fine, why they will work out. And these things *are* happening, she tells herself forcefully now. They are accessing it. But, like a patient in a coma who has never once responded to any stimulus, lying there day after day as new things are tried, it's hard to keep the hope alive. Rationalizing worry or lying to herself. She isn't sure. Her mind chunters away at this particular worry, thinking and thinking and thinking about it. All pointless.

Joe's face falls into sympathy. 'It's me,' he says immediately. 'I bet it's me.'

'It's not fucking you,' she says. She turns away from him. His bluntness, his anxiety, it is so selfish, sometimes. 'It's nothing,' she adds. 'It's neither of us.'

'It is nothing,' he agrees immediately, to his credit. 'It'll happen. Nothing ever stays the same.'

He's right. People conceive all the time, don't they, even after they have struggled? People who go on holidays. People who have arranged the first adoption interview. People who have one-night stands. Desperate people. Relaxed people. It can still happen for them. Lydia raises her eyes to the bedroom window. She will be a mother, she knows it, and she can't wait to meet her children. Although she is certain they will be delinquents, raised by somebody who is – already – obsessed with baby-led weaning and the no-cry sleep method.

Joe comes right up to her and kisses the very end of her nose. 'Is my Lydia sad?' he says to her.

'She is sad,' Lydia says back to him, leaning into him.

'The end of your nose is wet now,' Joe says, still kissing it. 'Like a lovely little dog.'

Lydia laughs. God, he can always make her smile. He's as mad as she is.

She wonders how it is for him. Infertility. She asked him, once, and he lolled his head against the doorframe like a teenager and said he was fine.

The thing is, he has Paul. He is Joe's compensation, but Lydia doesn't have that, doesn't speak to a single member of her family. It was shortly after she met the Plants that it all went wrong at home for Lydia. A prying teacher at school, asking how come Lydia sometimes seemed so sad. A concealed bruise uncovered. An accidental secret told, and then the rest. The social workers. The anger-management classes her father failed to attend and her mother laughed off. The *temporary relocation* a social worker told her would take place as she collected her from school on a Thursday one November. How Lydia watched temporary become permanent, as the trees lost and regained their leaves, though nobody said as much. A Christmas with a foster family who had different traditions, who did presents *after* lunch.

Even now, when she finds herself socializing with the Plants, with these glamorous beautiful vets, whom she would only have ever admired from afar, she allows herself a small smile. For them, and their normal parents, but also for her, and how far she's come. She is not there any more, back in her childhood, in that house where her mother never opened the curtains, where her father smoked so much the entire room looked grey, and thank fucking God for that. She is here, about to have her own child, and to right some past wrongs.

But it isn't quite the same. Paul is adorable, but he isn't hers. She has nobody to anchor herself to.

She lies on the bed and checks her phone. She might have a nap. The heat out there is too much at lunch-time.

'Lyds,' Joe says. He looks at her, a familiar expression on his face. 'We can't solve everything, you know? It's a kestrel-in-the-shower situation.'

Lydia feels a grin crack across her features. In the early days of Joe joining the practice, he began a pattern of behaviour that he has yet to break. Lydia still remembers that first time. It was only a few weeks after he'd started, his first set of nights. She'd woken in the morning, Joe sleeping next to her after getting in sometime after six. It had been a deep winter morning, the heating creaking, no light from outside. Lydia had stumbled into the bathroom, reaching for her towel in the half-light. All she remembers is turning on the bathroom light to find an injured kestrel sitting in the shower tray, staring at her in equal surprise. She'd screamed, and Joe had rushed in, and said, 'Oh, yes, there's a kestrel in there,' and they'd doubled over in laughter. 'He's had better days,' Joe had said, pointing to his leg. 'I couldn't leave him.' Joe had turned and gestured then to a handwritten sign he'd attached to the door of the bathroom. *Warning!!!!!* it said. *There is a kestrel in here!* 'Hardly an explanation,' Lydia had said drily, and Joe had kneeled down to check the bird's leg and said, 'Don't kick a kestrel while he's down.' Other animals had followed – most memorably, an owl sitting calmly on the arm of their sofa, which Lydia discovered when getting a glass of water – but *a kestrel in the shower* became marital shorthand for trying to take on too many problems at once.

'I know,' she says, flashing him a small smile. 'We haven't had one for a while.'

'I'll bring you home a real nice kestrel soon,' Joe says easily, moving some clothes off one of the chairs.

Her phone makes a noise, the BBC Breaking News noise. 'Wow – have you heard this?' she says, showing him. Joe finally stops tidying and looks at her.

'A major search is under way in the hills just outside

Verona, Italy, as British national, William McGovern, thirty-one, is missing,' Lydia reads.

'Oh.' The bed dips with Joe's weight as he sits down next to her.

Lydia keeps reading. 'He lived near here,' she says looking up at Joe. 'He was a policeman, apparently. An Italian policeman but half British.' Joe is completely still next to her, as though she hasn't even spoken, likely not even listening.

Maybe the test was wrong. It was too early. Not enough HCG in her system yet. She calculates it. It's possible. It's just possible. Hope ignites for Lydia. Yes. She hasn't yet had her period – due sometime today but still not here. She may yet be a mother. She might *already* be a mother, she thinks, wondering if sperm has met egg, after all.

'Do you think I should do another test – tomorrow?' Lydia says, putting down her phone. 'I know I sound mad,' she adds, expecting him to laugh, to indulge her as he usually does.

'I don't know,' Joe says tightly. He reaches for her phone and reads the news article. Typical Joe. He can't engage with difficult topics except about animals and his bloody sisters.

No, she's just jealous, Lydia tells herself. Stop being petty. They are not more deserving of their beautiful, cohesive family unit than her. It is just luck, just bad luck.

'I haven't had my period yet,' she says, but that makes him stare at her phone even more intently.

'I can't believe about that policeman,' he says.

'I know.'

'It's too hot in here,' Joe says, opening a window. He leans over Lydia to do it, and she breathes him in. But, for just a second, she sees the Joe the rest of the world sees. Caustic, *difficult*. Not her Joe, interior Joe, soft as butter. Usually.

19.
Joe

Joe hears Cathy sigh through her nose. 'A policeman,' she says. The three of them have locked themselves in the main bathroom in a panic, hiding from Lydia.

The bathroom is hideous – truly, enough to give you nightmares, but not enough to make you renovate it when it's hot outside. A monstrous white bath tub with three stairs leading up to it. The sort of bath you'd have an orgy in. Beige stone tiles everywhere, up the walls, up the steps to the bath, across the ceiling . . .

'It shouldn't matter,' Frannie says from her position on the bottom bath step. She is fiddling with an expensive glass bottle of bath oil, taking the cap on and off. Joe wishes she wouldn't, feels like a teacher with a fidgeting student. Every time she does so, the room is filled with the cloying scent of roses. Her gaze is fixed in the middle distance as she does it, and he wishes she would concentrate.

Lydia isn't pregnant. Lydia isn't pregnant. She retreated into the toilet, came out pale-faced and wan. Her period had arrived. Amazing how much that fact still bothers him, even in this mad, surreal, murderous context.

He and his sisters have been in the bathroom, discussing the fact that William was a policeman, and getting their stories straight. According to the news, *local police in Verona are going to begin interviewing any potential eyewitnesses this afternoon.* Joe had wondered why it was so fast, and now he knows: they haven't killed a civilian. They have killed a fucking cop.

'Do you have that piece of paper?' Cathy says to Joe.

'The incorrect PIN?'

'No,' Cathy says, her voice just slightly sharper than usual, the only variance Joe has been able to spot since he told her about his botched cashpoint attempt. 'That piece of paper, remember, the thing from his pocket with the – with the blood on it.'

'Oh,' Joe says. 'Sorry. Sorry, my brain doesn't work as fast as yours.'

'Nobody's does,' Frannie says. 'Cathy is the hare and we are the tortoises.'

'Oh, thanks,' Cathy says.

'A beautiful hare,' she says to Cathy. 'And a handsome tortoise,' to Joe, which makes him smile.

'Can tortoises be –'

'The paper?' Cathy says.

'Yes. Sorry.' He unlocks the bathroom as quietly as he can and creeps down the stone hallway to his bedroom, sliding the wallet and the piece of paper out of the pocket in the lining of his suitcase.

Back in the bathroom, he passes it to Cathy. She sits down next to Frannie – who is, typically, being of no assistance – and spreads it on the step between them, looking at it. Their tanned legs stretch out in front of them. They're both in denim shorts, Frannie in a halter neck that exposes too many ribs, Cathy in a pale denim shirt that shows off her tanned arms.

'Let's just google it,' Frannie says.

'We can't translate it online, remember?' Joe snaps. 'In case . . . in case anyone ever looks.'

'Oh, yeah,' Frannie says. 'Sorry. I forgot.'

'Again.'

'Look – I'm trying, okay? I'm sorry.' She starts fiddling with her phone.

'I hope you haven't told the cavalry,' Joe says, which is how he refers to her many friends and acquaintances. Frannie is the only thirty-something he knows who has a TikTok account.

'Of course I haven't,' she says, hurt.

'Ignore him,' Cathy says kindly. 'Look. This doesn't mean we can't decipher it in some way. He was a police officer. You know?'

Joe stares at her, waiting.

'We have new information,' she says patiently. Joe feels a sting of shame that she is always three steps ahead of him.

'He must have been off-duty in the market,' Frannie says. She pulls the cap off the bath oil again and Cathy takes it from her. 'What?' she says.

'Stop messing with stuff. Everything. Your phone goes off all the time.' As if on cue, it makes a noise, and Frannie looks at it, her cheeks red.

'It's Mum,' she says. 'In the group WhatsApp.' Joe pulls out his phone and looks at it.

Have you seen about the missing man near you? she's written. They stare at each other, saying nothing.

'If only she knew,' Frannie says softly.

'I know,' Cathy says.

Joe puts away his phone, ignoring his worrying mother,

and looks at the piece of paper. It's illegible. Even if it were in English, he wouldn't be able to make out much of it. It is in four pieces, torn and soft around the edges, like a used tissue. Already the blood dashed across it has faded from red to dark brown, disturbing inkblots patterned across whatever the document once was.

'*È stato mandato*,' Cathy says.

'Sorry?' Joe says.

'That's what I can make out, just here . . .' Cathy says. She lifts the pieces to show him. Dried blood floats off it, a burgundy grainy sand, and they stare at it. Frannie's cheeks flush. She stands and wets some toilet paper, wiping it up carefully from the bathroom tiles. Nobody looks closely at the smear of red on the tissue, old blood reinvigorated.

Joe is staring at the pieces of paper. 'I don't know what I'm looking at,' he says. 'We've done this once already. Let's just forget it.'

'Joe,' Cathy says, while Frannie washes her hands. She cocks her head a second, listening out. Joe starts. Is that somebody on the stairs?

'Look, it's here,' she says slowly to him. 'You're not being thick, don't worry.'

'I didn't say I was,' Joe says, though that is exactly what he thought. Cathy traces the words in front of him, looking down at the paper and then up at him, to check he has understood.

'Okay – and?' he says.

'I don't understand either,' Frannie says reliably.

'Well.' Cathy stands and goes to the window, holding the documents in the light. Frannie catches Joe's gaze and rolls her eyes. Joe gives a soft half-smile to his ally.

'Joe?' Lydia's voice calls out in the corridor.

'Shit,' Joe mouths. 'Be down in a bit,' he shouts. He is met with silence. Lydia isn't replying or moving. 'Go down – I'll be down soon.' God, the last thing Lydia needs is this, the implosion of the closest thing she has to a family as an adult. She will refer to her upbringing casually now to him, but he was with her a few weeks ago, at her work summer party, when some distant lawyer enquired about where she'd grown up. Lydia had been vague and stiff, and had turned to him, sad eyes and shoulders, and said, 'There is no way to bring up domestic abuse at a summer party without putting everyone on a downer.' But then he'd watched as she deliberately calmed herself, got another drink, took off her shoes and danced with him, his Lydia. A beautiful flower that grew up through a crack in concrete.

'Where is everyone?' she says. He hears Paul say something illegible. Frannie's gaze goes from indolent to alert, staring intently at the door.

'Not sure.'

'Okay, then,' she says, her footsteps finally retreating.

'I know what this is,' Cathy says to Frannie and Joe. She goes back over to them, holding it out. 'It's a police document.'

'I'll be by the pool, with Paul, then,' Lydia calls, from further away.

'Okay,' Joe shouts in a panic, though he feels bad.

Paul used to cry on walks with Joe, but only if they went at night. He couldn't work it out. In the day, he seemed to love being walked around the country lanes, but in the night, screams. Joe tried different routes, warmer clothes. Until one day he followed Paul's gaze and realized: he was terrified of the moon. The fucking moon! Joe had bought Paul a book all about what the moon was and read it to him, and eventually he'd clapped when he saw it, and Joe's heart became a sunburst, the moon reflecting the light back to Paul, his nephew.

Frannie stares at the door with big, wet eyes. She turns to Joe. 'You're going to have to tell Lydia. She'll – she'll figure out something is up.'

'Frannie,' Joe snaps.

'What?' Frannie says, her eyes round and hurt, staring at him.

'Just – we're already trying to fix this mess,' he says tensely. 'Stop adding to the chaos.'

'I'm not.'

'Just grow up,' he says tightly.

'Excuse me?' Frannie says. Joe ignores her.

'Listen,' Cathy says, a rare urgency imbuing her voice. She holds out the pieces of paper in front of her. 'Look at this, on this one. *È stato mandato*, right? The edge of a seal, up here in the corner, maybe like a local police office or something? And down here, on this one – what do you make that out to be?'

She hands it to Joe. It feels like an exam. He reads it slowly. Then again. Then a third time.

'It says Plant,' he says, as confused as if Cathy has sprouted another head right there in the hideous bathroom. 'It says Plant?'

'What?' Frannie says, standing too.

'It says Plant, and you can just make out 03/07, under the seal, 3rd of July,' Cathy says. 'It's a warrant. It's a warrant.'

'*What?*' Joe says.

Cathy's gaze swivels to Frannie. 'This cop had a warrant for our arrest.'

20.

Joe

'Whose arrest?' Frannie says, frowning, and Joe is pleased she is as confused as he is, that maybe he isn't as thick as he feels.

'I don't know. I can only make out *Plant*.'

'Maybe it isn't to arrest. Maybe it's just to search?' Joe says. 'I don't know, we have a lot of people in the villa over the year . . . maybe one of them did something.'

'Right.'

'You met him for the first time in the market?' Cathy asks Frannie.

'Yes.'

'He's got a warrant dated three days before that.' Cathy's words hang in the air around them. She's staring at both of them in turn, her eyes wide.

The messy truth is dawning on Joe. They have buried a policeman who had a warrant for one of them. 'Frannie, who have you killed?' he says hoarsely.

But it is Cathy who gets to the centre of the issue. 'Warrants aren't issued in a vacuum,' she says. 'The police will know. They will know he was coming for us – for whatever reason.'

'Shit,' Joe breathes. Downstairs, he hears a commotion. More than just Lydia. There's somebody else there. Somebody is knocking.

*

Joe stops in the hallway. He's so aware of every part of his body. What his hands are doing, his shoulders, his facial expression. He's going to give himself away; he's not an actor. He's not cut out for this.

It's the police, the Carabinieri. Joe can see that through the glass window in the heavy wooden door. A black hat, black suit, red stripes down his trousers. There is something frighteningly official about it. The pomp and circumstance, the military undertones. He's only glad that it is not the Polizia di Stato. That it is not the people who threatened him outside the bar on that first night.

'*Ciao*,' the policeman says. 'You may be aware – maybe? We are looking for William McGovern.' Joe takes in his lilting Italian tones. 'We are interviewing everyone in the vicinity to see if they have any useful information.' His cool, dark eyes scan across Joe's face. Cathy arrives behind Joe, stopping on the penultimate step, waiting. Frannie has stayed upstairs.

Joe tries not to let any tension set in in his body, uncurls his hands from fists, drops his shoulders. 'I'm Mario,' the policeman adds. 'At the station,' he says, 'if I may have a word or two with you, first?' He addresses Joe.

'Right,' Joe says. 'I'll come now, if I can help.'

The Carabinieri holds the door open for him, leaving Cathy behind. 'You come after,' Mario says over his shoulder. She nods. Her face is so pale. None of them has slept yet. But it is almost finished, Joe is hoping, as he gets into the police officer's car, in the back seat, like the criminal he is. They've disposed of the body, and they will be interviewed by the police, and then, in a few hours, that will be that. It has to be that way. He has to tell himself it will be that way.

21.

Now

Jason's Office, early March, 5.00 p.m.

'All right now, cycling past the crime, why don't you tell me about the steps you took to mitigate things.'

'I know you mean the cashpoint bungle,' I say immediately. 'The thing is – none of us wanted to be doing that stuff. Joe just – he felt he had to, I guess. I now know.'

'Yes, I see.' I can hear the ball bearing in Jason's pen moving up and down across his pad.

'Committing other crimes. After – after the first,' I stammer.

'Don't worry,' Jason says. 'This is all stuff we know, remember.' He checks his watch discreetly. Almost the end of the day. Almost ten to six. 'I just need to finalize this.' He looks at the window. We're into early March and it's getting lighter earlier in each session. 'We need to explain your thinking.'

I laugh, a small, sardonic laugh. 'Er, none?'

He throws me a wry smile. 'Right?' If only he could meet my family, to ask them too. But I haven't spoken to them for over a year, so he surely can't.

'Where do you *go*, after these sessions?' I say suddenly.

'Everyone asks eventually.' Something about Jason's body language is childlike, his leg kicking the underneath of his chair just once. It reminds me immediately of Paul.

I am assaulted by another memory. A beach day last December. Paul wanted to get in the water, even though I kept showing him how cold it was, dipped his little fat hands in it repeatedly, but all he did was wrinkle up his nose and laugh.

In the end, I took off my shoes and socks, wet sand yielding underfoot like chocolate puddings. Then I rolled my jeans up and paddled in, holding him while he shouted with joy, up there in the warmer air. It was a day much like today. March looks pretty much like December in Birmingham, like the world stops turning for three months and it just rains and rains.

Jason has one of his feet up on the chair next to him now, and he rubs at his eyes while yawning, not covering his mouth. I like this about him, this intimacy, this earthiness. Like he doesn't care at all how well I get to know him. He has no boundaries. Most people treat me like a leper, so it's nice. That's all.

'Why didn't you confess sooner?' he says, changing the subject, and asking the first truly barbed question he's asked me. 'It seems there were a lot of opportunities.'

'Because I only felt I could . . . when we reached the point of no return.'

'Which was?' Jason clicks his pen.

'In the outhouse. At the bottom of our gardens.'

PART III
Perverting the Course of Justice

22.

Then

Joe

The Verona Police Headquarters is a brown-stone building right in the centre of the city. A blue Polizia car is sitting outside it when they approach.

Inside, the station has sea-green carpets and smells of cigarettes and coffee, even in the bathroom, where Joe currently stands, in a panic. The interview is conducted by a prosecutor, not a police officer. This has rattled Joe, who has asked to use the toilet.

He is staring at his reflection in a cracked mirror above a grey ceramic sink. Isn't it seven years of bad luck if you smash a mirror?

If he thinks of Frannie, he can see her features shifting underneath his, like one has been traced from the other. They used to share a bathroom and get ready together on Saturday nights. They'd narrate their outfit choices, the way they were doing their hair, their faces side by side in the mirror. They called it their Saturday Show. Cathy thought it was ridiculous.

Joe reaches out to run a finger over the length of the crack. It's jagged, the broken glass rugged terrain underneath his skin. Maybe one day, he thinks, looking at himself, index finger looming large in the mirror, he will forget today. This sink. This crack. Surely, in a year, maybe two, they will all forget, they will all relax.

He meets his eyes in the mirror, then looks away. He leaves the mirror, the crack, the bad luck behind him.

'So,' the prosecutor Matteo – Matt – says to Joe. 'Can you answer our questions?'

The room is old-fashioned. A meeting suite that looks more like an office. A dark-wood desk in the corner with red felting stitched into it. A table in the centre with two cheap plastic chairs. A tape recorder whirring next to them. This man is a lawyer for the state. Should Joe get his own? Or would that say more than anything about his guilt?

He meet's Matt's eyes. They're a pale, ashy kind of brown, the colour of driftwood. He has a square-shaped face, an upturned nose like a child's. Maybe early forties.

'That's fine,' Joe says. 'Happy to. But I don't know how much help I can be.'

'You are here on a holiday, yes?' Matt says, upending his pen on the table with a soft click but not looking at it. He is staring intently at Joe, his other hand across his mouth, obscuring his expression.

'Yes, with my sisters, that's right.'

'You have been having a nice time?'

'Sure.'

'Sure . . . okay,' Matt says.

'The usual.'

'Right, yes, yes. And what do you mean by *sure* and *the usual*?' Matt says, putting on a faux-British accent as he says the words.

Joe is sure that Matt is not a nice person, but, then, he thinks that about most people. He is blinking deliberately often, as though he has been told to, like somebody imitating a human. He nurses a coffee in a squat cup that rests on a white saucer. Joe has a plastic cup of water that has three melting ice cubes in it.

'We've had a nice, relaxing break,' Joe says tightly, the lie steaming into the room out of his mouth. His breathing is fast. He is hanging all his hope on the story they concocted being enough, like putting up a fake painting and hoping it fools people into thinking it's real.

'Here I have a photograph of Will,' Matt says, sliding a laminated A4 piece of paper over the table to Joe. Matt has large, leathery hands that look older than his face. Hands that could definitely punch, that could cause damage. Joe looks at his own hands, surgeon's hands, elegant hands, and thinks that even if he wanted to, he couldn't get out of here.

He tries not to show the physical reaction he has to seeing Will, alive, young, in Carabinieri uniform, minus the hat. A bright, white smile, an American smile. Eyes that slant downwards at their edges. Pink cheeks. Joe swallows, but his throat doesn't seem to be working, is too dry. He takes a sip of water to cover up a cough.

He waits a beat. He should remember this man from the market, he knows he should, but he simply deletes it from his memory. He can't admit to it. Not now he's here in this stuffy little room with this *lawyer* waiting for him to slip up. Sod it. He'll say he wasn't at the market.

He looks at the prosecutor and thinks, Let Cathy and Frannie say they recall him from there, and let me remove myself. If Frannie is ever rumbled, let Joe not be – let Joe not be involved at all. He closes his eyes in self-loathing. He knows it's dishonourable. But he also knows a lot of people would do the same.

'Never seen him,' he says, trying to smile Will's bright, white smile at Matt. 'Sorry.'

Matt says nothing, his face expressionless. The only movement in the room is the rhythmic clicking of his pen and the ticking of a clock on the wall. Joe counts the seconds. Three. Four. Five.

'You not recognize him?' Matt says, inching the paper over again towards Joe.

'No,' Joe says, after three fake seconds' thought.

'What have you done – in beautiful Verona?' Matt says conversationally.

'Oh, you know. Relaxing by the pool in the villa, and in town,' Joe says truthfully. It is nice to tell the truth, the same feeling as playing a trump card. *See*, it says. *I'm not always a liar.* He shakes his head. He's got to get out of the mind-set that Matt knows him to be lying. He doesn't. This is so routine to Matt. One interview of many. Joe doesn't tell him about the bar. The first night. He will say it didn't seem relevant if they ever find out. God, he can't believe Frannie has put him in this position. That his past indiscretions against pricks with Vespa helmets might loom large.

'What have you been doing over the past, say, twelve hours?' Matt says. 'Sightseeing? Drinking?'

'We had a –'

'You were out early-ish? This morning? Eleven?'

'I . . .' Joe hesitates.

'I knocked,' Matt says, looking Joe directly in the eye. 'Early this morning.'

Joe puffs air into his cheeks. Matt won't let him finish. 'Yes,' he says loudly. He takes a breath and speaks more quietly. 'I was – I was taking the car back.' He can't lie. There'll be cameras at the hire-car place, paperwork.

This is the sticky bit. He just wasn't sure it would come up. Or wouldn't come up so soon anyway.

'Yes,' Matt says, still staring at him. 'And you are off home soon?'

'The day after tomorrow. Avoid the queues.'

'The queues right next to the airport,' Matt says lightly. He very deliberately puts the pen down and looks at Joe. His eyebrows are drawn together, quizzical rather than suspicious. Joe is no good at this, can't tell if Matt's bluffing or genuinely confused. Cathy would know. Joe always says exactly what he thinks, and can't read people who don't.

The late-afternoon sun slants in through the window. Joe turns his face to it, trying to look unconcerned. It could be a musty police station in the UK. The signs are in Italian and the coffee – not offered to him, *grazie* – smells better, but that's all.

'Yes, by the airport,' Joe says, looking back at Matt. 'But isn't it always better to get those things out of the way? Save some money – we didn't need it for the last few days?'

'So you would then get a taxi to the airport later?' Matt says. His tone is neutral, his face impassive, but his words are incisive, like a firm, gripping handshake that won't let go. Joe is drowning in these logical words. Of course he wouldn't have taken the hire car back ordinarily.

'Exactly,' Joe says.

'To save money?' the prosecutor says with a wry smile.

'Yes.'

'And so last night, before you took the car back?' Matt says. He upends the pen again.

Joe tries to turn his mind to the story he agreed with Frannie, but he's no good under pressure. It's why he prefers surgery to consulting. Surgery, for him, is stress-free. The patient unconscious, not looking at him, no expectant owners. He is alone. He is the hero, the father-figure, the God.

'Yes, I . . .' Joe says. The clicking of Matt's pen. The ticking of the clock. He reaches for his water and sips it, the ice cubes bobbing against his lips.

Either Matt knows, or everybody is a suspect, Joe is thinking, as he looks at Matt's even features. Large eyes. A high forehead. Hair swept back like a Gillette advert. But he can't know. Wouldn't he arrest them if he did?

Sweat prickles under the neckline of Joe's top. He narrows his eyes as they meet Matt's. 'Last night?' he says, stalling.

'Yes – what did you . . . do?'

'The usual, you know, holiday stuff,' Joe says. God, why can't he think? Barbecue. They said a barbecue. But all Joe is thinking about is how he is choking. How he can't seem to find any air. What time did the barbecue start? He can't remember, and Matt will ask him. His mind is empty.

Matt lets a little laugh out of the side of his mouth. It's contemptuous. 'Can you be a little more specific?' he says.

'I was with my family.'

'. . . yes.'

Joe can't breathe for just a second. His throat seems to catch as he tries. Is there enough air in this room? His eyes dart to the closed window, the door that has a blue jacket hanging from it. He takes a stifled breath, moves his t-shirt's neck away from his skin. Will's dead eyes. His curled grey hands. The smell of the earth. Frannie, Frannie, Frannie. His littlest sister, who bought him a stone statue of his old cat Peanut that sits on his back-garden patio. Who buys the exact wine he likes for their Friday-night drinks, who sends him a photo of the bottle on the checkout in Sainsbury's when she shops on Thursdays.

'We do not have all day . . .' Matt says.

Joe's jaw twitches. 'Amazingly enough, neither do I,' he says tensely. Anxiety so easily converts to anger for him.

'Why don't you want to answer the question?'

'I do,' Joe says tightly. 'I had a barbecue with my sisters. Pretty late.' He surreptitiously tries to wipe the sweat off his upper lip with his finger. His stubble scratches against his skin. What if Matt knows everything about the document William had on him? Is waiting for Joe to say?

'A barbecue,' Matt says. 'No wife? Girlfriend?'

'She wanted an early night.'

'Where did you have this barbecue?'

'A little way from the villa.'

'I see. Nice food? Wine?'

'Yeah, all that.'

'See anyone else?'

'No. We had a salad-type meal, around five, with my sister's baby, Paul. Then –'

'Is this Catherine or Francesca?'

Joe freezes. So he knows his siblings.

'Frannie,' Joe says. And now it's his turn to blush. There it is. He has spoken the name of the killer.

'I am looking forward to interviewing her. So – your barbecue was after your dinner, yes? A second meal?' That neutral expression again as he unpicks Joe's lies as easily as pulling at a loose thread. Oh, you think you're so fucking clever . . .

'Yes. We just had some – we had some sausages later . . . none of us could sleep.'

'I see. So you – you texted each other?'

'No! We were just – we had a bit of alcohol and then decided to cook.'

'I see. So not trying to sleep, then.'

'Oh, do you know what?' Joe says. He pushes the table away from him and towards Matteo, then stops himself, stops himself from telling this lawyer to go fuck himself.

Matt cocks his head to the side. 'What?'

'We weren't tired,' Joe says, backtracking, trying to recover it. God, he is a bad liar.

'So nobody else came to your barbecue, didn't see anything unusual?'

'No. Nothing.'

'What time did it go on until?'

'Early hours.'

'One? Two?'

'Something like that. I had a lot of beer,' Joe says, letting out a fixed smile.

Matt waits, quite what for Joe isn't sure, then scrapes his chair back, tosses the pen on to the table like he is disappointed and reaches to shake Joe's hand in his huge one. 'Again,' he says, 'if you think of anything you might've missed. If you hear anything about Will. You will let us know?'

'I will,' Joe says. 'Are we done now?' He places his fingertips on the edge of the table, ready to go. He is sure he sees Matt's eyes flick to his brittle, dirty nails, just momentarily, but it could have been a blink. It could have been anything.

'Yes, done,' Matt says. As he rises, Joe sees that he's thick-set. A face like a Roman bust, so perfect in its proportions, but a wide stomach that swells as he stands. Matt catches him looking and avoids his gaze for a second.

He asks for Joe's number, and he gives it.

As he has his hand on the panel of the door which in the UK would say PUSH but here says SPINGERE, Matt speaks again. 'Where did you hire the car from, again?'

Joe's body stills. That *again* is a lie. Falsely casual. 'Holiday Rent Now,' he says, not looking back at Matt, not trusting himself to.

'No problems,' Matt says.

Joe leaves. Outside, he looks up into the sky. There are two clouds floating next to each other. They're round, like somebody has blown smoke rings into the sky. His mind is spinning, spinning, spinning. As he walks off, free, to buy a packet of cigarettes – finally – he still feels like he's in there. Still captive and claustrophobic. Still under watch.

23.

Cathy

Cathy has been sitting on the second-to-bottom step where Joe left her, thinking about the millions of paths they could and should have taken last night. They could have collectively blamed it on another, unidentifiable car. Said William was drunk, and weaving in the road. Maybe the police wouldn't have remembered what had happened with Frannie at the market. Maybe they were too hasty, led by Joe's cynicism and Frannie's fear. And now it's too late, it's too late, it's too late.

She has been thinking too about why an Italian policeman was walking alone on a Verona road, towards their villa, carrying a warrant with their surname on it. For the first time, Cathy sees a different perspective. What if there's much more to this than meets the eye? What if William was coming to find them? What if he knew something about a member of her family? Joe? Frannie? Lydia? Cathy herself?

But, just as she thinks it, the perspective disappears, and she can't quite catch it again, no matter how hard she tries.

The police station is nothing like anything in the UK. There is evidence everywhere that Italy is old, and old school. From the outside, it looks like an ancient ruin. Brown-stone, blocky. Dirty in that charming way of old buildings, marred with centuries of people's living. The fawn-coloured stone is water-stained, a huge blemish above the door that looks like coppery old blood.

A man in a black stab vest with POLIZIA written on it greets her at reception. She is led into a room that smells of newspapers and coffee. As she stares at an evidence bag in the corner of the room, she thinks of Will's skin, bluish in the moonlight. His fingernails dirty with grime by the time they got him into the earth. The way, in the end, because of the depth of the hole, they had to throw him in like a rag doll.

A prosecutor sits opposite her. He is clean-shaven, not handsome exactly but perhaps interesting to look at.

'We are interviewing anyone who might have seen something connected to Will,' he says to her in perfect English. His name is Matt. 'Last night between eleven o'clock and noon today.'

'Okay,' she says, trying to sound normal.

Will. Such a simple piece of knowledge but meaningful too. He preferred Will over William. The same way she prefers the shortened version of her name too. Maybe his parents were – like hers – stuffy and traditional. Catherine, Francesca and Joseph and Rosemary. So formal.

'Eleven o'clock?' she says, stalling for time. That must be the time he was last seen by anybody. Except them, of course.

The prosecutor is holding a biro, his grip loose. He checks his watch and writes the time along the top of the lined pad. Cathy is good at reading people, and, in her opinion, there is nothing to suggest that this man knows what's going on.

Matt seems, to Cathy, to be running through an entirely routine list of questions.

'So your siblings and you were – up late?'

'Yes, that's right – we stayed up having a few drinks outside.'

'And the drinks became a barbecue?' His tone is mild but his brown eyes are watchful, flicking across her like she is in a scanner. His gaze on her eyes, then her hands, her fingertips, her legs drumming rhythmically underneath the table. It causes a slight tremor, and she knows he's noticed. Perverting the course of justice, she is thinking. Right now, right this second, she is committing another crime.

Briefly – only briefly – she imagines telling the truth. Sailing Frannie up the river to save herself. But she could never do it. She loves her too much. Frannie would never do it to her. Is that right? Cathy hopes so, but sometimes thinking about her place in the family is too raw, since what happened with Rosie.

'Yes.'

Matt hasn't written a single other thing on the pad. He is just waiting for more detail. When she doesn't give it, he asks, 'Where exactly were you?' He breaks to sip a black coffee.

'A little away from the villa. We didn't want to wake Joe's wife.'

'Lydia.'

'Yes.'

'Did you do anything else? Take a walk?'

She stops for a second. What if the police check their phones? They were tracking their locations, most probably, in the woods. There will be a record, somewhere, of

Frannie's phone call to Cathy, even though they have deleted their call logs. 'No, I don't think so,' she says. 'Er – things are a bit hazy. We were drinking.' She tries not to feel shame. Tries to live the lie, getting so close to it that she becomes it, like taking on somebody's accent or stealing their body language. It's fine to drink on holiday. To stay up late. There was no body. No accident. Only alcohol, her siblings, the crickets, the moonlight. The elements of it that she chooses to keep.

'That is what your brother said,' Matt says, and Cathy picks up the subtext immediately, like a gun in the small of her back.

'No idea of anything else?' he adds.

'Hmm. I haven't had much sleep.'

She isn't thinking as strategically as she should be. They didn't think this through. The certainty that they've made a mistake flashes up and down her body. Her armpits become damp. She takes a sip of water from the white cup, but her hand is shaking. It's all so obvious.

'Okay,' Matt says, his tone sceptical. 'And then – and then what?'

'Then we went to bed,' she says.

'At . . .' She can hear the trailed-off sentence. The *t* comes right at the end of the word, a soft click of his tongue, a full stop.

'I'm not sure.'

'Same as Joseph,' he remarks. Don't respond to it, Cathy thinks. Don't think like a guilty person. Don't be on the defensive. 'You were drinking . . . lots, yes?' he says, inclining his head. A lock of his dark hair falls forwards, stiff with gel.

'Yes.'

'Anything can happen,' he says softly. Cathy looks up at him sharply, but tries to keep her features impassive.

She says nothing. She is the Cathy who never answered the phone call. A different person entirely.

'You all right?' Matt says dispassionately. He glances to her armpits. 'You're hot?'

'I'm fine.'

'And on this night when you were drinking – you saw nothing, you heard nothing? Nothing unusual?'

'No.'

'Do you know this man – the missing man?' Matt says. He holds up a printed sheet containing a photograph of the man whose body Cathy buried last night. He is not exactly how she remembers from the market. He is bigger here, has especially red cheeks. Two round, perfect circles, like a cartoon boy. 'You seen him anywhere?'

Cathy takes the print-out between her fingers, looking into Will's eyes. *Why did you have a warrant with our surname on it?* she asks him silently. She glances up at Matt, wondering if he knows the answer.

She looks down again at Will. She's got to be honest about the market. There will be CCTV, witnesses. It is only his killing she must erase from history.

'Maybe,' she says carefully. 'I think my sister might have spoken to him.'

'Your sister?'

'At a market. He was smoking – she asked him not to. One of your colleagues was there too,' she says. 'Well, the police.'

Matt nods. His face remains closed. If Cathy had to

132

guess, she would say that he already knew this information. Nobody's poker face is that good. Suddenly she's no longer hot, she's freezing.

He picks up his pen. 'When was this?'

'Friday,' she says. 'About two.'

'Okay, so this man was smoking . . .' he prompts, and Cathy explains what happened while Matt writes it down.

'It might not be him, I don't know. They look a little alike,' she finishes. 'We went home afterwards.'

'You and Frannie.'

'And Joe.'

'I see,' Matt says, his face blank again. 'All of you, your sister, your brother, were there.'

'That's right.'

Matt says nothing for a beat. 'And you – your family, you're going home the day after tomorrow?' he eventually asks.

'Yes,' she says, raising her head, her eyes meeting his.

'You have enjoyed Verona, yes?'

'Definitely,' Cathy says, her shoulders beginning to relax. She shifts her chair back, just slightly.

'You will take the hire car back on your way to the airport, I am guessing?' His body language is completely still, like somebody peacefully watching something unfold in the distance.

'It's been taken back already,' she says.

'Already? By . . . family?'

'Yes.'

'But the airport and the hire-car place are right next to each other,' Matt says to her. His expression isn't suspicious. It's open-hearted, as though he's waiting for her to clarify, sure that she will.

Cathy shrugs. There's nothing else she can say or do, except hope.

'Okay,' Matt says, like a disappointed teacher. 'Free to go.'

When she gets back, she finds Frannie and Paul by the pool. She offers to have Paul while Frannie goes for her interview, a team involved in a grotesque relay.

She sits with Paul on the sun-lounger, resting the side of her head against the top of his, breathing in his biscuity smell, thinking how she hopes he never has to go through something like this.

He turns to her and their eyes meet. 'You'll never know what we did for you,' Cathy says to him, knowing he won't understand, won't take it in. 'We did it because we love you.'

Paul catches the last couple of words and recognition flares his eyes with light. 'Same!' he half shouts, which makes Cathy laugh through her tears.

24.

Joe

Last night Joe dreamt he was arrested. A sympathetic arresting officer, who said off the record that he would've done the same thing for his sister. The cold slice of the handcuffs against his wrists. A stone cell with an arrow-slit window that let in a slice of sun that blinded him unless he moved around to avoid it.

He heard two phantom knocks in the night, checked outside the window twice, waking Lydia, but there was nobody there. Nobody who stayed around anyway.

The heat of the summer is always there every time Joe opens the door. It never goes away, not even overnight. He can feel his legs burning as he walks to the breakfast room. It's the second morning, almost thirty-six hours afterwards.

The breakfast hall is a large, double-height room with floor-to-ceiling mullioned windows, made fashionable with the black frames everybody is choosing lately. Two wooden doors are propped open either side of them, letting in sunbeams. A dog roams around the stone floor, a German shepherd who is maybe one or two kilograms overweight. A spiral staircase in the corner of the large, sunlit room leads up to living quarters. It smells of fried butter, croissants, coffee and sun-cream.

Lydia helps herself to a juice, getting Joe one too, even though he needs something soothing, not acidic. She goes to look at the buffet. He rakes a hand through his hair. He's so fucking tired. He kept thinking of things they'd forgotten last night, but he became tangled up in the thoughts. There were too many of them, overlapping and entwining together, and he was too nervous to write anything down, to make a record of it. Did Frannie get every last drop of blood? Did she clean the shovels? Will a forensic team be able to trace skin cells Will left behind on the road? Is the fire they set actually a warning sign to the police, a semaphore signal they have sent up into the night? *Here* is where something was covered up, they have inadvertently said. What are they going to do with Will's wallet and the warrant? It traces him to them; they need to keep it with them, hidden, but they can't take it through fucking airport security, can they? Joe starts sweating again as he thinks of it, sipping at his too-sweet orange juice.

'Police,' Cathy says under her breath to him. Joe stares at the windows. The Polizia di Stato and the Carabinieri are moving across them, their figures distorted by the uneven glass. Five of them. Hanging around the building. Frannie starts jittering next to him, and he throws her a look.

They help themselves to breakfast. 'Just act normally,' Joe says to Cathy.

'I'm not the one covered in sweat.'

Joe has a full fry-up every morning, and so he does today too. He adds three sausages and a spoonful of beans from a steaming silver bowl. The plate is warm in his hands. He's served coffee as he sits with Cathy, Frannie opposite him, Paul in a highchair by her side. Paul has emptied a four-piece wooden puzzle on to the tray of his chair and is intently studying one of the pieces. Joe reaches for it, and Paul grabs urgently, like a dog guarding a ball, says, 'My,' and taps his chest. Joe cannot help but feel the slow drip of love for Paul, who mashes together two puzzle pieces, unconcerned and unaware. This is all for you, this is all for you, this is all for you, Joe tells him internally.

Lydia joins them after a few seconds. He glances at her, that turned-up nose he's loved for nearly two decades. He wonders what she'd do if he told her. They've always identified as over-thinkers. Lydia once said, 'We're mad as hatters, we are,' when they had spent their whole evening worrying about ovulation sticks and a skin rash on a French bulldog, respectively. They'd cackled into their dinner. The next day, a tiny set of worry dolls had arrived at the practice, with a note from Lydia, via Amazon Prime: *For your worries, and mine*, it had said. But those dolls can't help him now, and neither can she. This isn't a worry. This is a real problem.

'I'm tired,' Joe says, rubbing at his head, trying to explain his behaviour. Cathy's eyes light on him.

'You were rolling around in bed last night,' Lydia says, through a mouthful of fruit. 'Lunatic.'

'I know. I was hot.'

As he chews on a sausage, his bowels seem to liquefy. He can hardly believe yesterday ended and today came. That a world like this exists. Cathy accepts a cup of tea from a teapot. Joe watches it pour from the spout, a not-quite-cylindrical stream.

'I slept fine,' Cathy says. Her face is serene. She's a great actress. Joe can't help but study her. Is it easy for her?

'I want pancakes,' Joe says pointedly to her. 'Do you?'

'Sure,' she says, scraping her chair back. They walk over to the buffet and stand a few metres away from everybody. Joe ladles the pancake mixture on to the hotplate and glumly watches it. He glances over at Paul. He's still clutching at the jigsaw pieces. He loves to hold as many things as possible in his fists.

'How do you seem so fine?' Joe says to Cathy.

'I'm not fine.'

Joe's always been a ruminator, even though he tries not to be. He called Evan a twat under his breath at work three weeks ago and has thought about it most days since. Evan had performed an unnecessary scan, the money from which enabled him to hit his financial target, which shouldn't have been a surprise to Joe, who has always known him to be a tosser. His entire personality is formed around the fact that he one day wants to own a Maserati, when, actually, he is flat broke following his divorce. He uses *myself* when he means *me*. So, he *is* a twat. But still.

He wishes he could be a pragmatist, like Cathy.

'I couldn't sleep,' she says in a low voice, eyes down to the buffet, ostensibly looking at the pancake batter swirling in a vat. 'All right? I slept fucking terribly.'

'Did you dream?' Joe says.

'Yup,' Cathy says. She smiles sadly as their eyes meet, an eerie feeling settling over Joe of dreaming the same dream as his sister. 'You?'

'Yeah, arrests, mostly,' Joe says, prodding at the pancake, wishing he did have his worry dolls, after all, if only to confide in. It's so funny how the sky is still so blue, Paul still loves holding things in his tiny fat fists, pancakes still cook, in this, the afterlife.

'Mine were about him.' Cathy bites her lip and looks to her left.

'What about him?' Joe says.

But that is as far as Cathy is willing to go. She shrugs, biting at the edge of her thumbnail, and doesn't answer.

He glances over at Paul as he thinks it and wonders if, when it finally comes out, Lydia will look back on this holiday and be able to pinpoint the day. The day he stopped sleeping. The day everything changed. Would she forgive him? For the initial act, and then for the secrecy? He skews his mouth to the side as he ponders it. Yes and no, he decides. Lydia is tidy in both a physical and a mental way. If people piss her off, they're gone. She could forgive a crime but not a lie. She's not only estranged from all of her family but from several friends too, a direct result of her childhood.

Cathy's body language changes. She stiffens. 'There are eight police now, in the foyer,' she says, her brown eyes searching over Joe's shoulder. 'Don't look.'

'How can I not look?' Joe says, wanting to turn around.

'You said about the market, didn't you?' Cathy asks quietly. 'I've been meaning to ask.' She turns the pancake. Everything about her body language is a study in nonchalance, weight on one hip, but Joe knows her well enough to spot where the edges aren't quite sanded down. Her shoulders are a millimetre higher than normal.

'No,' Joe says, shocked. 'I didn't.' He blushes with the shame of it, a micro-betrayal already. But who wouldn't try to protect themselves in the situation he finds himself in?

'What?' she says. 'You didn't say about the market, to the police. That Frannie saw Will?'

'No?' Joe says again, not offering an explanation.

'Why not?'

'I just figured it was better to omit everything.'

'But I said you were there, Joe.'

Joe goes cold. 'I didn't think. What do we do? Do we clarify it?'

'No,' Cathy hisses, drumming her fingers against her lips. 'Okay – you didn't actually see him at the market, did you?' she says. 'Just – from afar?'

'No, he was pretty close to me.'

'*Joe.*'

'Right – I see. Okay. No. No, I didn't see him.'

'So if they ask – which they won't' – she looks at him sharply – 'we say that.'

The feeling of his t-shirt being too tight again descends on Joe. He's lied to the police and now he has hidden his true motivation from his sister, and she, altruistic Cathy, is trying to get him out of it.

She stares at him, saying nothing. He wonders if she knows, if she knows he tried to extricate himself from the blame in the interview room. She has so much power over him. She could call up the police, right now, and say, *My brother lied.* The vulnerability of each of them strikes him. Adrenaline begins pumping. What the fuck's happening to him?

He's going mad. He can't get any air. He gulps. He's breathing, he thinks he's breathing, but it doesn't feel like he is. What the fuck, what the fuck, what the fuck? He leans forward, his hands on the table. The pancakes are two round shapes in front of him, filling his entire field of vision. Pancakes and panic. 'I can't breathe,' he says to Cathy.

She looks at him gently. 'You are breathing,' she says in a low voice.

'I can't do it. I'm going to die,' he says. His chest is tight. He really can't breathe. He really actually is not breathing.

'All right, come on, out of here,' Cathy says calmly. She leads him out of the dining area, through the fire door at the back, propped open so it lets a rectangle of sunshine in. Joe holds up a hand to Lydia, telling her he'll be back soon. They stand there together. 'In for five,' Cathy says, her eyes on Joe's.

Is he breathing? How would he know? Will he ever feel normal again?

'Out for seven,' she says.

'I don't have seven.'

'This will pass,' she says nicely. 'Okay?'

'No, this one is different.'

'You always say that.'

'We've kil–'

'Stop. Breathe.'

Already, Joe can feel the adrenaline burning dry, like a kettle boiling empty and switching off. There's nothing more in him. His limbs feel exhausted.

Panic attacks. He's had them before. Hundreds of them. Cathy's the best person to talk him down from them, not because she takes them seriously but because she doesn't give them credence, doesn't fear them like he does.

'In for five,' she says calmly, a half-smile playing across her features. 'Some things don't change,' she adds.

She leans a hand on the bar of the fire door and glances over her shoulder, inside. 'Pancakes have burned.'

A car door slams around the side of the building where the main entrance is. It's a white-stone building, almost too bright to look at. Snowflakes dance in Joe's vision when he tries. The palette of the day is a royal-blue and clean, intense white. It helps, the contrast between this and the brown and the red of the night before last.

Another car door. A dull, metallic thump. Joe turns instinctively towards the noise. He can't see, so he looks at Cathy, waiting for a clue. She is staring just behind his shoulder again. She's lit up by the sun, her skin peach-coloured, her hair caramel, eyes a bright oak. But it's her expression he can't stop looking at. Eyebrows drawn together. Mouth slack.

'Don't look,' she says in just a whisper. He turns around anyway. His muscles are tensed, ready.

'What? The police?' he says, looking back at Cathy. She brings a hand to her mouth.

'No.'

'What?'

Joe steps back, joining her. They stand there, together, side by side, and stare.

'Cane corsos,' Cathy says. A breed of sniffer dog.

25.

Joe

There are tens of them, the cadaver dogs. Each on a lead, each with a police officer, each straining to go. They're large, black dogs, like a Staffordshire bull terrier but on taller legs. Joe treated one, last year, brought in by a Spanish man who lived in Kings Heath. It had eaten the skin of a tennis ball, according to the man, in *one whole gulp*. He'd made the noise of it, the gulp. *Unk*. The dog needed a big operation. Recovered well. He could smell Joe coming through the prep room into the dog ward. He would always be looking up when he arrived, nose quivering.

Joe can't stop staring at them. Lydia is probably wondering where they are, but he doesn't care. He's transfixed by the spectacle of the dogs, like a herd coming together. Yet more are being let out of yet more police cars. There must be twenty of them.

Joe turns to look at Cathy. Together, they go around to the front of the building. They are acting suspiciously, but they can't help it. They stand next to an orange tree that is so perfect and round it looks fake, the oranges hanging like lanterns. Joe lights up a roll-up.

He tries to look natural as the police file past. Then the media, news reporters with fluffy microphones looking for soundbites, looking for suspects. The pretence of all this. He's going to have to keep it up forever. He can barely stand the thought of it.

'We wanted this,' he says to Cathy in a low voice when they've gone.

'I know.'

She looks ashen now in the bright sunlight. She makes a flicking gesture with her fingers, and he hands her the cigarette he's rolled, though she doesn't smoke. He lights it for her while it's in her mouth, both of them trying to manage with shaking hands. Their eyes meet, his face close to hers, but neither of them speaks.

'Do you regret answering?' he asks her.

She knows exactly what he means. She always does. Whether she will confide is another matter. 'No,' she says. 'No.' She shrugs. 'It's Frannie.'

The police are letting the dogs off their leads and into the distance. Their tails are up. They block the sun, light and shadow, light and shadow, as they move towards the horizon.

'They can't smell below six feet,' Cathy says quietly, when the police are out of earshot, and they're alone again. 'We thought it through.'

'The blood,' he mumbles around his cigarette.

'Just have to hope she's cleaned it up.' Cathy holds her cigarette between her middle and ring fingers, close to the knuckle, like a seasoned smoker. When she puffs on it, her face is right next to her hand. 'You look like a Mafia boss,' Joe says with a tiny laugh borne out of a manic kind of anxiety at the situation they find themselves in rather than anything light.

Cathy throws him a wan smile.

Joe finishes the cigarette and scuffs it out in the dirt.

His legs feel like he has been exercising, the muscles trembling with fear.

'There's no way we haven't got his smell on us. On our drive . . . our clothes,' Joe says, thinking aloud. 'Can't those dogs smell a treat about a mile off? I operated on one once, and he knew exactly where I was at all times.'

'I've washed all the clothes,' Cathy says. 'Don't worry. I've taken care of it. They are trained to smell decomposition. He was . . . he'd only just died. I think the scent is different.'

Joe nods. Relief rushes up through him. She's got it. She'll sort it. 'You're so fucking smart,' he says to Cathy. 'Can't believe you've never found someone.'

He's astonished when Cathy takes an actual step back from him. 'What?' she says, her voice just a whisper.

He blushes. He allowed his relief at her knowledge, at how in control she is, to let him run his mouth. 'You know,' he stammers, 'just — a, you know, a nice man to share your life with.'

'I haven't *not found* someone,' she says, making air quotes.

'Sorry,' Joe says uselessly. 'Ignore me.'

Cathy does. They stare into the distance, the air hazy and shimmering with the heat, both thinking.

Perhaps Will was here before he unthinkingly, unknowingly, walked to his death. What was he doing, walking on that road towards their villa late at night? The man that his sister killed before the mystery could be solved, a man dying with his own secrets intact, like an unopened box sent out to sea.

Cathy breathes out cigarette smoke into the summer air like icing sugar, then turns to look at him. 'It'll be okay.'

'I feel like we need more of a plan,' he says. He thinks

for a second. What would his dad do? What would his dad want him to do? 'There's a hotline, isn't there?' Joe says. 'That you can text in.'

'7070. It was on the news. Why?'

'What if we said we'd seen him?'

Cathy understands his meaning immediately. 'But not us,' she says.

'Get a pay-as-you-go phone. And text in. Say we saw him today.'

She seems to shiver in the sunlight, her shoulders rising up as she turns away from him and breathes smoke out of the side of her mouth. 'Up to you,' she says. 'I feel like we should maybe leave it for now.'

'Why?'

'I just think – the cashpoint stuff . . . you know? We dodged a bullet there.'

'Yeah. Maybe. Stop playing with fire,' Joe says softly, looking at the amber tip of his cigarette, slowly turning to ash, orange to grey like a fast cremation.

'Exactly. And . . . I don't know.' Cathy scuffs the ground with the toe of her trainer. 'It's just – I don't know. It's all a bit distasteful, isn't it?'

'Yeah, I think we've really crossed the Rubicon with distasteful,' Joe says drily.

'Maybe,' Cathy says.

They stand in silence for a few minutes more.

'She said she couldn't stop,' Cathy says, so quietly he has to strain to hear.

'I know.'

They stop speaking, letting the words and the suspicion hang in the air between them.

'Cath,' he says quietly now.

'Yeah?' She looks up at him, round brown eyes concerned.

'Would you have done the same for me?'

Cathy waits a beat, still looking at him. 'Of course,' she says. She waits a second, seemingly thinking, then adds: 'Of course I would. I am.' She doesn't ask the question back.

'You are?'

'I am keeping your crimes a secret,' she says simply.

Joe takes out another cigarette and offers one to Cathy. She takes it, unlit, holds it until she has finished the previous one. Joe lights them both, then plays with the lighter, pulling and pulling on the little wheel, looking at the small, contained fire that pops up, and is easily put out, over and over again.

She is keeping their crimes a secret. The beginning of the crime doesn't matter, because of the ones they have committed along the way, like a train that just goes all night, on a loop, with no end or beginning, so nobody remembers where it came from.

'It's about Paul,' Cathy says quickly. 'For Frannie.'

'I know,' Joe says, smiling a sad half-smile as he thinks of how Paul is terrified of his own reflection in the mirror. Joe can't wait for him to realize it is himself, for that wide-open toothy smile to break. 'And it's about Rosie. Isn't it?' he asks, wanting to talk about it, even though it's a place they hardly ever go to.

'It's absolutely about Rosie,' Cathy says, surprising him.

26.

Now

Jason's Office, early March, 5.00 p.m.

'Ms Plant,' Jason says with a nod as I arrive for my session.

I say nothing, sitting down opposite him. I know I've avoided it long enough now. I cross my feet at their ankles.

Jason is in jeans and a jumper today, dressed casually with no explanation. He rubs at his left eye with his index finger as he gazes down at some papers. 'How are you feeling?' he says, kind of listlessly, it seems to me.

'You know,' I say. 'Up and down.'

Outside, I hear the hiss of a bus pulling away. We're into March, though the weather isn't yet warming up. Somehow, the turn of the year from February to March seems to have focused both of our minds.

'Right, we need to get to it,' Jason says crisply.

'I know,' I say. I sink my face into my hands. 'I know. I have talked around it for weeks, I know.'

'Look,' he says gently. My hands are still covering my eyes, and I feel him begin to move around the room, tidying up; an obvious diversionary tactic but one I'm grateful for nonetheless. 'Would it help to hear of all of the people I have been through this with? You're in safe hands, I promise.'

'Are any of them in prison?' I say sadly.

He puts the papers on the shelf and gets out a new, blank pad, a deliberate gesture maybe. He sits and leans

148

forward, looking at me, his elbows on his knees. 'Going over it – it's a necessary evil, okay? Like – like the dentist. And, yes, some of them are in prison.'

I give a sardonic laugh. 'God.'

'Look,' he says, 'I have most of the information, and now we just need to . . . to shape it.'

'Into a statement,' I say sadly.

He leans forward and gets file number one. He has four of them now. They seem to multiply each time I visit. Four teal bundles, pink ribbons wrapped around them, tied in careless bows by Jason himself, who seems to have no secretary, no assistant.

'I think our strategy should be that we just tell your version of events to the court, at the trial,' he says, pointing to the pad where the statement will rest. 'Play as straight a bat as possible. Exactly what happened, from start to finish. Okay? No games, no narrative. No lies.'

'Right,' I say. 'Yes, I understand that.'

The crime. The fallout. Everything that followed. Everything that happened following it. 'The trial is in two weeks,' he says. 'So we need to get on it.'

27.

Then

Cathy

It's the middle of the night. Cathy is sitting with her back against Frannie's headboard, working on her phone, doing stuff that doesn't really need doing.

They're lit up only by the rolling Italian news. Their legs are the exact same length, bare feet completely level with each other. Their skin flashes bright red from the pictures on the television.

'Not sure I'll ever sleep again,' Frannie says, rubbing at her forehead. She's wearing a t-shirt that says RIOTS NOT DIETS. She's fiddling with the baby monitor in her hands, periodically gazing down at Paul's sleeping form. 'This reminds me of after-school,' she says, leaning her head back against the wall.

Cathy, Joe, Frannie and Rosie would let themselves into their house each afternoon, around four. They'd walk back together, along the river, then through the fields, up the hill and home. Frannie was always late. Joe walked too quickly. They complained about these same things to each other, most days. 'God, slow *down*,' Frannie would huff to Joe, who would turn and walk backwards, laughing at her. In some ways, not much has changed. Only a few weeks ago, they stayed up chatting in Frannie's kitchen until half past one in the morning. Cathy and Frannie painted their nails. Joe drank six beers.

'Granted, we didn't watch Italian news after school,'

Frannie says with a laugh. She takes a sip of black coffee. Frannie is a huge coffee drinker, at all times of day. It doesn't seem to affect her at all. Cathy stares at her sister's profile, the perfect features, straight nose, eyes that turn up at their corners. Even her fingers are attractive, slim but not bony. She looks like Rosie.

Rosie was the original baby of the family, two years younger than Frannie. She died when she was eight. Sudden Infant Death Syndrome. A rare case of a child, and not a baby.

Just that, Cathy thinks, looking at the delicate slant of Frannie's nose. A rare event. Bad luck. Just the total and complete devastation of their family, and everything they knew.

In the post-Rosie world, their parents became strange and difficult. Their mother risk-assessing – she once banned them from going on bouncy castles – their father repressed. Rosie's room is still completely preserved, photos of her on the wall that stop aged eight. The month following her death, some photographs of her came back, newly developed, and those ended up framed, too.

In the wake of this, the remaining siblings began to forge ahead, alone, three siblings who wanted to be together, no matter what.

'I can't believe how little I'm sleeping,' Frannie adds. Cathy sometimes thinks Frannie lucky. She was ten when Rosie died, and she hardly remembers her. She hardly knows what they have all lost. Cathy, who was thirteen, and Joe, who was fifteen, remember almost everything.

'Let's just turn this off,' Cathy says. 'We'll only see something about him again.' Already, the footage of the sniffer dogs has cycled around twice, a sea of black and tan on the horizon, a forensics team accompanying them, eerie, tall, white figures among the dogs.

Frannie mutes it but doesn't turn off the picture. She finishes her coffee and puts the mug in between her shins on the bed. Her phone is charging on the windowsill, and Cathy can see it lighting up, even at this hour. Why are all her friends awake?

'Why do you think he had that piece of paper?' Cathy asks her, rather than asking her about her friends – and how she came to make so many of them, so easily.

'I mean,' Frannie says, reaching for the mug again and tossing it from one hand to the other as she thinks, 'he was a police officer.'

'Yes, exactly.'

'It could have been *anything*, couldn't it? A safety inspection of our villa? A hire-car thing? We have no idea.'

Cathy shifts her position on the bed, crossing her legs underneath her. Frannie unconsciously rests an elbow on Cathy's knee. Despite the sombre situation, Cathy still manages to locate her old anxieties and their counterpoints. That Frannie is closer to Joe than to her. That she finds Cathy incomprehensible, boring, *weird*. That elbow says differently, and Cathy pats it.

'What if he was investigating someone?' Frannie says.

'Who?'

'Well, not you or me.'

'Right?'

'Joe? Or *Lydia*? What if Joe went after Will and – you know how he can be –'

'I know,' Cathy says. 'Maybe Joe got in more trouble the other night with Lydia and that man than he said.'

152

'Yeah. Maybe we could ask him. Where is the document?' Frannie says, extending a hand to Cathy.

'In my room.'

'Let's look at it again. Tomorrow. With him, when we've all slept. See what he does.'

She stares straight ahead, at the television, but her features look troubled. Cathy can tell she is going over whether Joe is involved in some way more than he says. She looks gaunt tonight. The sockets of her eyes are clearly defined, incongruous against the holiday tan, the highlights and shadows exaggerated by the monochrome glow of the TV.

Joe's in the shower down the hall. He can't sleep either. They can hear the water hitting his body, collecting and running off in thick ropes of water.

'Look,' Frannie says suddenly, staring at the television. Cathy turns her attention away from Frannie's cheekbones and to the screen.

Omicidio. Cathy's body reacts to the word before her mind can translate it. She sits forward, looking at the English subtitles. They scroll past, painfully slowly, like the football news on Ceefax they would sometimes watch after school together.

Police open homicide investigation due to forged cashpoint transaction.

Cathy feels the veins in her skull pound. She puts her head in her hands as the room dips and spins around her. 'What?' she whispers.

She raises only her eyes to the screen, keeping her head low, watching the subtitles play out as an Italian police officer speaks. Frannie has got off the bed, is standing in the corner of the dim room. Cathy can hardly see her.

We have reason to believe Will McGovern died in suspicious circumstances, though no body has yet been found, the scrolling white text reads. *The person who knows the whereabouts of Mr McGovern has gone to great lengths to make it appear as if he is missing, not dead. A failed attempt at a cashpoint has come to light due to the fast actions of HSBC Bank. The cadaver dogs picked up the scent of a dead body nearby. We now believe his killer is trying to make it look like Mr McGovern is alive.*

Cathy's entire body feels as dry as a desert. Her mouth. Her eyes. Like somebody has sucked all of the moisture out of her, leaving only a husk in place. Frannie's bedroom door opens, and they both tense. It's Joe, with a pink towel wrapped around his waist. 'Can I get changed in here?' he says, clutching a pair of tracksuit bottoms and a grey t-shirt. 'Lydia's fast asleep. And I don't want any more fucking questions.'

'Sure,' Frannie says faintly, staring at the television and going to sit back on the bed.

Cathy looks at her. As her eyes adjust to the dark, she sees that Frannie has raked her hair back from her forehead, her hands now holding it there, elbows out to the side, her body otherwise rigid.

'What's happened?' Joe says immediately.

Cathy and Frannie exchange a glance. 'What's happened?' he says again.

'Look,' she says, pointing to the television. 'The cadaver dogs – the cashpoint . . .'

Cathy goes to stand by the windowsill, looking out. As she turns back to look at Joe after a few seconds, breathing deeply, she sees a crucifix right above the centre of his head. An oak-coloured cross. Another silver Jesus. Two red spots on his hands. She can't stop staring at it.

Joe pulls on his t-shirt. It clings to the wet parts of his skin, the grey material turning to black inkblots.

Cathy takes a breath. In a low voice, she says, 'They know he's dead.'

'Fuck,' Joe whispers, staring at the breaking news. He's still in the pink towel and his t-shirt. He glances over his shoulder to the door, which sits ajar, checking nobody is out there. 'We need a new plan.'

'No, we don't,' Cathy says firmly. 'We need to stop. Just stop.'

'But –'

'Look – let's just . . .' She crosses the room to him, a hand on his damp arm. 'We need to stop.' She takes a breath. 'We could stop.' She turns around to look at Frannie, still looking at the television, the whites of her eyes shining exactly as they did on that night, animalistic, flashing. Joe looks at her too. Cathy stares down at the windowsill, thinking. As she does so, Frannie's phone, charging there, lights up again in front of her. Frannie is in almost constant contact with her best friend, Deb, so Cathy isn't surprised to see a waiting message.

Frannie met Deb when they were twenty-one, when she brought in her Manchester terrier for a consult. Cathy observed in real-time how easily her younger sister made a friend. An open question or two, and then they were giggling as they tried to weigh the dog on the scales. Numbers were swapped and that was that, a best friend arrived; something Cathy has never had. Deb goes over to Frannie's most Tuesdays – *by far the worst day of the week*, Frannie says – and often, as Cathy falls asleep at home, she can hear their high laughter through the walls or the open windows.

But it isn't from Deb. It's a branded text message. *'Thank you for contacting Jason Granger Law . . .'* is previewed on Frannie's screen.

Cathy blinks. Jason Granger Law? She averts her gaze from Frannie's phone, gets her own phone out, then googles him.

Jason Granger, his website says. *Birmingham Criminal Lawyer.* Cathy stares at it.

Why has her sister got a lawyer's reply text? Is it her own lawyer? Before she can persuade herself otherwise, Cathy adds Jason's number to her contacts, for her to investigate, feeling guilty about yet another thing: she would be mortified if Frannie looked at Cathy's own phone, at her message to a man she went on a date with two weeks ago, who, she now knows, doesn't want to see her again, after Cathy texted to no reply (twice). She knows why: she answered his questions too awkwardly in the pub, was probably boring too about animals, maybe spoke too much about Macca, her rescue bulldog.

Cathy stares as Frannie and Joe argue. Cathy is motionless, thinking only of this secret, this secret Frannie has chosen to keep from her.

She can't help but feel, in the dim light of the villa, that they are turning on each other, slowly, so slowly you might not even notice it, like three warships that started facing forward and are now facing backwards, without anyone on board feeling any movement at all.

'How haven't they found the body, if they know he's

dead?' Joe says, looking at her. Even after a shower, he still smells of cigarettes, has brought the smell into the room with him.

'I don't know,' she says. If she is going to ask Frannie about it, she should do it now. But something stops her. The cards have been dealt, and it only remains to play the game, to keep them close to her chest.

'Are they going to find it?' Frannie asks. Cathy's gaze swivels to her.

'I don't know that either,' Cathy says, rubbing at her forehead. She pauses, thinking. 'You didn't send that text, did you?' she says to Joe.

'What text?'

'The hotline. Tell me you didn't send that text.'

Joe tenses, turning only his head to her.

'What?' Frannie says. It's a sharp *what*, like a lemon.

'Of course I didn't,' he says tetchily. 'I said I wasn't going to.'

Lydia appears in the doorway in her pyjamas, hair piled on the top of her head. 'What text?' she says.

28.

Lydia

Lydia wakes in the night to the sound of voices and experiences a familiar sensation: loneliness within a crowd. That's sometimes how it is with the Plants, especially on holiday. They don't even mean to leave her out, but they do.

Joe's side of the bed is empty. She checks the clock: 1.32 a.m. She listens intently. She can hear all three of them, talking animatedly.

Moonlight shifts outside, illuminating the bed with two moving squares of bright white.

She gets up, puts on a dressing gown and ventures out of the bedroom. Where *is* he? It's late even for him. He did the same thing last night too. And yesterday when he was in the bathroom, clearly with his sisters, discussing something, and he dismissed her like she was an annoying child. She asked him four times what had been going on, and received all sorts of nonsense in response. A work crisis, which he wouldn't elaborate on, then something to do with his mother . . .

Lydia had to learn, throughout her twenties, how to stand up for herself. No one else is going to, she realized very slowly, as she – with the help of the therapist – phased out problematic and toxic friends who would say things like, 'Does it bother you that you've gained weight?' Lydia hadn't known any better when she made them.

And so Lydia decides, as she rearranges her hair on top of her head, that she needs to draw a line here, now, tonight. She's on this holiday too. She deserves to be treated as such.

She hears voices as she moves along the corridor. It's stone, cold underfoot, like a crypt. She can feel its imperfections on her bare feet, some parts rough, some parts undulating and uneven. It smells like an old church, this villa. Lydia always forgets until their holiday rolls around again. Even when they've just cleaned it, it still has that kick. Wood, old tombs, ancient incense.

Cathy is speaking, Lydia thinks, her low, calm register combining with Joe's raised one in Frannie's room. She stops, feet getting colder the longer she stays still. She knows she shouldn't eavesdrop, but the opportunity has presented itself, and Lydia has been fascinated by the Plants since she was fourteen. Even though she is now a Plant herself, her curiosity has hardly waned. Their glossy, dark hair, their athletic limbs, their closeness.

Maria and Owen – their parents – served full English breakfasts on weekdays before school with sunshine-bright orange juice in actual *jugs*. Their pink landing carpet was always hoovered in perfectly even stripes. Lydia used to think back to her own home, mouldy windowframes and unpredictable atmospheres, and wince. And now here they are, that perfect family, uninhibited, unaware they're being overheard. Lydia feels suddenly strange, like a voyeur or a creep.

'Yes, they can,' she hears Joe say in Frannie's room. The orange-juice jugs disappear in Lydia's mind like popped balloons. This family, she has learnt over the last few years, is not perfect. Frannie is of the opinion Cathy and Joe are unhappily ambitious. Joe and Frannie think Cathy is emotionally stunted. Cathy and Frannie think Joe's temper is too quick and too hard. They form tessellating circles, interacting in different ways, confusing ways to Lydia, who once thought love was black and white.

Lydia stays in shadow in the corridor. The door is ajar. Joe's whispering. She can barely hear him. Underneath whatever he's whispering, she can hear the tedious hum of the news. The missing man. She's glad it isn't a woman who's gone missing, at least, not here, not on her holiday.

'Tell me you didn't send that text,' Cathy says loudly. Lydia takes another step forwards, almost walking into the light. Cathy never shouts. Never raises her voice. Is never anything but calm, composed, put together. Before either of them can say anything more, Lydia takes a step forward. She hesitates, just once, at the door. Her fingers illuminated but the rest of her in darkness. Something in Lydia's gut is telling her that she can't ever return to this moment, her fingertips pushing into the light, against the point of no return.

'Of course I didn't,' Joe says and, despite herself, Lydia feels herself sag with relief. 'I said I wasn't going to.'

'What text?' she says, and steps into the light. She is looking at her husband, but she is absorbing too the atmosphere between him and his sisters.

Cathy has her shoulders up. She catches Lydia looking and crosses her arms against her body. She glances at Joe, then seems to make a decision. Immediately, she strides towards the door, glancing at Lydia as she walks past her.

Time seems to slow down as she does so, like they are two ballroom dancers, faces side by side, bodies heading in different directions. Something is communicated from Cathy – the queen of subtext – to Lydia. 'Sorry,' Cathy mutters. Somewhere between *excuse me* and an apology. Lydia stands aside and lets her go.

'What text?' she says again to Joe. He turns in a tiny, useless circle, his hands in his hair. He pauses, then speaks again. 'Let's . . .' he says, but doesn't finish the sentence, as he leads her down the corridor, back to their neat, small room full of the moonlight she only just left behind, when everything felt different.

'I don't know where to start,' he says, standing by their bed.

'What?' Lydia's eyes narrow as she watches him, mystified. He's wearing a pink towel and a t-shirt, an absurd combination. What is he doing? He puts his hands in his hair and the motion pulls up his top.

'Something's happened,' he says. He sits down and his bare feet dangle off the high bed. Then he stands again, whips off the towel and pulls on a pair of jogging bottoms. Lydia watches in the dispassionate, intimate way of the married couple.

She is eerily calm. She never thought she would be, if her worst nightmare came true – some betrayal by Joe, quite what she is not yet sure – but she is completely calm.

'What's happened?' she says.

Joe knots his hands together in his lap. 'I wanted to send this text,' he says, biting his lip. Behind him is a kettle and set of cups, dusty with disuse, and three white crosses on the wall. His eyes go to the left and the right. Lydia tries to hold his gaze to her, but she can't. It's like trying to anchor a boat to the air.

'What text?'

'To Evan.'

'At the practice?' Lydia says in surprise.

'Yeah – he –'

'He's in charge, right?'

Lydia stares at Joe. He is so obviously thinking on his feet. She raises her hands, palms to him. 'I don't deal with liars,' she says. 'Get your story straight.'

'No, no,' Joe says, panic crossing his features, turning down his mouth, drawing together his brows like he is a cartoon of himself. She's shocked him. He once called her ruthless, and she's never forgotten. 'You have to become ruthless in my situation,' she'd told him icily. When you are forced to cut off your parents, no other subsequent separation is as difficult. All around Lydia, she notices people putting up with things, settling, living alongside people who make them miserable, and she swears that will never be her.

'How can you say that to me?' he says.

Lydia feels a stab of guilt. It's fair to say that Joe is her ally in life, has never given her reason to doubt him. Doesn't have a phone passcode; it contains only photo albums full of dogs and cats anyway – he takes a photograph of every animal he cures, adding them to an album called *Homeward Bound*.

'I promise,' he says now. 'It was Evan.' He rubs at his forehead. 'Sorry. The practice is – I didn't want to worry you.'

Lydia sits on their pillows, waiting for the explanation.

'It's struggling a bit – Evan's had a . . . he's fucked up. We're deciding what to do about it.'

'What's he done?'

'Just did an unnecessary procedure,' Joe says.

'Right. What did he do?'

'Ultrasound because he knew the owners were rich.'

'I see.'

'Yeah, I mean, he shouldn't have done it. He's flat broke. And I won't make him partner,' Joe says, a small, self-deprecating smile sneaking out.

'Why is he broke?' she asks.

'His divorce,' Joe says. He's edging more closely to her and, God, she can't resist this man. He smells of musk and sun and he accepts her exactly – *exactly* – as she is, empties the bathroom bin each week of its many pregnancy tests, only smiling wryly, not saying anything at all. She feels high on the relief of this, that the text is nothing. Thank God for nothing! 'He actually got a second job, a delivery driver. I think his wife really stung him on maintenance.'

'Oh, wow.' She smiles at him, shifting closer. And it is then that he does it: he angles his phone just slightly away from her. A tiny movement she wouldn't usually notice.

'Can I see your phone, please?' she asks. She tries to breathe deeply, not let herself get suckered by this man who loves animals and her.

'See what?'

'Your phone.' She holds out a palm, flat, expectant.

Joe looks exactly like somebody who doesn't want to give his phone to his wife. His body turns away from her again, physically curling in on itself like somebody with stomach pains.

'Joe,' she says softly.

He reaches a hand to his pocket, but it's merely a gesture. It's going to accompany his explanation of why he can't hand over his phone. There is no smoke without fire, to Lydia, and so she simply says, 'Okay,' and turns away from him, stalking into the bathroom to get a glass of water.

'Lyds.'

'You've made your position very clear,' she says to him when he arrives. 'There is something on that' – she points to his pocket, at the rectangular embossed shape – 'that you don't want me to see.'

'I deleted Evan's text. It was stupid. Because it made me anxious.'

'Show me the phone or fuck off.'

Something flits across his face, but Lydia can't read it. Can't name it. Something like anguish. His eyes crease at their corners. He shows his teeth. '*No*,' he says.

In 1995 Lydia's mother was given a choice. Leave with Lydia to keep her safe, or stay. And she stayed. And so Lydia will never stay. Not with somebody who hurts her. She lives with Joe's sharpness on the basis that she is never on the receiving end of it. He might be rude about dog owners and people who cut him up in traffic. He might say he hates how Evan has to say, 'The mighty, mighty York,' whenever he talks about where he's from, but Joe never ridicules Lydia.

'Okay, then. Your choice,' she says.

Joe starts brushing his teeth. Lydia looks at him in the mirror for a few seconds, wondering what all this means.

As they get ready in silence, she looks at Joe's body

from under lowered lashes. He looks hunched. Despite herself, Lydia feels a rolling wave of sympathy for him, like shivery thunder moving across her body. No, she tells herself. No. We do not feel sympathy for people who cause us pain. She gets into bed and turns deliberately away from him.

Lydia wakes because Joe isn't sleeping. It's impossible to sleep next to somebody who is turning over, disturbing the sheets, obviously frustrated. Like trying to sleep through an argument, only Joe seems to be having it with himself.

She rolls over and opens her eyes, looking at Joe's back. He must sense this, and turns to face her. They look at each other for a few seconds in the darkness.

The whites of his eyes look blue in the shifting moonlight, which moves in shadows across their bed, like the night sky is turning over as he is too.

'What's going on, Joe?' she whispers. She can only say it here, eye to eye in the night-time, not able to see any of his body language.

'Nothing,' he says, but he comes closer to her. A warm hand arrives in hers underneath the duvet, and she closes her eyes.

'I promise, there is nothing happening that you need to know about,' he says, but his words are sad, dampened, laced with fuzz. 'I want you to trust me.'

'I don't trust you,' Lydia says immediately. 'Not when you're like this.' She lies back, removing her hand from his, thinking. 'What do you mean, *that I need to know about*?'

He shifts closer to her, and he rests his head on her

chest, their legs entwined. He breathes deeply in and out, an almost-sigh. It's the only sound in their room, even though the window is open.

'I mean that – okay. Something has happened that – if you know about it – will make your life worse.'

'About Evan's ultrasound?'

There is just the slightest hesitation. 'No.'

'Well, I think I need to know what,' Lydia says, sitting up, moving him off her.

'You don't,' Joe says.

'I'm – *Joe.*'

'Look. Something's happened. In the business. And, if I tell you – then –'

'Is it illegal?'

'Yes.'

'Does it affect me?'

A beat. 'No.'

'You can't –'

'I'm not going to tell you, Lyds,' Joe says gently, lying propped up on one elbow. She can't make out anything except the vague shape of him, his shoulder and his eyes.

'What *sort* of thing is it? I should know, shouldn't I? Even if it is illegal.'

'You won't want to know. It's for . . .' Joe's gaze shifts to the window, then back at her. 'This is for your own good. I promise,' he says. 'When have I ever given you reason not to trust me?' He waits for her to answer, and then, when he catches her expression, he adds, 'Not them, not your family.' An earnest hand to his chest. 'Me. Me.'

'There's no need for that,' she says.

'What?'

'You don't need to say it that way.'

'I'm sorry,' he says immediately, earnestly. 'My bad.'

'You haven't,' she says softly. 'You haven't ever given me a reason not to trust you.'

'Then,' he says, like it is a full sentence.

'Are you helping somebody?' she says. 'Is this a kestrel situation?'

He smiles at that. 'Yeah,' he says. He flaps a hand uselessly in the night air, then lets it fall back on to the bed. 'You could say that.'

It's light, but early, when Lydia wakes. Joe is gone again. She stands at the window. The sky is stippled, violet clouds with pink edges, like a messy child's painting. She wonders where he is. She sees him in the distance, with Cathy again, at the edge of the grounds of their villa. She has her hands on her hips. His position is defensive. She knows it well. Lydia stares at both of them.

She will keep an eye on this, she decides. Listen out.

The longer she looks, the more she sees.

29.

Joe

Joe did send that text.

He went back into the city. He travelled in on an evening bus, the sky an intense peach beyond the dirty windows. He'd stayed standing up for the duration of the journey, even though it was empty, wanting to burn off some of his nervous energy, his fingers sliding down the plastic pole in the centre of the bus.

A man sitting behind a grey, old-fashioned till greeted Joe in a long Italian sentence, and he shrugged his shoulders apologetically and said hello in English. He reached into one of the cabinets and pulled out a Nokia. Black. It easily fit in the palm of his hand. He took it to the man and paid for it.

'A second phone for the second woman!' the man said. 'Very private.' He had a knowing smile. Joe left in a panic, his hood up, the area checked for CCTV, out into the blazing orange sunset.

It was, he reasoned, better to take the risk and lessen their chances of getting caught. Better to do x than y. Better to risk a than b. Joe's life had become a series of bad situations, of rocks and hard places, and he was tired of it. He was so tired of it he could have sat down right there in the street and cried. He could have almost walked right over there to the police station and handed himself in.

Handed in his whole family. Bought a gun from a similar shop to this and shot himself in the head.

Instead, Joe went into a dingy side alley with the phone and powered it up. Good. It had ten euros on it. Joe could hardly work it. It was so old, the keys made sounds as he pushed them, an electronic, retro sound like playing Tetris. He typed out the message into Google Translate, then checked it over. God, he wished Cathy had come.

I served the missing man this morning. I work in a bar in Padua.

Ho servito l'uomo scomparso questa mattina. Lavoro in un bar a Padova.

Before he could talk himself out of it, he had pressed *send*.

On the way back, he bought three Italian pastries. Whenever he's stressed, he eats, always has done. He usually mitigates this by counting calories on an app he's too embarrassed to admit he uses. But he scoffed these, all one thousand calories of them, as though the butter and the sugar could fill him up, could cover up his secrets, could squash them down and suffocate them completely.

30.
Cathy

Cathy is no stranger to moping, though nobody knows it. She is sitting at the kitchen table, alone, as she does often in England, only this time with a different brand of tea. Manuel. Italian tea. It doesn't taste the same.

She is thinking about Lydia's stricken face and wondering what sort of husband her brother is being at the moment. How Lydia must feel. So in the dark. Knowing, surely, that something is happening, but not *what*. It is strange to consider her brother in this way. As a spouse and not as a sibling.

She sat just like this at home, in the early spring, drinking Tetley. She'd been on a date with the owner of a giant house rabbit called Leonard. In the second consult, when she'd diagnosed the dacryocystitis – blocked tear ducts – the owner had asked for her number.

'For a consult?' she'd said.

'For a coffee.'

'Oh.'

'Oh – no,' he'd said, looking for a second at her expression. He was huge, this Pete Green who liked giant rabbits and daytime consults. A mountain of a man. 'That's fine. Don't worry.'

'Oh – I just – sorry,' Cathy had said. 'Coffee would be good.'

She'd looked forward to it all week. She'd practised in

front of the mirror, adopting Frannie's easy body language. She'd made a list on her phone of topics to talk about, if she dried up. Because that is what always happens to Cathy. She can't think of anything to say. What a stupid problem to have, she often thinks, but it is a problem nevertheless.

They'd met in the evening in a venue that was a cross between a bar and a café. It had been one of those glum, rainy spring evenings that felt like it could be autumn. Dark-wood beams rested up ahead, pendulous lights hung down like stars. 'It's so dark in here I can't fucking see,' Pete had said, which had made her smile. Rain spattered the floor-length windows and washed the street outside.

They'd drunk coffee and shared carrot cake, then ordered a pot of tea, which was brought to them by a waitress so stroppy they'd been shaking with laughter. They'd watched the sky fade to black outside. Cathy remembers odd details of it: wrapping her hands around the warm mug. Seeing a virtual stranger's eyes in candlelight. Parting ways on a cold spring night.

She thought it had gone well. They'd laughed, hadn't they? There weren't as many awkward silences as usual? She hadn't panicked in the bathroom about small talk, or blushed so much she wanted to run out?

Cathy had made a cup of tea when she arrived home and sat at her kitchen table, just as she is now. She buried herself in paperwork, and then the text came through. Credit to him, he was straight up. *A lovely evening but better off as friends.* She had put her head into her hands, then, looking at Macca and feeling her loneliness. Macca couldn't speak. He couldn't ease it. Sometimes it was so bad that she wanted to phone some sort of hotline. Hire an assistant, a robot, to sit opposite her and simply witness her drinking this cup of tea. Otherwise, basically it's as if it didn't happen, it didn't happen, it didn't happen.

In Verona, she goes to bed eventually, around four or five. She's woken at nine by a knock on the door. She goes downstairs, pyjama-clad and anxious, and sees two shifting forms through the window. It's the police again. Carabinieri. Black and red uniforms, a warning sign, like poisonous insects. Her stomach falls off a cliff. They know. They know. They've seen her. They've seen Joe. And now it's time. They could only keep running for so long, like trying to stay ahead of a tsunami.

Cathy opens the door with shaking hands. 'Hello,' she says.

'Catherine,' one officer says, a new one, a blond, tall man. She meets his eyes and tries not to look terrified, waiting for him to speak, for him to arrest her, to caution her in Italian, to ask for Frannie. They've found the body. They've found CCTV footage. They've found the blood. The hire-car company has reported them. She holds her breath as he opens his mouth to speak.

'We have come to inform you,' he says. Cathy's chest is tight.

But, as she roots around herself she finds, lodged in next to the fear and the shame, a little shard of relief. That it is over. That the worst has happened.

'We just wanted to let you know that as things are now, you are safe to fly tomorrow,' he says. 'But if we say we need you for longer, to assist the police with their enquiries, you must not board. We thank you for your help in the investigation. We may be in touch. But, for now,' he says, an unreadable expression on his face, 'in case you were wondering – you're free to leave.'

Cathy says something, she's not sure what – some pleasantry – and closes the door. Her entire body is covered in sweat, her shoulders up around her ears. There's no way they didn't notice.

She sits back at the kitchen table where she was a few hours or days ago, she is no longer sure, and thinks about that relief. And now, in its place, she finds disappointment. A not unusual combination to her, but she wonders if, this time, it'll be the time she leaps. That one day she might confess.

She presses a hand to her stomach where the guilt is living and tries to squash it down, but it doesn't work, nothing works. Only confession would work. She looks up at the Jesus above the door and confesses to him, out loud, the first person she tells.

They're flying home today, but Frannie is still by the pool. Cathy has been thinking about her. About her explanations for Will's injuries and the lack of ambulance. About how she said she couldn't stop, after she hit him, but changed the meaning of that just slightly when pressed, like a media spin doctor. *I couldn't stop*, she said. And then she said she meant she couldn't stop *immediately*. How fast was she even going? Why has she got a lawyer?

She stands to go and pack, and as she does so she stares across the pool at Frannie. A perfect lemon tree sits behind her. She looks like she's on a photoshoot for a magazine. There are almost more lemons than leaves, hanging point-downwards, like teardrops, waiting to fall. Frannie is staring back at Cathy. Goosebumps break out across Cathy's shoulders, though she's not sure why. Eventually, Frannie puts on her sunglasses, covering up her eyes. Cathy waves and points upstairs, wanting to dispel the atmosphere. When she looks up, she still can't see Frannie's eyes, but she's sure they're on her, tracking her every move.

31.

Lydia

Lydia is pretending to pack, but really she is going through Joe's things, a task she has never once undertaken in their entire relationship. But he is keeping something from her. She isn't an idiot, so here she is, with his iPad, the quiet of the villa beyond.

She has all of his dirty clothes here too. She starts her search methodically. First, the clothes. She pauses, his shorts in her hands. If she looks, she can never go back. If she finds something.

What is she looking for? She knows Joe. She *knows* him. He wouldn't – what? Cheat on her? Here in Verona? The thought is ridiculous. She puts down the shorts.

But then she remembers his facial expression. And – worse – Cathy's. They looked guilty. All of them did. Maybe it's something financial. Gambling. IVAs. Business debts. Personal guarantees given. Lydia can't help her mind spiralling.

There's nothing in the shorts. A voided prescription with the dose scribbled out. A used tissue. Three euros and an Italian car-parking ticket.

She goes to the iPad next. It doesn't have a passcode. She goes through his emails, social media, search history. All present, and nothing sinister. He has googled recent veterinary cases, things to do in Verona, and – she will forgive him this one, if this is all it is – 'Megan Fox hot'.

Her heartrate is slowing down the less she finds. Maybe it's nothing. Old traumas resurfacing, a gut feeling that is still misguided. Maybe her Joe is good, the man who looked at an error message on a recent pregnancy test and said, 'Yep, you're a nutcase.' Maybe he is still hers.

She navigates to his WhatsApp next. He has the app on his iPad. There's the family group. She was added to it only last year, after she asked. Joe had downplayed it – *It's boring, honestly, full of photos of Paul and vet questions* – but, last year, just before Christmas, when they did a secret Santa, Lydia had finally been added. She'd felt a thrill at it, at the proximity to a proper family, with all its complexities and simplicities. Frannie had wanted a higher budget – 'What can you even get for twenty quid?' she'd said, and Joe had said, 'A better vets' receptionist?' Lydia had enjoyed reading it, the barbs and the easy banter of a functional family.

She looks at the rest of his texts. Banter with two friends. Professional communications with Evan. She lets her shoulders sag.

But . . . something is niggling at her. She pauses, wondering what it is, before she realizes. *Look for what's missing, as well as what's there*, one of the lawyers at work once told her when she helped him with a disclosure bundle. What's missing?

His sisters. He hasn't texted either of them for – according to his phone – three days. But . . . he texted Frannie. The morning after she had Paul. Didn't he?

That can't be true. She stares at the threads of text messages and WhatsApps, neither name present. She goes into the deleted files of both. Nothing.

She sits back, the iPad held loosely in her lap, thinking. Thinking about what to do next.

And feeling relieved too that at least it isn't an affair.

But what is it? Something to do with the three of them. And something that – he thinks – doesn't concern her. But something that requires him to cover his tracks.

She will have to ask him, she decides. She will have to ask him, and not take no for an answer, until he meets her eyes and tells her the truth. They're married. They share a bed, sleep naked, share showers, sometimes. Rescue animals together, laugh together, want a family together. It's only right that he tells her the truth.

32.

Cathy

Cathy can hear Lydia packing next door. She's decided to burn the wallet and the warrant, and she hopes Lydia won't come investigating.

A couple of matches does it, in an old bowl by an open window, the leather catching fire and curling, giving off an acrid smell. She has a jug of water handy, but luckily it smokes and burns to ash, and then to nothing.

Next, the warrant. It's tucked in the side of the suitcase, and, as she gets it out, she is still thinking of Frannie and Jason Granger. She spreads out the pieces on the bed and leans over them, hands either side of them. They've dried out since that night when they got covered in blood and Frannie's tears and the sweat from their panicky hands. Some parts are harder to read, but some are easier, the blood having paled.

But wait, what's that? Her eyes scan, trying to make out any further words. An *s*, maybe. An *o*. A *p* . . .

She stands and holds up one of the pieces to the light like it's an X-ray. There is something, down there, right before that rip.

The letters have been torn horizontally through their centres, that missing piece discarded somewhere so the remaining parts don't fit together. But Cathy recognizes what is half written there. As easily as she would recognize her own name. *Joseph Plant.*

*

Cathy is standing in the airport next to Joe, wondering quite who he is. What does her brother know? Was Will already known to him? She thinks about his lie to the police, that he never saw Will, and of Frannie hiring a lawyer, and can't help but wonder if they're playing some sort of game that she doesn't know the rules of.

'Where do we check in?' Frannie says, holding Paul, twenty minutes after everyone else has done it while she was in duty free. Cathy tries not to be irritated by her as Joe shows her where. 'I can't believe you did it without me!' Frannie says to him as they walk off. 'Your old Saturday Show colleague.'

They're all nervous. But, so far, nobody's told them there is a block on one of their passports. Nobody's said they will be searched, and Cathy is pleased about that too, because before she burned the wallet and the warrant she took a private, encrypted photo of them on her phone. She knows it is a risk, but she couldn't part with them entirely. Couldn't quite leave the mystery alone. Might need them one day, to atone. Or to solve the mystery of who he was and what he wanted with them.

And yet Cathy knows they are all expecting sniffer dogs and armed police and a last-minute announcement over the tannoy on the plane.

Lydia has been quiet. She's now browsing the perfumes in duty free, but in the manner of somebody who isn't really looking. Cathy is privately worried. Lydia doesn't miss a trick. And it is impossible to act normally when you have been complicit in the burying of a body seventy-two hours earlier.

'Giant Toblerone?' Joe says, walking over to Cathy as he holds one up. Cathy looks at him, her complicated, tender, brittle brother. How can he act so normally? She's got to raise it with him.

Together, they drift into the make-up section. Their eyes are reflected all around them in a hundred mirrors, bouncing off the bright, white spotlights up ahead.

'Joe,' she says.

He looks at her wordlessly.

'Why is your name on the document Will had?'

'What?' Joe says. His mouth falls open in shock, his eyes squint up, as though he is studying something very close up that he can't quite make out.

'Why is your name on the warrant?'

'Not here,' Joe says, and Cathy feels a flash of relief, of hope that he might explain. Cathy leads Joe out of the shop, away from the multiple refracting fairground mirrors and the CCTV.

They leave through one of the automatic doors that fronts the runway, leading to a smoking area. A plane, just taken off, banks and loops back on itself as they watch it.

'What are you talking about?' he says.

'Your name is on that warrant, Joe. Right at the bottom. Along a rip.'

'*What?*' he says.

'You don't know why it says Joseph Plant?'

'I have no idea,' Joe says. He waits a beat, then says, 'What kind of a conversation is this?' It's become a family phrase, that sentence. Frannie started it. She'd been through a phase of drinking, smoking, skipping school. She used to try to control her tellings-off, like she was a CEO or something. 'What kind of a conversation is this?' she'd said, bold as anything, standing in their hallway, an

180

hour past her curfew, in a skimpy dress, smelling of cigarettes. Joe had caught Cathy's gaze and they'd both dissolved into giggles, much to their parents' annoyance.

'I don't know,' Cathy says quietly.

They walk further outside. A gust of air carries the smell of hot engines and petrol on it. It whips Cathy's hair around her face. She pushes it impatiently behind her ears and carefully hands Joe her phone, keeping it angled close to their bodies.

Joe stares at the phone cradled in his hands. His body is bent over it, his head dropped downwards. He stands with his weight on one leg, the toe of the other foot resting behind him. He looks both curious and casual. Totally natural, Cathy thinks as she assesses him.

'I have no idea,' Joe says eventually, his tone mystified. If he's lying, he's convinced her.

They stand there in the sun for a few seconds, Cathy feeling like a police officer, hoping the silence will be filled. But Joe doesn't provide any further information.

'Could it be the – you know, the punch, you said about? In the bar?'

'I mean, maybe?'

'Okay, well,' Cathy says, still looking closely at him. *What kind of a conversation is this?*

'I don't know what to do about this,' Joe says. Another plane roars along the runway and they move instinctively away from it even though they're nowhere near it. 'Should I . . . I mean –'

'Well, you can't tell anyone.'

Now in the shade of the building, Joe turns to Cathy, his eyes dark, his skin sallow. 'We should use an untraceable computer, when we're back,' he says. 'Put in as much of this document as we can. Internet café or something.'

'Yeah, maybe,' Cathy says, though it's useless. There are only four legible words. *Stato, Mandato, Joseph* and *Plant.*

He hands her back her phone as they enter the departure lounge and sit down, waiting to be called for their flight. Cathy watches the officials. The people scanning the bags. The cabin crews. Customs. And the police too, by the gate. Two German shepherds with them, different sniffer dogs. Joe is watching them too, as they sit there like sentries.

She closes her eyes against the sniffer dogs and the airport and the Italian police and wishes as hard as she's ever wished for anything that her family, in ten years, will have got away with it, and have forgotten about this holiday, will never, ever reference it, like an event that truly never really happened. She wishes and wishes for it, the world black against her closed eyes. She stays there, the world black, and wonders if they will ever go back to Verona.

'We can't ever sell the villa,' she murmurs to Joe, her eyes still closed.

'I know.'

'And we can't go back.'

'What if he's on us?' Joe says. Cathy opens her eyes. He's turned to her, his elbows on his knees, body bent over double in the plastic chair.

'On us?' Cathy says.

'His smell.' There's something about Joe's expression that makes Cathy uneasy. She blinks, trying to dispel the feeling. Joe has never once made her uneasy.

'They're airport sniffer dogs. They're looking for drugs.'

'I think they'd raise an eyebrow at a dead body,' Joe says bluntly.

'Who knows. We've washed a lot,' she says. A throw-away bit of reassurance. An alternative scenario plays out in front of her. One where he cracks a joke. *Can dogs even raise their eyebrows?* he'd say, and Cathy's smile would turn into a laugh.

Their flight is called: 1573A to Birmingham International. Cathy will be relieved to be in her own bed, away from it all. Back to before, she hopes, and away from her siblings; somewhere she's never before wanted to be.

She passes her bag through the scanner. A bored-looking airport worker looks at the screen through heavy-lidded eyes, head tilted slightly backwards. There's nothing in my bag, she repeats to herself. She doesn't look at Joe. Her whole body is tense as the scanner stops, then restarts again, as though God himself, Jesus from the Verona crucifixes, is toying with her.

She steps next into the body scanner. It beeps. Her heart speeds up. A man waves a scanning wand over her. She finds she is holding her breath. It moves between her arms and the sides of her body. It moves between her legs. It comes back up, down the length of her arm and, just as it does, she meets his eye, just briefly. A dark-brown eye, long lashes, a moment of contact. And, as she meets it, she thinks, *I buried a body just a handful of days ago. There's a manhunt for him, and I need to escape.*

The airport worker can't read her mind, of course, and Cathy passes through without incident. But the thoughts still burn on to the inside of her brain. As though they are all there, queued up in her head, waiting to tell somebody. Waiting to be spoken.

In Birmingham, Frannie, Joe and Lydia have gone to the car while Cathy waits in the airport. She is working on her phone, chasing up scans and prescriptions. Her bag is missing. Only hers and a stranger's, a tall, lithe man who stands next to her. He has a shaved head and is tanned, one hand resting on a hip. He's wearing a white t-shirt that has three distinct purple blobs down the front of it that for a second Cathy thinks are blood.

He catches her looking. 'Aeroplane wine,' he says with a shrug. 'I hate flying.'

Cathy nods. There is something about his body language that makes her want to keep looking. His weight on one hip. The way his waist is slim compared to the width of his shoulders. The blond hairs on his forearms.

She forces herself to turn away. She's tired, her feet cold in flip-flops. Gone is the refrigerated air-con of Italy but so too is the heat. It feels blustery even here, inside at the baggage claim, as though a door is open somewhere.

'Yours lost too?' the man says. He doesn't appear to be particularly annoyed. He sits down, right there on the baggage carousel. Cathy stares at his slim ankles and feet bare in his trainers and feels a swoop deep in her gut.

'Apparently so,' she says tightly, wondering why she finds this hard, an attractive man sitting near to her, solo, evidently waiting too and wanting to talk to pass the time. Cathy's shyness is doubled in weight by the shame of it. Why can't she learn from her date with Pete the rabbit owner? Why can't she just be like everybody else?

'Probably being lobbed around somewhere.' He leans back on his hands and looks at her. His face is open, a wide, white smile aimed at her. Right where his t-shirt meets his shorts is a thin slice of tanned skin, only a millimetre wide. Cathy can't stop staring at it. The hint of a curl of dark body hair. Her cheeks flush against her will, against the knowledge that she shouldn't be attracted to anyone right now, not in the current circumstances.

Their bags land on the carousel, which starts moving, startling him to his feet. He laughs, looking at her. She blinks, staring ahead as her suitcase approaches. As their cases arrive, pressed close together, he reaches for hers, first, and drops it by her feet. 'Later,' he says. As he turns away from her, she catches his scent. It's like a summer. The smell of stepping into a hot greenhouse. That night, Cathy smells it suddenly on her, on her arms, and sniffs and sniffs until it's gone.

33.
Joe

Joe is back home, and back to work, as though none of it ever happened. He's in the backroom, which runs along the width of the building behind the consultation rooms that open out on to it, centrifuging blood, and making a coffee, and being careful not to mix the two up. He held his breath this morning while drawing this blood. The metallic smell of it. Sharp and cloying. He'd almost been sick.

'Yum, blood and coffee,' Frannie says as she drifts by. She has no shoes on, and is carrying a can of Coke.

'Might check my coffee for diseases,' he says, and he hears Frannie's laugh bloom as she reaches the reception.

He did bloodwork on his first work experience, much to his disappointment. He wanted to treat animals, and instead he processed results for two weeks. He still remembers now, seventeen-year-old Joe, who hadn't yet grown into his nose, peering through the window into the treatment room, hoping for a glance of a cat or a dog.

Evan comes in through Consultation Room One. Joe's back stiffens. He can't be bothered with Evan at the best of times, but especially not today. He glumly dribbles milk into his coffee and tries to ignore him. Evan is good at client care, Cathy tells him all the time. He hardly ever has to write down a bill, never gets complaints. 'That is because he is a fake,' Joe had said a few weeks ago, deadpan, and Frannie had barked out a laugh. 'He's not a fake,' she'd said, laughing. 'He's totally upfront about what a twat he is.'

Evan is a terrible medicine vet. That's the truth of it. He's okay at surgery, has steady hands and can talk the talk, but that's about it.

'We can't bully the only non-Plant,' Cathy had said with a sigh.

Joe moves across the office, away from the spinning blood and the freshly made coffee, and begins signing a worming prescription for a cockapoo. Something about the sterile snap of the lemon disinfectant, the coffee, the mostly mundane list of problems: vaccinations for cats and dogs, conjunctivitis, Labradors having eaten knickers – these things are comforting to him after the blood and terror of Verona.

Cathy is in Room Three, directly behind him. Frannie is out front, on reception. It's their mother's day off, but she will probably come in at some point, almost always does. Cathy's dog Macca is sleeping in the corner.

Evan flicks on the kettle, which comes to a boil again quickly. 'How was Verona?'

'Yeah, fine. Hot.' Joe thinks of the hotline text and the fucking cashpoint and wonders how long he's got. How long until they find him? Will he get a couple more weeks, months? This box of worming medication expires next year. He's sure he won't see it.

'You go to the place I told you about?' Evan crosses his legs, the toe of his shoe hitting the floor. 'Where the locals go?'

'Yes, yes, we went to the restaurant, and we said *Evan is*

so cool and authentic,' Joe says. *'He knows only the places off the beaten track where the locals eat.'*

'I'll take that as a no,' Evan says, unfazed. 'I don't know what to do about my patient,' he adds, jerking his thumb behind him, indicating the consultation room. 'And I'm knackered.'

'You always say that after our holiday,' Joe says. Evan's parents are lawyers, and he once joked he'd get them to sue the practice for stress.

'That's because it's always a nightmare,' Evan remarks mildly. 'I mean – what do you call a vet who is so busy he just issues prescriptions without thinking?'

'A doctor,' Joe deadpans. Evan practically falls over laughing.

Joe double-checks the signed prescription against the cockapoo's weight and reaches for his coffee. It's too hot. 'Well, I can't help with tiredness,' he says, quietly relishing this moment of . . . of what? Of superiority, he supposes. He is the partner and Evan is the employee. God, Joe thinks. He needs to get a life if he gets off on things like this.

'Yeah.' Evan rubs at his forehead. 'Was working last night.'

'Here?'

'No – Deliveroo. Absolutely knackering.'

'I can't string a sentence together after leaving here,' Joe says sympathetically.

'Right,' Evan says tightly, obviously embarrassed. Evan is a curious combination of wanting to be seen as a big shot and a victim.

'How bad is it?' Joe says. 'Money-wise.'

'I pay Ali over three grand a month, mate.'

'Wow. Beans on toast for dinner, then,' he quips, but, internally, he's wondering if there's something they could do. Increase his salary, maybe.

'Not even that,' Evan says with a short, sad laugh.

'Are they in there?' Joe asks, nodding to the consultation-room door.

'Yeah. Two-year-old bitch – toy poodle. It has a history of weird test results. Intermittent odd symptoms.'

'She. Not it,' Joe says. Evan turns on the charm for patients, but doesn't ever bother out back. 'How old, exactly?' Joe leans back against the counter, more relaxed than he was. Evan's financial situation has made him feel better about his own crisis. *Schadenfreude*, is it called? He can't be that bad if there's a word for it, Joe hopes.

'Two and a half next month.' Evan takes off his round glasses and rubs at his eyes. '*She's* fine, sort of. Losing weight sometimes. Not always eating meals. Intermittent vomiting but by no means often. Seems a bit stressed. Slightly low glucose. Latest test showed raised renal parameters, but she's so young . . . the weird thing is she's worse after the vets'.'

'Is the glucose artefactual?'

'Tested in-house. No.'

'What else have you tested for?'

'Parasites. We've done a food-allergy trial. We've done a faecal parasitology. Checked for UTIs. An abdo X-ray for foreign bodies, a cPLI for pancreatitis. All negative. But that's how we got the kidney result,' Evan says. He rubs at his hair with his hand. He has a wrist tattoo which says *Love your life* on it. Twat, twat, twat.

'Tricky,' Joe says. 'Why is she worse after the vet?' He hears the skittering of claws against linoleum in Evan's consultation room and raises his eyebrows.

'I don't know. I said I needed to think,' Evan says, a half-apology on his face. 'Without them firing questions at me and the fucking dog trying to get into everything. It must be something gastro with that range of responses.'

'Does she have diarrhoea?'

'Sometimes. Look.' He gets out the blood results. Joe instinctively turns away from them. The breakdown of everything contained in the blood: antibodies, plasma, red blood cells. The same as humans. The same as Will. He can smell it.

Joe disguises his reaction by sipping his coffee. It's still too hot, and burns his lips like an allergic reaction. He stares at the wall in front of him. She's worse after the vets'. Something is niggling at him. He whirls the coffee around in his mug and takes another burning sip.

Stress.

'Do a basal cortisol test,' Joe says. 'Or, better yet, an ACTH stimulation test. I reckon atypical Addison's. In toy breeds it's different. The tell is that she can't handle stress.'

'God,' Evan says. 'Right. Really?'

'We'll see. Try it.'

Satisfied, sort of, Joe goes into the reception to see Frannie. She's usually a great morale booster. She keeps Chinese waving cats on the reception desk and has treats for the dogs and Dreamies for the cats that she gives to the owners with their receipts. She makes it a nice place to be.

'All right,' he says to her, leaning his elbows on the desk. 'Just had Evan in, whingeing.'

'Oh, be kind to Evan,' she says.

'You sound like Cathy the conscientious objector.'

'Really not,' Frannie says, making a face. Joe helps himself to a Twix lying on her desk and she waves him away. 'Have it, I can't eat,' she says.

'I can't stop.'

Evan arrives out in reception with the dog and her owners. 'Thanks, mate,' he grins, as they pay. 'Told them it was my idea.'

'Of course you did,' Joe says. He finishes the Twix and holds out his hand. Frannie gives him a bag of Quavers.

'Said I had a brainwave out back,' Evan says with a laugh. 'Sorry, not sorry. You eating for two, or what?'

Joe stiffens. 'You're a twat,' he says. Evan thinks he's joking and laughs loudly. 'Looking gorgeous as ever,' he says to Frannie, when he's seen out his clients. He can never resist flirting with her.

'Piss off, Evan,' she says dispassionately.

Joe finishes his crisps, then goes back to his blood-spinning.

As he's working late, he receives a text from Frannie. His bottle of wine – a Yellow Tail merlot – is sitting there on the checkout next to – he snorts – a packet of cigarettes and a huge cheesecake.

'Perfect,' he replies to her, and she sends a smile.

Joe thinks, now, as he works, of all the animals he's ever treated, and saved. The happiness they bring to their owners. The care and attention he treats them with. Wonders if that will ever outweigh it.

34.
Cathy

Cathy is in a consultation with a woman whose Dobermann is off his food.

'Try the paste for two days,' Cathy says, her hand on the Dobermann's head. He's fine. Eyes bright. Tail wagging. Stomach feels relaxed and non-tender. 'Stick to the bland diet, hand-feed him chicken and rice rolled into balls if you need to. Little and often. Come back if that doesn't work, but he should be fine.' She meets the owner's eyes – a woman in her sixties. 'I'm not worried,' she says. She always says this, if it's true. She would want to be told it herself, if it was Macca who was sick.

The woman blinks at her, smiling, a hand going unconsciously to gesture to the dog. People's pets mean so much to them. Cathy sees the Dobermann and his owner out into the reception. Frannie – a pen holding up her hair, Facebook open on the work computer, her desk littered with chocolate bar and crisp wrappers – quickly task-switches and sorts out the bill. She glances at Cathy. 'Got time for a quick fashion parade?'

Cathy raises her eyebrows.

'Look – I shop when I'm stressed,' Frannie says, getting an ASOS parcel with its distinctive black-and-white packaging out of the top drawer. 'What do you make of this?' she says, opening it and pulling out the clothes. She holds up a top to Cathy. It's blood-red.

'Too much,' Cathy says quietly. 'Red doesn't suit you.'

Frannie keeps rooting in the bag, oblivious. Cathy doesn't say, *How can you think of shopping right now?* It wouldn't be fair. They all cope in different ways. Frannie drags Cathy into the prep room, the room with the best lights, where she tries on a floor-length patterned dress which swamps her. As she pulls it off, Cathy can see her ribs.

'Maybe,' Cathy says. 'It's a possible.' It's a phrase she used to say to Frannie all the time when the clothes came to the practice, but she doesn't mean it this time. Everything's changed.

'I'll ask Deb,' Frannie says, balling up the dress and putting it back into the clear plastic wrap.

Back in the consultation room, Cathy cleans the table with antiseptic spray and blue roll.

She hears her mother arrive in the foyer. Cathy has always been tolerant of her mother's inability to completely relinquish control of the business to her three children, but she can't see her today. She'll know.

'How was the break?' Maria says, poking her head around the door.

'Good,' Cathy says.

'You look tired. You all do.'

'We're fine,' Cathy says.

'You eating enough?'

'Mum,' Cathy says, a warning signal in her voice. She's thirty-five. She doesn't need to be parented. And, if she does, it isn't this – this anxiety her mother demonstrates. If Maria wants to parent her, then they could at the very least discuss the elephant in the room.

'I'm just asking,' Maria says.

'Are you consulting?' Cathy says. 'Today?'

'No. But Frannie told me there's a Rottweiler with epistaxis?'

'Yeah – he's in the back,' Cathy says, wondering if, when she's sixty-five, she won't be able to resist coming in. God, she hopes not. 'Joe's going to CT him.'

'Really? Already?'

'It's not just a bit of sneezing,' Cathy says, sighing with frustration at having to explain their reasoning, at having to reiterate a conversation they've already had. If only their mother would either work full time or not at all . . .

Maria is already heading out. 'We've got it under control,' Cathy calls after her.

She checks her phone before her next patient, sitting on the floor next to Macca, her rescue bulldog, brought in three years ago with a broken toe and an owner who didn't want to pay to have it fixed. 'To be honest, I wish I'd never got him,' the man said, and, right that second, Macca's brown eyes met Cathy's, and it was love.

'Sure there's somebody here who could rescue him,' she said lightly.

'Oh, yeah – God. I'd love that. He's just got too much energy.'

Cathy stared at him, wide-eyed, thinking, *How could you?* Macca went home with her the week after, heaved himself up on the sofa. His toe hadn't even needed any treatment except rest.

She browses her phone but there is no news. Her blood turns fizzy in the checking of it. She sits there alone in the backroom, her face flushed, in the premises that she used to be so proud of part-owning but that now feel like a prison. It is no better, being in the UK. It is worse, actually, because they are so far from the body. Cathy has no idea if they've found it. At this very moment, as she looks at her holiday manicure resting against Macca's fur, somebody could be unearthing Will. The stench of him, his rotting skin. What they have done is *so* wrong, so manifestly wrong. They are monsters. What would their mother think? Their mother would ... what? Cathy cannot imagine it. She'd fall apart. That's what would happen. That is what has already happened once.

She gathers Macca to her. He grunts, and she releases him. Usually, she would work. She would see patient after patient, letting the aftercare stack up and up, she'd order prescription dog food and new oxygen cylinders out back, each task breeding others. She'd get home at ten o'clock, too tired to think. But she doesn't do that today.

She asks Evan – eating cheese sandwiches alone in his room – to cover her next slot, even though she knows he is knackered and put upon. Nevertheless, she makes an excuse and walks through the reception, Frannie's huge eyes tracking her. They're a practice almost in the middle of nowhere, just three shops in a row, flats above them, fields behind. A pharmacy, an independent café and their veterinary practice. The rent was cheap out here in the sticks, and they marketed themselves as a discount vets, much to their mother's annoyance. The business soon rolled in. People didn't mind travelling for a bargain and an easy parking space.

It started raining this morning on her way in. Biblical rain, the sort spoken about on the news as well as the weather bulletins. A month's worth of rain in a morning, and more still coming down. It's so stormy that the sky is becoming dark and heavy in places, the colour of a black paintbrush dipped in clear water. Outside, it smells of wet grass and hot pavements.

In the café next door, she orders an Americano and adds milk at a small wooden station at the back. She will just take ten minutes, here, alone, to get her head together. Sitting down, she raises the mug to her lips and thinks of Will. Maybe if she thinks of him, pays her respects, perhaps it will help somehow.

As she watches the quiet café gradually fill up with people shaking out their umbrellas, self-consciously pushing their wet hair back from their faces, she sees him. The man from the baggage claim. Cathy blinks, amazed he is out here in the countryside. He has a brown bag with him, a laptop bag. He is wearing glasses today, but it's definitely him. He has on a parka and dark jeans turned up at the ankles and the hotness is back in her cheeks.

She tries to catch his gaze, and she sees out of her peripheral vision that he stops as he recognizes her.

He walks over to her table, bypassing the counter. He brings with him the smell of the countryside in the rain, and, underneath that, that hot summer smell again. She looks up at him as she breathes in.

'The baggage-claim girl,' he says, his face easing into a smile. He's older than she first thought. Maybe early forties. Dark eyes but pale lashes.

'That's me,' she says.

How funny, Cathy thinks. If her bag hadn't gone missing, she still would have crossed paths with this man here in the café, but she wouldn't have known him, like two dominos falling over in a row, the first required to tilt the second; something Cathy thinks about a lot when she relives the phone call Frannie made to her.

He turns away from her, an arm raised in a half-wave, and Cathy finds something sweeping across her skin. Disappointment. She wants that hot-cheeked feeling.

'Was anything broken? In your bag?' she asks desperately.

He turns back to her, a smile spreading over one half of his mouth and then the other, a lopsided half-knowing grin, and says, 'Nope. You?'

'Tom,' the owner of the café calls out, looking over to Cathy's table. 'The usual?'

'Please. To go,' Tom says, turning away from her again.

Cathy finds herself downing her Americano faster. She has to get back to work, after all.

She times her stand just as he touches his contactless card to the machine. And then they're walking out together into the rain. He's holding a reuseable cup, his weight on one hip again. Her work uniform is getting wet. What is she doing, having rushed her coffee break to walk out with him? She's always the one doing the chasing. But she can feel the heat off his body, even here, standing outside in the rain together.

'You work at the vets'?' he says, gesturing with his coffee to her tunic, pulling up the hood of his parka with the other hand.

'Yeah.' Cathy looks past his shoulder, to the vets'. Joe and Frannie emerge together. Cathy absent-mindedly checks her watch. Joe is supposed to be in afternoon surgery. And Frannie is supposed to be on reception. Where are they going? She keeps looking. Something about their body language is self-conscious, sheepish, maybe. They walk down the road together, to where Cathy can't imagine.

'You a vet, or –' Tom says.

'Sorry,' Cathy says. She points to them. 'That's my brother and sister.'

'You work together?'

'Mmm,' she says, still looking. Still thinking. Still thinking about Frannie's lawyer, about Joe's name on the warrant, at how alone she suddenly feels in the family, as though they're holding her over a sheer drop, and she has to rely on them not to let go.

'Pretty rainy for a walk,' Tom remarks, watching them too.

She turns her gaze back to him. 'You're getting so wet.' She looks at his jeans, already dark in places from the rain.

He shrugs, a big clumsy shrug, like he just doesn't give a fuck about anything and Cathy, who gives far too many fucks about absolutely everything, moves to him like a flower to the sun.

'Yes, I'm a vet,' Cathy says, answering his question with flaming cheeks.

'Oh, lovely!' Tom says. The rain is battering both of them, and Tom starts laughing again. 'Jesus Christ,' he says. 'It's not Verona, is it?' But he still stands there, smiling down at her.

'No, it's not,' she says.

'Should we . . .' he says. Cathy waits, wondering if he might feel it too. She stands there, hesitating as droplets track down her neck, looking at his take-out coffee. Their eyes meet. 'You want to – go somewhere less wet?' Tom says. 'Share my coffee? Or buy another?' He shrugs, another big shrug.

Cathy became shy when she was twelve. It started with glandular fever. The day before it, she had played hockey, then gone to a café, then come home and tidied her room. Unlimited energy, which she spent however she wanted. She stayed up late. She kissed boys. She finished essays at the eleventh hour and played sports to destress afterwards.

But then, the illness. She caught it off a classmate at school, who recovered in about a week, no time at all. But it felled Cathy. First, the heat of the fever, the intensity of the fever dreams. Then the fatigue, like her limbs were under water. She doesn't remember much about the weeks and months that followed it, only little snatches. Reaching up to put her hair in a ponytail, the motion of her arms unexpectedly exhausting her. Falling asleep while cradling a cup of tea, and sleeping so deeply that when she woke up it remained in the exact same position, only cold.

She got sick on New Year's Eve and it was April before she made lunch for herself. She would get up at ten, watch television until lunch-time. Nap. Watch television until the evening, when she was often in bed before nine. The doctor said her immune system had gone into *its overdraft*, that it needed to spend time repaying it, an explanation which made sense to Cathy, strangely logical in the chaos of the illness she found herself living in.

Cathy continued to recover over the summer and into the autumn. Everything she hadn't been able to do during her illness was tentatively done, sometimes in small scale, in miniature, that autumn/winter. She baked a cake and lay down while it was in the oven. She took small trips out, but she rested in the back of the car on the way there.

And then suddenly, in the following January, she was mostly better. She had been talking to a boy on MSN on her laptop, sometimes, when she was ill, reclining in bed. He was in her school, in the year above her, had been off for almost as long as she had, with a broken femur that wouldn't repair.

He'd come over that night, when she was in charge of Rosie. Rosie had been eight, Cathy thirteen, Joe fifteen. Everyone else had been out, at a family party that Cathy said she wasn't interested in, but really just still did not have the energy for. She hadn't wanted to hold everyone back, so said she'd look after Rosie instead.

Rosie was fast asleep. Cathy and the boy had headed into the den, closed the door, watched a movie.

Even now, with everything that happened after, and since, Cathy can remember odd details of that evening. The pavements glassed with frost outside. She'd lit three candles, three orange dots in the darkness on the mantelpiece. Never again would Cathy take for granted an evening spent with enough energy, not sleeping, not even the most mundane one, she was thinking, as she held hands with a boy called Sean she hardly knew but wanted to. Nothing bad would ever happen again, she really did think, on that exact evening. She'd had her dose of bad luck.

They'd emerged from the den after the film ended. She'd gone to check on Rosie, found her in her bed.

Completely still.

Cathy had paused in the doorway, dismissing the

anxiety she felt. She crossed the room and reached out to touch Rosie, just to check, and she'd been cool. Cooling. Not quite cold but not body temperature either. Cathy's own body had reacted to the shock by turning boiling. She still remembers that panicked heat even now.

Sudden Infant Death Syndrome, they said. It could happen to any child. Nobody knows what would have happened had Cathy been listening, checking more often.

The rest Cathy hardly remembers. The 999 call, her parents meeting her in the hospital. She only remembers that frost outside, those three candles, the last, bottled feeling of happiness as she had sat hand in hand, a teenager, with that boy Sean, whom she's not ever seen since.

The only other thing that Cathy remembers is what she overheard. Mother-to-father, wife-to-husband, in what they thought was the quiet privacy of their kitchen, Cathy heard it.

Well, she's always done whatever she wanted to do without thinking.

Cathy can see as an adult that that is an unfair assessment – she was a normal teenager; active, yes, selfish too – but nevertheless. It has come to define her adulthood. Every word ventured on dates is second-guessed. Life lived in greyscale, muted, always at work. It must be self-sabotage, she realizes now; bad things happen right after good things, right after you let go.

Cathy looks up at this man who doesn't seem to give a shit about anything at all. And see how happy he is, getting pissed on and smiling at her. Living his life in the rain. 'Do you know what?' Cathy says, looking up at him, rain dribbling down her forehead. She could try. She could try to be less shy. She could try to reach out. 'Fuck it. Let's.'

35.

Now

Jason's Office, mid March, 5.00 p.m.

'All right,' Jason says. 'We have what we call disclosure in – from the other side.'

'Oh,' I say, the term vaguely familiar to me, as legal jargon sometimes is. Proceedings, witnesses, defendants, the accused . . . I stare at my hands in my lap as I sit opposite him.

'So I have been through it,' Jason says, and I feel my shoulders sag with relief. It's not my job, I sometimes have to remind myself. It is actually his job, to finish this, to help me, to end it.

'Okay,' I say in a small voice. Now that he's told me, I see that the disclosure is spread out in lever arch files with my name on their spines. Three, four, five of them. They seem to crowd in. All that documentation about something that happened in a split-second.

There are three half-drunk mugs of coffee on Jason's desk and his hair is more snarled than usual.

'And matched it up to your statement that I took.'

'Right. Is it bad?'

'No, it isn't bad,' Jason says, but his voice elongates on the final word, emphasizing it, like shining a spotlight on to it.

'But it isn't good?'

Jason's eyes slide to the side. 'I mean – look,' he says, his gaze turning directly towards me and locking on to mine.

For a moment, my heart seems to spasm and I think he's going to tell me that none of this is good, that everything is over, that we're done for. 'Joe has disagreed with your version of events.'

I close my eyes. It's funny how, even in estrangement, I still feel close to Joe. We might no longer live in those beautiful, tiny cottages with their mullioned windows and stone floors, work at the vets' together, hang out every night. I might be here, in a lawyer's office, and he in his own, and yet . . . I feel I could reach out to touch him, my brother Joe.

'How bad?' I say. The statements were taken separately, as they have to be. Maybe, maybe, maybe there are just small inconsistencies. Maybe our recollections are only slightly different. Maybe it's nothing.

But, like everything that followed Verona, the best-case scenario just simply doesn't materialize. It is a run of bad luck, like throwing a one on a dice a hundred times in a row.

'It's very different,' Jason says plainly. He reaches for the file marked '*R.* v. *Plant* – File 1', and, as it sleets outside in random flurries, he starts to explain it to me, and we get to work. With fixing it. With fixing the mess we all made. I stare as the sleet becomes rain as it hits the dirty glass in Jason's office. Of course we are done for, I think. It was foolish to have hope.

I blink as I look back up at Jason, underlining a section of Joe's statement. The crime is done, and now to the punishment.

36.

Then

Cathy

Cathy gets out of her car, her feet submerging immediately into the puddles that surround it, and walks up to Frannie's front door instead of her own. She barely saw her today, at work, and she has decided to speak to her after she saw her wandering the country lanes with Joe. They need to clear the air, and Frannie is an easier person to do that with than Joe.

Cathy has exchanged numbers with Tom but hasn't yet heard from him. As they parted, he'd touched her shoulder, and Cathy's body moved towards his like it was no longer within her control. Other than that, though, the coffee date ended like many dates have before. A half-hearted promise, an intended plan. It will be cancelled by him, she assumes, a new plan made, cancelled again, the potential dying off like snow that falls but doesn't settle.

Frannie answers the door with their parents, who have their coats on. Frannie is wearing a colourful headscarf and holding Paul, who's in one of those towels with a hood. His eyes are dark brown, framed by straight, wet lashes. He smells of lavender and biscuits and milk. Paul startles at her, surprised to see her, then hides his face for just a second, a game he often plays.

'You all right?' Frannie says, smiling.

'We're off-duty now,' Owen says to Cathy, pulling her towards him for a quick hug. 'Nice to see you briefly.' As ever, when he looks at Paul, his face transforms. Gone is the stoicism. And gone is her mother's anxiety. They hide behind their hands as they walk backwards up the drive, peeking out to make Paul laugh, displaying a whimsy Cathy never remembers them having with her. So many parents are better off as grandparents.

Frannie's hair is piled on her head around the scarf. Her make-up has faded. She's so thin. Cheekbones with deep cuts underneath them, like somebody with a wasting illness.

She steps aside and lets Cathy in, as she always does. 'Joe with you?' she says, and Cathy feels a pang. Like Frannie would rather Joe were here than her.

'No. How're you?' Cathy asks.

'You know,' she says, her back to Cathy. 'Up and down.'

'Yeah.'

'Glad we're back. Tea?'

'Yes, I'd rather be on today than a few days ago,' Cathy says. 'How were Mum and Dad?'

'Oh, the same,' Frannie says drily. 'Exemplary grand-parents. Dad actually sang to Paul. Was singing "You are My Sunshine".'

'Unbelievable.'

Frannie laughs, picking up a stack of post as she walks down the hallway.

Her house has a different smell to Cathy's. Play-Doh, fresh laundry, old cooking. She is always making things with and for Paul. Finger-food, kitchen experiments, papier-mâché.

Frannie walks down the wooden-floored hallway with him, knowing that Cathy will follow. It is always at Frannie's cottage where they congregate, never at Cathy's. Cathy knows why, knows it's logical, but it still stings. She could host them at hers, even though her small kitchen table is always covered with paperwork, even though the beamed ceilings are so low she needs the lights on in the day. Her house might be a poorer version of Frannie's, but it still has nice features. Neat stacks of logs by the real, open fire. Wood-panelled cladding in the front room that she painted a navy-blue. A bell by the door that she kept from when it was a Victorian post office.

Cathy goes to sit by Frannie's modern bi-fold doors, as they almost always do. Frannie brings over two teas, and they sit there, their legs hanging down over the patio, together.

'Joe says you told him that his name is on that warrant,' Frannie says casually to Cathy as she passes her the tea. Her tone is not accusatory. The world, to Frannie, is quite simple and benign, has none of the complexities Cathy seems to find in it. Joe once threatened to punch a boy who dumped Frannie when she was fifteen, and Cathy still remembers her saying to Joe: *But I'm not bothered. I liked him, but not that much!*

'What?' Cathy says, but, really, she is thinking, There is a triangle here, and Cathy is at the point of it. The angle that's most likely to bear the brunt of any impact. That's how it feels anyway. Immediately, she wants to leave. To go to sit alone in her house, the doors and windows closed to her siblings.

'He says you asked him about it?' Frannie says.

She is tinted green by the glow of the cottage garden in front of her. Frannie's house is effortlessly stylish. She buys things Cathy would never think to – sheepskin rugs draped on benches, old-fashioned movie posters framed on the walls. She buys almost everything off eBay.

'I did – because his name is on that document,' Cathy says. 'Isn't that weird? That it says Joseph?'

Paul toddles over and Frannie picks bits of something yellow out of his little fists. 'Bath sponge,' she says, unable to resist smiling at him. 'The paper could be anything – couldn't it?' she continues. 'A traffic offence. He did a lot of driving there. *Anything.* He thinks you're suspicious of him.'

'Well, maybe I am.'

Frannie straightens and Cathy just catches her expression. Troubled, somehow.

'Sorry,' Cathy adds quickly. 'I just . . . you have to admit it's weird.'

'Yes, it's weird,' Frannie says, her face clearing. 'But Joe says whatever he thinks. He couldn't keep a secret from us even if he wanted to.'

'Same as you,' Cathy says.

'Right,' Frannie laughs. 'I'm just too dumb to tell lies to you two. Is Joe around? Should I make him a tea?'

'I don't know,' Cathy says, wanting suddenly, forcefully, to be alone with her sister, wishing that Joe weren't right next door all the time. She would maybe even tell her about Tom.

Their parents had been shocked by Frannie's pregnancy. She'd told them all over dinner, but it was clear Joe already knew. What had surprised Cathy most was Frannie's drive to keep the baby, to raise him alone. She – previously somebody who spent the generous wage they paid her on trainers and jewellery – started saving immediately.

She'd intended to take leave but had been lonely in the

cottage, so instead brought Paul into the practice in his pram every day, Macca sitting next to him.

Frannie gets to her feet and starts getting things out of the fridge. 'We can't turn on each other,' she says to Cathy.

She goes to the cupboards and gets down a bowl. She puts something in it and presses a button on her microwave and turns her back to Cathy. 'That's what he said.'

'Yeah,' Cathy says.

Paul lines up three dinosaurs in a careful row on the wooden floorboards. Cathy watches him, thinking.

She stares at the rain splattering into Paul's paddling pool, the drops little eruptions, like somebody is blowing bubbles from beneath the surface. Frannie's garden is wild, full of herbs and flowers and bushes all mixed up together. At the moment it's a riot of green and purple, a moving painting along the back of the house.

'Don't you think?' Frannie prompts.

'I'm not turning on anyone,' Cathy says.

'No. We know that.' Frannie folds her freckled arms, looking at Cathy. *We.*

'Just forget – *forget* I said anything,' Cathy says, her voice as tense as a glass clasped too tightly.

'Oh, there's no need to be like that.'

'Like what?'

'Difficult.'

'I'm not being difficult. You seem to be being so . . . finding it so . . . easy.'

'What?' Frannie says, turning to Cathy in surprise. She frowns, obviously confused.

'Nothing,' Cathy says, already feeling guilt – an effect only the baby of their family can have on her. She was lashing out because she felt isolated from them, she tells herself.

'No, what?' Frannie says.

Cathy thinks of the lawyer's details, and of the warrant, and of Will's blood, and how much of it there was, and finds she doesn't quite know where to start. 'I just wondered how you really are, underneath everything,' Cathy says.

'I'm really fine,' Frannie says shortly.

'I mean – exactly.'

'What?'

Cathy says nothing. Frannie's eyes widen as she looks at her. 'Oh, I'm *too* fine, am I? Classic you.'

'Classic *me*?'

'Draconian self-punishment.'

'Jesus, Fran. I was only concerned,' Cathy says, but it's a lie. She wasn't concerned; she was suspicious. Frannie does seem too fine. Shopping in duty free and – right now – wearing a pair of feather earrings she must have put on that morning. Cathy can't imagine doing such a thing. She is barely getting through the days.

Frannie stands and gets some potatoes out of a drawer and throws one at Cathy. 'Peel this and stop being moody,' she says. 'Ready?'

Cathy catches the second and third potatoes while Paul shrieks with laughter, trying to do as she is told, but still thinking. She could ask about the lawyer. Frannie is already pissed off. Cathy may as well seize upon it.

She sits, looking out over the garden, a bowl between her knees, and curls the peeler around the wet, fleshy texture, thinking. Wanting to ask a million things. How often she and Joe discuss her. If they trust her. Wanting to ask if Frannie is sorry. If she is thankful, for what they did. For what they have done for her. Or if, perhaps, she doesn't think about it. Cathy glances across the kitchen at her sister as she chops a carrot. Is she as straightforward as she makes out? Or is the directness actually cover, a deflection, like somebody who pretends to be direct but is actually a ball of neuroses, like Cathy herself?

'What I mean,' Cathy says, while peeling the potatoes, 'is just . . .'

Frannie's expression has hardened. She waits, silently, for Cathy to finish, like a police officer with the upper hand. 'Just what?' she says eventually.

'I saw your phone in Verona. I know I shouldn't have looked. But I saw that lawyer contact you back.'

Frannie's eyebrows rise. 'Right,' she says archly.

'Don't be mad.'

Frannie sighs and leans against the kitchen worktop. 'To be honest, I thought it would be sensible to have a lawyer on hand – for all of us. In the current climate. If anyone is searching my phone and finds his details, then it's likely too late anyway . . .' A sad laugh escapes through her straight, white teeth. And in that moment Cathy believes her. That laugh is vintage Frannie.

'There was *so* much blood, Fran. There was so much. And not calling the ambulance –'

'I know.' Frannie shifts her weight on her bare feet.

'Were you going faster than you said?'

'No. I wasn't.' Frannie looks Cathy dead in the eye. Cathy holds it for a moment, bolstered by her own honesty.

'Were you drunk?'

'No.'

'I feel like – you and Joe –' Cathy starts, but at that moment, she hears him enter through the door, calling out to Frannie. 'Speaking of.'

'You feel like me and Joe what?' Frannie says. Joe raises a hand in greeting to both of them and pours himself a Coke from Frannie's fridge. They stand there, both of them in Frannie's kitchen, looking at Cathy, a united front.

'Sorry I'm late,' Joe says. 'Let's just say: a Labrador and a Nerf bullet walked into a bar . . .'

'Any survivors?' Frannie says drily.

'All.' Joe smiles. He's a great vet. He always, always wanted to be one. Cathy remembers him very seriously pressing a fake stethoscope to his cat Peanut one afternoon after school and listening intently.

'Do we want the wine you got too?' Joe says. He wordlessly carries his Coke across Frannie's kitchen and joins Cathy, sitting cross-legged at the open door. 'It's been a wine kind of week.' He turns to look at his two sisters. Frannie grabs a bottle from the fridge and pulls out the cork with a pop. 'The Wards wouldn't pay their bill this evening. Almost went full Woolworths.'

'Oh, for God's sake, Joe,' Frannie snaps, looking at him. 'It was twenty years ago.'

Cathy hides a smile, though she understands where her youngest sister is coming from. The Woolworths tantrum when she was ten has become folklore in their family.

'Now you really do need wine,' Cathy says.

'Cheers to that,' Frannie says grimly.

'I'm going to get a pizza,' Joe says, bringing up an app on his phone.

'No – I'm making homemade healthy chips.'

'Healthy chips is an oxymoron,' Joe says.

And suddenly it's the same as it is most nights. All three siblings. Food, drink, banter, but Cathy is stifled by it, tonight.

'Make yourself at home,' Frannie says with a laugh. She leans over him, adding mushrooms to it, which he protests at. She puts the potatoes in water and places them in the fridge.

Cathy rubs at her forehead. What is happening? It's a completely normal scene between them, and that's what's wrong.

Her sister seems absolutely fine, having killed somebody last week. There is something uneasy about it that she can't untangle. Usually, she feels so comfortable sitting here by Frannie's open doors. Whether it's raining or snowing or sunny. But not tonight.

'What do you want?' Joe says to Cathy, holding up his phone. 'Anything?'

'No, I'm fine,' Cathy says, knowing she sounds uptight.

'Oh, honestly,' Frannie says, looking over her shoulder at Cathy. 'Just have a pizza. Will's still dead whether you have one or not.'

'Is that how it is for you?' Cathy says. 'We just – get on with it?'

'Cath,' Joe says softly. 'It's just a fucking pizza.'

'Fine,' Cathy says, sipping her wine, wondering why she's the only one with a guilty conscience.

They talk of other things while they wait, sitting overlooking Frannie's garden. The business, the various ongoing cases – Joe and Cathy do a deep dive on a Labrador with recurrent giardia until Frannie tells them to stop. They don't talk about the holiday, or the body. Two glasses of wine down, Cathy has to admit, she finds it better. Maybe Frannie's right. Maybe dwelling on it does just make it worse.

Their pizza arrives, and Frannie heads to the door. Cathy hears Evan's voice before she can really consider if that's right.

She looks at Joe, opening another bottle of wine. He inclines his head. 'He delivers,' Joe says.

'*Does* he? Why?'

'Money,' Joe says flatly.

'For what?'

Joe fiddles with the cork. 'He pays loads of child maintenance.'

'Wow. God. Now I feel bad.'

'I don't,' Joe says tensely. Cathy's eyes track across his fingers, still fiddling with the top of the wine bottle, and she can't help but wonder if he knew Evan was on shift tonight.

'Maybe we should pay him more,' she says.

'He earns a fine salary. Up to him if he wants to leave his marriage and kid.'

'*Joe*. You're so mean sometimes.'

'I'm not mean. I just say what we're all thinking,' Joe says. Cathy can't resist going into the hallway to help Frannie. And to see Evan.

'. . . if you wanted to,' Evan says. 'After this?'

'Not really,' Frannie says lightly, imbuing her voice with laughter.

'Right,' Evan says, holding out the pizza boxes to her. 'Well, then. You paid on the app, right?'

'For the pizzas, or the proposition?'

'Don't flatter yourself,' Evan says, while Frannie takes the boxes, still laughing.

'Did he just ask you out?' Cathy says, as Frannie closes the door.

'Yeah, again,' she says dismissively, in that way that only beautiful people can afford to. Cathy feels a stab of jealousy. How does she do it? Frannie would never go on a singular date. She would never be ghosted: they would always want more.

'Evan?' Joe says, as they walk into the kitchen and start arranging the pizzas boxes on Frannie's giant table. 'What'd he do?'

'Just asked me out, over a fucking pizza delivery,' Frannie says. 'Here are the pizzas, also, are you down to fuck?'

'That's disgusting,' Joe says, but he's laughing as he roots in Frannie's fridge for mayonnaise. Cathy knows that is what he is looking for without his having to say. 'Should have ordered a hot dog,' he adds, his voice muffled as he searches.

'I can't believe he has a second job,' Cathy says.

'I might complain that the pizzas are cold.'

'Don't,' Cathy says, reaching for Joe's arm. 'He's obviously – I don't know. Going through some stuff.'

'He's a tosser,' Joe says. 'Who chats up women in their own homes when delivering pizzas?'

'Lonely people,' Cathy says.

They eat in companionable silence, Cathy feeling more relaxed as each minute goes by. Maybe they can learn to forget. Maybe they can eat pizzas and drink wine just the way they used to. Maybe they can take the piss out of their colleague, behind closed doors, be the worst versions of themselves together. Maybe, maybe, maybe.

It's the same mood as Rosie's funeral, that volatile mix of panic and gallows humour. Cathy remembers it well. The wake. All their friends and family. Their mother in a stiff nineties skirt suit, their father in a black jacket so dark and old it was a kind of bottle-green. After everybody had left, Cathy, Joe and Frannie had been washing up in the farmhouse kitchen, as they often did. Cathy washed, Joe dried, and Frannie put away, which actually involved Joe putting most of the stuff away because she couldn't reach. Cathy had glanced towards the ceiling. Their parents were speaking. 'They said a ten per cent discount,' their mother was saying.

Joe looked at Cathy in alarm. Their mother continued: 'And they haven't applied it. Look – we paid in full for everything, the pizza slices, the cheese and pineapple sticks –'

'Wow,' Joe had said, evidently unable to help himself.

Frannie was looking smilingly from Cathy to Joe. 'What?' she'd said.

'Nothing,' Cathy said quickly. She'd glanced at Joe. 'Do not,' she'd said, holding up a hand, her mouth quivering.

'It's funeral food,' Joe said. 'A discount for . . . for funeral food.'

'We'll go to hell if we laugh,' Cathy had said. But Joe had already been doubled over with laughter, and Cathy and Frannie soon joined him. 'God, they're becoming tight,' Cathy had said. Over the following years, their mother's small but sharp traits – frugality, a kind of anxious fussiness – loomed large, while their father seemed to fade away entirely into nothing, repression, quietness, tears on Christmas Day and Rosie's birthday that he explained away as *just feeling a bit under the weather.*

Joe, Cathy and Frannie eventually responded the only way adult children can: by withdrawal.

Thinking of their closeness, of how much they have vested in each other, Cathy says, spontaneously to Frannie: 'Have you told Joe about Jason?'

Frannie's gaze turns shocked, pizza crust suspended over Joe's mayo.

'The lawyer?' Joe says. Cathy stares and stares at him. 'We thought it would be good to have someone in case we ever need him,' he says. Too much explanation. His tone too earnest.

'So you know who he is.'

'Yes,' Joe says.

'The two of you – but not me,' she says. She's burning with it. With the ancient sibling rivalry, the feeling of being left out, but with something else too, something she's been trying to keep a lid on: resentment. Bitterness. That Frannie did this to her. That she's in so deep she can't get out.

Frannie and Joe don't answer her.

37.
Joe

Saturday night at their parents' house. Joe looks forward to it each week, but always returns home in a bad mood. Lydia didn't want to come tonight, has been strange with him all week, each night asking him what Evan did, each night being moody when he refused to tell her.

Cathy has left Macca at home this time. 'He'll just beg for cheese,' she'd said glumly, evidently feeling tense too.

Their parents live in an old farmhouse on the edge of Warwickshire – far enough away from their cottages that they have to call before swinging by, which suits them just fine. It's an L-shaped house with two annexes – one they use as a bar and one for storing wood. They're sitting in the bar now with two old yellow Labradors, the door flung open on to the July rain, which drips in, fat splashes ricocheting off the wooden floor. It's a tiny room, six stools around a little island, a few bottles of wine and beer, a dartboard in one corner. Not an actual bar, as Joe often points out. More of a shed.

Paul has gone up to bed, and the atmosphere has soured somewhat since he left. There is no conduit through which they can channel their love for each other. No hilarious dinosaur outbursts – *Stegosaurus!* – shouted with a lisp at dinner-time – or the word 'yes', said over and over – recently learnt, but in an American accent. Joe heard his father imitate it, earlier – *yayus* – and had been so surprised by the lightness in his tone.

'Glad Italy was good anyway,' their father says stiffly to them. Joe looks steadfastly down into his half-drunk pint so that he won't exchange any glances with his sisters.

'It was,' Joe says into his lap. He looks at his father, smiling benignly, and Joe feels ten years old again, wanting so badly to impress him, wanting to confide and to confess. Wishing he were still that age, that Peanut was still alive, waiting to curl up on his pillow. That Frannie and Cathy were still his father's responsibility and not – somehow – Joe's.

'Is Verona safe?' Maria says.

'Honestly,' Joe says. The question irritates him more than usual, because Verona, evidently, isn't safe: or it wasn't for Will anyway. 'It's fine,' he adds tightly. 'Honestly. It's Italy. We didn't go to Iraq.'

Maria doesn't smile. Their father ignores the exchange, gets the darts out of the cabinet and sets up the dartboard. 'One game?' he says hopefully to Joe, ever the stifled diplomat, ever the peacemaker.

As they play, their mother asks about the outcome of a terrier with a luxating patella, and Joe thinks of the limping Jack Russell he saw back in Verona the day he used Will's card in the cashpoint. Yesterday, a nurse asked him to cannulate a tricky chihuahua and he wanted to hide under the desk rather than open a vein and smell the blood. Surgery is meditative for him usually. Cathy prefers medicine, figuring out the Rubix cube. She knows every single drug interaction off by heart, can give you a differential on protein in the urine in five seconds flat. It's why they've always made such a good pairing. But now he's lost, and he suspects she is too.

'We operated. He's fine – on cage rest,' Joe says.

'The owners won't adhere to that,' she says. 'They're – you know.'

'We had to do it,' Cathy says.

'I'm not sure I –'

'Are you retired or still micro-managing?' Joe says, then immediately regrets it as his mother's face falls.

'You all look thoroughly depressed,' she remarks, instead of answering. 'Post-holiday blues?'

'I'm fine,' he says.

'Don't be grumpy,' she says, while he shifts uncomfortably underneath her gaze.

'It's just – we have to explain all our decisions to you. Because you don't want to work, which I understand. But you still want to be involved,' Joe says.

'Sorry,' his mother says, her voice higher pitched than usual. 'Forgive me for wanting to know what's going on in my own business.' She spreads her arms wide, then drops them. Joe shakes his head in irritation. So totally unreasonable.

'Forget it.'

'Tell us more about Verona,' Maria says. 'You hear about the man – the missing English guy – while you were there?'

The atmosphere tenses like a muscle. It's hard to imagine she doesn't know, or won't work it out, Joe thinks, as he finishes his beer. She's their mother.

But what is atmosphere, really? It's only body language. Nothing more or less specific than that. The molecules of the air don't change because they know something their parents don't.

'Yeah,' Joe says. 'You already texted.'

'I know. Nobody replied to me.'

'There were a few police around, they did ask us some stuff.' He darts a look at Frannie. 'It wasn't a big thing.'

He sees Cathy shift across the bar from him. She's looking downwards, at the Labradors, but he knows she heard him. She reaches a hand to grab her Coke. It's steady.

'Were they scary?' Maria says. This is how her mind works: always, always, always to the worst-case scenario. Joe's had enough, even though on this occasion, her maternal instinct is bang on. Look where they've ended up. Solving problems themselves, instead of asking for help.

'No,' Joe says testily.

'Poor bloke,' Owen says, and the atmosphere immediately descends into sadness. Their parents are thinking about Rosie, but his siblings – Joe is sure – are thinking about William.

Frannie's gaze is watery as she looks across the room at him and Joe wills her to hold it together.

'Yeah,' she says thickly, once the grieving sister, now the perpetrator of another family's grief. They lapse into what their parents must think is a companionable silence as Joe, Frannie and Cathy sit there, feeling like ghouls, like villains.

Joe feels a buzzing in his pocket and brings his phone out. It'll be Lydia.

It's a +39 area code. His whole body goes cold. He stares at it, then holds it up to Cathy to show her. 'Italy calling,' he says, his voice strange and hoarse.

'Do you want me to take it?' she says immediately.

'No, I can,' Joe says. He can feel his parents' eyes on him.

'Why don't you want to take it?' Maria asks shrilly.

He ignores her and ducks outside, the dew and rain on the grass soaking through his trainers. 'Hello?' he says into the phone.

'Joe,' an Italian woman's voice says.

'Speaking,' he says. His heart feels like it's pumping electricity through his body.

'It's Carina, sorry – new number,' she says. Carina lives a few villas down from them. They know each other to pass the time of day with, to take post in for, but he's not sure she's ever called him.

'How are you fixed for September?' she asks him.

'We're fully booked,' he says. 'Why?'

'Oh – it's nothing. We have a couple here who wanted to check if their family could join them – spill over into your villa.'

'Sorry,' he says, thinking he could do without all bookings, that he wants to fence off his villa forever, and certainly never stay in it again himself. 'Sorry,' he adds again, just wanting to get off the phone. Cathy and Frannie will be concerned, sitting inside, pretending everything's fine when it's anything but.

'No worries. You hear about the development?' Carina says lightly. 'While I am speaking to you.'

'What development?' Joe pulls the hair back from his forehead.

'The woods behind your villa, at the side of mine,' she says. 'They're finally developing. They got planning permission last week.'

Joe thinks he's going to faint. 'Nobody told me,' he says, like that will undo it, this news that's landed in his lap from nowhere. 'Aren't they supposed to say?'

'I'm sure the ancient Italian planning system has written you a letter you won't understand,' Carina laughs, then rings off. Joe stands there in his parents' garden, wishing, for just a second, that he didn't have a mother and a father who had already experienced too much tragedy. He might otherwise reach out to them. He extends an arm into the darkness, imagining somebody could grasp it, somebody who could help him. He stands there for a second, arm outstretched, listening to the rain.

'What're you doing?' Cathy says, emerging in the lit-up doorway, her face concerned. Her eyes travel to his extended arm and her frown deepens.

'They're digging up the woods. Development,' Joe says, aware he isn't making any sense.

'What?'

'They're going to find it,' he says, just as Frannie emerges.

A thick silence descends between them.

'We need to go,' Joe says.

'Do you know,' Cathy says, walking back into the bar, 'we have to deal with something back at our cottages, sorry,' she says quickly to their parents, her tone so firm it's impossible to argue with. 'We have to . . . The neighbours have said Macca is barking.' It's a thin lie, but it seems to pass, because Cathy never lies. She gets her coat and ushers out Joe and Frannie. Their parents might be speaking, might be saying goodbye, or wondering what's going on, but Joe is on another planet, reliving and reliving the phone call, wishing he had appreciated last week, yesterday, when things were bad but not this bad.

Like a parent in a crisis, Cathy ushers them all out into the rain and into her cold car.

She turns on the old heater and drives them half a mile down the road in silence, then pulls over. She reaches up to turn on the interior light. Joe watches her movements, deliberate and slow. He can't cope. He can't cope. He's panicking.

'Shit,' she says. She kills the engine. 'What did she say, exactly?'

Joe repeats it, word for word, glad to be giving it to Cathy, this problem that weighs too heavily on his shoulders.

He looks at the back of Frannie's neck from his position in the back seat. Her ears stick out more than they used to. His stomach rolls over in fear for her. He wishes she would eat. She didn't touch any of the cheese and crackers tonight, had only water. Unlike him. He had about sixty crackers. A kilo of cheese.

'How big are the woods?' Frannie says to Cathy. Their faces are distorted by the overhead light, grotesque shadows forming from their noses.

'I need to get out,' Joe says. Cathy's car has no rear-passenger doors, and he bangs impatiently on the back of her seat.

'All right, all right,' Cathy says, getting out and holding open the door for him. They stand there, by the side of the road, in the glow of the headlights, as they did a week ago.

'A fucking development,' he says hoarsely to her.

'It might not be where we – where we . . . put him.'

'Of course it will,' he says. He leans his hands on the top of the car. He's going to be sick. It's a panic attack. 'Of course it will. This is – this is . . . fate.'

'You need to calm down,' Cathy says.

'It's better this way,' Frannie says faintly. They're in the complete darkness of the countryside, standing on the road on which they used to walk home from school. The same sibling dynamics at play but in a different situation, an unimaginable situation.

'There is nothing we can do,' Cathy says. 'We just need to sit tight.' She gets out her phone and types something. 'Look,' she says, showing them a website. 'It can take ages from planning application to first build.'

Joe takes the phone from her and reads the article. 'Or not much time at all,' he says. 'It says here it varies.' He wants to throw the phone on the soil, suddenly. That fucking man from the market. Frannie's fucking late-night trip for wine. How did they end up here?

'It's not bureaucratic,' Joe says. 'Not like here.'

'It will still take time,' Cathy says.

'But then what?'

'I don't know.'

'We need to go back over there and move it.'

Cathy scoffs. 'I think that is the worst idea you've ever come up with.'

They stand in silence for a few minutes.

'Do you dream about him?' Frannie asks.

'Yeah, I dream about him,' Cathy says quietly.

'No,' Joe says honestly. 'I dream about myself. Getting arrested.'

'I dream about the moment,' Frannie says. 'And the way we buried him. That earth . . . the smell. You know all this rain?' she says. 'I had the doors open last night and that hot earth smell – I was sure I could smell dead bodies too.' She says all this in a low voice, staring into the distance.

'Our DNA will be on that body.' Joe looks at Cathy as he says it.

'They didn't take our DNA.'

'But they could recall us for testing. And if we don't go, we'll look –'

'Let's deal in realities, not hypotheticals,' Cathy says. 'It's easy to stand here and imagine the worst all the time.' She looks up at him, eyes clear and smart in the darkness, and he trusts her. He has to.

Joe sighs, staring at the ground. 'I wish it were different,' he says.

'I know,' Cathy says. 'We buried him pretty deep. I don't know how deep foundations go. Maybe not that deep.'

'I wish we'd left him,' Joe says. 'We could have faked a suicide.' Cathy winces.

He glances back towards their parents' house. 'They're so . . . don't you wish we could tell them?'

Frannie exhales quickly. 'Definitely not,' she says. 'They'd fall apart.'

Joe huffs. 'I mean . . . don't you wish they wouldn't?'

'Oh, yeah. But they're stuck in the past. With Rosie. That's what Deb says.'

'What does Deb know?' Joe says nastily.

'They used to be – they weren't always this way,' Cathy says, ignoring him. Neither he nor Cathy have many friends. It's the demands of the job. He knows he's jealous, but he can't help himself. He can't imagine telling a friend all of the inner layers of their family.

Cathy continues. 'They were . . . do you remember when we went to France? On the Haven Holiday?'

Joe nods quickly. Their father had lost his glasses while drunk. They'd laughed for hours while he felt his way around the campsite like a mole, eventually uncovering them in a bush. He remembers so much about that holiday. Zipping down waterslides, riding horses. Picnics with inaccurate French produce – apricot buns they thought were normal bread, and had to eat with burgers regardless.

'Apricot burgers,' he says, smiling at Cathy, who smiles back. 'Do you think they'll ever . . . I don't know. Loosen up?' he asks. 'Acknowledge her birthday?'

'No,' Cathy says sadly. 'Some things scar you forever.' She looks away from him. 'They just can't handle it. That's why they go into hiding.'

'I wish I could remember,' Frannie says. 'I don't remember this.' She brings her hands to her forehead. 'This – this fun.'

'They were fun,' Joe says, bringing an arm around his younger sister's shoulders, the three of them silhouetted against the sky. He wishes for just a second that Rosie was still here too, or at the very least that their parents could have dealt with losing her, somehow. Somehow differently to the way that they have. The loss of it chokes him. She would be almost thirty. He can't begin to imagine what she'd look like. If she would have come to Verona with them.

'Joe,' Frannie says. There is something light in her voice. Joe suspects she is steering the conversation away from

Rosie, and away from Cathy's guilt that hangs between them, unspoken.

'What?' he says.

'Do you know you've come out in your fucking slippers?'

Joe glances down. Jesus. He wore them the whole evening without realizing. 'Fuck,' he says. 'Is this old age?'

'Definitely,' Frannie says. Cathy, Frannie and Joe get back in the car together and leave. 'Don't forget your pipe,' Frannie says to him when they reach their road, their white cottages glowing like three lighthouses in the distance. Joe closes his eyes in pleasure. It doesn't have to happen to them. They can still laugh, they can still have fun, they can still love each other, even in the darkness.

38.

Now

First Day of Trial R. v. Plant

'All right, then,' Jason says to me fourteen days later, though you wouldn't know it. The same blank, shallow skies. The same brown spindly trees. Late March looks like December too, it turns out. Another month has zipped by, another month of estrangement from every member of my family. Until today.

We're standing outside Birmingham Crown Court. He has a proper suit on, even though on the way over here I caught a glimpse of his pink socks as we walked.

'Ready?' he says. He won't let on, but I think he is tired, his beard greyer than when we first met last year.

The door to the courthouse is dark wood, imposing, exactly like the police station in Verona. I stare at it, at the defendants and lawyers coming and going. Juries, judges.

'You're listed for ten,' Jason says in the foyer. His breath smells tarry, of coffee. Lawyer's breath, he once joked in that base way of his.

'Will it be awful?' I say in a low voice to him. I've tried to be an adult throughout this. From the police station in the middle of the night, to all the rest of it. The unfurling of what I did in Verona to now. But I can't, not today. Not now it is upon us.

'Yes,' Jason says, and I like his honesty.

'Damn,' I say, an attempt at humour which falls flat.

Jason leans a hand against the stone building. 'You do this all the time,' I add.

'Not too many high-profile trials, to be fair,' he says. He looks directly at me as he flares his lighter, a little tick he has.

'What do you want to happen?' I say. Another click of the lighter. A little blue-and-yellow ball of flame appears, like magic.

Jason doesn't seem taken aback by the question. He's in only a suit, no coat. It's well cut, the sleeves finishing precisely at his wrists.

'Justice,' he says eventually. 'The prosecution do their bit. The defence do theirs. And then what happens in the middle – the judge, the jury – that's the justice part, isn't it? The bit in the middle.'

'So you don't want to win?'

'We're beyond winners and losers, aren't we?' he says, looking at me directly. He's shaved his neck but not his beard. The result is an eerie, stuck-on look, like he's painted on a polo-neck jumper.

'I guess so,' I say, still looking at him. And he's right. Whatever the outcome, Will's still dead, my family still obliterated. We won't recover. We can't.

We head into the courthouse and sit together in the foyer. I'm halfway through a vending-machine cup of tea which tastes like plastic. A steamy, clammy warmth, definitely hardly any tea in there. Jason touches my shoulder just once, and that's when I see them.

My eyes track them as they enter Courtroom One before me. Mum, Dad. Joe. God, Joe. He's much bigger now, his chest a barrel. Lydia isn't with him, of course. His hair has greyed out at the temples like somebody has spray-painted them. His forehead has three distinct lines across it, great grooves of stress. I remember how hard he tried to keep everything together. Too hard, probably. We all tried so hard to stay moulded that we crushed us, our family.

Mum and Dad are older. I blink, unable to believe it's really them. There's a hump forming at the top of Dad's back. I look at them dispassionately.

I am unable to stop myself acknowledging them. I'm not sure exactly what I do. A combination of raising up my chin, waving, an attempt to pin down their gaze. Only Mum looks at me, just once, a quick, sharp look, the way somebody might glance at the sun accidentally before turning away in pain. Something sad and small pops inside me. It's all so unnecessary.

They move across the courtroom, my family, in one cohesive mass, like a ship that can't veer off course, even if it wants to.

I turn to Jason. His mouth is turned down in understanding, and he bows his head to me, almost in a gesture of respect. 'I'm sorry,' he says softly. Another little touch to my shoulder, almost a punch.

'Me too,' I say. 'I mean – it was bound to happen, wasn't it?'

'The law is not kind on families,' he says simply, as we watch them go.

They enter and let the courtroom doors swing behind them and I think of Jason's cigarette lighter, flaring and being put out over and over again.

'Ready?' he says lightly. His status as a lawyer is comforting to me. He does this every day. It isn't frightening to him. There is nothing at stake, only money and financial targets and promotions. Not life. Not death. Not family or love or honesty or truth, not really. Not to the lawyers.

'Ready.'

'Ms Plant to Courtroom One,' an announcement says over the tannoy. Jason and I head in the same door as my family, their DNA no doubt imprinted on the door handle that I have just touched. 'Should I go now?' I say, pointing to the centre of the courtroom. 'To the box?' It's practically spotlighted. The place where thousands of defendants have had their say before me, taken oaths before me, ruined their lives before me.

'No, sit here for now,' he says, indicating a chair by him. 'We wait to be called, for the charges to be read.'

'All rise,' a clerk in a sweeping robe says. I'm struck for a second that, if everything changed on that night in Verona, everything is about to change again now. A play in three acts. Then. Now. And the future, whatever it may bring.

The judge enters and we bow our heads to him, exposing the most vulnerable parts of our necks, and then, it begins.

39.
Then

Lydia

As Lydia slides the gearstick into reverse, going for a late-night run to Tesco for comfort food, the sound system clicks on. Expecting the radio, she reaches out her index finger to turn it off, but Joe's voice comes over the speaker system. The display lights up with a call as Lydia stares at it, confused.

'What is it?' a woman's voice says clearly. Lydia stares at the house, her mind whirring. Joe must be on the phone, which has transferred to the car's hands-free when she turned on the engine. She sits there, waiting, frozen, hoping the call continues.

Joe must realize, because it stops. Lydia stares at the display, then gets out her phone and takes a photograph of the number. He's calling a woman. He's calling a woman when she's out. Lydia feels hot, her raincoat sticking to her chest and bare arms. Maybe he's deleted his group WhatsApps with Frannie and Cathy because he's told them. Maybe he plans to leave her.

The anger hits her next.

She will be calling that number, she thinks, as she wrenches the car into gear. For the first time ever, she is glad she is not pregnant. That she isn't in too deep with this man who is keeping secrets from her.

40.
Joe

It's the next week, and it's late. Joe is locking up the practice, as they have no overnighters tonight.

He switches off the lights in the backroom and stands there in the gloom, blinking, doing nothing except thinking. Some of the time, he's able to cope with it. He's okay if he's busy. He's worst in the morning, in the lag of the few seconds between waking up and remembering. His brain goes from nothingness, to *something's wrong* to *that*. When he sleeps, he is the Joe of before, and when he wakes, he has to go through the painful process of becoming the Joe of today. Joe the accomplice. Joe the criminal.

He sighs, walking through the prep room, through Cathy's meticulously neat consultation room, and out into the reception.

Frannie is sitting at the desk in the dark, playing Solitaire on the computer.

'Fran?' he says, surprised. 'Where's Paul?'

'Mum and Dad's,' she says. 'I was supposed to go out to dinner, but . . . I don't know. I didn't want to.'

'Oh,' he says, stopping and standing in the dimness next to the dog scales. He reaches a toe out to press them and they spring to life, illuminating the room a harsh blue that he knows will last exactly thirty seconds. 'Who with?'

'Deb.'

'How come you didn't go?'

She shrugs, angular shoulders rising up and then down again, her body a triangle. 'I don't know.'

'Are you struggling?' he says.

She looks at him, her face entirely neutral. 'I'm worried about Cathy,' she says.

'*Cathy?* Why?'

'She isn't herself.'

'But who even is Cathy?' Joe says.

'I know,' she says. 'I *know*. But –'

'But what?'

'She is suspicious of the warrant.'

'Aren't we all?'

'It has your name on it,' Frannie says. 'I don't know. I'm worried she doesn't feel –'

'Feel what?' Joe says. The light of the scales goes off, leaving them in the gloom, the room the bottle-green of the Solitaire background.

Frannie says nothing, just looks at him in the dimness. 'I think we should be nicer to her,' she says in an almost whisper. 'Keep her – on side.'

'What? We are nice to her,' Joe says, shocked by the manipulation underneath Frannie's statement. They've never suggested anyone should keep anyone *on side*. As though this is a game only one person can win.

Frannie raises her shoulders again and then drops them. She has her face cupped in her hands. 'I just – Joe. She has so much power over us.'

Joe puts his hand against the wall, trying to think. 'What are you saying?' He raises his voice.

'Let's not fight,' she says plainly. 'I'm your co-host.'

Joe ignores her. 'I still don't understand what you're saying.'

'Nothing, really. Just –'

'So what, then? Cathy holds the cards? She could hand us in?'

'Maybe.'

'We could hand *her* in?'

Frannie stares at him, eyes round, two little surprised *o*'s. 'What? No. I definitely didn't mean that.'

'Me neither,' Joe says quickly.

They travel home together. Cathy's house is in darkness. Joe wordlessly heads into Frannie's after her. He opens her doors and sits there, on the kitchen floor, feet on the patio, just thinking, thinking about what she said. Thinking about how, when he asked whether she was okay, she said she was worried about Cathy.

She points wordlessly to his Yellow Tail merlot sitting on the worktop like a loyal friend. 'You always remember to buy it,' he says.

'I do.'

She pours him a glass, not asking where Cathy is, not inviting her over. It's the first time they've done it alone. They clink glasses and she sits down next to him. 'Are *you* okay, though?' he presses.

'Don't worry about me,' she says.

'I'm kind of worried if you're *not* okay,' he laughs.

'What's that supposed to mean?'

'Just – I mean . . . we buried a body,' he says, pleased that their only neighbour is Cathy.

'Yes . . . I'm aware of that, Joe.'

'I just – I don't know.'

'Drink your wine, Joe,' she says.

'Cheers,' he says softly.

Frannie looks sideways at him. She slides off her shoes, sips at her wine, saying nothing. They turn their eyes to the sky and sit in silence. Joe knows they are both thinking of their conversation earlier in the reception area.

After a few minutes, she clinks her glass against his. 'To the future,' she says.

41.

Now

First Day of Trial R. v. Plant

'I swear by Almighty God,' I say, 'that the evidence I shall give shall be the truth, the whole truth, and nothing but the truth.'

But what is the truth? That is what I am thinking as I enter the witness box, looking out at the courtroom. It is more mundane than I expected from the grand exterior, and from television and films. The seats are foam chairs covered with a teal wool. The room has the quiet atmosphere of an office on a weekday in January. Hard working, reflective, slightly dreary.

In the public gallery, Dad's hands are on the wooden bench in front of him. There is something assertive about the gesture, like we're here to sort out a load of nonsense. And maybe he does think that, I don't know. He won't take my calls, not since it all ended, not since it blew up on that August night.

All truths are different, and mine is different to Joe's. I look down at my feet in tight, new black shoes, take a breath, and meet the jury's eyes, one by one.

'Ms Plant,' the barrister says, exactly as Jason said he would. 'If you don't mind, will you take us through the afternoon leading up to the – to the incident?'

'Yes,' I say, my voice clear in the courtroom.

Jason catches my eye, drawing my attention towards him, back towards the process, I guess. The reason we're here. He's my solicitor, but I am questioned by a barrister, who is old and male. Way past retirement age. Lithe, tanned, big ears, a large nose, wild eyebrows under the wig.

'Go ahead,' he says nicely to me. My eyes dart to the jury, the judge, back to him.

'We were on holiday, in Verona,' I say. 'We had been over many times, mostly in the summer. We own a villa there.'

'And is that villa in your three names?'

'Yes, we bought it collectively, me, my sister and my brother, Joe,' I say, staring ahead, not letting my eyes stray to them again. 'Now sold.' I glance at Joe as I say this, who looks away.

'Okay. So talk me through what happened, then, in Verona.'

'It had been a normal holiday.'

'Completely normal?'

'Until that point, yes. Just – you know. We'd been enjoying the sun and seeing the sights nearby. Cooking together, drinking.' I pause, wishing I could take back that word.

'Okay, and where were you, exactly, on the afternoon before the death of William McGovern?'

'At the market,' I say. I can't help but give a gulp. My digestive system betrays me, my guts clenching against my will. 'Shopping together,' I say softly. And, for a moment, I am in the before. Just me and my siblings, on holiday. In a phase of our life, a past phase, when we all lived in one row of houses together, in and out of the others', looking after Paul, a little community. Working together at the vets'. It's all gone. It's all gone.

Tears move up through my body, carried on a tidal wave of sadness. 'We were at the market. It was a normal day,' I say thickly. And now what? My cottage is under offer. The vets' practice disbanded. Calls unanswered. Facebook pages defriended. Estrangement.

I try to distract myself. There are four rectangular windows along the top of the courtroom, the kind you might find in an old school hall, and I stare up at them, those four little boxes of light. The March sun seems to have finally come out. They're bleached completely white.

I tell the courtroom about the market. The barrister waits patiently, then begins to probe.

'So, then – after that,' he says carefully, 'the rest of your afternoon was uneventful, but your evening was not, is that right?' He folds his arms across his body, disturbing the line of his black gown.

'Yes. It was late.' I wince. 'Sorry,' I say, trying to breathe, trying to collect myself. Trying to remember, here, for this courtroom, and to forget, all at the same time. The car. The body. The blood. That first unknowing step away from everything. Our homes. Our business. Our family dynamic. It was dysfunctional, sometimes, like everyone's, but it was ours.

'Can you talk us through it – please? Minute by minute?'

'Okay,' I say in a small voice. Jason told me this is exactly the way the questioning would go, but, now that I am here, it feels hostile. Like everything I will say will be met with scepticism.

I look across at the jury. Twelve completely ordinary men and women. Some in suits. The man on the far left surely will become the foreman – he has on large gold-framed glasses and a navy-blue expensive-looking suit, complete with waistcoat. Otherwise, an amorphous mass. *The general public.* These people who vote in elections and work in offices and shop in supermarkets and watch soap operas. A mainstream group who will take a view – guilty or not guilty – on the events in Verona. Only I have no idea which. I have no idea how it's going to go. Will they go home and talk about us – my family, me – like we are villains? Corrupt, self-serving? Or like how it *was*? The desperation, the panic? The accidental cover-up. The cover-up that has its roots in something beautiful, in love, that turned sour, like curdled milk.

I blink, and look straight at the barrister. What is going to happen to me? After all this is over?

I close my eyes against it all, just for a second. I hear somebody clear their throat and I know it's Joe without even looking. I know because of the tone of it, the pitch, the length of time on the *uh* before the *huh*.

I open my eyes but look down at the wood of the witness box, the white plastic cup of water. Anything but look at him.

Jason is seated behind the barrister, encouraging me with his eyes. Unblinking, solemn, reassuring.

'As carefully as you can, will you take us through it?' the barrister prompts. He flicks his eyes to me, then back down at his notes, a hint of irritation beginning to creep in. We could be rattling through this, I am sure he thinks, much more efficiently than we are.

I nod, again. 'Yes,' I say. I take a breath and let it out slowly. 'Okay,' I say.

'Shall we start at, say, one o'clock in the morning? Is that right?'

It is as though a trapdoor to hell has opened up in me. It's hard to describe unless you've been through it. Trauma, I guess. Goosebumps break out across my shoulders. Something starts off in my gut, a constant, rhythmic pulsating, like a generator making enough energy in order to release something horrible. I swallow a few times, knowing that everybody's eyes are on me in the silent courtroom. The silence is weighty now, like before an important press conference or solemn announcement.

I raise my eyes to the barrister but say nothing. The generator is still going, but it's started to make panic, which sweeps over me like a sandstorm. All our mistakes. Everything we've lost. The walls look like they're tilting.

'Okay?' he says. 'Ms Plant?'

'Yes, yes, okay,' I say.

Think. Think. That night. Before. And then after: the strangely calm, methodical days after it, the happy moments, even, until everything fell apart.

I can't do it. My hands are trembling so much that the jury's eyes follow them as I reach to tuck my hair behind my ear. 'Can I – sorry – can I take five?' I say, directing this question to Jason. He snaps to attention, springing to his feet, my lawyer, my protector.

'Your Honour, I know I may not have the right to speak but –' he starts, but the judge waves a hand.

'Adjourned,' he says softly. 'Jury out, please. We'll break for five minutes, Ms Plant.'

I nod my thanks at him, saying nothing.

Jason comes for me and leads me out to a bench adjoined to the wall of the courtroom. It smells nice out here. Of central heating, of coffee, of that very specific smell people carry on them, having just got out of a warm car in winter. Frost and the synthetic scent of dusty heaters. The comforting stuff of normal life. I can sit and pretend I am here for bad reasons but not horrible ones. A driving offence. An assault, even.

My family haven't filed out of the courtroom. They've chosen to wait in there for me to resume, an expectant, judgemental decision, I think.

'I'm sorry,' I say. 'I'm sorry.'

Jason sits next to me, closer than other lawyers to other clients, I imagine. Tears squeeze at my throat. 'I'm sorry,' I say again.

'It's fine, it's fine,' he says, in the tone of voice I sometimes have to use with Paul when he gets overtired. His voice is low. 'Technically legally speaking, we shouldn't talk.'

'Since when are you about technicalities?'

'True. I have even dealt with jurisdictional conflicts for you . . . to get the trial here.'

'I knew it would be hard. I thought I was –'

'You are ready,' Jason says, chewing the skin on his lips, which are dry. He's staring down at the floor and not at me. 'Look. I'm not going to lie to you. You have to be ready.' He looks at me and I realize that, while it isn't a threat, it is a command. The strong arms of the justice system are around me now, and there is no choice in this, no freedom, not really.

'Okay,' I say in a small, sad voice. 'How long have I got?'

'We need to make some progress before lunch-time,' he says. He gets out the blue folder with my name on it and taps it.

'You aren't going to your evening appointment today,' I say, trying to buy time, trying to buy some normality too, to let my heartrate return to normal.

Jason throws his head back and laughs, grey hair catching the dim courtroom lights. A couple of barristers turn to look at him, but he doesn't acknowledge them.

'You want to know what it is,' he says, looking sideways at me.

'Absolutely.'

'All right, but only because you're mid-trial,' he says lightly. 'I don't trust just anyone with this level of intel.'

'Okay,' I say softly. I look at the door to the courtroom.

'Is the barrister good?' I say.

'Not bad,' Jason says. 'It's AA.'

'What's AA?'

'Where I go. I am an alcoholic.' He says it as though he is remarking on the weather, sips his coffee and looks at me.

'Oh.'

'So there you are. I am afraid you are represented by a madman.'

I let a little laugh escape. 'We all have our vices.'

'I've been sober ten years.'

'And you go every day?'

'The alcohol masks the problem.'

'And what's the problem?'

Jason finishes his coffee. 'Oh, a whole host of them. Getting obsessed with stuff. Filling the voids, you know. Like you say' – he glances at me – 'we all have our vices. Anyway – I'm very glad to say I'm quite level these days,

243

and more than capable of being a good lawyer . . . technicalities or not.'

I feel a rush of hope, right there, in the courtroom, halfway through a murder trial. That, when this is over, I might regenerate too. A phoenix in the ashes. That there is hope for damaged people, for people who have made massive, massive mistakes.

'I'm rooting for you,' he adds.

That's all it takes. A little glimmer. Of support, of coffee, of warmth. I can't see the road there, but that doesn't mean it doesn't exist. Jason can see it for me. I get to my feet. 'Okay,' I say, the two syllables tumbling out in one hot breath. 'Okay.'

Jason gets to his feet again and follows me in, leads me to the witness box, past the empty jury seats, past the empty judge's bench. The courtroom gradually fills up again.

'Okay, Ms Plant,' the barrister says in a bored tone. 'We won't redo the oath but can you please reconfirm your name for the courtroom record?'

I nod, ready this time. I turn directly to the jury. 'Catherine Plant,' I say.

42.

Then

Cathy

Tom has been texting. And now – just like that – he has called.

'At work,' she says, in response to his asking where she is.

'You work a lot,' he says. 'Like – *a lot*. Want to come out with me instead?'

She closes the screen on her computer, where she's been researching Italian planning. She can't seem to find an answer on how long they have until they start digging. Weeks, months, years. Italy concerns itself less with bureaucracy and timescales than England.

'That's the job,' she says, then clears the history on her computer, turning her attention to him.

Cathy has never been on a second date in her life. She can't believe he wants to. She could leave work, she thinks, looking around the back office. She could leave that prescription. She could hand over that German shepherd to the night nurses . . .

'I know,' Tom says now, a long, drawn-out noise, a pleasant one. 'I could come to help. I'm a brilliant vets' assistant, I promise. I'm unflappable.'

Cathy lets a laugh escape. 'That must be nice.'

She walks into the empty reception, still on the phone. Frannie's gone home now – she works three long days per week, when Paul goes to nursery and their parents', and two short.

Rain moves down the plate-glass frontage so fast it looks like it's shivering. Wheat will soon be harvested in the field opposite. Autumn is almost upon them, this weird, awful summer soon to be in the past, in the season before, and then in the season before that.

Who knows how long they've got left before they find the body? How many seasons – two or three maybe? They're on borrowed time. It makes her fatalistic.

'Come be my assistant,' she says to Tom.

'Already on my way,' he says, and Cathy hears the chink of his keys in his hand.

She goes into the staff room and, right there on the table, as though it's a message from above, is Frannie's ASOS parcel, still not yet posted back. She hesitates, then carries it into the toilet cubicle, undresses, unwraps the dress and slides it over her body. Her hair has become static where the dress touched it, and she smooths it down, looking at herself. Where the dress swamped Frannie, it flatters Cathy. The sleeves are billowy, the dark material swirling around her feet. It's casual but chic, a deep, almost-black patterned with autumn leaves. She pulls the ochre drawstrings around the middle and – ah – there she is. A Cathy with a waist emerges from the depths. She takes a photo of herself and sends it to Frannie, saying, *Can I keep it?* Frannie replies immediately: *Of course! It's on me! Stunning.* Cathy stares at those texts, those sisterly, generous texts, and at herself in the dress, and tries to grasp and keep hold of these relics of normality.

Tom's smile is broad when he arrives. He rocks back on his heels, looking at her, Cathy thinks perhaps flirtatiously.

'In the back is a spayed German shepherd,' she says, ignoring his expression. 'She had a pyometra.'

'Right, boss,' he says. 'Nice dress. Strange attire for a vet.'

'I changed.'

'For me?'

'We need to check her obs.'

'Okay,' he laughs.

He's in a pale denim shirt, sleeves rolled up to just below his elbows. She pauses, standing by the door to the recovery room. He stands right next to her, body heat emanating off him. He doesn't kiss her, but his hand comes to her waist and his index finger curls around it, just for a second. 'Okay,' he says again.

She pushes open the door. The German shepherd still has the oxygen tube in, is lying on her side in her cage. 'Looks worse than she is,' Cathy says over her shoulder to him.

'God,' Tom says, looking shocked for the first time.

'She's really fine.' Cathy kneels down and puts on a pair of gloves, easing the blue tube out of the dog's mouth. 'Right, then, Thomas,' she says over her shoulder to him, 'please can you get me a syringe out of' – she points – 'that drawer there.'

'Yes, boss,' he says easily, springing to his feet and passing it to her. 'Next?'

'That's all for now,' she says with a laugh. She draws up and injects painkillers and anti-inflammatories. The dog moans softly, and Cathy cups her face gently. 'Okay, let's give her a few minutes. Prescription duty for me. You – keep an eye on Bella.' She points to the dog.

247

'Absolutely, dog sitting,' Tom says, settling down cross-legged in front of the cage. 'The best job in the world.'

Cathy checks the prescription pile in the backroom and authorizes them one by one, but she keeps sneaking a look at Tom. She can see him through the little window, sitting diligently, intermittently stroking the dog's head. He doesn't check his phone, never looks around, never noses through their things. Just sits stroking the dog, exactly as she told him to.

He leans back on his hands the way he did at the baggage claim and Cathy's heart turns over in her chest.

The prescriptions are almost finished, but she wants to go now. 'All set,' she says through the door to the recovery room.

'Bella is in fine spirits,' Tom says easily. 'We've been chatting about all sorts.' He dimples as he turns around to look at her.

'Good,' Cathy says, smiling back. She stretches out her hands to him to pull him up and suddenly his body is right against hers in the dimness of the recovery room. She leans back slightly, tilting up her head to him, wanting nothing more than to be completely enveloped by his smell, to have those lips on hers.

'Cathy,' he says, a note of mock admonishment in his voice. 'What will Bella say?'

'I don't care,' Cathy says, discarding every single thought about Verona, about how she shouldn't get close to some-body new.

'Okay, then,' Tom says, and he brings her body towards his, but he doesn't kiss her, not yet, just whispers something incomprehensible but nice, his words travelling from his mouth, right into hers, until their lips meet.

'Wait, there's two more,' Cathy says, as they go into the backroom to get her bag and collect Macca after a few minutes. 'Two prescriptions of Joe's,' she says. 'Then we can go.' He leans his elbows on the desk right next to her, peering at what she writes.

'Joe's thyroid cats,' she says. 'Two lots of methimazole. One is tablet form, one a cream.'

'A cream?'

'You wipe it on the flap of their ear,' Cathy says.

'Nice.'

'And done.' Cathy bags up the prescriptions and puts them into a yellow plastic basket. Tom is so close to her. His clothes smell of the rain outside. His skin of cut grass and chewing gum. 'Okay?' she says.

'Joe the brother?'

'Yeah.'

'What's he like?' Tom says as they walk through to the prep room. He pulls at one of the gas tubes coming from the ceiling. 'Shit, sorry,' he says, when it moves more than he expected.

Cathy laughs as she flicks off the main light. Her entire body feels lighter for Tom's kiss. All she wants is more. 'Joe will probably hate you,' she says. 'He's not as amenable as Macca here.'

'One of those.'

'Exactly.'

'Over-protective?'

'Sort of. More of Frannie than me,' she says, and she

must say it darkly, because Tom's eyebrows raise in surprise. 'He would do absolutely anything for her,' Cathy explains, and, as she does so, she tastes the truth of the words. He *would*. He would do anything for Frannie. So where, exactly, does that leave Cathy?

'And for you?' Tom says incisively.

'Less sure on that,' Cathy says lightly.

'Ah – odd one out?' he says, leaning against the doorframe. They're still in the darkness. Macca sighs and lies at their feet. 'One of my friends feels that way. He always says that he wouldn't choose them as friends.' His words are as light and as powerful as settling snow. Cathy thinks of the various snatched conversations her siblings seem to be having without her, the secrets they might be keeping, and shivers. *Would* she be friends with Frannie and Joe?

'What about your mum?' Cathy is glad he's moved the conversation on.

Cathy thinks as they stand there in the darkness. 'She's a traditional kind of vet. She was lectured at. We learnt through doing. She's still so theoretical,' Cathy says, thinking of how her mother is so smart with differentials but misses easy physical tells.

'Amazing that there are types of vet,' Tom says, and Cathy laughs too. Being a vet is as normal as driving a car in her family, and it's nice to see his perspective.

'Will Bella be okay?' Tom says.

'There's a nurse here to look after her,' Cathy says.

'Oh, so you were merely occupying me.'

Cathy laughs. 'Didn't you enjoy it? Your task?'

'I did.'

All she can hear is the stirring of the animals. She can

250

just about make out the X-ray machine attached to the wall, in the dimness. The blink of the lights of the machines. 'Nothing seems to bother you,' she says to Tom. 'You are — like, so light-hearted. It's so easy. You don't care that I'm weird.'

He throws back his head and laughs, no doubt startling the animals. 'You're not weird. I'm just really dumb,' he says to her earnestly. 'Promise.'

'No way.'

'Definitely.'

'How so?'

'I mean, I really do fuck about for a living.'

'Do you?'

'Yeah. Today I taught one single guitar lesson. I'm an extremely lazy freelance person,' he says easily. Just like that. A small self-judgement, laden without any shame whatsoever.

'What else do you do? If you don't work a lot?'

'Er, well, I am a vets' assistant on the side.' He flashes a grin at her.

'I literally never fuck about,' she says.

'I have noticed. You should try it sometime,' he says casually. 'Bunk off. Stuff something up. It feels good.'

'No way,' Cathy says, and he laughs again.

'Okay,' he says, the word still imbued with humour. 'That's cool too,' he says happily as they leave the surgery and head out into the rain. He glances over his shoulder at her. 'We could go get some dinner, if you wanted? Whatever.'

Internally, Cathy laughs in delight. *Whatever.*

43.
Joe

It's seven o'clock in the evening. Joe's been operating almost all day, his arms aching with the effort of it. He's in the backroom now, doing post-op admin.

His mother passes through. 'All right?' she says to him. She stops and leans over him in a waft of perfume as she looks at what he is doing. 'Why is that so cheap?'

'It's a long story,' Joe sighs. And it is. A fraught negotiation to get the owners to agree to this much. A heavily discounted operation because Joe knows that otherwise it wouldn't have happened at all.

'It should be twice that,' she says.

'I know.' He looks up at her. 'You're not even working today. Stop – just – stop fussing.'

Joe is immediately assaulted by a memory of a different Maria entirely. The mother who waited, smiling, for him at the bottom of a slide so hot it burned his thighs in the summer. The mother who – he is sure – used to tell him never to be a vet, that the hours were punishing, the work hard and miserable, sick animal after sick animal. He can't help but look curiously at her as he remembers, the mother before and the mother after Rosie died.

'Why did you want us to do this job?' he says, covering the invoice with another piece of paper.

'What?' Maria says, but it doesn't sound like a question.

'I just . . . I'm sure you told me once not to do it,' he

says. 'When I was little. When I got Peanut.' He could almost cry, saying Peanut's name. Jesus, what the fuck is up with him? Crying over a fucking dead cat.

'It was just hard when you were all young,' Maria says, and Joe guesses it was. A career woman in the eighties, married to a career man too.

'I bet you look back on it fondly,' he says, trying to invite it into the room. But what, exactly? Rosie, definitely, but also just Maria as she once was. The boy that lives in him is always looking for that, for that glimpse. He can see how badly damaged Cathy was by Rosie's death, and he supposes he worries he might be similarly affected too.

His mother looks away from him. 'Don't you?' he presses. Rosie would have been thirty next week. He knows what will happen in a few days' time: his mother and father won't answer their phones, will emerge a week later pleading busyness, stomach bugs, a tough DIY project. It's the same every year. Her birthday goes both unmarked and marked in equal measure.

When she looks up at him, her eyes are wet. 'I look back on a lot of things fondly,' she says, and then she leaves, as though that sentence was a goodbye.

Joe looks down at some cat prescriptions, trying not to cry himself. God, he wants his mother. That smiling slide mother, as she once was, her arms open to him and all of his hopes and fears and problems.

The prescriptions. He was only co-signing them to occupy himself, but they're wrong. He huffs.

'These have the wrong dose on,' he says, walking into the reception and waving them at Cathy. 'You signed them yesterday?'

'Do they?' she says, but she isn't looking at him.

'Yeah – they're ten times the dose. Cath?'

'Oh – sorry,' she says. 'I must have – I don't know. Lost my head a bit.' She flashes a smile at him, just for a split-second. Blink and you'd miss it. Cathy's way. What is going on with her? She never makes mistakes. And she seems pretty sanguine about it.

She's told somebody. The paranoia arrives like a truth in Joe's brain, the way anxiety always does. His chest constricts. His hands begin sweating.

'Tough on all of us, isn't it?' he says, trying to dispel the panic and to open her up.

'It's fine,' she says.

'Right, nought point one mill, not one mill,' Joe says, scribbling out the dose and signing it himself. 'Okay?'

'Yeah. Sorry.'

It's dusk. Frannie left for the day at four, working one of her short days, so it's just the two of them. The television is tuned to the news, as it always is, but is now, of course, rendered sinister for all of them.

Evan's out the back, somewhere, reluctantly finishing the stitching. They need to be better with Evan, he is thinking, somewhere in the back of his mind, and stop giving him the shitty post-op tasks to do. Joe saw a coupon on his desk the other day: £2 off in Tesco, carefully clipped and folded. Maria would hate a non-Plant joining the partnership, but maybe Joe could do something for him . . . something magnanimous. Something good.

'Sorry,' Cathy says again to Joe.

'Do you need to take some time off?' Joe says. 'We can't be killing cats . . . or anything.'

Cathy looks at him. They both hear the unsaid *else*.

'No. I'm fine. I just wasn't thinking straight, was rushing yesterday. It's not because of . . .' Cathy turns away from him, straightening some of the prescription food they have out on the shelves. 'It's not because of him,' she says over her shoulder. And then, to change the subject, he assumes, she adds: 'We need more Hills i/d.'

Joe puts the prescriptions in the drawer, ready for Frannie to hand out tomorrow, and tries not to wonder if there are any others he should double-check. Maybe he should just go through some of the ones in the system, just in case . . .

He turns to ask Cathy if he should, and that's when he sees it.

Search being narrowed in woods for Verona missing Brit, is flashing up on BBC Breaking News on their reception television. Joe's stomach is in his feet. His body seems to still, pointing to it in slow motion. Cathy hasn't seen it yet, is looking at the packets of food and a list she has on a clipboard, and he watches her clock his sudden movement, sees her blink once, twice, everything moving like sand through an egg timer, slow and granular in the detail, and then she sees it too.

Sweat blooms across her as she reads it. Joe sees it happen, little droplets across her collarbones like she's exercising. Her cheeks go red in two distinct patches, and then pale immediately, like lovers whose lips never quite meet.

'They know,' Joe whispers. He wants to cry out, but he can't. He can't catch his breath.

Adrenaline is rushing up and down his arms, making him shivery, like he has the flu.

'Stop that,' Cathy says gently to him, and he looks down to see he's rubbing at his arms.

'What the fuck are we going to do?' he says. 'It's a matter of time.'

She comes closer to him. 'I don't know. Nothing,' she says. 'We can't do anything.'

'I've done enough of that. Nothing.'

'I know. I know. I know,' she says, and she reaches for him, and he remembers, he remembers the same gesture when she slapped her palm into his. The day of Rosie's funeral. They'd both thrown a white rose on to her pale coffin. Cathy's right hand had held the flower, her left had slapped his, and he'd immediately enfolded it, like a stone being absorbed completely into a still pool, and thrown his flower too. They'd stood there, holding hands, watching the petals float down, saying nothing. He clasps her hand as it lands on his.

'This is fucked,' he says. 'This is so fucked.'

'It's not. It's not,' she says. 'They haven't swabbed our DNA.'

'So, what – we'll go on the run if they ask for it?'

'I'm just saying – we might not be suspects,' she says. 'We don't know where.'

'But the cashpoint . . . I don't know – Frannie said –'

'Frannie said what?'

'Nothing. Forget it. We had drinks last night and she seems, I don't know. Worried.'

'You had drinks without me?'

'It wasn't like that,' he says. He pauses. 'I did text that hotline, you know,' he adds, partly to distract her, partly to confess, and she closes her eyes, just briefly, like an insect flapping its wings.

'No.'

'I did. They might trace the burner phone I used. Find everyone who bought one that day. They might have CCTV of the cashpoint by now. You know? They might know to come to us to swab us, when they find the body.'

'We have to wait, Joe,' she says. They hear a noise, towards the corner of the room. Cathy crosses the reception and pulls open the far consultation-room door. And there is Evan, standing. Listening to every single word.

44.

Cathy

Cathy jumps as she stares at Evan in horror.

Her panic is immediately interrupted by three rings of the buzzer outside. She turns and looks out of the window. A soaking-wet man in a navy-blue anorak is holding a French bulldog in his arms. There's blood everywhere. Cathy is vaguely aware of Joe, who has his hands braced on the reception desk like he is about to be sick, but all she's doing is moving to the door to let the man in. Not thinking of the search. Not thinking of Evan. Not thinking how everything has fallen apart in a single moment. The day after she got everything she wanted.

'He's been knocked over,' the man says. 'We're not – this isn't our vets' – but please help.' He's young, maybe early twenties, blond. Instinct takes over for Cathy. She assesses the dog immediately. They need to operate. That much is clear.

'Bring him in,' she says.

The dog is prepped and under, cut open, internal bleeding stemmed, and Cathy is stitching him back up by the time it feels like there's any space in which to think, and not just *do*. He's going to lose a leg.

They need to speak to Evan, who is monitoring the anaesthesia, as all of the nurses have gone home. To explain. 'What you heard . . .' Cathy says, as Evan watches the dog and then adjusts the dial on the anaesthetic machine. His hand is shaking.

'Let's just concentrate on this,' Evan says tightly.

What are they going to tell him? It's all Cathy can think, as she stitches and checks, stitches and checks. The room smells of rust and iron. Joe holds her gaze across the table. He looks as lost as her. He isn't doing anything at all. He's abdicated. Cathy continues the operation while he watches, uselessly.

'We will talk about it, though,' Evan says. Cathy accidentally pulls a too-tight stitch across the dog's abdomen which makes her wince.

She looks at Joe and he picks up the thread, working quietly alongside her, their hands performing a dance they can remember off by heart, like piano players, like sportsmen.

She has no idea what Evan will do. She tries to think what she would do if she were him, but she can no longer think that way. She will forever be the Cathy who answered her sister's call in the middle of the night, however much she'd like not to be.

And now they're searching a wider area. They've only been home for four weeks. And the crossroads that Cathy has been avoiding is suddenly there, right in front of her. As messy and as sick and as hopeless as the animal she is operating on.

Afterwards, they're alone with Evan in the recovery room. The dog is recovering, sedated, the owner still out front. It's absurd, she finds herself thinking, as Evan places his hands on the table and looks at them. There's no way they can't tell him. Is there? They implicated themselves with a conversation that should have taken place somewhere else. Isn't that always the way? People become more and more complacent, until they slip up.

But it was their reaction to it too. Like a silent bomb had gone off. They should have shrugged it off. Made something up. The amount of time that's passed in which no excuse has been provided means they have given too much weight to his eavesdropping.

Evan is squinting at her and frowning, like she is in bright sun and he in shade. 'You obviously know something about the missing man on the news. Right? You were in Verona. You were saying . . . I mean, call me crazy but . . . I can't see how this isn't . . . that.'

Joe is unhooking the gas pipes, not looking at either of them.

It's the middle of the evening. They would both usually be at home. Her eyes are heavy. 'Evan . . .' she says, with no idea how to end the sentence.

'I mean – am I right, here?' he says, speaking in that way that he always has. Joe says he talks like he's watched too many sitcoms.

'I . . .' Cathy says. She's had the entire operation to think, except she hasn't, can't multitask in that way, not when a life is at stake. Immediately, she thinks of resuscitating Will, of how fucking hard she tried, of the position she's been put in. And where is fucking Frannie when it all falls apart?

'It's nothing,' Cathy says lamely. 'We were just watching the news.'

'Cathy,' Evan says. 'Do you think I am an idiot?'

Cathy's eyes fill with tears. She gets angry, trying to blink them away, betrayed by her body and her heart. She can't do it, can't deny it. It's like saying black is white. Evan is too smart for this.

'You were talking about . . . that man,' he says. 'And now you're crying.'

Joe turns to face her and gives her a nod, a silent, tiny nod. They've got no choice, that nod says. It's too late. Time has run out. It's better to switch to damage control than it is to lie and to increase suspicion.

Cathy breathes in the smell of the antiseptic, looks at the fluorescent lights above and opens her mouth.

'Evan,' she says, not looking at him.

'You know where he is,' he says softly, and she cries even more.

One path leads left, and one right.

She turns right.

'On holiday,' she starts. She feels no relief, despite this confession having bubbled inside her for weeks. She doesn't want to tell just anyone.

'Right . . .' Evan says.

'Frannie killed someone,' Cathy says. Three small words. Three big words. The truth.

'What the fuck?' Evan says. 'What the actual fuck?' His mouth is parted, his eyes round and unblinking. 'What?' He takes two steps away from them, like they are monsters.

But they are not monsters, she thinks sadly, checking on the French bulldog's breathing. Everything is unreal to Cathy, a poisonous pit of fighting snakes in her stomach.

'It wasn't malicious. We did what we had to do,' she tries to say.

Evan is still staring at them, his hands in the exact same position they were when the words left her mouth, up by his hair.

'She hit a man with her car. It was an accident,' Joe says, and she's so glad he's there with her, her brother, to try to bend the story, as tough and unyielding as metal, into what it *really* was. Into love and loyalty and – anyway – into the only viable option that they had. Wasn't that the case? They're not wrong, are they?

Evan has brought his hand down to wipe at his forehead, which is now covered in sweat. 'I mean . . .' he says. 'I didn't think . . .'

His expression changes as he looks at Cathy. She must not have the words for anything, at the moment, because she can't name his expression. All she knows is that his face has changed. From something to something else.

Suddenly, she's frightened. Here, she and Joe, alone with this man.

'How . . . how could you?' Evan says.

'You don't understand,' Cathy says. Can she ever explain it to anybody? The dead-of-the-night phone call. The blood. Her fear for her sister, greater than her fear would be for herself. Their long, shared history, Rosie . . . everything in Cathy's life led up to that moment, or that's how she feels anyway.

She meets Evan's eyes. 'You just – what? You just . . . you what, you hid a body?' He directs his questions to her, and Cathy can understand why. She has shocked him more than Joe ever could.

'We didn't have a choice,' she says.

'I just –'

'You can't tell anyone,' Joe says loudly.

Evan still says nothing. A hand over his mouth, thumb rubbing at his chin.

'Frannie rang me,' Cathy says, jumping to explain. 'It was after one o'clock in the morning. She'd hit somebody. She was so frightened she'd go to prison – she was on the wrong side of the road, she just forgot, she just forgot they drive on the right.'

Evan nods, hands still over his mouth, skin in greyscale.

'She needed me. We didn't know what else to do . . . we – the blood . . . we had no choice.'

'Right.'

'Wouldn't you – wouldn't you do the same? If it were your sister – your brother?'

Evan looks at her for a long moment. There's sweat along the very top of his hairline. The sheen catches the overhead lamps. 'I'm an only child,' he says eventually.

'We'll all go to prison,' Joe says. Cathy glances at him. It won't help, this aggressive line, but she understands why Joe takes it.

Suddenly, Cathy is not glad he's there with her, after all. That she is on *that* side, and not on Evan's. They *are* monsters, they must be. She wishes fervently that she weren't here, trying to make a murder, a body burial, and the rest, sound necessary, and that she was there, with Evan. In shock. Aghast. The Cathy from before the phone call.

'It's . . . this is . . .' he says.

'I know,' Cathy whispers, trying to breathe deeply. 'I know.'

'How . . .' Evan starts to say, but the pieces are falling into place around him, clearly. Evan is a total news junkie. He will know all about that case.

'He was a cop,' Evan says and for just a second Cathy feels almost proud that she was able to call his reaction, to know him. 'Who decided to cover it up?'

'I mean. Everyone. No one.'

She stares across the room, thinking. Trying to employ the skills she's been using all her life: logic, reasoning. But it's impossible when it's personal. When she's involved.

'What am I supposed to do with this information?' he says. He looks at Cathy. He's in profile in the dimness, turned sideways on to her.

'I mean –'

'We'll all go to prison,' Joe says again. 'We will all go to prison if you say anything. Paul won't have a mum. He already doesn't have a dad.'

Evan says nothing at that, his mouth twisting up on one side in some sort of ironic smile. Cathy thinks of him delivering those pizzas and winces. Something about the situation feels more precarious because of that, because of who he is, because of what they know about him and witnessed him doing.

'Okay, great,' Evan says, with an edge Cathy's not sure she's ever heard in his voice. Joe's never liked him, but Cathy doesn't mind him. He isn't especially interesting to Cathy, doesn't incense her the way he does Joe. But interesting is overrated. Interesting is having had sex only twice, aged thirty-five.

'You weren't there,' Joe says.

'No, I wasn't!' Evan says. 'How can I not tell anybody

this? This is – I mean . . . it's actually mad. I'm committing a crime, aren't I, in covering up your crime?'

'I'm sorry,' Cathy says earnestly. 'But – for someone you love. If they rang and . . .' she starts, but it's no use, not really. Nobody understands the dilemma until they face it. Cathy wouldn't.

'Would I shovel soil on a human being?' Evan says.

'There's no one you'd do it for?' Cathy asks tentatively, knowing exactly who he would do it for. The same person he works a second job for. The same person he pays child maintenance for.

He drops his eyes to the floor, evidently thinking. 'God,' he says, maybe finally comprehending it.

Evan leaves shortly after that. Joe too leaves her alone with her work, the way it's always been.

The urge to end it strikes her, as she checks on the post-op Frenchie. To end it in the easiest, simplest way, before it ends them: for the person with the least to lose to take it on the chin.

She could confess, say it was her. Take the blame for her sister.

She'd lose Tom, but what even is that? A stupid fling.

After all, Cathy thinks, in the dark of the practice at night, another life saved, what difference does it make? It would be the punishment Cathy ought to have received twenty years ago. If she came out and said that it was her, then this whole thing would be over, without her having lost anything at all. Not really. Not compared to everybody else.

45.
Lydia

Lydia finds the photo she took of the call Joe received and dials the number. She is at work, where she knows she won't be disturbed. It's an Italian number, and she recognizes immediately the international flat dialling tone. She almost hangs up, there on her lunch hour in one of the back meeting rooms at the law firm, losing her nerve, not wanting to know, but she doesn't.

'I'm Joe's wife,' she says simply to the woman who answers. It's a technique she's seen the lawyers use here at work: play a straight bat but provide as little information as possible. People usually fill in the gaps with their assumptions.

'Oh, hi,' the woman says to Lydia. Lydia doesn't recognize her voice. Her palms are hot and slick with sweat, not only at what she might find out but because of the invasion of it. Joe will sometimes wave a hand rather than explain his siblings' in-jokes. Almost like he's decided she can't possibly understand. 'I spoke to Joe the other night,' the woman adds.

'Yes . . .' Lydia says. 'And you're in Verona?'

'That's right.' A puzzled note enters the woman's voice. A pause while she waits for an explanation, which Lydia is supposed to provide.

'I just wondered – sorry – but would you mind filling me in on what you discussed?' Lydia says. Affairs circle in her mind. And the lies people tell to cover them up.

'He was asking about the location of the new development – near the villa,' the woman says. Lydia's chest feels alive with relief, like a dam somewhere has burst and allowed only good feelings to rush in.

'Oh, yes, he said about this – so sorry,' Lydia says. 'I was trying to find somebody else.'

She cups her face in her hands, allowing a smile to spread. No affairs. No bankruptcy. Just a woman in Verona that Joe spoke to because he was worried about their villa.

'No problem,' the woman says. 'He wanted to know when we're starting and what the area looked like, how it would affect the value of his villa. I have been meaning to call back – it's been postponed because of the police investigation. They have a particular area of concern just off the track road. They're searching everywhere around there, it's such a pain . . . there is not an inch of Verona untouched, it seems.'

Lydia thanks her and rings off. Well, she can't tell Joe that, can she? He'll just have to find out for himself. It's only a development. Nothing sinister.

She spends the rest of the day smiling.

46.

Joe

'Emergency,' Joe says, rubbing at his forehead. Even though he has washed his hands, his wrist still carries the metallic tang of blood on it. At least, he thinks it does. He smells it sometimes, the blood from that night. It's a memory, a phantom. He sniffs again, just checking.

'Yeah?' Lydia says, her eyes tracking the movement of his arm. She's sitting on their blue sofa, her socked feet poking out from underneath a white throw. Her body language is easy.

'What?' Joe says. He sits down next to her. Even his legs ache. What's the matter with him?

Fucking hell, he is thinking. They're searching a specific area. What does that mean? Evan now knows. The ship is sinking, water pouring in faster than they can stop it.

Joe unclenches his jaw and looks at her properly. 'What's with you?' he says.

'I owe you an apology.'

'Do you?'

'I'm sorry I was suspicious. I know what the Verona thing is.'

Joe's heart rolls over in his chest. 'What?'

'I know you're only worried about the development. So – what? Have you tried to stop it? In some illegal way?'

God, Joe thinks, raking his hair back from his forehead. The guilt. The fucking guilt of this. He can't cope with it.

At every turn there is no *right thing* to do. Everyone else has aces and kings, and he has a dummy hand.

Joe scoots closer to her on the sofa, small compensation for shutting her out. 'How do you know about that?'

'Oh, just Google.'

'You don't owe me an apology. Yes, I was trying to stop the development.'

'Of the woods?' Lydia asks.

'Yes.'

'What did you do?'

'Just wrote letters . . .' Joe says feebly.

'And you rang a woman? Didn't you?'

'No.'

'I know you did,' Lydia says. 'You're still lying, Joe. But I thought this was just about –'

'I've said I can't tell you.'

And then she gets up and walks away from him like a skittish animal. She goes upstairs and slams the door to the bathroom. He hears a bath start running, one that she probably doesn't want. Lydia is prickly about her role in the family. Won't accept she will always be once removed.

Joe stares up at the ceiling, where she's likely sitting in that way that she does, perched on the side of the bath, toes in their bathmat that she launders religiously once a week, and puts his head in his hands, wondering what to do. Wondering if there's a possible solution he could think of that doesn't hurt anyone. That keeps Frannie safe. That keeps Lydia safe but not excluded. But there isn't. He sits back down again, his eyes closed, tears budding, listening to the sound of the bath filling up, the water rising and rising but not yet spilling over.

He can't tell her. It'll break her. That he has done something illegal, something connected to violence. Her father hit her and her mother. The first time, he held her wrists so tightly they left marks, Lydia says. The second was a punch to her stomach. Lydia told a teacher only after the twentieth time. She'd lived through all that violence.

She would leave him. He lifts up his head. But is that the right thing to do – to take that choice away from her? Or is the right thing to do to continue to protect her from the knowledge?

He climbs into bed next to her later that evening. She is sleeping, he can tell. Deep breathing. She's on her front, the way she always sleeps. It's hot in the bedroom, and she's thrown the covers off herself, the soles of her feet exposed to the air. He sits, looking at those feet, that bum, the limbs of his wife that he promised to love forever, to honour, to forsake all others for. So what is he doing?

But it isn't that simple. Nothing is. Frannie – in some ways – means as much to him as Lydia. Which is the right choice?

Lydia must feel his eyes on her, because she stirs. 'Spare room,' she mumbles into the pillow. It has a small wet patch on it, a drool patch. Joe loves the intimacy of marriage, that he is allowed to see these things about another person. But it no longer seems to be something he is allowed. He must throw it away, to save his sister. Can that be true?

'I want to talk,' he says gently to her, not wanting to startle her, to scare her away.

Lydia sits up, saying nothing. She's naked, but she draws the duvet up her body, covering her breasts.

'Let's say that I'm helping somebody who's done something illegal. Something really illegal.'

'How illegal?' Lydia says immediately.

Joe lowers his gaze to the bedspread, to that patch of drool on her pillow case. 'It would get life in prison,' he says softly.

Lydia blinks, looking at him. 'What?' she whispers. And then she moves her foot away from his, that beautiful, round heel of her foot that looks exactly like a peach, and asks him one question only: 'Why are you doing that?'

'Love,' Joe says.

Lydia stares straight ahead and nods slowly, appearing to think. And then she says: 'Why are you telling me now?'

'I want you to be able to decide what to do.'

'Then you'd better tell me the whole story,' she says, turning to him, her hair still mussed from sleep.

He pauses for a second, thinking. Evan already knows. Doesn't he owe it to her?

'Okay,' he says, slowly, painfully.

And so he tells her. The whole thing. Frannie, Verona, the blood, the body.

At first there is recognition when he says his sister's name, but then, after that, Lydia's face seems to fade, like a message written in sand being slowly, slowly, slowly erased by the tide. By the end of the story, there is nothing left. And that's when he knows. Lydia is easy to predict, lives her life by rules she's had to construct to make sense of what happened to her. And this will breach one of those rules, Joe is sure.

Nevertheless, his heart full of hope, he stares at her and says, 'I hope I've done the right thing in telling you.'

'I don't know,' she whispers, looking at him, eyes huge and sad, basset-hound eyes. 'Joe. How could you do this?' Still, she doesn't raise her voice.

'No – I . . . she . . . what could I do?'

Lydia wraps the duvet more tightly around herself and shivers. 'Joe.'

'What?' he says.

'Nothing,' she says softly, looking beyond him, somewhere, in another room. Thinking, he supposes, in that way that she does.

'What do you think?' he asks plainly.

She meets his eyes and tries to form her face into a smile, but it's a hopeless imitation. 'I get it,' she says thickly, sadly. 'Yeah. I get it. It's family, right?'

'Right,' Joe says quietly, not sure what to think, what to make of her expression, of her rigid body language, of her eyes.

'Joe?' she says, a few minutes later.

'Yeah?'

'Is the body in the woods that they're developing?'

Evan's hands are shaking in surgery the next day, though Joe thinks it ought to be his. The police are searching the woods where Will is. They know, they know, they know. They're going to find the body, covered in his and his siblings' DNA, unless he does something. But what?

Lydia was still strange this morning, like somebody with a hangover or morning sickness. Removed from him. Existing mostly in her head, making coffee in silence, taking ages to answer him. Joe went in early, told Cathy what she'd told him. Cathy's skin turned the colour of off milk.

It's eleven o'clock. A joint effort to X-ray a Labrador's leg. An easy procedure. Nothing Joe would ever think about.

Evan is trying to keep the Labrador still, but his hands . . .

Joe stares and stares at the movement. Tremulous fingers. His short, neat, little nails.

Joe is fascinated by them. Is Evan afraid of him? Or nervous? Or what?

The thoughts keep coming. Will Lydia leave him? He cannot, he cannot think of that. He will be sick.

Will they find the body? Will his phone ring at any moment? What the fuck are they supposed to do – go on the run?

Evan looks up at him, sensing Joe's stillness.

'I'll position him,' Joe says. He gets the Labrador lying still. 'Just X-ray him with me here,' Joe adds.

'Er, no,' Evan says. 'I will not irradiate you.'

Joe stares at the wall. What's the point of safety procedures when he's doomed? But he obeys Evan, says, 'Stay,' to the dog, then absents himself while the X-ray clicks. He rewards the dog with a bit of sausage.

Evan says nothing, turning away from him. He sighs and turns off the X-ray machine, still looking at Joe. Another puff of air escapes his lips, but no words.

He takes the dog out front, then comes back and starts to wipe up.

'Does anyone else know? Maria?'

'No.'

'Did you lie to the police?' he says, his back to Joe.

'Yes.'

'Wow.' He turns to him, expression unreadable. 'What was it like?'

Joe shrugs, not so much trying to convey the feeling but trying to remove an uneasy weight from across his shoulders, as though an uncomfortable arm has been placed across them. 'It was horrible.'

'And you . . . you buried a body,' he says flatly.

'We tried to revive him,' Joe says. 'He was dead, but we still did the CPR.' His voice catches as he says it. 'It was –'

'What?' Evan says, but his tone is more gentle.

'He just . . . I don't know.'

'Was it awful?'

'Yes.'

'I always hate how people assume vets will be good at CPR,' Evan says conversationally. 'I can't imagine.'

Joe looks at him. Maybe it'll be okay. 'Yeah,' he says. 'We had no adrenaline or anything, obviously. It was hopeless.'

'I bet.'

'Plus, he seemed not to respond as well as I would have expected.'

'Really?'

'The whole thing is a blur,' Joe says. Despite himself, despite the circumstances, it's nice to discuss this with somebody else, somebody not in his family, not interested in the dynamics. 'We were probably too late. Frannie left it too long.'

Evan's mouth falls open in shock. Oh, shit, Joe thinks,

looking at him. He's said too much, as he often does, the relief of Evan's understanding making him deflate and leak information. And Evan's forensic, scientist mind won't be able to let this go. 'Why?'

Joe says nothing, which seems to be the best and only option these days.

'How long had she left it? Like – hours?'

'No! Half an hour.'

'*Half an hour*,' he says incredulously. 'You can do a lot in half an hour.'

'I know,' Joe says. And he can't explain it. The panic, the fear, the shock of it. How the events are not cemented in his mind, even now. The smell of the blood. Frannie lit up in the headlights. 'It's a blur,' Joe explains again. 'Anyway,' he adds, 'will you review the X-ray, then call the family?'

'Sure,' Evan says easily. 'Sure, Joe. You're the boss.'

47.
Cathy

'Can I stay?' Cathy says.

'Of course you can stay,' Cathy's father says to her as they cross the wet lawn. 'Bed's made up.'

It's late. Friday night. Cathy's seeking refuge at her parents' house. She wants to call 999. To falsely confess. To end the nightmare for all of them.

She came here instead of doing that.

Tom has called her twice, but she didn't answer either time.

'You're all right, aren't you?' Owen says. Cathy turns to him in surprise in the darkness.

'I'm fine,' she says.

'Well,' Owen says, and then he reaches out to clasp her shoulder. 'You seem down.'

She looks at him. How could she tell him? She thinks of the days, weeks and months after Rosie's death. They never, ever mentioned Cathy's role in it. Cathy was waiting for them to. They came home from the hospital without Rosie. They arranged the funeral. The topic was dropped, a radioactive family secret they unsuccessfully tried to bury even though it throbbed underneath the earth. And their behaviour towards Cathy changed, cooled, became resentful, in some ways. She was struck by the distinct feeling that her mother was acting around her.

Three months after Rosie's death, it was Cathy's

birthday, and they got her a card and a voucher. That was it. Cathy still has the voucher. Unspent, kept forever, a gruesome memento of what happens when you make a mistake.

'Well, you know,' she whispers to her father now, desperately wanting to ask, suddenly, in the aftermath of her sister's mistake, about her own. He holds her gaze for a few seconds, saying nothing. 'Do you think sometimes good people just – pure and simple – mess up?' she says in a low voice.

'Of course they do.' His eyes seem to harden in the night air in front of her, and she has a sudden feeling that she is crossing some point of no return that she isn't ready for. 'Why?' he asks.

'Just asking,' she says softly, through tears. She's sure she sees his eyes shining too.

'Did something happen on the holiday?' he asks. All around them, Cathy can hear the drip of rainwater falling off the plants. She's surprised by the direct question. He is usually repressed, usually feels it would be better to say nothing than something, no matter what. She looks up at him.

'This and that.'

He would be one of the last people she would tell, she thinks sorrowfully. He wasn't there for her during that most crucial part of her life, and now she is damaged forever.

'Well, I hope nothing serious.' He holds her gaze for a second and she wonders if he knows. He can't. But perhaps some parents can just sense certain things.

'Since you've come back you don't seem as – as close.

And – you know. It's a tough week for us all. I thought I'd see if you were all right.'

Cathy almost takes a step back. It's Rosie's birthday. Cathy has been over her late sister's features so much that she can hardly recall them now, needs photographs, all of which she's already seen. She can't imagine the adult she would have become. Perhaps she would have been Cathy's ally, perhaps the triangle would have been a square instead.

'Rosie,' Cathy says. Her father stops walking and nods. 'You never usually do anything in the week of her birthday,' she adds softly.

'Your mum doesn't,' he says simply. Something slots into place for Cathy. Maybe now because she's seeing Tom, she has a different perspective, a relationship perspective. Her mother is the one driving their behaviour, the anxiety, the reclusiveness, maybe. Her father puts up a front to avoid revealing that.

'I see,' Cathy says. 'Well, we all . . . we're all flawed, aren't we?' she says, thinking whether she deserved those perfunctory birthday presents, the lack of joy, the shortage of love. Thinking about whether anything can be done now to undo it.

'We are,' her father says, and his hand trails softly down her arm to grip her hand. He squeezes gently. 'Your mother is. I am.'

'What about me?' she says.

'You're perfect,' he whispers. His eyes dart to the house. He grasps Cathy's hand tighter and pulls her in for a hug. 'She would have been thirty this year,' he whispers in Cathy's ear.

'I know,' she says. The quiet and dark of the garden, lit

only by the reflections of lights from the house, makes the conversation easier. 'I'm so sorry.'

'You don't need to be,' he says. 'You don't need to be.'

'But I do,' she says to him. 'We never – we never discussed it.'

'We don't need to,' he says.

'I think we did,' Cathy says to him. He turns his mouth down in a show of what might be agreement or ambivalence. It's not perfect, but it is something. Cathy nods, releases his hand and walks towards the house. It's the best she will get.

As she leaves him downstairs, she hears him call up to her. 'Have a look in the trunk,' he says. She knows exactly where he means.

She walks upstairs, alone. Owen and Maria have kept each of their children's bedrooms almost exactly as they were when they left. This is more her mother's impulse than her father's. She cleans the rooms each week, irrespective of guests, like a well-kept museum.

Cathy's room is the last, the door at the very end of a long corridor with wooden, uneven floors. She creaks it open. The bedroom is cold in that way of unoccupied rooms, and she reaches down by the bed to turn on the old brass radiator, the metal tap cool under her fingers. She used to tuck the duvet behind this radiator and lie right next to it when she was a child, her legs slowly cooking.

Somebody has left a pair of folded pyjamas on the trunk. Cathy rubs the soft material. They're an old pair of hers. She must have left them here ages ago. She moves them and opens it, a kind of ottoman, with a creak. Inside is a box. On it is her name, written in calligraphy-style print. She opens that, and finds all her old school reports, a few Babygros, a few photographs of the four of them, and a few of just her too. One of her having dropped an ice-cream, a shocked expression on her face. One of her and Rosie wading in a lake – something their mother would never have let Cathy do after Rosie died. She closes the box after a few minutes and sits with the notion that her mother cares enough to at least keep hold of this stuff, even if she created it before Cathy's mistake.

She goes into the en suite. It's perfunctory. Just a shower, toilet and sink, but Cathy always liked it. Sometimes, on the bad days after Rosie's death, she'd pretend this room was a self-contained apartment, one where nobody could come and bother her.

She changes into the pyjamas, putting her clothes in the laundry hamper, like the Plants still do here. Laundry is forever changing hands. Even though they have all left home, none of them quite has altogether, like they are actual plants whose roots still tangle.

And why haven't they? Cathy swipes off her make-up in the mirror, looking into her own eyes. They are so like Frannie's. So like Joe's. So like Rosie's. The shape, the colour, the size. All identical. She thinks of what her father said. How, twenty years on, she got a grain of truth out of him. How it is so little, so late.

The Plants must seem so functional to outsiders. Cathy finishes taking off her make-up and piles up the dirty cotton balls. They're covered in the lightest amount of make-up. But we're not functional, she thinks, as she watches herself emerge, her face red and new-looking from the chemicals, from the wiping.

She stares at her reflection in the bathroom mirror, thinking about how funny families are. That they are still here, sharing pyjamas, combining their laundry. Regardless of everything. Cathy isn't sure whether that is a positive or a negative. Isn't that what families do? Paper over the cracks, still love each other regardless of the black holes trauma leaves in their past? Some of them have tempers, like Joe. Some of them are blissfully unaware, like Frannie. And some of them are like Cathy, cold workaholics, frightened of new experiences. Of *any* experiences.

After Rosie died, the family seemed to mould itself into new shapes, like clay that had been softened again to make something new. Joe and Frannie joined together. Her parents too, her father in his repression, her mother in her anxiety. And Cathy, culpable Cathy, had been left alone. But had that been fair? She thinks of just now, in the garden. How they came closer to the topic than they ever have before. Her father's hand-squeeze. Her tears. His apparent forgiveness. It might be enough. It might still be enough for her.

She thinks about how the circumstances now seem to mirror that. That, deep down inside, she has a painful gut feeling that she is alone once more, the vulnerable one on the point of the triangle, about to be betrayed. That she feels she should act before she is forced to.

She pads back into the bedroom. The rainy night is blackening and charring the window. The radiator creaks and hisses as it fills. She lights a candle by the bed, a candle she bought a lifetime ago, when she was sixteen. It's an old-style church candle. A big, fat pillar of dusted wax.

She lights the others on the windowsill too. Dark-green wax sticks in old silver candlesticks. Like a little vigil, just for her.

She stares out at the street down below as she imagines her mother gathering the photographs, sifting through them.

A soft knock at her door, which then eases open. Cathy turns and is surprised to see Frannie. 'Dad said you were up here,' she says with a small shrug.

'Oh,' Cathy says, standing there in pyjamas. The room smells of burnt matches and the hair-straightener smell of the central heating. It's slowly warming up, her limbs relaxing in the pyjamas, in the warmth. 'How come you're here?'

'Paul's being such a pain – he's just fractious, I think it's because he's learning so many words. Mostly dinosaurs. I thought we'd come and stay,' she says. She wraps her slim arms across her waist. 'Great minds. How're you?'

'I'm okay,' Cathy says.

'Really?' Frannie says, her brow wrinkled. They hear the sound of Paul's cries downstairs, and Frannie stiffens, looking watchful. Then they hear their mother. They can't make out the words, only a high kind of babbling, a happy sound, and Frannie smiles wanly.

She moves Cathy's bag and sits on the blue cloth ottoman at the end of the bed. 'Joe told me they're searching the woods by the track road.'

'I'm sorry,' Cathy says. 'I wish . . . I don't know. Hopefully . . . we're not suspects . . .'

'Yeah. Hopefully. How are you really?'

'I'm fine, Fran,' she says.

'I don't want us to turn against each other,' Frannie

says. 'I know Joe's name on that document is . . . it doesn't make sense to me either.'

'We're not turning against each other – who said that?'

'Nobody,' Frannie says, louder than Cathy was expecting. 'I'm just – I don't know. You're not yourself.'

'Why do you think his name was on the document, then?'

'I have no idea. It doesn't make sense, like I said.'

'So much of this doesn't make sense.'

A question flashes across Frannie's features. 'Like what?'

Fuck it, Cathy thinks, remembering her dark eyes in the mirror, thinking of Tom, every lie she's told, how they are now fractured, because of Frannie, unable to form the kinds of relationships they formed before. And all for this, a momentary act of altruism that Cathy suddenly, and for the first time, truly wishes she could take back.

'Do you really think Joe is –' Cathy says.

'I think he hasn't got a clue.' Frannie brings a pink hand to her breastbone. 'I know Joe, and he isn't lying.'

'Yeah.' Cathy plucks at the poppers on the duvet cover. 'They've had this since the eighties,' she says, picking up the end of it and flapping it.

'At least,' Frannie says. 'They never fucking buy anything.'

Cathy laughs at that. 'I know. They used to, you know.'

'Really?'

'Used to go every Saturday. Mum would go to town – take us.'

A globule of wax tracks its way down the side of one of the green candles. Cathy watches it gain momentum, leaving a wet trail behind it like a snail.

'I can't believe we have to keep it forever,' Frannie says. 'Tell nobody. You know?'

'I know.' Cathy could almost tell her now about Tom. *Look what you have taken from me, before it could even begin*, she would say. But she can't.

'But this must be the worst part of it. Right?' Something about Frannie's tone brings to mind their childhood. Frannie, as the new youngest, asking for reassurance from the elders.

'I'm sure,' Cathy says. Her chin trembles as she says it. 'Fran,' she says softly.

'Huh?'

'Is there anything I need to know?'

'What?' Frannie says. Her mouth parts in surprise.

'I just – I'm feeling . . . I don't know. I met this guy,' she says, the pull of sibling intimacy too great for her to resist.

'A *guy*?' Frannie says, a quick smile spreading across her features like a sunrise. 'You?'

'Me,' Cathy says laughing. 'I met him at the baggage claim.'

'From Italy?'

'Yeah – he'd been over too.'

'Why?' Frannie says quickly. Cathy frowns, not following.

Frannie says nothing. And then: 'You haven't –'

'What?'

'You haven't told him, have you?'

'Oh – no,' Cathy says. 'No.'

'You just never know –'

'What?' Cathy says, fiddling with the ancient plastic poppers on the duvet cover.

Frannie stands up, which is what she does when she wants to move on the conversation. 'Isn't it so weird that our rooms are just the same?' she says. She runs a finger over the chest of drawers. It comes away completely clean.

'What do you mean – about Tom?'

Frannie looks directly at Cathy. 'You just – how do you know he's who he says he is?' she asks.

Cathy almost laughs in horror. 'What?' she says. 'What – you think he's an undercover cop?'

It's a joke, but Frannie doesn't laugh. 'I just find it weird that he was in Verona. And you've – I don't know. We've not been back long –'

'Oh, so it's too quick, is it?' Their eyes meet, and then Frannie looks away, eyes glassy.

'No,' Frannie says. 'Do what you want. I'm just trying to help you. I just – you have helped me. And now . . .'

Cathy lets out a breath. Finally. Finally. Finally. A thank you, of sorts.

'Do you need to hit up ASOS? If you have a boy-friend?' Frannie says.

Cathy can't help but laugh. 'Yes,' she says. 'I really do.'

'Let's do it,' Frannie says.

Cathy agrees, and they sit in companionable silence for a while.

'I know Evan knows,' Frannie says. 'Joe told me.'

'I know,' Cathy says. 'It's . . . hard to be optimistic.'

'It is.'

The warmth of the central heating, the dancing flickers of the candles and their reflections in the window, her sister's belated thank you. They all combine within Cathy, and she forgets herself, just for a second, real Cathy oozing through a crack like melted chocolate. 'Do you ever think you might want to end it?' she says, thinking of that triangle again, of how she can't bear the waiting.

'End it?'

'I don't know,' Cathy prevaricates. 'Like –'

'Like?'

'I could say it was me. For you. And it'd end it. I'd be out in ten years, maybe, and no more lies.'

Frannie is looking at her in shock, and Cathy adds a smile, a split-second after the sentence is uttered, and she thinks she just about saved it, just about caught it, just about pretended she didn't mean it.

'It's so quiet here,' Tom says. He texted her. *Fancy a walk someday soon? Can do mornings, evenings, weekends, whatever to suit you.* And she couldn't resist replying, despite everything.

And now he is standing outside Cathy's front door wearing his parka. Cathy likes that he is wearing the same coat today as the other day. Something about it comforts her, as though he is living his life completely honestly, no continuity errors.

It's cloudy today, the relentless rain paused. It feels almost autumnal out here, Cathy thinks, as she locks her front door behind her. The bite of wood smoke on the breeze, the slight chill across her shoulders.

It's nice to be doing this and not *that*. Nice not to be thinking about the search of the woods.

She raced into the shower after work, washing off the antiseptic. She's blow-dried her hair like Frannie's, and now here she is, feeling strange dressed up, wearing make-up, in the evening, in the twilight.

Tom is wearing white trainers and dark skinny jeans. He gives his half-smile, his face almost childlike in the surrounds of his fur-lined hood. Maybe he's nervous.

Next door, she hears Joe's television through an open window. She can almost always hear what he's watching with Lydia. Sometimes she can hear Frannie too. She wonders if they notice how late she stays up working. If they judge her for it, working alone in the spare bedroom she converted to an office.

Frannie bought the first cottage when she was pregnant with Paul. Their parents helped her. Later on, her neighbour talked about selling, moving closer to the centre of Birmingham, and Joe made her an offer. And then, when the next house came on the market, Frannie got the Rightmove alert and sent it to Cathy. They couldn't believe their luck, the fortuitousness of it. They'd congregated at Frannie's while Paul was in bed. They'd sat around her kitchen table and drunk Indian tea – Frannie was going through a phase of drinking only this, and insisting the same of everybody else, Cathy seems to remember – and laughed at how wild it was that they were all going to try to live together, all three of them in a neat little row. 'Oh, we'll be able to do our toenails, and you'll be able to do bed and bath with Paul,' Frannie had said, her eyes alight with something. She wanted Cathy near her. Not as much as she wanted Joe, but it was enough. She looks back now and wonders how much of Cathy was involved in that decision, and how much was her following her siblings' lead.

They live on a track road. It has no tarmac and no road markings. The hay the nearby farmers use to put the animals to bed at night scents the air, together with flowers, somewhere, wet roses, the kind of homemade perfume she, Frannie and Rosie used to make.

'Where to?' Tom says, falling into step beside her. She walks him quickly past Frannie's and Joe's windows. She's not ready for them to meet him. Not while she's feeling like this, wondering about their motives. Wondering about everything, really. If they're too close. If it's dysfunctional.

'This way – there's a public footpath,' Cathy says. 'It goes over some fields.'

Tom's shoulder very deliberately bumps against hers. No, not bumps, that's the wrong word, Cathy thinks. Grazes, brushes. The softest of touches. There is something delicious about his proximity, as though somebody has just struck a match in the air between them. It hums and sings with heat.

'So, wait, all your siblings live in these houses?' Tom says.

'Yep,' she says lightly. Something in her is embarrassed by it, though she doesn't know why. Is he a bit *too* interested in this set-up? What if Frannie was right about him?

'Wow – that's intense,' he says. 'You must really like each other.'

'Sometimes,' Cathy says wryly.

She appraises him, his calm facial expression. What would he even be doing, trying to get her to confess?

'What have you done today?' Cathy says, trying to ignore her racing brain.

'Hmm, hard to say,' Tom says. 'Eaten four mint Aero yoghurts.'

She laughs in surprise and he glances down at her. 'No, really,' he says.

'Four?'

'They come in four packs,' he says, shrugging.

'What else?' Cathy says.

The thing is, she thinks, as she looks at the off-white skies, it is all just too lovely. Even this, in the summer twilight. It is too lovely for her. She is frightened to enjoy it. She's never told anybody that. She's aware of it, but she can't change it, can't seem to.

But here she is, trying, trying, trying again. And something feels different this time.

'I did do four lessons,' Tom says, Cathy thinks reluctantly. They turn down a bridleway, thick with overgrown grass, barely a single-person path through it.

'You?' he asks. He is completely oblivious to her awkwardness, she thinks, turning her head to look at him. 'How many mint Aero yoghurts did you have today?'

'None,' she says. 'Operated on a cat,' she adds. 'Thyroidectomy.'

'*Wow*,' he says. They go over the stile and into the fields. Something cracks just behind her. At first she thinks it's something falling on to the road, but then Tom says, 'Thunder.' He pauses for a second, then adds, 'That is so interesting that you know how to do that.'

'Oh,' Cathy says, laughing shyly. 'No, really. It's so normal.'

'Do you know how to operate on a cow?' There are cows in the distance, but Cathy is not sure that is what made Tom ask. He seems kind of random, which she loves; his questions get her talking.

'I could have a go,' Cathy says, laughing again.

'Let's do it,' Tom says. 'I'll hold the head.' He flops down on to the grass, sitting with his knees bent, his weight on his hands, just as he did at the baggage claim. She sits down next to him and looks at the sky above. Bluish-grey clouds are gathering. It's going to rain again.

'Where would you even start?' He leans towards her. 'Like – say, that one.' He points to the largest one.

'That's a bull,' she says.

'How do you know?' He laughs and looks sideways at her, and she thinks suddenly that he is goading her to say it. His smile spreads as he looks at her, that lopsided smile. 'Horns, right?' he says.

'Not horns – they can both have horns.' She leans towards him and points, making sure his eyeline is with hers. 'No udder,' she says, laughing.

Tom tips his head back and laughs. He lies down properly then, his bald head in the grass, and closes his eyes. 'So you're operating on one of those cows,' he says. '*Are* any of them cows?'

'Four of them are.'

'Right. Okay. Go,' Tom says, his hand flapping up into the air and accidentally – Cathy thinks – touching hers. Her stomach swoops again. She can't think about anything except his slim, tanned arms. His bare feet in his trainers. The way his t-shirt is riding up again as he replaces his hands behind his head, the archetypal image of a relaxed man. She shifts closer to him. She doesn't care. She doesn't care about what Frannie said. She doesn't care how she thought she should be the one to hand herself in, about how she doesn't have anything to lose.

'You really want to know this?' she asks.

He opens his eyes. 'Of course!' he says. 'For starters, I

think you're fucking hot. And as it goes I think this is pretty fucking interesting too. So that's perfect,' he says happily.

Cathy is thankful he's closed his eyes again, because she can't look at him. Her cheeks feel like they do when she has a fever. *I think you're fucking hot. I think you're fucking hot.* Round and round it goes in Cathy's mind, in Cathy's stomach, in Cathy's groin. What if she lay right down there next to him? Her eyes rove over him. That tight waist. That white t-shirt. She creeps towards him. Somehow, he knows, without his eyes being open, and he does the rest. One strong arm pulls her down, down, down, until her body is lying along the length of his, her head on his chest. That greenhouse smell all around her, finally, finally, finally.

'So – first step,' he says, and Cathy's glad that he has cut through some of this tension with a surgeon's skill, that he has guided the conversation back.

'First step – the cow is nil by mouth,' Cathy says. Tom rolls on to his side, looking at her, so she does the same, both propped up on their elbows. They could be in bed. Her eyes feel wide as dinner plates. What is she doing, lying in a damp field with a man she hardly knows? 'Administer NSAIDs,' she says, with a laugh. 'You really want me to go on?'

'Absolutely.'

'Okay, so next you cover it in chlorhexidine,' Cathy says. Tom widens his eyes, and she says, 'Like iodine. I mean – I think. I'm pretty rusty on farm animals.'

'The cow needs this C-section, Cathy,' he says. 'Or the calves will die.'

His hand drifts on to her hip. When she meets his brown eyes, he bites his lip and shifts his body on the grass.

'Next is an L-line block,' she says. 'A local anaesthetic. And fit the sterile drapes around it, so you have only the abdomen available.'

'You're so smart,' he says. 'It's so cool.' He looks into the distance, at the cows. 'I hope they make it.'

Cathy drops her gaze, unable to stop smiling. 'You want more?'

Tom tilts his head, looking at her.

A fat drop of summer rain strikes him right in the crown of his head, and Cathy isn't sure she's ever wanted to cup the back of somebody's head so badly as she does now. She shifts closer to him. Their torsos are pressed together. Cathy raises her head to look at him, and he isn't ridiculing her, or backing away, or laughing. He's just waiting, that half-smile quivering, eyes smiling. Just waiting for her. She leans towards him just as the rain really begins. Their lips meet, a soft, careful brush just at first. He opens his mouth immediately. It's warm and then hot. His hand moves from her hip, coming around the small of her back to encircle her completely, pulling her towards him. Even though Cathy's eyes are closed, she can tell there was just a flash of lightning, like a photographer's bulb. Two seconds later, the thunder. They break off. Their faces are wet from the rain Cathy can't feel. She looks into his eyes.

'Well,' Tom says after a beat.

'It's very rainy,' Cathy says.

'And we were talking about operating on *cows*.' Tom raises an eyebrow. 'Isn't that kind of – a crime?'

Cathy giggles into his chest. 'Maybe depraved,' she says.

'Call the vet police. Call the cops,' Tom says. He pulls her even closer to him. His chest is firm. Her hands find their way in, inside the warm parka, and underneath his t-shirt and – she lets out a breath – finally. To that skin. She glances up at him and says something she's never once said, not ever: 'Want to come to mine?'

48.

Now

First Day of Trial R. v. *Plant*

'By the woodland, yes,' the barrister says. 'And, as we understand it, he was put there immediately?'

'Yes,' I croak, in the witness box. Immediately, I think of exploring the countryside with Tom, and feel a pang.

Joe is staring steadfastly ahead. I wish Frannie were here. She understands exchanging glances, she understands a loaded look in a way that Joe doesn't.

I am distracted momentarily by just how many participants there are in a trial. The judge, the solicitors and barristers, the jury, but the press too, the clerks who bring the Bible for the oath, the stenographer. They must all have their opinions of me, though they hide them well, beneath professional veneers.

'And you did not actually own that woodland, did you, Ms Plant? It was not your land – is that correct?'

'Yes. None of it is, now,' I say. We sold the Verona house. We would never go back, of course we wouldn't, even if we weren't estranged. We sold it at a grotesque undervalue to an ex-pat couple who apparently went around it without saying a word and, at the last second, asked to see the spot in the woods, which they photographed, later selling the images to an Italian newspaper.

'Yes, you sold the villa last year, didn't you? And the profits went to –'

'We divided them up.' I can't look at Joe as I say it.

'Right. And so going back to the day after, say, after the body burial in July. Was there any indication that was where Will was? Or was he very well buried?'

'I . . ,' I say.

'Ms Plant,' the barrister says, like I am being difficult. Jason reaches to touch my barrister on the shoulder, who rises to his feet immediately, like he's mechanized, a slow jack-in-a-box. I didn't realize how powerful Jason was until recently, when I googled him properly: the Midlands' most successful criminal solicitor. No wonder Frannie chose him initially, even though she now can't use him.

'Your Honour,' the barrister says, 'the witness is being asked the most difficult questions, and I rather struggle to see where they are headed.'

The judge looks wordlessly to the other barrister, who says, apologetically, 'I am merely trying to ascertain how well hidden the body was.'

'Then proceed,' the judge says. The barrister turns his gaze back to me, expecting me to answer.

'No, you couldn't tell,' I say softly. 'You couldn't tell at all.'

'Thank you, Ms Plant. Now that wasn't so hard, was it?' he says, so exasperated that he turns and pours a cup of water so he can get in a few more shakes of his head in the time he buys himself.

'Your Honour,' Jason says, getting to his feet. 'While I am aware this is not convention – our witness is . . . she is in a difficult position with the –'

'Mr Granger,' the judge says, his tone surprised, 'whatever betrayal or otherwise is going on in the Plant family,

I am afraid it is imperative that your client *must answer the questions given.*'

Jason sits back down and throws me a helpless look, an apologetic look. I try to smile at him, but the line of my mouth will be wobbly, I know it will, through barely contained tears and emotion; a child's carelessly drawn smile.

'No, no,' I say, trying to be stoic in the witness box. 'Please just carry on. Just get it over with. Ask them all.'

49.

Then

Joe

Evan is in Joe's consultation room when Joe walks back in after surgery on Friday night to get his wallet and phone. Joe has nowhere to be. Lydia isn't speaking to him. Carina hasn't returned his latest call asking for an update on the woodland search. And now this.

Evan is just standing there, doing nothing except waiting. He's got changed out of his Vets 24 tunic and into jeans and a t-shirt, a jacket slung over his arm. He looks like he's waiting for a bus.

'Got the wrong room?' Joe says to him.

'Glad you're still here,' Evan says. He glances at Joe, an unreadable expression on his face.

'Only just,' Joe says tightly. 'On my way out. Shall I just lock you in here for the night, or –'

'I was thinking.' Evan glances upwards, with all of the time and confidence of a man with the upper hand. He's standing next to a poster about the appropriate weight for dogs, the royal-blue wall of Vets 24 behind him.

'About what?'

'About what you and Cathy told me.'

'Right . . .' Joe says, and he feels the words die on his lips, he really does.

He can see exactly where this is going. He's not an idiot. Just when they think it can't get any worse, it does, like a disease progressing relentlessly through a body. He stares impassively back at Evan.

Joe suddenly wonders if he could defend himself against Evan. Evan is shorter than him. Stockier, but it isn't strength. Yeah, he could probably win a fight with him, he finds himself thinking, especially with the weight he's put on. Jesus. Where is this coming from? 'Look. What's the situation here?' he says to Evan.

'I think this practice could benefit from some non-Plant input.'

'Right.'

'Right? New blood on the board.'

'There's no board,' Joe says tightly. 'It's a partnership.' He turns off the cat scales and screws the lid tight on the glass dog-treat jar, just for something to do.

'Look,' Evan says with a loud laugh, and all Joe is thinking is that he should have seen this coming. Evan is mercenary. Evan is an opportunist. Evan is broke. Joe winces as he thinks of it. How obvious it is.

Evan is acting completely in character, only Joe was expecting him not to. Why? He has been so foolish.

He turns away from Evan. It's too painful to look at him right now. He concentrates on switching off his computer. *Are you sure you want to quit?* it says.

'Well?' Evan says.

'You're threatening me.'

Evan laughs again. 'I mean – Joe. I'd be mad not to use this, wouldn't I?' he says. He's genuinely asking, Joe thinks, looking at him in astonishment. Would he use it? No, he wouldn't. He would try to fucking forget the knowledge he'd been given, if he were in Evan's position, he thinks darkly.

'I'll let you think on it,' Evan says. He reaches behind his back without turning around and opens Joe's door, then walks across the dimly lit empty reception and out the front without looking back. 'Am looking forward to quitting the second job that you never cared I had, though,' he adds softly.

'I did care,' Joe shouts.

He forces himself to stop. He's got to breathe, to let his heartbeat slow. He had a panic attack last night in bed, thinking of Paul waking up one morning without his mother if they fuck this up, if *he* fucks this up.

He feels like he's going to explode some days. He stares out the front of the practice. The windows of the reception are steamed up, the relentless summer rain marking them on the outside like a thousand fingers tracing their way down the glass.

He's got to get out, get out into the rain and away from the oppressive anaesthetic smells, the dim lights. He wrenches open the door and gets in his car.

He leans his head on the steering wheel, which feels cool and waxy. God, he wishes he could call Lydia.

He dials Cathy's number instead. Lydia won't speak to him until she's ready, he knows it. 'I need to see you. Now.'

'Now? Joe, I'm in bed.'

Joe checks his watch. 'It's eight o'clock.'

Cathy doesn't dignify that response with an answer.

'When can you see me?' he says.

'What's happened?'

'I need to speak to you.'

He hears her say something, muffled beyond the reaches of his phone, and he frowns. 'Is someone there?'

'No,' Cathy says. A beat. And then, her voice wet: 'Joe.'

'What?'

'Don't make me come.'

'Evan is going to blackmail us.'

The pause stretches so long Joe pulls the phone away from his ear to check the call hasn't disconnected. And then, her voice imbued with something heavy, like a rain-cloud ready to burst, Cathy says: 'I'll come now.'

'Go to Frannie's,' he says, though it hardly needs saying. 'She needs to be there too.'

'We need to do something about Evan,' Joe says dispassionately. 'He's just threatened me.' They're sitting in a row by Frannie's back doors. He's looking out on to her wild garden. Mint is currently ravaging it, entwined around buddleia bushes and lavender. She doesn't care.

The windows are giant, floor to ceiling, covering the entire back wall. Joe, Cathy and Frannie are fish in a bowl, looking out.

'What?' Frannie says, and Joe irrationally thinks, for just a second, that she is about to faint. Her hands are up by her face. Her waist is minuscule, her striped t-shirt tucked into jeans.

And then she laughs, a hard, sardonic laugh, a bitter laugh. It is so un-Frannie. 'This could not really be going any worse, could it?'

'It isn't funny,' Joe says.

'I'm not seriously fucking pissing myself,' Frannie says, drawing her arms around her waist and looking levelly at him. 'So keep your sanctimonious lines to yourself. This isn't a TV show.' She opens a bottle of his merlot – still bought for him, every fucking week – not looking at him. Their sacred ritual, now tainted too.

'What is up with you?' he says to her, but she turns away from him, refusing to answer. 'Evan is going to tell,' he says.

'What does he want?' Cathy says. Her face is drawn, like she hasn't slept or has a virus. Dry lips, eyes downcast, rings underneath her eyes. Joe wonders briefly what's up with her, but he can't ask. They each hold so much power. He doesn't feel it with Frannie, but he does with Cathy. If any of them annoys the other, crosses a line . . . any one of them could end it.

'Partnership.'

'For nothing, I assume,' Cathy says. 'One fifth of the business, in exchange for nothing.'

He hadn't thought about that. God. So they'd be giving it away.

When will this end? When will the tendrils of it stop spreading like Frannie's mint outside?

Something is simmering underneath every word he speaks, each breath he takes. The kind of thing that only reared its head occasionally in the past. When he was stuck in traffic and somebody pulled out in front of him. When he had five minutes to prep for a meeting and Windows started a mandatory update. Momentary rages, punches thrown. Little groans of frustration. Stroppy texts sent. This, though, is a dangerous kind of sadness, not anger, but it feels related. As though at any moment he might shout or cry, he isn't sure which.

'Call his bluff,' Frannie says. She fiddles with the baby monitor in her hands, then stands and begins to clear up, like the conversation is over. Cathy looks at her curiously.

'He'll fucking shop us,' Joe says. 'He will. He will. He'll tell Mum. He'll tell the police.'

'Okay,' Cathy says, folding her hands in her lap. 'Don't panic.'

Joe stares at Frannie's back as she tidies. Where's *his* Frannie gone? Gentle, smiling Frannie who could always ease an atmosphere?

He tries to calm and slow his breathing. In and out. In and out. Come on. Pretend you're operating. Pretend you're doing something involved, and fiddly, and meditative. A simple bitch spay on a nice slim dog. The first cut, a straight, beautiful line that would heal easily. The parting of the skin, then fat, then organs. Something he could do with his eyes closed.

'I think we should give it to him,' Cathy says quietly. She looks at Joe, her eyes clear and glassy. 'Don't you?'

'I mean – it's the . . . it's the family business,' Joe says.

'I don't think we have a choice.'

'It's blackmail, isn't it?' he says. 'Fuck him,' he shouts. 'Fuck everything.' He's so angry now. He's so angry they spoke about it so openly, in the fucking reception. He's so angry Evan has capitalized on it. Without any further ruminating, he reaches over and punches Frannie's wall. A satisfying, fast strike that stings the skin across his knuckles. And then – release. His shoulders sag.

'What the fuck are you doing?' Cathy says sharply. A piece of previously neat plaster falls to the floor. They all stare at it in shock.

'Grow up, Joe,' Frannie says.

Cathy turns away from him, staring out of Frannie's window and so too does Joe, looking at the endless rain,

302

at the spreading weeds. The thing is, he thinks, staring at it, weeds don't stop growing because you constrain one part of them. It's too late, it's too late. It's out there now. He could cry about it, now that the anger has left him, looking at those little wet green leaves, spreading because it's the only thing they know how to do. The natural thing. The thing they were always going to do. The inevitability of it.

PART IV

Conspiracy to Bribe

50.

Joe

They've moved to the kitchen table. 'That's not fair. It's *ours*. We can't just give it to him – this . . . opportunist.'

'Well, life's not fair,' Joe says with a stiff gesture, more an upward creaking movement of his shoulders than a shrug. 'Will's fucking dead. Hardly fair on him.'

Cathy winces. She has her face cupped in her hands, is gazing at him over the table. She's flushed and sad-looking. 'But – I mean. We've got to be sure. We can never take it back. And, whatever we do, Evan will know forever.'

All three of them ignore the piece of plaster sitting near Frannie's doors, the redness blooming across Joe's knuckles.

'That's just it,' Frannie says. She's wiping her already-clean worktops in huge circles. She's always enjoyed cleaning, the same way Cathy enjoys work. Joe once asked how she was so good at it. He always leaves a tidemark of filth on his consulting table when he wipes it, and she ends up doing it for him. She had said, 'The trick is to stop when it's actually clean?' and they'd got the giggles for ten full minutes.

'What's to stop him blackmailing us again?' Joe says.

'Nothing,' Cathy says. They exchange a glance that Joe can't read, can't interpret, their identical eyes flashing in the dimness. Frannie starts removing hob rings and putting them in the sink, rolls up the sleeves of her striped top.

'Do you need to do that now?' Joe says irritably.

'Do you need to punch my walls?'

'Let her clean,' Cathy says.

Frannie sprays something on to the hob. 'I don't want us to give away part of our business to Evan. He's a lech. Fuck,' she says, her voice louder, scrubbing hard at the splashback tiles behind her hob. 'I can't believe he's doing this.'

'We have no choice,' Joe says again.

Cathy's cheeks have gone even redder. She blows air out of the side of her mouth. 'I agree.' She gets another bottle of wine and pours everybody a glass without asking. Frannie ignores her.

'We're not giving it to him,' Frannie says, standing there with one sleeve rolled up and a spray bottle of Flash in her hand like a gun. Something swoops in Joe's stomach, like a dove has just taken off. 'Really, I'm not giving it to him,' she says again.

Annoyance rises up through Joe, replacing the horror of the image of his sister with the makeshift gun. He is suddenly irritated by everything about her. Her beautiful house. Her total disengagement with practising veterinary medicine even though everybody wanted her to. Her stupid mistake that landed them here.

'You're being an idealist,' Joe says. 'Life isn't the fucking Green Party.'

Frannie's eyes are wide, still standing there by her oven. 'What?' she says.

'Who knows?' Cathy says with a sigh.

'Excuse me?' Joe says.

'I said *who knows* what you're talking about.'

'Er, why?'

'Because you are not making any sense.' Cathy picks up a glass coaster with bright colours blown through it, and begins turning it around, upending it on one side, then the other. 'You're ruining Frannie's walls and offending everyone.'

'Piss off. We have no choice but to make Evan a partner,' Joe says, his teeth gritted. God, he doesn't want to feel this way. Full of poison, of jealousy, of anger. But if they fuck it up, if they don't manage to control this . . .

Joe drops down his head, massaging the back of his neck, which is tight with tension. He wishes Lydia were here with her soft, warm hands to push his muscles around. Lydia. He's filled with nostalgia about his wife. For how it used to be, how it once was. When he'd tell her every single appointment he'd had throughout the day, and she'd tell him the ludicrous excuses the criminals at work had provided, her legs in his lap.

'It's pretty simple,' he says eventually.

'What?' Frannie says. Her eyes look massive. She has two scoured lines underneath her cheekbones.

'I mean . . .' Joe says again. 'If everybody viewed payoffs as pointless, there would never be any, would there?'

'Guess not,' Cathy says. She looks at him warily. 'What are you saying?'

Joe folds his arms over his chest. 'You've not seen enough movies,' he says, and Cathy gives a wan side-smile.

'This is . . .' Frannie rolls her shoulders and lifts her eyes to the ceiling. 'I can't do this,' she says.

'Same,' Cathy says drily.

'No, I mean.' Frannie covers her face with her hands, her shoulders beginning to shake. 'I've tried and I've tried . . .' she says. 'To be – to be okay. But we're not okay. Are we?' Her voice rises a few octaves.

Cathy is up, standing next to her, within seconds. Joe stays at the table, watching them.

'It's okay,' Cathy says. 'We all feel like this sometimes. It'll pass. We'll pay Evan off. It'll be fine. It's only money. Better to lose twenty per cent than one hundred.'

Frannie makes a low, moaning sound and Joe gets over himself and joins them, there in front of her oven, the bloody Flash spray smeared across it, the hob rings in the sink, leaving greasy brown imprints where they sit. Cathy's hand grips his in the group hug, Frannie's head lolls against his shoulder. 'I'm sorry, I'm so sorry,' she says.

'I know,' Cathy says.

'We'll pay him. We'll make him go away,' Joe says.

'This wasn't your fault,' Cathy adds. 'It could have happened to any of us.'

'It was my fault,' Frannie says. 'And now they're going to know what I did, when they find him.' And the anguish with which she says it is what stops Cathy and Joe's reassurance. Instead, they stare at each other over Frannie's head. Cathy is completely still, just looking at Joe.

'That you hit him?' she says softly.

'That I hit him twice. Okay?'

Goosebumps cover Joe's shoulders. His teeth begin

chattering. He thinks of the image of Frannie with a gun. How natural it looked. How anybody here could be in danger in the right circumstances, at the whim of anybody's temper, their volatility, their desperation. No, he thinks. Not this.

51.

Cathy

'I'll just – I'll just hand myself in,' Frannie says. Her nose is running, two clear tracks of liquid dripping on to her philtrum like a child's.

'What . . .' Cathy says, but she's speechless, truly speechless. All the blood. That's why. Something has gone very cold inside her, right in her middle. Who is this woman standing in front of her? How could she have lied to her the other night at their parents', when she thought they were finally being honest?

Cathy thinks of Tom suddenly, and how she left him high and dry in her bed, his face disappointed, his naked form embarrassed. *Fuck*. Why is she like this? So loyal to these two? He's right. He's right. It *is* claustrophobic to live near to her siblings, this near, to keep their secrets, to bury bodies for them. If she could choose, would she choose Frannie and Joe? She doesn't know, despite loving them, but she does know this: she would choose Tom. She hardly knows him, but already she prefers him.

And it is that which cements the decision in Cathy's · mind: she is not going to sacrifice herself any further. Not even for her sister. Not for the stranger her sister has become.

'I hit him accidentally,' Frannie says. She pulls at the neck of her t-shirt and wipes her nose on it. 'And then he sat up, just as I stopped. I was so . . . he started yelling at me. Saying I was mad, I was the mad woman he'd seen earlier, he was going to tell everyone. He kept gesturing to his side, where I'd grazed it. Saying he'd call the cops. And I just . . . there were just a few inches in it.'

'In it?'

Cathy glances at Joe. She's stepped back from Frannie, but his arms still encircle her. His face has changed and hardened. She shivers, there in her sister's kitchen, though she isn't cold.

'Between the brake and the accelerator,' Frannie says into Joe's chest. 'The worst had happened, I don't know. It was – you probably know a word for it. Fatalistic, maybe? He was . . . it was just – I panicked.'

'You hit him again,' Cathy says, staring at the tableau of her brother and sister. God, they're fucked. They're absolutely fucked. She looks at the ceiling and tries not to cry. They should have handed Frannie over. Testified that she wasn't in the wrong. God knows, but, right now, it feels as though they have chosen the worst path of them all. Burying a fucking body. What were they thinking?

'I ran over his legs,' Frannie says thickly. 'And then I waited. I just . . . how can it be a crime? To move your foot slightly over one pedal rather than the other . . . and then to just – do nothing? I was so scared. You've no idea.' Her eyes seem to turn down as she tries to explain herself. 'You have got no idea how that situation felt to me. How frightened I was.'

Cathy says nothing, not knowing what to offer up. Jesus Christ. It was murder. It was murder, after all. The blood. The delay. Frannie's faux-straightforwardness, her simplicity: she relied on her own reputation within the family to get away with this. 'You never said. I asked you so straight-up the other night. And you never said.'

'Where?' Joe says.

'Mum and Dad's.'

'Oh, right. Without me.'

'It wasn't like that,' Cathy says. 'Don't be so petty,' she adds, even though she knows she would feel exactly as he does: vulnerable.

'I'll go now, to the police,' Frannie says, disentangling herself, her hands up, white palms out. She grabs her handbag.

'Don't be dramatic,' Joe says, his face red. 'It's too late. It's too fucking late. We'd all go down for all sorts. Sit back down.'

Cathy deflates right there as they stand apart, just look-ing at each other. One of Paul's paintings from nursery is pinned to the corkboard by the door to Frannie's kitchen. It looks like Frannie, a tall stick figure with dark hair, his handprint in pink beside it. Cathy sighs, the air leaving her like she is a popped balloon. Joe's right, of course. Angry but right. That ship has sailed. It is too late.

She was thinking of taking the blame for Frannie only yesterday. On the verge of just doing it, some days, to end the suffering her little sister never deserved, that – Cathy thought – had been thrown over her like a hailstorm, one that Cathy could weather better than Frannie, and with fewer unintended consequences.

'What the fuck were you thinking?' Joe says through gritted teeth. Cathy gets that uneasy feeling again, the one she first got in the market, when Joe puffed up like this.

Protective Joe. Short-fused Joe. Only his enemy is now Frannie, once his greatest ally.

'They're going to find him,' Frannie cries. 'I had to tell you before they found him and the injuries weren't . . . what I said.'

'Let's just – look. Let's speak tomorrow, about Evan,' Cathy says. 'Let's just go – go away and all sleep on it.' Something seems to be bubbling away in Joe and she doesn't like it. She feels it too. Anger. Justifiable anger towards their sister who has misled them. The circumstances are no longer the same, even if the outcome is. Frannie intended it, and now everything is different.

'No,' Joe shouts at Cathy.

'Joe,' Frannie says tearfully.

'*Fuck* this absolute *shit*,' Joe says. 'Nope.' His square shoulders, bigger than they once were, are now retreating down Frannie's dark hallway. 'And fuck you,' he says to Frannie. He opens the door and the room is blinded, momentarily, by her security light, a rectangle of brightness let in and then shut out again, the room still as dark as it once was, as though no amount of light can be held in here, preserved, to keep the darkness from them.

Cathy arrives home and goes immediately out into her garden. She can't be confined. She needs to look at the horizon, the fields beneath it, the sky above, and breathe.

She jumped into action, when Joe called, even though Tom was over. She ushered him out, his expression somewhere between confused and fine, as is his way. She feels the breeze cool the tears on her face as she stares and stares at the horizon. Who is she? Why does she answer these calls from people who cause her this pain? The questions seem obvious, all of a sudden, though she's never once asked them.

The night sky is still and ancient. Sometimes, if Cathy stares for long enough, she gets a dizzying feeling of her own insignificance, of the infinity of the universe beyond them. Similar to the feeling she gets when she visits old monuments and imagines how many hundreds of thousands of people have passed over there before her, each with their own set of problems and concerns. She breathes and thinks and stares up at the sky, gulping in the warm summer air as she cries.

At the bottom of Cathy's garden is a stone outhouse, with a slate-tile roof, boarded-up windows. Ivy creeps up the side of it. *Who else has sat here and cried?* Cathy thinks. Millions of people. People in the 1940s during the war. People in Victorian times, with a single candle illuminating their faces. Millions. Hundreds of millions. She once read that one hundred and seven billion people have ever existed, and the thought comforted her then, as it does now. She is here, by herself, not in her siblings' houses, wanting them to come to hers. She is alone.

Everything is unresolved. They've left it as they found it: a mess. Joe stormed off home. Cathy is alone now, wondering what the hell they're going to do. The components of their mess orbit around her as she stands there, shivering in the darkness.

When she feels calmer, she turns, ready to walk back inside. Only one window is lit up in their block of houses. Paul's bedroom, the second window on the left. An egg-yolk-yellow square in the night. Frannie is leaning over his bed. Cathy can see only her thick plait of dark hair, her slender arms. Even now, in the worst of times, the love is so obvious, the smile Frannie can't help but let tug at her features as she gazes down at him. An ironic smile, an indulgent smile, just for him. She loves him. She loves him so much. She wouldn't survive being parted from him. She loves him so much. Even now. Even in the darkness. It's there.

'This rain,' Cathy says, when Tom answers his door the next evening.

'I know,' he says, a hand to his chest as he reaches with the other to take her coat. 'It's mad.'

'It's impossible to do anything,' she says. Her hair is soaked through from just walking from her car to his door. 'Where's it all coming from?'

'Who knows,' he says. 'Never understood weather systems,' he says over his shoulder.

'So this is you,' she says simply.

'This is me,' he says. He hasn't brought up last night. Cathy can't work out if he minds, but of course he did. She doesn't know how to broach it.

He has two ragdoll cats milling around. There is absolutely nothing on his floors. His doors are farmhouse-style, painted such a bright white they shine. It's very tidy.

'You're very neat,' she says as he hangs her coat on a hook. His parka and a lighter jacket hang there. Nothing else, no jumble of scarves or reuseable bags that flap around. 'Where's all your stuff?'

He throws his head back and laughs in that way that he

does, his face creasing like a fan. 'Stuff's overrated,' he says.

He's cooked for her. Baked aubergines that swim in cheese as he removes them from the oven in a cloud of heat. She stares at the aubergines. It doesn't look like this is something casual. Something fun. 'What?' he says, a small laugh escaping his mouth.

'Oh, nothing,' she says, glancing away from them and up to him.

'No, what?' He puts down the tray and places a hand on his hip, looking at her, an amused expression on his face.

'You're, like, cooking for me.'

'I am cooking for you. Would you rather I didn't?' He goes back to the aubergines. 'Or what?' he says, throwing a sidelong glance at her.

'Maybe,' she says with a small laugh. Tom looks at her. It might be the first serious long look he's given her. Gone is the banter, the childlikeness, the laughs. In its place are a pair of serious brown eyes.

'What's the matter?'

'Nothing,' she says. She rubs at her forehead. 'I'm just mad.'

'Oh, crazy is the best,' Tom says, she thinks earnestly. He pushes away the aubergines.

'Last night . . . I didn't mean to . . . I didn't *want* to . . .'

'Come here,' he says. She crosses the short distance between them, into his waiting arms. 'Come up,' he adds. They walk upstairs, their bodies joined together, a three-legged race, into his bedroom. The third – and last – door on the right. It opens on to a room painted a pale, duck-egg blue. More immaculate emptiness. More clean lines.

'I like your skirting boards,' she says.

Tom laughs. He laughs so easily, like the laughs are queued up there waiting for him to release them. 'My what?' He glances at her then. It's just a glance, but Cathy's insides turn to burning liquid. They're standing so close together in the doorway.

'It's all so neat and lovely,' she says. And then she points to them, to the bright, white skirting boards.

His curtains are open, the twilight sky beyond them. Cathy heads further into the room, thinking that they should eat the dinner, that she should go. Should, should, should. Tom crosses the room and lies down on the bed, both a clear invitation and an act of relaxation. He pats the space next to him.

She sits, an elbow propped up on the pillow, feeling so warm and comfortable up here with him. He entwines his feet with hers, pulling her towards him. 'What's with the aubergine fear?' he murmurs into her ear.

She can't help but giggle, and he laughs too at the absurdity of it, of her. 'Oh, you know, just terrified of aubergines and painfully shy,' she says lightly. She feels him nod in comprehension next to her.

'Look,' he says, 'it's only me.' And that sentence is enough for her body to open up to his. They become a hot tangle of limbs immediately.

Afterwards, Tom offers her food – 'No aubergines, I promise' – and drinks, repeatedly, but she doesn't want them. Wants to lie in this warm room that smells of his clean laundry, with him. She can't risk him leaving and coming back, upsetting the balance, this room a rare eco-system that might change at any moment.

'So last night was . . .' he says. His tone is casual. He's obviously waited hours to ask why their evening was cut short.

'Oh, nothing,' she says. 'My brother.'

Tom messes with a cushion. Buying time, maybe. His chest is covered in deliciously dark hair.

'He's just – he's a bit, I don't know. Difficult,' she says.

Tom evidently draws a conclusion from his purchased time, but Cathy doesn't know what it is, because he says nothing, just looks at her.

'You know how you said – about us all living basically together . . .'

'And working together.'

'Yeah.'

'I'd never say a bad word about them,' she says truthfully.

'But . . .'

'Well – I just wonder now. How healthy it really is.'

Tom turns down his mouth, evidently considering what to say. 'What do you think?' he says eventually.

'I just wonder . . . no – I mean. I shouldn't gripe about them.'

'I hope they're as loyal to you as you are to them.'

'I'm sure they are,' she says softly, but she isn't, she isn't at all. Frannie lied to her about the crime. They keep things from her. They are the opposite of loyal. Aren't they? As ever, sometimes the facts are clear to Cathy when set out this way, but she can't seem to really see them.

Cathy draws up the duvet over her as she begins to fall asleep, even though her stomach is rumbling. She and

Tom are completely naked, their bodies giving off a special kind of warmth under the covers.

'They are loyal to me,' she says.

He draws her to him and it is exquisite. The feeling of his bare, hot, smooth skin against hers. It has been worth the wait, she thinks to herself as she goes under. It has been worth all the bad dates, it has been worth wearing pyjamas for all these years.

52.

Now

First Day of Trial R. v. Plant

'And what, exactly, Ms Plant, if you don't mind telling the jury, happened after the remains were uncovered?'

'There was a port-mortem,' I say. The courtroom smells of Pledge furniture polish today. The jury is silent, not even shifting in their seats, just looking at me. There is something papal about the court. The dark wood. The various signs and symbols – the justice crest, the wigs and gowns. They merge with the statues of Jesus in Verona in my mind.

I can't meet my family's eyes. Mum and Dad are stoic, looking straight ahead. Joe is staring at his feet. And Frannie isn't there – of course she isn't.

'Do you miss her?' Jason said, a few weeks into our meetings.

I knew who he had meant immediately. I had thought, in the past, that it would be hard to miss somebody when everything in your life had changed. If the world upended on to its side, could you still yearn for small things, a chat across the fence in the back garden before bed, a shared tea-making session in the middle of the working day? But I now know that emotions are organic, pushing up through the soil regardless of the terrain they will meet outside. 'Every day,' I'd said to Jason.

'You don't feel angry,' he'd said, in that way of his.

Direct questions, direct eye contact. Lawyers might some-times feel like your therapist, but really they only ever want to get to the centre of the thing, to absolute clarity.

'No, I don't feel angry with Frannie,' I said, thinking back to how she started it all, and is now . . . well.

Caring for her child is a curiously intimate experience. I was unprepared for the tasks that parenting Paul requires. Baths and walks and washing his tiny little clothes I expected. But not the juxtaposition of big questions – *Where is the end of the earth?* – and small – *Do you like pegs?*

And, anyway, it's almost impossible to feel angry with somebody when their innocent little avatar lives in your house, sleeps on a cot bed in your spare room, sometimes in your bed. Who still carries little clutches of puzzle pieces and model dinosaurs around the house with him. Who still walks a little toddler-like at times, picking up his entire feet, soles flat. Who still confuses *my* and *mine*, and it seems impossible to explain the difference to him in a way that he will understand.

He would look nothing like Frannie if you sat them side by side. He doesn't have Frannie's large eyes or her big mouth. Paul is delicate. But there are similarities that I can't even name that some days are so striking it is as if Frannie has appeared right there in the room. The way the light would hit her eyes. The shape of her frown. I can never imagine it, can only see it when it's right in front of me.

'And then what happened?' the barrister says in a bored tone, bringing me back to the courtroom, to my family over there, the empty seat where Frannie ought to be.

'They started to investigate,' I say. 'And that's when . . .' I take a steadying breath. 'That's when things started to go really wrong, I suppose.'

I look at Joe now, his face as familiar to me as my own. That heavy brow. His braced shoulders. He's trying to look upstanding, as he sometimes does. We'll never be estranged, even if we never speak again, not truly. It isn't possible for family, for our family.

'Okay, so, you were all worried you would be – found out?'

'Yes,' I say. 'It was a bit of that. But it was mostly the threat of the body being found, and what would be found, that made it unravel.'

'And why was that?' the barrister says, his tone a perfectly pitched curious. He's an actor. He knows the answer to this question. Everything is at stake for me, and nothing for him. I am a real victim caught at a murder-mystery party, and nobody will believe me about the danger. I take another big breath and steady my shaking hands in the witness box. 'Ms Plant,' the barrister says. 'I have to remind you that you are under oath.'

'Yes,' I say. 'I know. I know.'

'Well?'

I glance at the jury again. Roughly half men and half women. Glazed expressions. 'It was what we did in response to the fear,' I say.

'Who?'

'Me, Frannie and Joe.'

I'm sure I sense a frisson as I say Frannie's name in court.

'So in what ways did the fear motivate you all?' the

barrister says. A simple question. I wonder how much the jury knows about what happened next. Is it true that they can't have read the news about us? Or is that an American rule? Do they know that it wasn't the police who got to us, in the end? It was ourselves.

53.

Then

Lydia

Lydia is sitting in her back garden, smoking, looking up at the dark windows of Cathy's and Frannie's houses. She hasn't smoked for years, but she found Joe's roll-ups. She needs to think, and something about cigarettes aids that process. The quiet, the breathing, the night air. An owl hoots nearby, and she looks up at it, thinking.

Where is she in all this? That is what her old therapist would ask her. *Where are you in all this, Lydia?*

It's a valid question, Lydia thinks, staring at the seam where the cigarette meets the ash. It's lit up bright red like a wound in the night, everything else in darkness.

Has he considered her? Did he think of her, when he agreed to do it? Lydia frowns as she asks herself the tough questions, as she has been taught to do. *Where is she in all this?* The Plants are top, clearly. And then her? She can only hope for second.

Joe arrives home. She hears the door, then watches the house light up, window by window, as he looks for her. Eventually, he arrives in the garden.

He smells of the vets'. The twist of antiseptic lingers on his clothes. It is rendered sinister, tonight.

'You're smoking,' he says, a question in his voice. He's rubbed the gel out of his hair, making it fluffy and matt-looking. It must have been a bad day.

'Yes,' she says, not wanting to discuss that, not wanting

to let him distract her. 'Can I ask you something?' she says.

He sits down opposite her on a wooden patio chair. He's facing her; she's facing the house. He's left all the lights on in the downstairs, one on in the upstairs too; an advent calendar of their life.

'Okay,' he says easily, in that way he always does, with her.

'Where am I in all this?' she says plainly.

'What do you mean?' he says, predictably. Lydia lights a second cigarette and sighs. Do men ever get it on the first go?

'I mean – when you answered Frannie's call – did you think of me?'

'Of course I did,' he says, Lydia thinks honestly, 'I only thought of you. Waking up alone, with Paul –'

'But you went anyway,' she says. 'To rescue Frannie.' She throws the stub of the first cigarette on to the ground. 'That's the thing,' she says. 'I don't think I would have done that.'

Joe is immediately defensive. Big shoulders up. Fingers drumming on the wood of the table. He goes to speak, then hesitates.

'You didn't think of the implications of it – for us,' she says.

'What are they?' he says, his expression wounded, like a small child's. Joe the rescuer. Lydia, for the first time in her life, wishes she could erase that quality of his, that she could focus him away from helping others and on to himself, on to her.

'If you get found out – what happens?' she says. She

spreads her arms wide, the cool summer air moving across her flesh. 'I lose you. If I get pregnant soon – then what? You'd be lost to both of us.'

'I'm doing everything I can to stop that happening,' Joe says, lurching suddenly across the table towards her, his eyes imploring. 'Literally everything.'

Something about his urgency frightens her. 'Don't be like that.'

'Like what?' he says, hurt. 'I'm just trying to get you to see –'

'But if you hadn't picked up the call, we wouldn't be in this position,' Lydia says, but he's wearing her down with his desperate expression.

'How could I not pick up that call?' he shouts. His voice is hoarse with it. 'Fucking hell, Lyds.' He bangs his fist on the table, which rattles.

'Don't shout at me,' she says in a low voice, a warning tone. 'Don't do that.'

'What am I supposed to do, then?' he says. He stands and turns around, his hands on his head, a man who doesn't know what to do. He kicks the leg of the table, which makes her jump.

'*Joe.*'

'I'm sorry – I'm sorry.'

'If you do that again, I leave.'

'I'm sorry . . .' He runs a hand through his hair. 'How can I . . . what can I do?' he says. It sounds rhetorical, but it isn't. 'You think I shouldn't care about my sister?'

'Put. Me. First,' she says. Her hand moves almost unconsciously to her stomach. She isn't pregnant, but she is already a mother. She knows it. The eggs are in there, waiting for their moment. Her children are out there, waiting to meet her. She puts them first already.

'What do you mean?' Joe says. But Lydia can tell he already knows. Those intelligent brown eyes are on hers, asking her not to ask him.

'Stop rescuing the kestrels,' she says softly.

'Hand her over?'

'Just – just stop. She's killed somebody, Joe.'

'I can't stop. I can't.'

'What are you even doing?'

'You don't want to know.'

'But it's her problem,' Lydia says. 'It isn't your problem. She's your sister. I'm your wife.'

'We're being blackmailed,' Joe says. Lydia swallows. 'We're going to pay it.'

'Who by?'

'Evan.'

The word is like a cold breeze in the night. Lydia is suddenly freezing. Evan. Joe's original cover story, back when the lies to her began. 'Right,' she says softly.

'We're going to pay him off.'

'How much?'

'A stake in the business,' Joe says.

'God, Joe.' Lydia stands up. 'I can't be part of this,' she says. 'When we do have a child –' she sees Joe's shoulders relax at the *when* – 'I can't . . . I can't have them be involved in this. This is criminality, Joe. Murders. Blackmail. Bribery. What next?'

'It'll go away,' Joe says. 'I said – we're going to pay him off.'

'And then what?' Lydia says softly, looking down at

him, his skin bronzed and illuminated by the lights from their house.

'What are you saying?' Joe asks, looking up at her.

'I'm saying there's a choice here,' she says. 'You have a choice.'

'I don't.'

'They're the family you came from – but I'm the family you chose,' she says.

Joe hesitates again. Lydia can tell he's going to say it. The breeze seems to still around them, the night holding its breath too.

'But you . . . you don't . . . I don't mean this harshly, Lyds, but you can't possibly understand this.'

'Why's that?' she whispers. He might yet not say it. He might not. All this time, never letting her truly in, not in on the family WhatsApp group until recently, always on the sidelines with their inside jokes. He's going to say it. He is.

'You don't have a family . . . you don't have . . .' Joe says, but Lydia is already walking away from him, towards those lit-up windows, towards the house they share together, away from those words, those words that are so careless, so reckless with her feelings, they may as well be knives.

Lydia sits up in bed, alone, Joe banished to the spare room. She is half a bottle of wine down, and angry. She cannot believe he said it. She cannot believe it.

None of it. That he buried a fucking body. That he lied to the police. That he bribed Evan. But, most of all, that he said it. That he said she didn't understand family.

She brings the glass of wine to her mouth and finishes

it, then pours another. She stares at herself in the mirrored wardrobes that sit at the end of their bed. She looks deranged. She looks heartbroken.

They're going to find the body any day now.

And, when they do, it is Lydia who holds all the cards. It is Lydia who could ruin them, this perfect family. It is Lydia who could demand whatever she wants in return for her silence.

PART V

Misappropriation of Corporate Assets

54.
Joe

Joe goes into the room he uses as a study. It's right next to Paul's bedroom. Sometimes, at night, Joe used to be able to hear him crying, but the evening is silent tonight.

The room contains a pale wood-effect corner desk he and Lydia got from IKEA. 'Let's rescue this one!' she'd said to him with a wide smile. 'Look – it's called "Klimpen" – is there a better name for a desk?'

God, he has hurt her, kicking tables, throwing insults. What a fucking dick he is.

He sits in the quiet of the study, the computer firing up, little green rectangles flashing, and thinks. He needs to sort it right now. Amend the partnership deed. Just do it. Just do it now. Cathy would caution against haste, but Cathy isn't here. Besides, Cathy's been messing up prescriptions. Been strangely absent in mind if not in body.

What else is he supposed to do? He understands why Lydia feels what she feels, but if they don't pay off Evan, they will go to prison.

His mother will need to sign this transfer. It's a problem. It's another problem. He leans back in his chair, thinking, then goes downstairs and makes a pot of coffee. Halfway up the stairs, he turns around and gets two Snickers. He must stop eating but not tonight.

He logs on to the company bank account. There's the

overdraft. There's the float. He sits back in the chair, the bright white screen hurting his eyes, and thinking. The heating clicks on, the radiator by his feet warming slowly as he tries to work it through.

Is there any way not to do this? He rests his fingers on the keyboard and thinks for just a second more. And then he hears it. A shifting, and then a small moan, a toddler sound. A watery cry, Paul, just through the layer of bricks that divides them.

Joe prints off their partnership deed with an amendment sheet. They should probably use a lawyer, but it looks easy enough. He adds in Evan's name and 'twenty per cent' after it. Consideration: £1. And that's it. Who knows if somebody will see it one day, will work it out. If HMRC will accuse them of insider trading, a sale at an undervalue, is that right? But what can they do? At every single stage of this, their options have been poor. They've made the best of the hand that Frannie dealt them.

He leans his head on the desk for a second. Fucking Frannie. His ear hurts as he lies against it on the hard desk. He reaches to rub it and turns his mind away from the question of whether he would have helped her if he had known the full circumstances, the truth. He doesn't have the capacity to worry about it. He's full up.

He looks sideways at the partnership deed lying on the desk right next to his eyes. Frannie, Cathy, Joe, his mother. *The Partners agree to transfer twenty per cent of the Business to Evan Sawyer, to be held in equal parts of twenty per cent each.*

How is he going to get that through without asking Maria to sign it?

He stares into space. Nope, he doesn't have the capacity to worry about that either. He has sold off a controlling share of the business for a pound.

It's a small price to pay. But it's better than parting with what they really owe: Frannie.

55

Cathy

'I'm a stop-out,' Cathy says, smiling, leaning into Tom as he stands in the doorway.

He ran her a bath this morning. He flitted in and out, bringing her tea, sorting his washing. They had a shouted conversation from bathroom to bedroom while he put his clothes away. 'What's with the aubergines, then?' he'd said, from his room to where she lay.

'Oh – you know. Just never really had a long-term aubergine.' Tom only laughed.

'I had a very bad aubergine,' he called, then arrived in the bathroom, a stack of folded towels held on the flat of his hand like a waiter.

'Did you?' she said, turning to him. His bathroom was immaculate too. A low windowsill containing only his shampoo, a five-in-one he described as 'good for hair washing, shower gel, road tarmacking, whatever you want'.

'Yep, got divorced and all.'

'Oh, I'm sorry.'

He waved the hand not holding the towels. 'It's fine. You don't need to say that.' It was the second serious thing he'd said. Tom was suddenly vaulted from fun fling to . . . to something more. To potential secret keeper. To boyfriend.

She stands now, on his threshold, not quite able to leave. 'See you later?' he says. 'Tonight?'

'Maybe,' she says, and he smiles, then, into the kiss. 'I'm a poor lonely aubergine,' he says.

'Me too,' she says, turning to leave, waving to him from her car, wondering what she is doing. Wondering what he might do with those secrets, if she told them to him.

PART VI
Fraud

56.
Joe

Joe dials his mother's number. She picks up immediately. 'Everything okay?' she asks.

'Yeah. I'm just . . . Evan is going to sit in on some partnership meetings,' Joe says, his words joining up and overlapping as they rush out together, such obvious lies.

'Right?' Maria says. She, like Cathy, doesn't miss a trick. At some point, Joe is thinking, as he stares at the new percentages, even if he hides this document forever, Maria will find out. Evan will refer to himself as a partner, or give a casting vote in a meeting, or sign a cheque. He stares at the wall, but there's no solution. If their mother finds out, he will have to make something up. Yet another thing. When you've told so many lies, one more hardly seems to matter at all, not even one told to his mother.

'Yeah, he raised some concerns about feeling, er, pushed out,' Joe says. 'So I thought I'd let you know.'

'I mean – that's quite a change,' Maria says. Her tone is conversational, but her words aren't.

'Well, anyway. You're not around day to day, so I wouldn't expect you to understand the dynamics here,' he says, hoping the deflection will be enough, but still wincing as he says it. It isn't fair. She didn't ask for this. He rubs at his eyes.

'Well – hang on just a seco–' Maria says, but he's already making his excuses, feigning an emergency, saying a hurried goodbye, feeling like a tosser.

This is all such a fucking bodge job. How long can he keep papering over things?

But he's decided what to do and so he scrawls his mother's signature before he can convince himself otherwise. It's barely an approximation of it, but it doesn't seem to matter. Who would even check? He holds up the document to the light. Shit. He could at least have used a different pen to the one he signed with.

He only needs Cathy and Frannie to sign it now. He hopes Cathy will just do it without quibbling. What if she doesn't? He knows he's being irrational, but he can't help it. They're each so reliant on the others . . .

He goes out into reception, unable to wait, sweating around his hairline, but finds Evan instead of Cathy, seeing out a giant house rabbit in a box, with what looks like an ear infection – the fur around it is sticky. 'Got a sec?' Joe says, gesturing into his consultation room.

'What can I do you for?' Evan says, the same twisted phrase he always uses, and Joe bites his tongue. If Joe is a tosser, then at least Evan is a cunt.

'It's all here,' he says recklessly, even though it isn't signed. He gestures to Evan. 'Twenty per cent of the business sound reasonable.'

'Sounds great,' Evan says.

He takes the single sheet of paper that transfers Joe's business, sold off gratis, to him. Just like that.

'Joe,' he says. There's a laugh in his voice, though it isn't a friendly one. It's a powerful laugh. He can hardly believe his fucking luck.

'I'm happy to extend an offer of partnership to you,' Joe says. He was never a good negotiator. Too hot-headed.

Always laid his cards straight out on the table. Maybe he should have started at ten per cent.

'I'm happy to accept,' Evan says, and, despite himself, Joe is relieved. It's for the best.

He reaches for the lid of the dog-treats jar and fiddles with the glass stopper on the top.

'And if you . . . if you renege,' Joe says. 'You know what? What we're doing here is illegal.' He thought about it last night. Nobody would shop somebody for murder if they themselves would get sent down for blackmail.

'Right,' Evan says, another laugh in his voice. It is being laughed at that angers Joe more than anything else. On the football field, at work and now too, it seems, in situations he never, ever thought he'd be in. 'Sure,' Evan adds.

It's the *sure* that does it.

'Do you know, you really don't want to cross us.' He walks two steps towards Evan, getting right in his space, making sure his shoulders look big.

Evan says nothing, just looks at him, then steps back, just a tiny bit.

The veiled threat, the reference to what they've already done, the hint at physical violence, they come from nowhere. As forceful as a volcano erupting.

Evan stares at him, his expression both judgemental and frightened. 'I await the other signatures,' he says eventually. Joe nods up at the ceiling, even though nobody can see him except the God who witnessed the crime in Italy. Something about that omniscience comforts him. That somebody may have a wide view of all of this. Can see what he is doing, and why.

They walk into the reception, Frannie on some fashion website, no lunch-time patients waiting.

Outside, the rain has finally stopped, and the sky is a burnt-sienna. There's a dust cloud. It's been on the news this week, turning their skies peach and orange instead of blue. After the flooding caused by the rain, and now this, outside has a post-apocalyptic vibe, people stopping to take photographs, tapping the arm of the person they're with and pointing. The sun is barely visible through it, a haze amid the dust.

Evan moves to walk out the front door, to buy a sandwich from next door, Joe guesses.

He'll get Frannie and Cathy to sign now and . . . well, then Evan joins the fold. He joins the numbers of people forced to keep this secret. Extortion, bribery, fraud, threats. He's in as deep as they are, then. None of them can see the sun clearly.

'Clock's ticking on those other signatories,' says Evan, over his shoulder.

Evan turns back to Frannie. She is totally still, surrounded by those bloody Chinese waving cats in perpetual motion, just looking at him, eyes wide and sad.

57.

Cathy

'Mum signed this?' Cathy says. She stares at the document, then up at Joe. It's ten minutes before Evan joins them at the first partnership meeting. They're always at seven o'clock, every other Tuesday. Cathy likes the mundanity of them. The instant coffee, the quiet.

'Glad you think so,' Joe says, plucking it from Cathy's grip. 'I did.'

Cathy moves away from him in shock. 'What?' she says. She stares down at it. Of course. Of course he hasn't told their mother. That is a poor copy of the signature that she knows so well. Like it's been traced. The same shape, but that's about it. A facsimile.

'You can't do that,' she says softly. 'She needs to know. And – Joe. I need to know too.'

'What do you mean?'

'You're doing stuff without telling me. We need to be transparent with each other.'

'Is that a threat?' he barks.

'What?'

'She wouldn't sign it. What would we possibly say?'

'You sold a fifth of the company for a quid,' Cathy says. 'That's – isn't that fraud? Selling things off at an undervalue? The taxman will look into it – HMRC . . . I . . .'

'If anyone looks into *anything* we've done over the last while, we will be fucked,' Joe says, taking a sidelong glance

347

at her. 'You have anything constructive to add? Going to tell the police about me?'

Cathy feels her mouth turn down in sadness. None of them is their best self at the moment. 'I can't sign this,' she says quietly. 'I can't be party to fraud, to all this . . . forging signatures.'

Joe thrusts a pen forcefully into her hands. The plastic burns her skin as he presses. 'Just sign it,' he barks.

She looks down, trying not to cry, knowing she's going to do it, knowing she has to do it.

'What have you told her?' she asks.

'That he's attending partnership meetings.'

'Joe, I . . .' she starts to say, but he ignores her, staring down at the agenda Frannie's printed off. Suddenly, Cathy can't be bothered to raise it. The train they're on is almost at their destination, she finds herself thinking, a thought she will come back to again and again. A team somewhere is probably uncovering Will, and discovering everything they tried to hide anyway. The end feels somehow near. She can only hope that she's wrong. She signs her name.

'What?' he says, catching her expression. He doesn't wait for an answer, and instead goes into the staff room. Cathy follows him. They're all waiting there. Frannie, Maria, Evan. 'Evan's joining us today,' Joe says tightly. 'Just – because he's interested in the management perspective.'

Maria looks over at Joe. Her dark hair is gathered at her neck. 'Right,' she says, her expression clearing and darkening, as though she is working something out. She will think she is being phased out.

Cathy gives a wan smile to Evan, keeping up the front. She's liked her colleague well enough for the past decade, but she can't believe he took the bribe. What would she do? Be given a stake in a profitable, successful business in exchange for silence? She would have waived that, she thinks, even if her silence could be purchased. And it was, after all, by Frannie. For free.

Evan's brows are drawn together, looking from Maria to Joe. Cathy watches him work it out: that Maria doesn't know he's a partner, and so – Evan is no idiot – she still doesn't know what happened in Verona either.

'Not much to discuss,' Joe says. 'On target for the month. All going well. We've switched the supplier of blood tests to a cheaper lab that does them faster too.'

Frannie is taking a note, the tendons in her hand crisscrossing over each other as she grips the pen.

'Okay,' she says, nodding. She has on large hoop earrings that should look hideous but don't.

'What's the matter?' Maria says to Frannie. 'You're so tense. You'll snap the pen.'

'I'm really not.'

'You – I mean – I just worry.'

Frannie drops her head and massages the back of her neck as Cathy watches. Those three words – *I just worry* – are said so often. She appraises her mother across the staff room.

She shakes her head, looking down at her drink. The staff room is dim and smells damp this evening.

They discuss the practice's footfall, whether they need to advertise. Joe tells everybody that they need to stop underestimating surgical time taken, which he addresses – kindly – to the room, but he means it directly to Cathy. She never bills even half what she should. *That shouldn't have taken three hours*, she will think of a simple cruciate knee op. *I'll bill an hour and a half. That's how long it would take an expert. Someone better than me.* She does it all the time, shaving time off here and there, passing on the lab results only at cost. Feeling sorry for families who can't work but who still want pets, families dealt bad hands with Labradors with arthritis and insurance companies who exploit loopholes. Families who want to do the best for their animals – most of them do – but can't. Cathy bears the cost herself. Chipping away at the business. Putting them less in the black than they should be.

'That means me,' Cathy says, raising a hand, trying to dispel the atmosphere.

'Bill them for everything,' Evan says. 'It's the only way. Why wouldn't you get the most out of a situation?' he says lightly. He's leaning back on the rear two legs of his chair. His gaze strays to Maria.

'I know,' Cathy says quickly. 'I will – I just. Too much heart, I suppose.'

Goosebumps break out along her arms, but she ignores them. Tries to ignore this interloper in her family's business that they sold out to in exchange for his silence. Evan must surely know Maria doesn't know, and Cathy watches him smirk as he looks at her, but he doesn't say anything. Not yet.

Cathy's eyes light on Frannie, and maybe she is thinking something similar, because she's staring straight at Cathy instead of taking notes. Cathy ignores the chilly feeling across her arms and back, and grabs a pad from one of the desks to distract herself.

They discuss profit margins and efficacy of drugs. They

discuss how the conjunctivitis drops are never in stock. Frannie says she will chase it up.

They keep it short, Evan's first ever meeting. Cathy's shoulders sag in relief as Evan leaves. Another bullet dodged. The rest of them file out in silence, coffee cups placed in the sink and the doors locked up. In the carpark out back, Maria and Evan gone home, the hot bins making it smell of Verona, Cathy looks at Frannie. She's so striking. That wide nose, those cheekbones.

'I can't believe it's come to this,' Frannie says softly to Cathy. Joe, smoking again, looks up sharply. Macca sits at Cathy's feet, just waiting.

'What do you mean?'

'I just mean – it was foolish. The whole thing.' Frannie takes his cigarette. 'It was foolish to attempt anything other than to hand ourselves in.' She straightens up as she says it, a strange jerk of her body that Cathy finds impossible to read.

'There was nothing we could've done that would've been right – or easy,' Joe says. The sky behind him is luminescent. The smell of roses, somewhere, drifts towards them on the breeze. Cathy wishes for a second that this was a normal late August, just a mundane partnership meeting. She'd enjoy the smell of those roses. But they must live their August, their descent into criminality, their family crisis playing out in front of them like some Mafia movie.

As Cathy idles in neutral on the way home, Macca in the boot, Radio 4 playing softly, she remembers those goosebumps, and something repeats on her. Something ... something sinister. Some moment in that meeting. She can't recall it. Maybe it is just the fact that

Evan was there. A non-Plant, for the first ever time. Knowing what they had collectively done.

It is only later, at midnight, that Cathy realizes. She feels too keyed up, as ever, to relax, and is carrying an armful of wet washing up her stairs, the sheets and shirts making her arms cold.

It isn't general fear or concern. It is something Evan said. Something that seemed to Cathy like a veiled threat, or at the very least a hint at his mind-set. *Why wouldn't you get the most out of a situation?* he'd said.

Anxiety flashes up Cathy's body. She drops the clothes on the stairs and sits a step beneath them, trying to think. No, he just meant . . . no. She can't think it. Can't even think that he would blackmail them again. And again and again, until it's over.

58.

Now

First Day of Trial R. v. Plant

'We wanted to fix the mess we were in,' I say, shrugging helplessly in the witness box, under oath. I wonder if they will document this shrug in the courtroom transcript the stenographer is painstakingly tapping out. 'We were desperate. As time went on, we had less and less to lose.'

'Are you saying that it . . . that it was easier to commit a crime because you already had committed others?'

Right before it all blew up, Frannie had become about as thin as it's possible for an adult to be without being hospitalized. Gone was the beauty. What was left was a shaky frame on which her old, gorgeous features used to hang. Her hair had lost its thickness, exposing more of her hairline, like after she had Paul and she grew back a fuzz that she had hated. There was no fat in her cheeks. Her skin used to crease when she smiled. We met on that final night in the outhouse in the back of Frannie's garden. There was no wine, but everything else was the same. The same ritualistic feel of our old Friday nights, only this time it was made sinister.

An owl was out, hooting softly nearby. It was the last time I saw both of them, before the police.

I stare at Joe. He staunchly refuses to meet my gaze.

'And so your collective desire to *fix the mess* –'

'Yes,' I say quickly, knowing what's coming, unable to

stop looking at it, to move away, like it is a fast train approaching me. I'm frozen.

'That is what led to the second murder?'

'Yes,' I say quietly, looking at the blank space in the public gallery. 'Yes.'

59.

Then

Cathy

It's three days since Evan joined the partnership. It's late. Cathy is the only one left at work. She has two tasks left to do: check where they are against their target for August and read a report on probiotics for dogs that's come in.

Maria walks into the backroom. Cathy is surprised to see her there, both because it's late but also because it is the week their parents usually go into hiding. 'You're here,' Cathy says. She is tired, is three coffees down, not sleeping well. Tom surely knows she's keeping him at arm's length, but he hasn't said anything.

'No rest for the wicked,' Maria says lightly. 'This need checking off?' she says, gesturing to the prescription food. Cathy nods.

They work in companionable silence for a while. The room is quiet around them, the night sky dark beyond the window. There is a strange atmosphere, Maria's busyness almost deliberately studied, and Cathy mimics her, going through their balance sheet robotically.

'I thought I'd help,' Maria says after a few more minutes. 'Now – show me the profit and loss.'

'No, I . . .' Cathy stammers. 'It's fine. I've just finished it. I don't want to have to do it again.' She rubs at her forehead.

'But what about –'

'Mum. It's fine.'

355

Maria blinks, staring at Cathy. 'It's just worry,' she says.

Cathy crosses the room towards her mother. 'It makes us have to do everything twice,' she says quietly. 'I know where it's come from . . .'

Maria freezes, saying nothing, her gaze on the floor. 'Right,' she says.

'We're all fine,' Cathy says. It's a lie, but it's an important one. 'We are fine, the practice is fine – you know?'

Maria nods quickly, still not saying anything. They don't broach the Rosie topic, not directly. That's Cathy's own battle to put to bed, she guesses.

They work together in silence for a while longer. 'It was my only job to keep you all safe,' Maria says quietly, after several minutes. She says it to the wall, not looking at Cathy.

'I see,' Cathy says quietly. 'Well, we all feel guilty about that.'

'You shouldn't,' Maria says.

'Neither should you.' Cathy may have returned the sentiment but, inside, her heart is singing. *You shouldn't.* Two simple words to heal a twenty-year-old wound.

'I won't tell you that these need doing,' Maria says when she leaves, waving a stack of referrals.

Cathy can't help but laugh. 'Right,' she says. 'I can see you're reforming.'

'Never,' Maria says, coming closer to Cathy and ruffling her hair. 'Never. Anyway – best go to my calligraphy class.'

'You're learning calligraphy?' Cathy says, thinking of the swirl of her name on the box.

'Yes, I just learnt a few weeks ago to do your name,' her mother says.

Cathy's eyes fill with tears. So her mother saved her box of things in the afterworld. After Rosie. She only wrote Cathy's name on it recently. Suddenly Maria's refusal to let go of the business doesn't seem like micro-management or a refusal to trust. It seems like love.

Cathy and Frannie take a lunch break outside the next day. They never usually take them together, but Evan is covering. One of the positives, Cathy supposes.

It's finally bright and dry, a blustery kind of day that makes your cheeks sting from the combination of cold wind and the sun. Cathy can feel the beginning of autumn's tendrils. Cold nights and apples falling from trees and sitting outside with Tom in knitted jumpers . . .

Evan is staring at her through the back window in the staff room as she gets up. He's talking to Maria. 'I'll get us some coffees,' Cathy says to Frannie, who nods.

Cathy dashes inside, through the back. Something has evidently just been said, because Evan and Maria stop talking as soon as she arrives. 'What?' she says. 'I was getting a chair —'

'Evan thinks he has become a partner?' Maria says questioningly to Cathy. 'Which sounds absurd to me?'

Cathy's heart descends in a chute that seems to run from her throat to her feet. 'What?' she says, stalling for time.

Cathy's eyes meet Evan's. She is the David to his Goliath. She sends a signal to him with her expression. Her face feels stiff and dry. With emotion, with stress, with the constant rug-pulling of what they have done. 'Does he?' she says, staring at Evan, not knowing which way this is going to go, not knowing what his game plan is. What did he say to Maria? And why?

'My mistake,' Evan says. 'I said *I'm going* for partnership. It's my ambition,' he says to Maria, still looking at Cathy.

'Right,' Maria says. 'Well, it would be a big step for us to do that, you know,' she says. She widens her eyes at Cathy.

Cathy swallows and looks at Evan as he leaves the staff room, whistling. And that's when she realizes. Games *are* Evan's plan. He knows she doesn't know. He saw her coming in, and said something to Maria, designed to create exactly this effect. The actions of a man who has been powerless for years, and is now drunk on his fortunes. Cathy can't say anything to him, can't even look at him for fear the conversation will escalate, so she makes the drinks in silence and goes back outside.

'Evan just told Mum he's a partner and then retracted it,' Cathy says to Frannie.

'What? Why?'

'Games, I think. It's a threat, isn't it?' Cathy says.

'But he's got what he wants.' Frannie's voice is stern, but her hand is trembling as it worries at her lip.

'He's got the first thing he wants,' Cathy says, thinking of what he said last night: *Why wouldn't you get the most out of a situation?*

Joe arrives out back and lights a cigarette.

'You're a regular smoker now, then,' Frannie says, avoiding the subject. 'Just – like that.'

Joe rolls his eyes and doesn't answer. He breathes smoke out of his nose in two distinct streams, then turns his gaze to Frannie. Something seems to pass between them. Cathy intercepts it, but isn't sure what it means. She thinks of what Tom said: *I hope they're as loyal to you as you are to them*, and something moves inside her.

'What do you think's happening?' Joe asks softly. He directs his question to Cathy, who knows exactly what he's referring to.

'I don't know. I don't know.' The BBC News coverage has stopped. They won't google it. They're in the dark.

Joe drags on his cigarette, looking out into the sun. 'Guess we just need to wait,' he says.

Cathy fills him in on what Evan said just now, and on what she thinks he meant last night, too. Joe lights a second cigarette. 'What a fucking twat,' he deadpans.

'Hear, hear,' Frannie says, and Joe smiles around the cigarette.

'He's going to ask for more,' Cathy says. 'Or he's going to tell Mum. Or someone worse.'

'You think?' Joe says. The tip of the cigarette glows red, a warning sign. 'Leave it with me.' He goes back inside, leaving Frannie and Cathy alone.

Frannie begins picking at a sandwich. 'Do you know what?' she says softly, looking down into her lap.

'What?'

'I'm finding it harder and harder to keep this secret,' she says. 'Are you?'

'Well, yeah.' Cathy bites into her sandwich, squinting into the sun. The wind gusts her hair into her face, but she doesn't mind. These things feel like mindful things that keep her in the now, sensations of nature, things she feels instinctively that one day she might miss.

'Deb's dropping by in a minute.'

'Right,' Cathy says.

'I saw her last night. Left my purse.'

'How is she?' Cathy says conversationally.

Frannie says nothing, and Cathy moves her hair out of her eyes and looks closely at her sister. She has her bare legs crossed at the ankles in front of her. She's wearing a rose-gold anklet with Paul's name on it, white trainers and a strange expression on her face. As Cathy looks at her, Frannie brings a hand to shield her eyes and gazes back.

'She's fine,' Frannie says. She stands as Deb approaches. She's tall, over six feet, with a mouth that turns down at its sides attractively.

'Oh, nice to see you,' Deb says warmly to Cathy. She hands Frannie her black leather purse, bought from a Mulberry outlet store last winter for – apparently – a *steal*.

'And you,' Cathy says to Deb.

'Did you have to Apple Pay your coffee?' Deb says to Frannie. Cathy feels a pang in her stomach for this sort of intimacy. Of knowing someone so completely, their routines, what they like to do each morning.

'I did!' Frannie says. She looks at Deb and there's a beat – just one, and that's when Cathy knows. Something about the hesitation, their eye contact, the set of Frannie's mouth, the way she swallows, just as she does when she's feeling guilty.

'Anyway,' Frannie says. 'Thanks for bringing it.'

'Yeah, no problem. Hope you're okay . . .' Deb says, turning to leave. Cathy watches them go, thinking: Frannie has told her. Cathy would bet her house on it. The wine, the lost purse. It all points to chaos. A secret told. Another person involved.

But Cathy doesn't feel anxious about it: she feels enticed. Frannie's breached their trust. If Cathy's right, maybe now she can too.

Frannie's standing in reception, ready to go home, shivering even though it's August. She looks like an actor on a stage without an audience, just waiting. Cathy wants to wrap her up, those skinny limbs in clothes that now look too large, and usually she'd at least go over to her, give her a smile maybe, but something stops her tonight. A strange kind of feeling, like somebody has removed the foundations of their relationship and forgotten to replace them. Has Frannie actually ever considered how Cathy feels? And, just like that, with that one straightforward question, the sympathy dies before it can really begin, like a rained-off sporting match.

'It's late,' Joe says, shutting his consultation-room door behind him. He nods to his car, parked out front, and presses the key. It flashes orange, for a second, like a pair of eyes opening and closing. Frannie pulls on her coat and opens the door, letting in the smells of wet earth and thunder.

'What do you reckon one fifth of the business is really worth?' Frannie says, standing there, the glass door open. 'I'll pay it back to you, every penny.' Joe waves his hand, not exactly in a *forget it* gesture, more one of tiredness, jadedness.

'At least thirty thousand,' Cathy says, and Frannie winces. Joe is still gathering up his things, and Frannie lets the door swing shut.

'A pound,' she says, watching the door close. 'We gave away thirty thousand for a pound.'

'What're we going to do, though?' Cathy says, looking out on to the dark countryside beyond Joe's car, trying to elicit the conversation that they need to have. 'I just don't think — I don't think he's really gone away yet.'

'What?' Frannie looks at her sharply. She folds her freckled arms and leans her back against the plate-glass windows. Above her head, in backwards font, is the logo for Vets 24. They designed it one night almost a decade ago on a piece of paper in Frannie's cottage, the week after they formally took over the company from their mother, and now here it is, immortalized.

'I basically told Evan what would happen if he came back for more,' Joe says quietly. 'So,' he adds, rubbing a hand across his forehead, then evidently decides not to speak. The words hang unspoken in the dim reception.

'What?' Frannie says. 'What did you say would happen to him?'

Joe says nothing.

Cathy reaches out and straightens a few of the chairs, separating the cat and dog areas better, then sweeps up a load of fur. Something about this conversation feels volatile. The same feeling she might get if they were all drunk and speaking too many truths, or in a fast-moving car driven in a temper.

'Well — I just . . . there is no next step, is there?' he says, looking across at Frannie, who's messing with the buttons on her denim jacket, all that hair piled up on the top of her head. 'We can't exactly rob a bank.'

'Don't say that,' Frannie says quietly, tears pooling in her eyes that disappear with a blink, like she's become adept at suppressing her emotions.

Frannie's phone rings, breaking the atmosphere, and she answers it. Joe turns to Cathy and shrugs helplessly, in that way that he does sometimes, like Frannie is a child they are co-parenting. Cathy keeps busying herself, cleaning the front desk, running the cloth along the keyboard, between the mouse and the chip-and-PIN machine. Joe turns off the television, the rolling news gone for another day, and a sigh builds and escapes from Cathy as he does it.

She thinks of Tom as she cleans and as Joe straightens the products on the shelves and Frannie murmurs into the phone. It's probably Deb.

Something changes in the reception and Cathy's back immediately tenses. 'What did she just say?' Joe is shouting, and when Cathy looks up he's cornering Frannie, right against the door to Cathy's consultation room.

'What are you doing?' Cathy says.

Frannie is chuntering frantically at Joe. The phone is now somehow in his hands. It's happened too fast, like an altercation in a night club that nobody can quite pinpoint the beginning of.

'You've told her,' Joe says, after hanging up the phone. His tone is completely without emotion. There is nothing positive or negative contained in it. Only a strange kind of empty factualness which scares Cathy. He's so big these days, her brother. Chest like a drum. He's holding Frannie's phone and standing over her like a bouncer.

'No,' Frannie says.

'*Joe*,' Cathy says. 'What are you *doing*?'

'He's a bully,' Frannie shouts.

'She said *I've been reading about Will*,' Joe roars. 'She knows, doesn't she?'

'I'm sorry,' Frannie bleats, her eyes finding Cathy's over Joe's shoulder. 'I'm sorry.'

'How could you?' he says. 'We have *just* finished dealing with the fucking fall-out of one person, and now a second? What. The. Fuck?' His face has turned red, the whites of his eyes shining unnaturally in the light. He looks so different. He looks like a thug.

'What – I'm supposed to just forget it? Not need my friends to confide in?' Frannie says.

'*It didn't happen,*' screams Joe. 'That's what we have to do. Live it. Live the lie. There are no bribes. There are no threats.' He meets her eyes. 'There is no body.'

'But I can't. I can't,' Frannie says. She is trembling and crying. Cathy can't stop looking at her. If only. If fucking *only.* 'They're going to come for us, when they find him, aren't they?'

'No!' Joe roars. 'They didn't take our DNA.' He yells it right into her face. 'They'll see it was a hit-and-run. There's no CCTV out there. Nobody will know. Except, for some reason, you keep telling people.'

'Joe,' she shouts. 'Stop – just – stop.'

Joe turns away from both of them and rests his palms on the plate-glass windows, looking out to the street. After a second, he drops his head, his forehead touching the glass. The only light comes from a lone street-lamp outside, her brother a crucifix in the night – white-palmed and self-sacrificial. 'Do you know what?' he says.

'What?' Cathy whispers.

'I'd have to commit mass murder if I were to kill everybody who knows now,' he says.

Cathy blinks.

'I'd have to kill two extra people.' He rolls his forehead on the glass, turning to look right at her. His eyes land on Frannie. 'Five if you count family,' he adds softly.

'Please come and get me,' Cathy says into the phone.

'Where are you?' Tom says.

Cathy looks around the empty foyer, the misted-up mark where Joe's forehead rested still apparent. 'At work. I was supposed to come back with Joe and Frannie but . . . we've had the worst row –'

'On my way.'

She pulls the sleeves of her cardigan down over her hands and wraps her arms around her body. She lets herself into her consultation room. She doesn't lock the door. She can't quite go there, can't quite think that Joe might be . . . what? Dangerous?

Cathy can hear them still arguing, somewhere in the back. All around her are enemies, it seems to her.

She stands in the empty consultation room, holding the hot phone in her cold hands, not doing anything except thinking. She turns off her computer, and the light, and stands there in the dark, hoping to become invisible, blinking back tears.

Tom must have sped over, because he arrives six minutes later. She leaves out of the front, locking the doors behind her, and walks over to his car, her trainers squeaking on the damp grass. His cheeks are red. His skin has a slight sheen to it. He smells of showers. The synthetic lime musk of male shower gel.

He kills the engine and looks at her as she gets in. 'I'm here,' he says simply. His eyes are serious again. No jokes.

A car with blacked-out windows cruises by, doing five, ten miles an hour, evidently looking for somebody. A rap song blares out. Big beats dropping in the night. Is this how it happens? One crime begets another and – suddenly. They're . . . they've become a family who will do anything, absolutely anything, to keep a secret, to cover up a crime, to keep people quiet. Money. Violence. Mobs. Mafia. They're doing what hundreds of families have done before them.

Cathy's skin breaks out in goosebumps.

'What's going on?' Tom says.

'You wouldn't believe it,' she says.

'Try me.' There's something about his tone that she wonders about. A kind of eagerness. The kind of tone of somebody who might know what's coming, but she pushes the thought away.

Cathy watches the car cruise past, thinking. 'I . . .' she says. She looks back at him, this man who was supposed to be a bit of fun, and wonders if she could do it. *I hope they're as loyal to you as you are to them.* She thinks of that astute comment, of Joe and Frannie's united front, of his actions earlier, and pauses.

Could she?

'You really can tell me anything,' Tom says. He scoots back his seat, like he doesn't plan on going anywhere anytime soon. 'I'm a total idiot. I'll probably forget.'

'You wouldn't,' Cathy says, unable to resist a smile. 'It's unforgettable.'

Tom spreads his hands wide. 'I mean – whatever,' he says nicely. 'Whether you want to, or not. I'm here.'

'It's selfish to tell you.' Her voice is thick with unshed

tears. Snot is building in her nose. God, she must look a mess. Tom wordlessly hands her a tissue from a packet in his glove-box.

'It isn't,' he says. 'It isn't selfish to need help.'

Her eyes feel starry with tears. She can't believe Joe acted like that. Has she been foolish to protect Frannie? To be involved with Joe and his temper? To align herself with them? She thinks of the looks that pass between them, and suddenly she feels completely alone in the world.

Except for Tom. She turns her head to the right and looks directly at him. 'If I tell you, we can never go back,' she says, thinking how easy it has become not to be shy. It's so easy, like a flower that knows to open up at exactly the right moment in spring.

'Okay,' he says. 'Okay. Let's do it.' His hand lands on hers, soft as a butterfly. 'Let's go.'

If Cathy was worried that Tom already knew about the crime, those doubts are completely extinguished by his reaction.

'Cathy, that is ... that's fucked up,' Tom says. The impact of the word feels like g-force to Cathy.

'No – I . . .' She didn't expect this. She thought he'd be easy-going, understanding. 'It is,' she says. 'But it's not my fault.'

He swivels his gaze to her in the car. He's pale. They're in a lay-by. The road around them is as dark as the track road was in Verona, lit up only by occasional cars that pass in stripes of white and red.

'I mean – I thought this would be . . . like, a small crisis.' He gives a sad half-smile, the kind people give in disbelief.

'Well, it isn't,' she says. 'And it's not – I mean. Needless to say, it isn't the kind of thing that happens to me too often.'

'Me neither,' he says quietly. 'I mean – it's murder.'

'She didn't mean it,' Cathy says quickly, no longer knowing if that's true.

Tom doesn't say anything for several minutes, his hand rubbing thoughtfully over his chin. What was she thinking, bringing her baggage to him in this way? He's right. It isn't a *small crisis*. It isn't normal. They must be toxic, the lot of them. Delusional fools. Troublemakers.

'You know,' she says, a hand on the door. She can get a taxi. She can walk. Anything but this. 'I wish I hadn't said.'

'No, no,' Tom says. He reaches for her hand, enclosing it in his. 'I didn't say that. I didn't say leave. I didn't say deal-breaker.'

'You said it's fucked up.'

He looks at her, his eyes the only thing she can see clearly in the dark. 'Isn't it?'

She drops her head, unable to argue with that. She's tired. So tired of covering for her sister. Of taking on her crime as though Cathy killed Will herself. Tom releases her hand, but replaces it along the back of her seat.

'Can I ask you one thing?' she says.

'Sure.'

'If it was you – your sister calls you in the night. What would you do?'

Tom understands it isn't a rhetorical question and stares straight ahead, thinking. 'For someone I loved,' he says.

'Yes.'

His eyes slide to her and something implicit passes between them. 'Yeah, I'd do it,' he says. 'I would do it.'

'Well, then,' Cathy says, spreading her hands in front of her and letting them fall into her lap. 'That's where I am.'

'Yeah,' Tom says sadly. 'It's just —'

'What?'

Another car passes. The white noise of its engine, its headlights like a soundwave, reaching a crescendo as it arrives and leaves. 'It's just that I wish you hadn't,' Tom says simply.

'Me too,' Cathy says. And, for the first time, she realizes that that is true.

60.

Joe

Joe arrives home in a fury, mad at himself for snapping, for being scary, for losing control. Lydia is waiting for him in the hallway, looking more engaged than she has in weeks. Eyes bright, looking up at him. 'I've been thinking,' she says.

'Have you now?' he says. He isn't in the mood for this. For more problems, for more things falling apart.

'What?' she says, the word more of a movement of her mouth than a sound.

'I said, *Have you now?*'

'I was going to talk to you properly,' Lydia says, turning away from him. 'About the . . . about Verona.'

'Go on, then.'

'Not while you're like this.'

'Like what?' Joe says. He spreads his arms wide, then lets them fall to his sides.

She starts crying, make-up streaked underneath her eyes like a watercolour painting.

'What's going on?' Joe says.

'Don't do this.'

'What?'

'Don't be – don't be nasty to me. Don't be so . . . don't be so confrontational.'

'Ask me what you wanted to.'

'Joe.' She meets his eyes, and that's when his head catches up with his heart.

'What?' he says. He's half aware that his hand has flown to his chest, where it flits and trembles like a bird.

'Did you pay him?'

'Yes.'

Lydia nods. Joe has confirmed something more to her than the bribe. He has confirmed who he is. 'I need to go for a bit,' she says.

'Go?'

'I need to – this isn't . . .' She spreads her hands in a help-less gesture as she looks up at him. He thinks, suddenly, of how many days he's spent in her company. Thousands. He knows those hands he's staring at as well as his own. 'It's not –'

'What?' Joe barks.

Lydia stands then, trainers on the wooden floor in front of him. She is going. She is leaving now. She is leaving *him*.

'Don't go,' he says softly. Lydia is standing right in front of him now. There's a bag in the hall. He's staring right at her, but he can see it in the corner of his vision. 'Where will you go?'

'I asked you to stop this, and you haven't. You're kick-ing tables and being so – so unpredictable. So angry. I just – this isn't what I signed up for.' She holds up her palms, like somebody pushing something away from them.

'Look. Evan is all paid now. It's done. It's over,' Joe says, trying to grab for her hands.

'You paid Evan's blackmail, even though I asked you not to.'

'He was going to call the police.'

'You did it anyway. You've been very clear about where I fit in in all this,' Lydia says. She places a warm hand on his arm. It's so easy to be magnanimous when you're the one leaving, Joe thinks nastily, though he knows that isn't right – that it isn't fair.

'Lyds,' he says. 'What was I supposed to do? Hand my sister in?'

'Consider your wife,' she says. 'That's all I asked for. And you just – you just didn't. You *don't*. I can't compete with this.' She gestures towards Frannie's house.

'She needs me,' Joe says.

'So do I.'

'So what is this?'

'I just need to be away for a while,' she says. 'I'll call you.'

'Oh, right – great. A phone call,' Joe says, rage bubbling underneath his skin. 'You promised to love me forever, and now I'll get a phone call.'

Lydia shoots him a look, a wounded look, her cheeks red, and he wishes immediately he could take it back. To fall on to his knees and beg her. To hold on to her hands and plead. 'Lyds,' he says thickly.

She shakes her head, her mouth tight. 'Let me take it back,' he says. 'I'll do anything.'

'You won't.'

'I will.'

'Okay, then – end it. Truly end it.'

'Hand Frannie over?'

Lydia puts her hands on her hips. She looks tired. 'It won't end until you do,' she says. 'Not really.'

Joe hesitates. He imagines doing it. But he can't hand Frannie over. He can't, he can't.

'I could stop helping her.'

'So if the police reinterviewed you tomorrow –'

'What? I should hand her in?' Joe says emphatically.

'So you would lie for her again?'

Joe stares at his feet. They lost Rosie and they never got over it . . . he can't lose Frannie too. He tries to find a solution that isn't that, that isn't full of absolutes, as tears clog his throat.

'Lyds, I –'

'I thought as much,' she says.

She removes her hand from his arm, his little kestrel. Tears blur their living room as he watches her get ready to go.

As she's leaving, he can't help but ask her.

'Are you going to tell the police?' he says.

Joe will remember the look she gives him for the rest of his life.

Joe storms into their small, square kitchen and starts opening the cupboards, feeling angry at Lydia and angry at Frannie. Most of all, he is angry at himself. Grisly, broken Joe, lashing out at the people he loves. Prioritizing people in the wrong way, losing his lovely wife.

Who does he think he is? He reaches up for a glass. It's still warm from the dishwasher that Lydia must have put on. He brushes a hand across the buttons.

She's left him. She's left him. She's left him.

He goes into their pantry, where they keep the stuff they hardly ever drink. It smells musty and damp. He leans his back against the wall, breathing, trying to talk himself down. He finds a whisky and pours it, even though it's only ten o'clock. Whisky is for after-parties. For midnights. For early-on-New-Year's-Days. And for . . . whatever this situation is.

Next door, he hears Cathy's front door close, then two voices. He stands in the quiet of the kitchen, just listening, but can't hear any more. He must be mistaken.

He sits at the kitchen table. On it are a couple of Lydia's Yankee Candles, a clutch of sunflowers in a vase and a notebook. The washing machine has been set, ready to start in eleven hours' time. She is so organized. She'd be a great mum. The greatest. He watches the green blinking light of the washing-machine timer. 11h 22m. 11h 21m. He stares and he sips.

When the washing machine flicks to 10h 59m, he pours another measure just as he hears a rustle at his front door, a soft knock perhaps. After a few seconds, somebody lets themselves in. It'll be a member of his family, he thinks moodily, staring at the watermark his glass has left on the kitchen table.

Cathy appears, framed in the doorway. She's in pyjamas. He gestures to her, and she pulls one of the wooden chairs across the floor tiles and sits down beside him, next to the radiator, laying an arm along it. She looks tired, he thinks, peering closely at her for once. He almost never does it: Frannie usually steals the limelight in every way.

Cathy's face is scrubbed clean of make-up, still glowing with whatever moisturizer she's used. Perhaps she didn't intend to come here, maybe she decided on the spur of the moment. Something about it reminds him of their childhood. The intimacy of this, of seeing her in pyjamas, bare-faced, smelling of toothpaste.

'This can't go on,' Cathy says simply. The baby hairs around her forehead are wet. 'You know?'

'I know. I know,' he says. 'I'm sorry – I lost . . . I lost my temper. I've been, I don't know.' He thinks of his father, and how far back they'd have to go to put this stuff right.

'You've been what?'

Joe shrugs uncomfortably. 'Struggling, I guess,' he says in a low voice. Cathy stands and gets a glass out of the cupboard for herself. 'Lydia left me,' he says.

'What?' Cathy turns around in shock.

'I told her,' he says, his voice low and mournful. 'She doesn't feel – prioritized.'

'She'll come back,' Cathy says firmly, but she doesn't meet his eyes.

'Maybe it's the whisky talking, but I'm feeling pretty pessimistic here,' Joe says.

'What do you mean?' She has her back to him. She stops and looks at him. 'About Lydia?'

'Were you with someone? Just now?' Joe asks, thinking too of the other night, when he'd heard a voice in the background of the call.

'No,' Cathy says, and her expression is totally neutral when she turns to him, glass in hand. 'What do you mean, pessimistic?' She sits back down. He can only hear her soft breathing and the hum of the fridge. They are so comfortable with each other but not with the situation. They could sit here in silence or they could fill it with their darkest thoughts. And both would be okay.

He looks at his sister across the dimness of his kitchen. Their family business paraphernalia is everywhere. Vet-related notebooks, pens from drug reps, a pamphlet on microbiomes from some CPD they all attended together. Their sister is just next door. Their lives are so entwined.

'We dodged one bullet. But – now what?' He takes another sip of whisky. It tastes like a cough forming in his throat. He doesn't like it, but it isn't about the taste. It's about what it represents. Masculinity, sure. The amber in the glass. How neat it is, how hard he is.

'Look, we are where we are,' Cathy says, her hands stretching eagerly over the table to him. 'I know how bad it feels. I even wanted to take the blame for her.'

'What?' Joe says. The burn of the whisky has made his voice hoarse. He sounds just like his father.

'It felt like the only way,' Cathy says. 'You know?'

'Frannie said . . . something like this. Ages ago.'

'She's smart. Smarter than you think. I just figured –'

'What?'

'I have nothing to lose,' she says, with a small shrug.

'That's so sad, Cathy,' Joe says, his lips wet with whisky, his mind soft and yielding like honey.

'And, besides,' she says, ignoring him, 'neither of you would be willing to do it. But I was.'

'Was?' Joe says.

'Yeah. I mean – I don't know. I'm sort of inclined to wait now, aren't you? It's been a week since they said they were searching the area. They haven't found it yet. So far' – Cathy dabs at a spot of whisky on the table – 'so far so good,' she finishes huskily, looking at him with a curiously positive expression on her face, like she's just let it out briefly, and then covered it up again.

'We're fucked if they find out,' Joe says. 'They won't give us any leniency for confessing. We've done too much other bad stuff. Lydia wanted me to just – to just hand Frannie over. Just like that.'

'I bet she didn't,' Cathy says immediately. 'She probably just wanted to be – I don't know. To be considered. Not kept out.'

'It was for her own good that I kept her out.' He pauses, wondering how to word it. And then he just says it. 'You know. You don't need to take the blame. It wasn't your fault.'

Cathy stares into her lap, her eyes wet. 'You don't mean Frannie.'

'No. I don't.'

She raises her eyes to Joe. Those big watery eyes on his.

'I know,' she whispers.

'So you can't.'

Cathy, predictably, says nothing. She reaches for his bottle of whisky and pours herself a measure. She fiddles with the glass, raising it to her lips and sipping repeatedly, small sip after small sip.

'When you said it was about Rosie, for you –' she says.

'I mean. It's why we're all so close, isn't it?'

'Is it?' Cathy says, blinking at him like he's just turned on a bright light.

'Yeah – I mean, I always thought so . . . bonded by tragedy and all that.'

'Maybe it's time to move on,' she says softly.

He pushes the balls of his hands into his eye sockets. 'You know, I'm not feeling myself,' he says, his hands still covering his eyes like a child.

'What?'

'I just feel so fucking angry all the time, Cath,' he says.

Cathy reaches for his hand across the table, draws it away from his face. His are hot and clammy; hers warm and dry.

'You were always a hothead,' she says affectionately. 'Remember the sports day?'

'Yeah,' he says with a small and silent laugh. 'The post deserved it.'

'Sure.'

'I don't know,' he says morosely, still holding on to her hand like it is a buoy out at sea. 'I feel like I'm keeping everything together. This whole crime. But I'm doing it in – all the wrong ways. Aren't I? Is Frannie mad at me?'

'We love you unconditionally,' Cathy says. 'We know you didn't mean to be scary.'

'I'm fucked up because of it too, you know,' Joe says. 'I felt all this – I don't know. I *feel* all this pressure to be like – the patriarch, you know?'

She looks at him curiously across the table. The glass is to her mouth, her head tilted back slightly, but her eyes remain on him.

'I see,' she says.

'I just ... I could've done something, at work,' he whispers.

'Done something?'

'I really could've hit someone.'

She leans across the table again towards him. 'Who – me?'

'No.'

'We'll get used to this,' she says, his sister, a ray of positivity he takes for granted, like somebody who lives somewhere with constant good weather.

'I just mean ... I have said some mad things. I threatened Evan.'

Cathy winces. She finishes the whisky and stands up. She's already swaying. She could never hold her drink. She's so little compared to him. Something in his gut twists at the thought. His baby sister. Not the youngest, not Frannie or Rosie, but still a baby to him.

'I'm worried what I'll do,' Joe says.

'To Evan?'

'No. I have a plan for Evan. I don't know.'

'To Frannie?'

'To the people I care about the most,' Joe says, side-stepping the direct question. He balls his fists up on the table. 'This stress, you know? It lives in me.'

'What kind of a conversation is this?' she asks.

Joe's mouth moves in the vague direction of a smile at their family joke. 'I don't know,' he lies. All he can think is that if Frannie weren't here any more, none of them would have any problems.

Cathy nods, just once. 'What's the plan for Evan?'

'I'm going to tell him we'll rip up the agreement if he comes back for more. Nobody knows about it. We haven't registered it anywhere. If he tried to sell his share, we could all stop him.'

'Good,' Cathy says softly, then leaves his kitchen. He doesn't hear her close the front door behind her, she does it so quietly, almost as though she were never there at all.

61.

Cathy

It's the end of the day. Cathy and Frannie are in the back-room, Frannie has on red tasselled earrings, some attempted grab at normality, no doubt, but they only seem to highlight her skinny cheeks and pallor. Nevertheless, it's good, in a way, to see her trying. 'Going out?' Cathy says.

'Yeah. Mum and Dad have Paul. Just going to go for a quick burger with Deb. Come if you want.'

'I'm fine,' Cathy says, waving Frannie away, hoping she doesn't talk too indiscreetly with her. 'Nice earrings.'

'Thanks,' Frannie says, standing framed in the doorway. 'Haven't had a chance to do my make-up or hair.' She smiles in a breathless sort of way at Cathy. 'It's been one of those days.'

'Isn't it always?' Cathy says.

'I'm late already,' Frannie says. 'But, while I remember, the eye drops are out of stock again. So we're back on the ointment.'

'Okay.'

'You all right?' she adds, her head tilted slightly to one side. Cathy finds herself, despite everything, wondering how her sister knows how to act so beautifully. As though she chooses even the way the light hits her features.

'Oh, yeah. Fine. Going to spend some time organizing stuff here.'

'Okay,' Frannie says, waving a hand as she leaves, but,

as she walks away, Cathy sees that her features have fallen, just slightly, as though she is disappointed in Cathy.

The door closes behind her, and Cathy stands with her hands on her hips, surveying the room. She wants immersion. Not thinking about her siblings or the man they killed or how she has burdened Tom with it. They parted ways the other night, and he said he'd be in touch, but he hasn't. She's just . . . waiting. They all are.

Their cleaner Joanie arrives, carting the Henry Hoover awkwardly by her side. She's blonde, with tanned skin and impossibly long nails that reach a fine point at their ends.

Cathy works alongside her, as she has done a thousand times before on Friday nights. She does it without thinking, the way she always has.

She starts straightening papers and shredding unimportant items, collecting mugs and washing Joe's old coffee stains out of the bottom of them. By the time she begins a general drugs audit, she's immersed, ticking and crossing off what they have, ordering some of the chemotherapy drugs the nurses can't order.

She puts some music on the television in reception as she turns to the appointment system. She knows that she is looking for tasks to do, but her heart still lifts as she finds one. She will sync up the bookings so she and Joe can make them on their computers in their consultation rooms too. She's been meaning to do it for ages. Their system is old and creaky.

She sits at the desk and puts in the practice's password. Frannie evidently tried a few different pairs of earrings this afternoon and she left them out, so Cathy puts them in her drawer for her.

By nine o'clock she's exhausted. The systems are synced, she's working in the same way she used to, but she no longer feels the same way. Because of Tom.

Sod it. She'll text him. See how he is. She'll finish this task on Frannie's computer and then text. She sighs and navigates to the *start* menu, her face lit up in the darkness. As the computer considers her request, the fan whirring next to her, she cups her face in her hands and considers what *she* wants, not what her brother and sister want, for the first time. She looks out at the August skies, dark already, autumn racing ever nearer, summer having evaporated into a months-long spell of rain, and thinks.

The computer shows the desktop and Cathy presses *shut down.*

'Three items open,' it prompts. 'Do you want to quit?'

She tuts and task switches, irrationally annoyed at Frannie for leaving things open. asos.com, hotmail.com and their drugs portal are open. Cathy shuts the portal and the fashion website, but something makes her hesitate over her sister's email.

Cathy clicks on the tab and gazes at it. Mostly spam, mostly unread. It's organized, hardly anything in the main inbox. Cathy clicks on the deleted items. She doesn't know what makes her do it. Perhaps the feeling that Frannie might delete things she doesn't wish to see, that Frannie merely pretends to be happy and sunny and fine, that Frannie avoids, that Frannie moves real-life conversations into deleted folders.

An email jumps out at Cathy. Something hot and acidic flashes across her body as she sees it.

William McGovern.

62.

Cathy

Cathy reads every single email. She never thought she would invade her sister's privacy in this way, but then none of them ever thought any of this would happen.

And now, sated, all of her questions answered by a faceless Hotmail inbox, she puts her elbows on the desk and rests her chin in her hands, trying to think, trying to work it through. The desk gleams in the light from the street-lamp outside. All Cathy can hear is the whirr of the computer and her own thoughts.

Her hands leave sweaty patches on her forehead after a few minutes.

I will not be parted from my child in this way.

That is what William's latest email said to Frannie.

Of course. Frannie got pregnant three years ago in Verona. Cathy's mind circles over it.

And then she thinks back, all the way back, to the beginning. The altercation with the stranger in the market. To the blood loss. To the warrant.

William wasn't a stranger to Frannie. The market altercation wasn't a random event, bad luck, a rare overreaction from Frannie. She knew him. He was Paul's father. He'd been trying to get Frannie to give him contact for over a year. He wanted half and half, fifty per cent of Paul's time to be spent in Verona. His emails became increasingly aggressive. *What will it take for you to cooperate with me?* he said. And then: *I have to say, Francesca, I am disappointed by the tone of these emails. Children should see their fathers.* And then: *I am minded to use the full force of the Italian law over here.*

That last email, dated two days before his death, suggested they meet, said he had a document for her to see. She refused. He must have shown her in the market, maybe, or later on.

Cathy stares at the screen until her eyes sting. So there never was a warrant. There was only ever a legal document naming a Joseph Plant. But Joe isn't the only Joseph. Paul Joseph Plant, the *Paul* ripped off. It was some sort of residency order.

Cathy sinks her head back on to her hands and tries to work it through. No wonder Frannie panicked. But she also killed him.

She looks up, her eyes glassy, making the reception blur around her.

Her sister murdered the father of her child.

And it also means there is a paper trail, linking Frannie to Will.

Cathy sighs as she locks her front door behind her. She walks down her garden path and up Frannie's. She's waited until Frannie arrived home.

She lets herself in and steps forward, into the light of Frannie's kitchen. Better now than later. It must be faced. 'I know who Will McGovern was,' she says.

There's a silence as Frannie digests this. Cathy stares at her, becoming vaguely aware of something in her peripheral vision.

It's Joe, in the darkness of the utility room.

'Who is he?' he says.

63.

Joe

Joe's littlest sister is sitting at her table, looking up at him. He is so mad he could kill her.

Her jaw has jutted forwards in that way that it does before she cries angry tears. Her forearms lie parallel on their sides on the table, her wrists an inch thick at most. The truth comes from Frannie easily, like a river overflowing after months of rain.

Afterwards, Cathy is standing in her raincoat, holding her keys, her face like she's just detonated a bomb.

'And that's the truth,' Frannie says. Joe hears the bones of her arms thud against the wood of the table. 'I'd told him about Paul. When he was born I thought it was the right thing to do. But then he began harassing me. He was going to get residency of Paul using the Italian courts. So I thought. I said we'd talk it out when I was over, but he wanted a lawyer's meeting. It escalated so quickly. I told myself I'd just avoid him, in Verona. It's a big place, that it would be stupid to miss a holiday because of him. But then there he was! At the fucking market, of course. He showed me the document at the market on his phone and then, when I wouldn't engage, he rang, late, drunk, to say he was coming over.'

'So you deliberately killed him,' Joe says flatly. Frannie drops her head. Cathy is saying nothing, her brow crumpled, looking like somebody approaching forty for the first time ever.

'There was no cigarette, at the market?' Cathy says eventually.

'No. I saw him there and we rowed. And then when he called to say he was coming – I think he'd been out, in a bar – I went out to meet him, somewhere neutral – I didn't want him in the villa around Paul – I wanted to try and . . . to try and talk him down.'

'And then what?'

Frannie heaves a sigh, a long, sad sigh that seems to go on and on. Several Lego figures sit on her kitchen table, and she reaches over and messes with one, passing it from hand to hand. 'He said he would be able to get full custody of Paul,' she says in a soft voice. 'Because I hadn't negotiated with him over the years. Because I'd tried to limit access to his child. It sounded like it might be bullshit, but I didn't *know*. You just don't take the risk – not with your kid. I'd just always said I'd let him see Paul when we were over, but that's all. Each July.'

'What was he like?' Joe says quietly.

'He was just so . . . so forceful. So powerful, you know? He would. Not. Let. It. Go.' Frannie rubs at her eyes as she says it. 'Every morning, some days, there would be a new email. I tried everything.'

'Why didn't you say anything? Ever?' Cathy says.

'Oh, God, imagine, imagine the receptionist telling the vets,' Frannie cries. 'It's all so fucking unsavoury. Joe and Lydia are married and trying for a baby. You're happily single.' Cathy sniffs, not looking at either of them. 'It's so – I don't know. I felt like a fucking *EastEnders* character with problems with the one-night-stand dad.'

Joe blinks a few times, shaking his head and looking

around him. At Frannie's American-style fridge, a huge space-grey one with an ice dispenser in the front. Her luminous green garden beyond the bi-fold doors. Her huge table, the sheepskin rug draped stylishly over the bench. How are they here? In the most middle-class of kitchens, speaking of murders, of threats, bribes, burying bodies. It all seems so insalubrious, suddenly, that he wants to walk out of this kitchen, leave her house and get straight in his shower. Scrub it all off.

'So basically,' Cathy says, her voice unusually loud and clear in Frannie's kitchen. 'You let us –'

'We have almost no time, then, do we?' Joe says. 'The body will be found soon, but there's a . . . there's a paper trail.' Cathy throws him a look which tells him that she's had the exact same thought. 'Isn't there?'

'You let us,' Cathy says slowly, 'you let us take risks we didn't know we were taking. We thought he was somebody random. Not somebody connected to you through the fucking *courts*. God, Frannie.'

'I spent the half an hour before I called you deleting his emails,' Frannie says. 'I deleted every one off the Gmail server on his phone. When I was doing it I found –' She swallows, a tiny, almost imperceptible movement, but neither of her siblings misses it. Joe unconsciously braces his shoulders. He knows something's coming. Another confession, in a whole line of them. 'I found that he'd used a site to fake legal documents,' Frannie says. 'That look like they're from a family court.'

Cathy lets out a breath through the side of her mouth. It makes a whistling sound in the quiet. 'So he was never going to be able to take Paul. If the documents were fake.'

'So there's no trail,' Frannie insists, leaving the rest unsaid: *So I didn't need to kill him.*

'You still let us be complicit with you in something we didn't know the full facts about,' Cathy says. 'We didn't know it was murder. This began as a hit-and-run. And now it's – it's this – this grotesque, awful . . .' When Joe turns to look at her, he's surprised to see she is near-vibrating with rage, almost the exact same way Frannie was trembling with fear when they went to help her on that night. Joe reaches to straighten one of the fridge magnets – the Juliet Balcony in miniature form.

'Look. There's no paper trail,' Frannie repeats. 'No courts.'

'I find it hard to believe a word you say,' Cathy says icily. Joe looks at her in surprise.

Joe gets angry all the time, but Cathy never does. Joe glances at her just briefly and considers where her limit is. What she's capable of. What the future holds for Frannie.

'You've killed somebody,' Cathy shouts. 'Somebody you knew. And you've fucking roped us in. And you deleted emails off a *phone* – not a server.'

Something satisfying seems to release itself in Joe. He's glad she's finally blown her top.

'It was the server, I was careful. They haven't come after us yet, have they?'

'Frannie. Fucking hell,' Cathy says. 'You're a fucking idiot.'

'I'm sorry,' Frannie says, looking up at both of them. She shrugs so helplessly. 'I thought – I just . . . it's all for Paul. It's misguided, but it is all for him. He wouldn't want to be split between Italy and here – can you imagine? In a foreign country? Where he knows nobody?' She wipes at her nose. Her finger comes away wet. 'Believe me, anything you say to me, I've thought myself. And worse.'

Cathy deflates, right then and there, her temper already spent. Frannie turns to Joe. 'I thought I would lose Paul,' she protests. 'Neither of you actually has a clue what that feels like.' Her eyes flash, then she looks at Joe, her brow wrinkling. 'Sorry,' she adds. Anger begins rumbling in Joe's body, a soft thrum at first, like the new bubbles in a boiling kettle. Not only is she using this against him now, but he is no longer trying for a baby because of her.

That single thought, her throwaway apology, is enough to ignite Joe's temper, like a match that lights so easily with the merest touch against the phosphorous side of the box. 'Is that right?' he says. 'So let me get this straight. I risked my fucking *marriage* for you.'

'I'm sorry,' Frannie chunters, her jaw quivering. Joe advances towards her.

'All right,' Cathy shouts. Frannie and Joe turn to her in surprise. Frannie stands up. 'Enough. Let's just – Joe. Go home. Let's regroup tomorrow.'

'Fuck off,' he barks. Frannie takes two steps backwards. Her back is to the wall. He's making her do this, he's dimly aware. He can see her ribs underneath her V-neck t-shirt. Each freckled rib, her body a xylophone. He can see the glands that sit behind her collarbone. He can't stop himself reaching for her wrists. He can feel her pulse beneath his fingertips.

'Joe,' Cathy says, but he glares at her, a quick snarl, then back to Frannie. Back to fucking business.

'You have ruined everything,' he hisses at her. 'You have ruined our family. You have ruined *my* family.'

He throws down her wrists and turns his back to her.

'Leave,' Cathy says.

Tears are running unchecked down Frannie's cheeks, one after the other, like raindrops down a window. 'Don't say that,' she says softly. 'Don't say it like it's all over.' She crumples in front of him. She sits on her kitchen floor and loses all dignity, clear snot running down from her nose, tears, eyeliner everywhere. She is a tangle of angular limbs.

'Isn't it?' Joe says. If he doesn't leave now, the top of his head is going to explode, a whale blow-hole right in the centre.

He's being taken over by anger. His blood is lava. His bones fried, baked hot. He's got to . . . he's got to get out of here. He's got to get out of his body. His mind. 'You fucking, you fucking bitch,' he says to Frannie. His heart feels weird. Maybe he's having a heart attack. It's welcome, he thinks, as he massages his chest. Dropping dead is fucking welcome at the moment, the mess they're in. The fucking mess of it. The lies. The post-mortem. A homicide enquiry, his family at the centre of it. Lydia. He has nothing left to lose now, nothing.

'I'm sorry, I'm sorry,' Frannie says to him, reaching up to him. 'I'm sorry, Joe. I wanted to tell you – but I thought . . . I just thought it would make it all worse. And it didn't change anything if you didn't know.'

'How could you?' Joe says, his gaze meeting Frannie's at last. 'How the fuck could you?'

'But it doesn't change anything!' she says plaintively.

'You're a murderer now,' Joe says.

He turns and walks away from Frannie, slamming the door so hard behind him that all three cottages quake.

64.

Cathy

Later, as she lies in bed, finally calm, Cathy hears voices outside. She stumbles to the window and looks out. Joe and Frannie are talking over their fence, next to the outhouse. Joe is lighting a cigarette. His lighter momentarily casts his fingers in an amber light, then is extinguished again.

As Cathy watches them, standing just a few feet from the outhouse, a strange feeling overcomes her. Some sort of trepidation. It neutralizes the frustration she feels with her sister, but that doesn't mean that she likes it. She can't quite say what's bothered her. Something about the scene of Joe looking at Frannie over the fence. Cathy can't read his expression. It's tender, but it is something else too. Maybe withheld.

Cathy is overcome with nerves about what is to come. Thinking about the power that each holds over the other, the actions they could take, the lies that they could tell. Something tells her that this is far from over. That the cracks are going to get deeper, form chasms, enough to move continents.

65.

Joe

'It's late,' Frannie says to him in the dark of their gardens. Her voice is clear and high, like a bell. He didn't realize she knew he was there. 'Could smell your cigarettes,' she adds, as though he vocalized that thought.

'It is late,' he agrees.

'You're mad at me.'

Joe glances up at the moon, a nightlight for just the two of them. 'No.'

'No?'

'No,' he says sadly. 'Yes. I just wish I had known who we were burying.'

She advances towards him and reaches a hand over the fence. He can only just see the top of her head, dark hair illuminated by the moonlight, and her hand, reaching towards his. He grabs it tight. He can feel her bones.

'What can I say except I'm sorry?' she says. 'I'll say it as often as you like. Every day for the rest of my life. Every hour.'

She turns her head back towards the house momentarily, looking up at Paul's window. He can just see her forehead and the tip of her nose, painted a soft dark yellow by the lights of her house.

'What did you mean about your family?'

'Lydia's left.'

'Oh.' Frannie looks at him, her eyes just meeting his over the fence, like two children. 'Oh, Joe.'

'Hopefully we'll work it out,' he says woodenly, though he doesn't mean it.

'Would you do it again?' he asks her after a few minutes more.

'No,' Frannie says immediately. 'Absolutely not. I would give up everything to take it back. Despite who he was. Despite what he did. Because of what *my* crime put *you* guys through.'

'Well,' Joe says, in relief. He has arrived back at where they were: two family members who love each other, both in a situation they wish they weren't in. 'I'm glad about that,' he adds huskily.

Frannie squeezes his hand, then slides away from him.

'I'm glad you're glad about that,' she echoes softly. He reaches over the fence and ruffles her hair, the way he used to do when she was little, just the way he used to do to Rosie too, before they lost her. 'But he was a twat,' Frannie says.

Joe lets out an unexpected laugh in the night.

'Trust me when I say he really, really was,' Frannie says.

'I trust you.'

Frannie moves away from him, up into the blackness of her garden, her dark hair disappearing first, leaving her pale shoulders, her pale legs, until nothing is left of her at all.

66.

Lydia

Lydia is sitting in her car, across the street from the house she shares with Joe, waiting. Deciding whether to go in. Trying to figure out how much having a baby comes into this decision. But Lydia has lines. They're not the same as everybody else's, which are learnt through experiences and good parenting, good guidance. Lydia drew hers with a therapist, with the help of her patient foster families. As a result, Lydia's boundaries are firm, strong because they are artificial.

She assumes he is inside. It's late. He will be sleeping. She considers what to do.

There's a sound as another car arrives. The brakes screech. Lydia stares at it in surprise. The only traffic they usually experience is farm traffic in the early mornings. Lydia likes the rhythm of that. Noisy nature, cockerels and geese. Dairy trucks, tractors, the stench of hay that drifted by before she properly woke.

There is no reason for anybody to arrive now.

Ghosts fill Lydia's mind as she watches. Who arrives outside houses in the middle of the night, apart from heartbroken women? Highwaymen, her brain says. Beggars. Murderers. Convicts. That's who arrives at this hour.

She turns off the interior light in the car and watches as Joe answers the door. She holds her breath. He might surprise her. He might yet rescue this.

But Lydia watches it unfold and she thinks, *Despite everything, I married somebody just like my violent fucking dad.* She stares out of the car windows, and watches her line finally being crossed.

67.

Joe

Joe doesn't quite make it up the stairs to bed before his life changes. He's walking along his hallway when he sees the shadow outside his door.

He flings open the front door, his sister's sad form still in his mind, and comes face to face with Evan. With no warning at all, he feels as vulnerable as a kid whose parents aren't home.

'All right,' Evan says. His stance is strange. Joe scans it for a moment in shock, then realizes: he's drunk. He's trying to balance on his feet. Joe tenses his shoulders, making them look bigger than they are.

'What?' he says coolly. Inside his head, a mantra. This is my house. You are not welcome here. I call the shots. I make the rules.

'Been thinking about this situation we find ourselves in,' Evan slurs. He leans his right arm against the doorframe but lurches in so far that he loses his balance.

'Piss off,' Joe says. 'It's late. You're drunk. I know what you said to my mum.'

Evan shrugs, not saying anything. 'Your mum deserves to know who she's in business with.'

'More threats,' Joe says lightly, trying to take the power back. 'I wouldn't be making threats in your position.'

'What's that, then?' Evan says.

'Let's see: you've blackmailed us. That's one crime. You

have helped us to cover up . . . what we did. So you're an accessory after the fact,' Joe says, thankful for Lydia's knowledge of criminal law. 'And you are totally reliant on us for your income and your partnership capital, which is written on a meaningless piece of paper.'

'Meaningless,' Evan swallows. 'I have to say, I'm surprised you're saying this.' He smiles at Joe, a strange smile, wolfish under the security lights, which cast long shadows under his eyes. He looks like that painting, *The Scream*. Joe stares, trying to appear unfazed, not frightened, but he wants to take as many steps backwards as he can, to run into the house, to phone Lydia and leave, forever. Instead, he bundles Evan out of the door. 'We had a deal,' Evan adds.

'We had a deal on the black market,' Joe says. 'What're you going to do – sue us for the money?' He folds his forearms across his body. Feeling big. Feeling fat. Feeling good. The anger is productive. It feels more like vitality than fury. He begins to walk Evan down his front path, with no idea of where they will go.

'I could call the police right now and tell them that you committed murder,' Evan says calmly, his voice low. It's cold for August, and his breath hangs in the air like balloons of smoke. He brings out a phone and dials slowly, looking at Joe after each digit. '101 to report a crime, is it? One,' he says, keying it in. 'Zero. Shall I call? Test you for your DNA, won't they? Arrest your whole fucking family.'

'Right,' Joe says. He doesn't let himself react.

'Tell them to test the DNA on the body, and then test yours.'

Joe is trying to keep his head. Trying not to overflow. Trying to think straight too. Put one foot in front of the other. 'And if you did that, and we all went to prison, what would you get? How much money?' he says.

Evan stops still, at the edge of the field, and looks at him.

Joe narrows his eyes, appraising Evan's back. 'You don't have an answer,' he says.

'I do.'

'Go on, then. What?'

Without any further hesitation, Evan presses the green *call* button on his phone. As they stand in silence while the phone connects the call, he says, 'Fifty-one per cent of the business.'

Joe reaches out and snatches the phone from his hand, pressing the red button to hang up. 'Now you're talking,' Evan laughs. 'Now some action.' He meets Joe's eyes in the darkness of the countryside. 'What I will do,' he says, 'is call the police now, and you'll be taken away. And when you are, I will produce the signed partnership deed and inherit the business, all of the Plants' stakes having been voided for illegality.'

Joe stares at him. Evan's parents are lawyers. He forgot. And Evan's right. He knows he's right, he remembers the solicitor going through the options for how the partnership would dissolve.

But it isn't only that sentence that does it or how boxed into a corner Joe feels. It is Evan's expression, a beat after he's spoken. Triumphant. Full of testosterone. Somebody who has finally got one over on his boss.

Joe isn't having it.

398

For a second, right as he decides what to do, Joe thinks he sees Evan flinch. Just a slight shiver, the sort a child would make in their sleep. It happens right as they cross the threshold of a field, into the dark wilderness. Joe looks sideways at Evan, the moon right behind his ear, and he wonders what life will look like tomorrow.

PART VII
Murder

68.

Joe

If he will take down Joe's family, then Joe will take down Evan. He balls his hand into a fist, as he has a hundred times before, and connects it completely and squarely with Evan's jaw.

The punch lands with more of a thud than a smack, Joe feeling exquisite with the release of it, the power in his arm having bowled Evan over. He stumbles once, twice, his head lolling back as Joe watches. And then he falls backwards, another thud. And then a crack. His head hits two parts of the stile as he goes down.

Joe stares down in shock. The world seems to still around them.

It is a slow and soupy night, the air close and warm, like the air in an indoor swimming pool. Clammy. The moon he and Frannie looked at earlier is now partly obscured by a bundle of pillowy clouds. The rain that's troubled them all summer has finally gone, like the weather too knows the new phase they're in. He thinks of Frannie's hand gripping his over their fence.

The ground is soft underfoot, muddy tracks made by tractors and farm traffic. He's always loved living here with Lydia, close to his family, and he'll miss it. It was written in the invisible stars, he thinks, looking upwards. From that night in Verona. It was always going to end here.

Joe reaches down for Evan's wrist and holds it listlessly. There's no pulse. His head is bleeding profusely. Sweat rises from some deep, warm part of Joe, and he begins to tremble.

Alone in the field, tears bud in his throat and he finds himself wondering as he cries whether Evan has any siblings.

Joe reaches for his phone, afterwards. Finds the contacts with shaking hands. Finds Cathy. She will know what to do.

'Help me, please help me,' he says into the mouthpiece.

'What?' Cathy has panic in her voice, her usually muted tone immediately harsh, like she's been waiting for this. 'What?' The second word she utters is resigned, a full, disappointed glob of a word like syrup falling off a spoon.

When he's talking to her, he hears the BBC Breaking News alert in his ear. Confused, he pulls away the phone to look. *Body found near British family's second home in search for Verona missing man*, it says.

He looks down at Evan. It was pointless, this silence he bought them.

It was futile.

69.

Now

After First Day of Trial

'As the defendant has previously been granted bail, you're all free to go for now,' the judge says to Joe.

I let myself out of the courtroom and watch Joe leave the dock.

I am a prosecution witness in the trial of my brother. Jason was my defence lawyer, when I was charged with perverting the course of justice for my role in the cover up. But, on the first day of trial, I took a plea bargain in exchange for giving evidence against Joe.

It seems amazing to me that I am functioning, that the news is still on, that the moon is still out, that dinner is made.

I arrive home with Paul and put him to bed, looking at that very moon. The curtains in his makeshift nursery are open, letting in a slice of pale light. Frannie's house, next to mine, stands empty. Lydia is no longer next door, only Joe, though we are not permitted, by law, to speak.

Lydia got pregnant, last year. It's not Joe's, obviously. It is some guy's from work. Lydia moved on determinedly, not looking back, and fair play, I thought.

Paul holds on to his feet, the way he did when he was tiny, and stares at me. I wonder if he misses Frannie, and if he misses her in the same way I miss her. That visceral feeling that I want her arms around my neck, her chest close to mine. I guess, looking down at him, that he does.

The trial will race back towards me tomorrow. I'll be back there, in the box, speaking, answering questions. Paul will be at nursery, with no idea of what's at stake.

'Which book?' I say, staring down at him. I pick him up from the cot bed, not yet ready to part with him, and hold him close to me. He isn't Frannie, but he is part of her. The next best thing.

'*Gruffalo*,' he says. He brings the bottom of his jaw forward and his eyes catch the moonlight, and for a second he looks so like Joe that I clutch at my stomach, holding him even closer to me than before.

'Okay,' I say, plucking it off his miniature bookshelf and sitting in the dining chair I've brought up here. It has no cushion on it, isn't a long-term solution, but we do the best with what we've got.

'Mummy,' he says, rolling deliberately from his back on to his side in my arms.

'No,' I say, pointing to my face in the twilight. 'Auntie Cathy.'

'Auntie Cathy.'

'That's right.'

'Mummy?' he says.

'We'll see her soon,' I tell him, looking down into my sister's eyes. 'I promise, Paulie. I promise.'

'And we'll see the dinosaurs too,' Paul says, dinosaurs and his mother both of equal importance to him. I look away with wet eyes, wait for the tears to clear, then look back at him.

'Sure,' I lie.

70.

Then

Cathy

'I may be mad, but I thought – I wondered if we could have a coffee,' Tom says, even though it's late. 'And a chat.' He's standing in Cathy's living room, still in his coat. Cathy's entire body is light with relief. She knows this is not a goodbye coffee. She knows in the deep, wise part of herself that's only recently woken up. The part attuned to the way his eyes linger on hers, the way he stands self-consciously on one foot, the other toe-down to the ground.

'I can do coffee,' Cathy says. She touches his arm as she walks past him to boil the kettle. He follows her, watching as she gets out mugs and milk. He reaches over her to pour in the milk, while Cathy's inside sings with happiness. She hasn't lost it. She hasn't yet lost him.

Her mobile is ringing in the living room where she's left it. She almost doesn't pick up when she realizes it's Joe. Tom raises his eyebrows, but says nothing, so she answers.

'Help me, please help me,' Joe says into the phone.

As her gaze meets Tom's, his eyes darken just slightly. She closes her eyes and concentrates on her brother's panicked and tinny voice.

'What?' she says to him. She turns away from Tom, just for a second. 'What?'

'Please help,' Joe says. 'Please come – I'm in the big field to the left.'

Cathy knows it. It's where she and Tom walked on that funny third date of theirs. Completely secluded, with a single track weaving its way through the long grass. 'Why?' she says.

Tom comes in front of her, gesturing for the phone, but she nods, letting him know she's okay. His hand comes to her waist, instead, and rests there, a warm, supportive palm against the fabric of her t-shirt. She stares at the floorboards, trying to make sense of Joe's panic. For a second, as she looks at a particular whorl of wood that she's never noticed before, she is certain that Joe has killed Frannie. An eerie calm descends around her. A silence, like the room has hushed. All she has now is Tom's warm hand and that whorled floorboard.

'What've you done?' she says softly.

'I've killed someone,' Joe says hoarsely.

'Who?'

The whorl. The hand. The question that hangs in the air. 'Evan.'

Perversely, Cathy's entire body sags in relief. Tom's hand is all that is holding her together.

'He wanted more money.' She hears Joe gulp down the phone. 'I didn't want to do it.'

A thousand childhood memories walk into the living room with her. When he got a B in A-level biology and had to wait to hear if he had been allowed to take a degree in veterinary medicine. The way he carried Rosie's coffin. He carries it all, the eldest sibling.

'What?' she whispers in part sympathy and part horror; the potent familial mix they find themselves faced with.

'Please come. I'll come to you,' Joe garbles. 'Meet me in the outhouse.'

Cathy meets Tom's brown eyes. His hand is still on her waist, the other still extended in an open gesture for her phone. 'I can't,' she says. 'I can't – Joe.'

'What?'

'This has gone too far.'

'No, Cath. I didn't mean to do it. He – he fell.'

'How did you do it?'

'A punch,' Joe says. He swallows again. Cathy hears his Adam's apple moving up and down in his throat, a dry, dragging sound.

'Joe – I can't, I . . .'

Cathy wordlessly passes the phone to Tom, who hangs it up. He puts it on the table and stands there, his hands on his hips.

'I think I'm going to be sick,' Cathy says. 'I can't . . . he's fucking killed someone.'

The shade is back over Tom's eyes. He avoids contact with her for a second, sighs and sits down on her sofa. Cathy joins him.

'Look, I don't want to tell you what to do,' Tom says, a hand on her bare knee, his eyes on her phone.

Cathy puts her head in her hands and rakes her hair back from her face. 'What do I do?' she says. 'Tell me what to do, Tom.'

He says nothing, his hand not moving from her knee.

'I just want to go upstairs and get into bed and not wake up again.'

Tom laughs, a small, sad laugh. 'Sounds good,' he says.

He can't stop his eyes darting to her phone. The vessel through which they heard the news that changed their lives forever. Again.

'What would you do?' His body is completely still, and Cathy is grateful for his calm, her port in this storm.

He glances at the phone again, and that's when Cathy understands what he's saying.

'You think I should hand him in.'

'He's killed somebody,' Tom says, sitting back and making an expansive gesture with the wingspan of his arms. Her knee is cold where his hand used to be. 'This is . . . you've got to do the right thing.'

'For who?'

'For you,' he says simply. 'And for him. Everyone has a limit.'

He hands her the phone, and, this time, she takes it. 'I need to tell him first,' she says, taking the phone but pausing. 'I need to tell my brother that I'm ending this.'

Tom is waiting for her when she gets back from the outhouse, an exchange she is not ready to think about, not yet ready to dwell on.

He raises his eyes to her, and she dials.

The heat from outside is still on her skin as she makes the call. She speaks to a calm 999 operator, tells them what she knows, tells them the address and then she hangs up, just like that. This must be shock, she is thinking. Everything looks the same. Her sofa. Her boyfriend. She is suddenly tired, wanting to lay her head in his lap and fall asleep.

She shifts against him, moving her body underneath his arm, which clamps around her, like they're out to sea and he's rescuing her. She stays like that, half sitting, half lying, for several minutes.

There's a noise outside. She flinches immediately against Tom, as though her body knows before her mind does that it's all over. The living room takes on a strange tone. It's lit up blue. Sirens. They're coming. They're here.

'Will they be lenient with me?' she asks Tom, who puts his hand on her shoulder. She leans her cheek down on it. It could have been really good, being with him, she thinks. It could have been perfect.

She blinks at him. The sirens are loud now, surely on her street, the living room a blaze of blue and white, flashing on and off, on and off.

She steps away from him.

He leads her into the hallway and reaches for the door handle for her. The sirens are so loud. 'You've done the right thing,' he says, but, already, the noise of the sirens is filling the house. Police cars and ambulances.

'It's not – it's not – I'm sorry.'

The sirens strobe in the night.

Tom draws his mouth together in a tight line. And then his eyes meet hers. Sad eyes, like he knows something, can see something that she can't, that she doesn't understand. He raises his shoulders, just a fraction of a centimetre. If a stranger did it, she wouldn't know what it meant, but she knows him, her Tom. The half-smile, the shoulders. A sad parting of ways.

She turns off the light in the hallway and stands there for a few seconds, her house bathed in police-blue, like an aquarium.

'Stand down,' she hears a tinny voice say outside. Cathy

411

feels nothing. Not guilt at the betrayal of her family, not fear of her imminent arrest for her role in everything, not regret for everything that happened in Verona, and afterwards. Cathy feels nothing. Absolutely nothing.

'Show yourself,' the police say, and Cathy knows she should cooperate, but then she thinks of everything that's happened since Verona, every desperate action, every lie, and she thinks that all is lost except this moment, with Tom still in her kitchen, for only a few minutes more. So, instead, Cathy watches them creep further and further towards her, like a slow, incoming tide that will eventually reach her and drown her but not quite yet. Not quite yet. She reaches for him. They still have a minute together. Maybe two.

71.

Cathy

Cathy isn't handcuffed. Nobody pushes her head down into the back of the police car. Instead, she is read the caution, and then ignored, driven to Perry Barr Police Station, somewhere she has heard of but not ever been to, until now.

A separate police car came for Joe. An ambulance for Evan, though it was obviously futile. Cathy will never forget the sight of Joe, bloodied and mad, his eyes bright and feverish, in the outhouse as he pleaded with her.

The police car smells of synthetic-apple air fresheners and sweat. She is in the back. It's overheated, the fabric of the seats soft and yielding, old foam that feels like it might never let her get out. It reminds her of car journeys taken with her family when she was younger and would almost always be sick. Frannie insisted on eating pick 'n' mix in the back, even though the smell made Cathy worse. Joe always got the front seat. He was the eldest, he said, and those were the rules. Cathy leans her head against the window and closes her eyes to everything.

At the police station, Cathy is taken to an interview room. The calm that descended in her living room has stayed with her. She wonders if a jury might be lenient. Who will represent her. What their parents will think.

A police officer confirms in a monotone that Evan is dead.

Cathy stares at the wall for a while, waiting, with the artificial awake-ness that shift workers and people in crises carry with them. Two late-night phone calls in one single summer. Two bodies. Two sleepless nights. If they were here, in different circumstances, she'd make the joke they have about their father. 'Joseph, Catherine, Francesca, whoever you are!' She wouldn't even have to finish it before they'd laugh. Her siblings, the people they once were.

'The wait is because we're assigning you a duty solicitor,' a different police officer says to Cathy at eleven o'clock.

Cathy's eyes are gritty and she rubs at them. Make-up comes away and she wonders what she must look like. A criminal? She thinks of the animals at the practice and hopes somebody is looking after them. She wonders where Joe and Frannie are. If her parents have been informed. What Tom's doing. She is sequestered from it, here, from the information and the questions. A small self-contained room away from it all.

She stares at the wall before answering. It's painted white, in cheap paint that's bubbled like there's grit underneath it.

Suddenly, here in the white room, she understands why she's calm. The worst has happened. There is now a way out, even though she has had to detonate a bomb to expose the exit route from her family. She takes a breath. It's over. The guilt and the panic and the waiting are over.

'I have a criminal lawyer's details in my phone,' she says. 'Can I call him? He's called Jason.'

*

414

Cathy meets Jason in a meeting room an hour later. He has mismatched socks on, that's the first thing she notices. He is somehow shabby-looking, but she can't say why she thinks a lawyer shouldn't have a partially grey shaggy beard, or not be carrying a take-out Costa coffee that's dribbled down the side.

'I'm Jason,' he says to her, and sits opposite her, crossing his legs at the thigh.

'You're probably wondering how I got your details,' she says.

'Not really,' he says with a quick smile. 'Don't worry. Right. Let's start from the beginning.' He sips at his coffee. It is sweet-smelling, some sort of syrup in it.

He looks down at his papers, shuffling them, then gets out a brand-new blue pad and a posh fountain pen, which Cathy likes, and writes the date along the top. He gets it right: it's tomorrow. Just after midnight. It's a good sign. He's smart.

'So,' he says, looking at her again. 'Why don't you start from the beginning?'

'The beginning is so far back,' she says.

He makes a shrugging gesture, like, well, start there. 'We've got all night,' he says with a small laugh.

'It started in Verona,' she says.

'Ah,' Jason says. 'The body that was just found.'

Joe told Cathy in the outhouse. 'Right. How did they find it?'

'I don't know. I'll find out,' he says. 'Tell me the rest.' He reaches behind him and closes the door. 'Tell me everything. Go.'

72.

Now

Second Day of Trial R. v. Plant

'And that night in late August – you heard from your brother, Joe, is that correct?'

I nod, then say *yes*, in the witness box. I look directly at my brother, at the tufty grey hairs at his temples. 'Yes,' I repeat. For the first time, his eyes meet mine.

'And what did he say?'

'He said he'd killed Evan. And that he needed help.'

'Thank you,' the barrister says to me. 'Thank you, Catherine, for your witness evidence, which has been invaluable.' He looks towards the public gallery, where my family stand. And to the dock, where my brother stands, solo and handcuffed, at his murder trial.

'We will continue to hear evidence in the trial of the Crown against Joseph Plant,' the judge says. 'On the charges of' – he checks a sheet – 'preventing the lawful burial of a body. Criminal damage. Perverting the course of justice. Conspiracy to bribe. Misappropriation of corporate assets.' The charges go on and on. He finishes reading them, his face completely expressionless. This must be so mundane to him. Cathy blinks.

'Will there be any re-examination?' my barrister asks the other barrister.

'No,' he says. 'No need, I think. Thank you, Ms Plant. Hopefully justice can now be done.'

'They won't need me back?' I say on the courthouse steps to Jason, freezing in my nude tights and skirt suit. I was given a suspended sentence for my role in the crime, in exchange for giving evidence against Joe. He loosens his tie and stares down at me.

'They shouldn't,' he says. 'It'll be a few weeks, for the other witnesses. Then however long the jury deliberate for. There are a lot of charges.' He lights up a cigarette, seemingly in no hurry to escape the bleak March cold. I draw my coat around myself and look at the lit-up tip, a layered rosebud set on fire, remembering how much Joe smoked in Verona. 'So you're free to go, I'd say. What're you going to do?'

'Go and see Frannie,' I say, gesturing vaguely in the direction of the town centre.

Jason nods, inhaling on the cigarette, and breathing smoke out into the blank sky, creating his own dense clouds of winter.

'Well,' I say, unsure how to end it, but something about Jason's body language stops my sentence right there.

'Do you think I don't know?' he says, dragging on the cigarette, his face at an angle, but not breaking eye contact with me, not for a second.

'Know what?' I say, though I feel my cheeks heat up in the bone-cold winter air.

'Let's not pretend,' Jason says. He taps ash off the end, which disperses on the breeze like a dandelion clock. I step out of the way, feeling panicked, feeling exposed.

'Is it safe with you?'

'Your secret? Always,' Jason says. He reaches out to hold my shoulder. 'I would have done the same thing as you,' he says, before leaving. He rounds the angular corner of the Crown Court, his body disappearing, leaving a trail of smoke which hangs suspended in the air for a few seconds, then disappears too.

73.

Then

Cathy

'I guess I'm here to report a crime,' Cathy says carefully in the quiet room with this man, Jason, whom she barely knows.

'Okay.'

She thinks of Joe's eyes in the dark of the outhouse, his hands and face covered in Evan's blood. She thinks of Frannie arriving, also responding to Joe's call, and of her tears as he too became a murderer, both just normal people two months before, the transformation complete. She thinks of the pact they made.

'They've found the body,' Joe said, a bloodied hand on Cathy's arm, those alien eyes on hers. 'You need to say it was all me.'

'What?' she'd said, looking at the house containing Tom, not wanting to lose him, not wanting him to leave, even though she knew he wouldn't.

'Say it was me,' he said again. He glanced at Frannie, who seemed to know exactly what he was saying. 'I've fucked it,' he added. 'I've fucked it with Evan. There's no way out, so you should say it was me.'

'It was you,' Cathy said softly.

'Tell them everything.' He stood behind Frannie, his hands on her angular shoulders. 'Say it was me who killed Evan, and say it was me who killed Will. I did it all. Everything we did, I did. Say I confessed it all to you, right here.

I'll back up your story. Confess to perverting the course of justice when you covered for me. That'll explain your DNA on the body. But tell them the rest was me. Eventually – and it might be as late as the day of the trial – they'll offer you a plea in return for evidence against me. Hold out for it. Hold your nerve. Then take it. And then try to make your evidence reduce my crimes from murder to manslaughter.'

'No,' Frannie said, her voice hoarse from crying, her eyes wet. Cathy stares at Joe. He's nothing if not smart.

'We can't all lose everything,' Joe said. 'It doesn't make sense for us to. Let me go down for it.'

'You'll never come out.' Frannie turned towards him, buried her head in Joe's chest. 'You can't. You'll get fifty years. I can't do – I can't do fifty years without you.'

He shrugged against her, looking down at her, then across at Cathy. 'I love you,' he said simply to Frannie, his voice fractured and broken. 'I love you.'

'What's the crime?' Jason says now.

'My brother, Joe,' Cathy says. 'I think he killed somebody on our holiday.'

74.

Now

One Hundredth Meeting with Frannie

It's visiting hours at the hospital. My body is scanned, frisked, signed in. I have to confirm I have nothing dangerous with me. Sellotape. Pens. Knives. Drugs.

It smells of the specific smell that I know to be where my sister currently calls home. Vegetable soup. Sweat. Old clothes. Human stuff. Mundane stuff.

Frannie is waiting for me in her room. She's sitting up on the bed in a patch of bright winter sunlight, reading a novel. She's taken to reading at least two a week, something I've never really known her do in adulthood.

She has gained three stone in weight and been treated for major depressive disorder, triggered – though nobody really knows the full story – by the events in Verona. She is now almost ready for release from the institution we paid to get her into, and speaks with a wisdom, sometimes, that unlocks something for me often in the car on the way home.

'How's Paul?' she says as soon as I enter the room.

'Good – he's good. He's finger-painting at nursery,' I say. And then I add: 'It's done.'

Frannie knows exactly what I mean. There may be triple locks on the double doors, but my sister is still – gloriously so – my sister, in here. It is not as I thought it would be. There is no heavy, sombre feeling. There is no shame or madness. Only people who have been dealt hard hands by life, by their mental health, by their brains, and sympathetic nurses trained to ease the wounds in their psyches. It is a more comforting place than most, because this is recognized and accepted and treated, not hidden away as it is elsewhere.

'Did you look for my post?' she says.

'Yes, only an ASOS catalogue.'

Frannie smiles a half-smile. 'Did you bring it?' she says hopefully.

I toss it out of my handbag at her, and she places it very deliberately and squarely on her bedside table, like she is looking forward to it, this small treat for later. That very small and optimistic action makes something happy move around my heart and down my arms.

She's aged in hospital. I notice it now that I no longer see her every day. She looks like a woman approaching her mid thirties. Forehead lines. Rounded brackets stretching either side of her nose to her mouth, despite the weight gain. Frannie has sacrificed her beauty to what happened in Verona.

'Are you pleased you did it?' she says, squinting as she looks up at me, folding out the novel spine like a butterfly across the cover of her bed.

The topic of the crime is still a tight, knotty ball that sits between both of us. 'Yes,' I say, looking at her. 'It's what he wanted.'

'So he says.'

She stands and makes us two cups of tea. At the boiling of the kettle, the nurse outside her room turns his head just slightly, which seems to irritate Frannie.

She hands me the tea in a hot plastic cup with a quick,

embarrassed smile. 'It'll probably bloody taste of melted plastic,' she says.

'Don't worry.'

'Do you think your testimony helped?' she asks.

Because that's what I was doing. I was helping, so Joe's trial went ahead without Frannie under suspicion, like he wanted, but I was also trying to mitigate it. To explain why he did what he did. To tell the court he was of good character otherwise. We were trying to walk the line between the police believing Joe enough not to investigate but also to get them to treat him leniently. That was why it was so worrying that our statements didn't quite match: we'd had only those few minutes in the outhouse to cook them up. Still, I hope I've done enough.

Frannie, who wasn't charged for her role in burying the body because of her mental health, sits down, cradling her tea, and meets my eyes. The essence of Frannie still sits behind them. Sunny Frannie. She never lost that, in her depression. It was just masked for a while.

After Joe was taken in, and after I told the police the first handful of lies, Frannie didn't come out of her cottage for nine days after her interview. She lost more weight. Wouldn't answer her phone, not even to Joe on his daily call. Our parents thought she was sad for Joe. I knew exactly what the problem was, but couldn't solve it, and sat there most evenings of that strange, surreal week worrying for Paul.

Things escalated pretty quickly after that. A mental-health professional assessed her, asked if I would have Paul for a night, which, in the way of things that feel so disturbing they must be temporary, eventually became hundreds of nights.

'So-so,' I say. 'I just told everyone what happened really. The judge went through the crimes at the end.'

'Do you think he'll get them down to manslaughter? Do you think you helped?'

'Maybe.'

'What does Jason say?'

'Nothing. He's such a lawyer,' I say, which is unfair, really. Though unconventional, Jason still refuses to speculate, still won't cross certain lines.

'He's a hot lawyer,' Frannie says, which almost makes me spit out my tea.

'We'll have to see what happens,' I say. 'The jury seem fair.'

I reach for Frannie's hands across the bed. Somehow, she's made this sterile, medicalized room smell like her. Her laundry, her perfume. She lets me touch her. Her nurse outside the door watches carefully. He's standing on the royal-blue linoleum which we can see through the hatch-like window in her door. It looks like a lake. Frannie ignores him, but her body language changes.

'Joe was in the wrong too, you know,' I say lightly to her. Just trying to ease open the door to the conversation we need to have. We have circled it for so long. It's been surprisingly easy to do so, to repress it. To make small talk, to bring Paul to see her, bearing the cookies he's baked, to chat about the weather, the news, work.

Frannie freezes. She has gained weight in the fast, unnatural way of people recovering from something. There is fat in her cheeks and on her arms, but she looks uncomfortable with it, somehow, like an overfed baby. Her skin is pale. She doesn't exactly look healthy, not yet. But she's getting there.

She gets up from the bed and opens the window. I've been surprised by the freedoms she has, here in the hospital, under watch. It's not as you would imagine. Frannie washes her own clothes, has visitors, open windows, gets take-out McDonald's delivered. Browses ASOS catalogues. She isn't restrained or overly medicated. She is just my sister, as she's always been, closing her eyes against the open window, against the fresh spring breeze.

'He murdered somebody,' Frannie says, her eyes wet and wide as she turns to me. 'As did I.'

Wood smoke drifts in on the breeze. The room quickly cools, but Frannie leaves the window open, coming to sit on the bed. 'Do you know how it was?' she asks me.

'No.'

'It was like being put into somebody else's body.'

'Your illness?' I say. Blood rushes to my cheeks, not sure I'm ready for this conversation, not sure I can get it right, that I can listen and understand her, but not betray myself either.

I've been seeing a therapist called Stuart, who has been unpacking with me what happened with Rosie, and beyond. I've been experimenting with him. Working less. Observing that nothing catastrophic happens. Opening up more. Doing more things. Fun things. Letting the fuck go. We all have our own mental-health demons, I think, looking across the bed at my sister. Tonight, I am going to fight mine by determinedly having fun and observing that nothing bad happens. By telling somebody, anybody, how I really feel.

'Imagine if suddenly, everything you liked to do, you don't enjoy any more. You don't want to eat. Your body aches you're so tired,' Frannie says tentatively. 'That is what it's like.'

'I know,' I say quietly.

'Everything was grey. It's frightening and bewildering. You're snappy. You feel uncomfortable in your body. There is a constant pressing sadness.' She pushes a hand into her stomach. New rolls of fat protrude around it. 'Right here – you can't ignore it. Your whole mind feels like a wound. You could cry at anything. The stupidest stuff. I kept reliving what happened with Will – when I lost my temper in a way no human should.'

'Frannie,' I say, my eyes filling with tears. 'I'm so sorry you went through that.'

'You're thinking that if the guilt was that bad, I should have just said it was me, right? Joe says he was responsible for Evan, and me for Will. Carina called the police, said she was worried by how much Joe was calling. It was almost easy, how guilty he'd made himself look.'

'I . . .' I hesitate. It has crossed my mind. Joe slickly glossed over it. *Why would two people go down when one could?* he says simply. But Frannie has kept her counsel on that particular issue, right up to now.

'The truth is that I'm only just opening the windows,' Frannie says. She looks at Cathy, a small smile of disbelief on her face. 'You know? I had to deal with one trauma before the other.'

I nod. The windows are the perfect metaphor. 'I know.'

We sit in silence for a few seconds, sipping the too-hot tea, not quite sure where to go next.

'I wonder . . . I don't know. I think what happened with Rosie made us, me and Joe . . . I don't know.'

Frannie is nodding quickly. 'Yeah,' she says. 'I know. I've had enough therapy to know.'

Something lifts in my heart, even within the tragedy. A kind of space, enough to let in the light. We don't need to go over it. The past, our actions. We don't need to validate the others' pain. It hangs unsaid, in the air between us, where it needs to be.

'To call your siblings when you've fucked up,' Frannie says. 'I don't know. That's kind of childish. Isn't it? To want your family to bail you out. And I was still the baby. Still a kid.'

'You were the baby of the family because we liked you that way,' I say. 'Loved you that way,' I add softly. 'We needed a baby of the family, because we lost one. We needed you. We babied you.'

'Yeah. But I'm not Rosie.' Frannie's voice is warm, her eyes crinkled. 'You have to sometimes move on. You know? Into adulthood. Away from the flowerpot you grew up in together.'

'I know,' I say. Maybe we won't live in the same row of houses together. Maybe we won't work together. Family's complicated, isn't it? I go to ask for her view, for Joe's view, on my part in Rosie's death, and if it contributed to my slight distance from them, but then stop myself. I don't need to. What I believe is what matters. And I believe it wasn't my fault. That, even if it were, I've got to stop paying for it, or we'll all lose another life too.

'And thanks,' Frannie adds softly to me. 'I owe you and Joe . . .' She touches a hand to her chest. Her breasts are ample and full again, womanly. 'Everything.'

'It was nothing,' I whisper.

427

I scoot closer to Frannie on the bed and hold her to me, my head resting on top of hers. I feel my chest become damp with her tears, thankful tears, regretful tears. Tears of relief too maybe.

'We love you,' I say to her, right in her ear. She nods quickly against my ribs.

'I know you think I should do the right thing,' she says. I say nothing in reply; I don't. 'But I just can't leave Paul. I just – I know what the right thing to do is but I just . . . I can't bring myself to do it.' She shrugs, the motion a heavier movement than it used to be. 'It's so easy to say you would do the right thing,' she says, rubbing at her nose. She puts down her tea on the bed, where it wobbles precariously.

I think of those emails from Will, aggressive emails, scary emails, and of Frannie's position as a single mother, and everything that's happened since. Joe's stoicism in the dock at his trial. Frannie's weight loss, and then weight gain. The way she seemed to deliberate, sometimes, before doing things, as though they required the effort of a marathon. The way the waterline underneath her eyes was red for a year. She lost Paul temporarily in her depression, but that doesn't mean she deserves to lose him permanently. What is justice, anyway, if not suffering?

I reach across the bed and grasp Frannie's hand. It's warm, where it used to be cold, even with the window open letting in the spring breeze and the sun, a sharp-and-sweet combination. Frannie grabs the throw from the end of her bed and scoots closer to me, wrapping us both up in it.

'I think it's time to move forwards,' I say. 'Don't you?'

Frannie smiles at me, a wobbling smile that only partly

resembles her old, unhindered grin, and grasps tightly at my hand. 'Let's,' she says.

I squeeze her warm hands, inside the blankets. Together, our grips are encased within the kind of forts we used to make when we were little.

Tom is waiting for me in his house.

'How was it?' he says to me, opening his front door wide. He's wearing a cream-coloured woollen jumper and holding a cup of half-drunk coffee. His feet are bare. 'Made you a pot and then drank almost all of it myself,' he says with a smile.

'It was okay,' I say. 'I saw Frannie too, after.'

'Tough day,' he says softly.

My nose must be red from crying in the car, thinking of Frannie tucked up under that blanket. Her nurse said on the way out that she will be strong enough for release soon. That Paul will begin to spend overnights with her shortly after that.

'Yeah,' I say, looking into his brown eyes and thinking that I never would have done it if it weren't for him. Who knows where they would have ended up. A worse place, surely.

'What now?' I say to Tom. 'Now that it's over?'

'Whatever you want,' he says. 'Whatever you want.'

'All rise,' a clerk says. The jury and the judge file in. I watch from the public gallery, only a few feet but several hundred light years away from my mother and father. They say they don't understand why I have testified against Joe, but I hope one day they will. Maybe one day we can tell them the real story. When they're ready.

When everybody is settled, the judge addresses the jury. 'Have you reached a verdict on all charges upon which you are all agreed?'

'Yes,' the foreman says. He is exactly as you might imagine a foreman. In a jacket and shirt, where everybody else is tired and casual. Glasses. I wouldn't be surprised to spot a briefcase at his feet.

'And have you reached that verdict unanimously?'

'Yes.'

I stare as we wait.

They recite all the counts. Murder. Preventing the lawful burial of a body. Criminal damage. Perverting the course of justice. Conspiracy to bribe. Misappropriation of corporate assets. Fraud. Murder again.

'On count one: murder. How do you find the defendant, guilty or not guilty?'

'Not guilty.'

Joe's head drops.

He is found guilty of preventing the lawful burial of a body, criminal damage, of perverting the course of justice, of bribery and the fraud charges. He is found not guilty of the second murder charge.

They are instead replaced with reckless driving and manslaughter by reason of loss of control.

'A family man,' the judge says. 'You were driven to the edge of sanity by trying to cover up your first crime. What you did was unforgivable, hostile and violent, but it wasn't murder.'

The judge doesn't know it, but he is speaking exactly the truth.

Joe's shoulders have dropped. He's looking directly up at me.

I see my older brother, in all of his guises. The first flash of that temper I saw when he was eleven and somebody fouled him on the football pitch. What a good, incisive vet he was, logically making his way down differential diagnoses, trying *a*, trying *b*, trying *c*, noticing things other people didn't notice. That dog was licking its lips. That cat was holding its head tilted slightly to the right. Always calm in the veterinary theatre. We have had to pretend to be estranged. So that everybody would believe my evidence. The evidence that brought his charges down.

'Please remain standing for sentencing,' the judge says to Joe. I stand. I can't bear to watch. I walk out of the public gallery, shuffling past my parents. I open the door to the foyer and let it close softly shut behind me.

Epilogue

It's summer again. Cathy is in Birmingham city centre, sitting on a blanket that Tom thoughtfully brought along with him. They're in St Philip's Square. He's brought strawberries and wine; she's brought six doughnuts. 'A mixed picnic,' Tom says with a laugh. 'But a good one.'

He takes a strawberry and holds it up to the light. His hair has grown in in the past few weeks. He's forgotten to shave it, and his head is covered in a kind of babyish fuzz which Cathy finds adorable.

He deheads the strawberry and pushes it into her mouth. Cathy feels the rough texture of the seeds, the sweet bite as the flesh resists, then yields beneath her teeth.

She lies back, her head in his lap, sunglasses on, an arm across her forehead to stop her burning across her hairline. 'Good day?' she says dozily to him.

'Sure,' Tom says easily, lying back against her. A blade of grass tickles her ear. Clouds pass above them as they lie there, relaxed in the hazy summer sun, not speaking, not needing to.

After a while, she rolls on to her stomach and looks at him. 'I miss Paul,' she says.

'Me too.' The sun passes behind the cloud, just for a second, reminding Cathy she's here, in England, not there, where the sun blazed, baking the body they buried. 'He'll be here in a bit,' Tom says. His words convey misunderstanding, but his eyes don't.

'I miss living with Paul,' she says explicitly. 'With a kid.' She thinks of the dinosaur mural she painted across the wardrobes in her spare room that she's left there. Of how Paul rushed up the stairs to see it every time he visited. How she hopes it will never be painted over.

'I know.' Tom sits up and eats a strawberry, evidently thinking. Soon, he will come to a decision in that slow, careful way of his.

'There they are,' Cathy says. Frannie is in the distance, hair piled on her head, sunglasses over her eyes, Paul's hand in hers. He's over half her height now, a child more than a baby, and Cathy's heart rolls over as he comes into view.

'Oh no, we've got double strawberries,' Frannie says when she reaches them. She gives Cathy a hug.

'You can never have too many strawberries,' Cathy says, gesturing to the pile. 'We have doughnuts too.'

'Good.' Frannie takes one out of the packet and halves it to share with Paul.

She sits down on the blanket, cross-legged, her maxi dress spreading taut across her leg. Paul keeps his hand in hers. He now has knuckles instead of dimples. 'Cheers,' she says, raising a glass. 'I saw Lydia, just then,' she adds conversationally.

'Did you – where?'

Frannie licks the sugar off her lips and jerks her thumb behind her. 'Down there. With her baby.'

'The father is some guy she worked with,' Cathy says.

Frannie chews while thinking, swallows, then says nothing for another minute more. 'I mean –' she says.

'I know,' Cathy says. Tom frowns, not following, but he wouldn't be able to. Frannie, Cathy and Joe have always been able to communicate in this way.

Frannie's and Cathy's eyes meet. Lydia wasn't Joe's family. Not really. Not in this way, this primal way where love is unconditional. Where crimes are forgiven and covered up for each other, no questions asked. You can't invent that. You can't manufacture it. It just is.

They go back to Frannie's cottage after their picnic.

The evening has turned dank, even though it's the height of summer. The sky is pale and gloomy. The sunset will turn it white to grey to black, no colour to it. It's strange for Cathy to be back at the cottage. Joe's was sold recently, and hers too. She lives with Tom now, works at a different practice. The space is nice. The space to be herself, to forget, to move on, to let her sister and brother be each other's favourites if they want to. It's a shame their parents thought Cathy betrayed Joe, but she finds she has a new freedom without them.

Cathy goes to Frannie's fridge while she and Tom sit at her large table, where a thousand things went wrong before. She watches them for a moment, the garden a blaze of flowers behind them. You'd never know.

She gets out a bottle of wine and some sparkling water and mixes spritzers.

As she's making them, listening to the chit-chat of Frannie and Tom, to Paul's constant dinosaur commentary,

434

she sees something poking out from underneath a bottle of merlot.

It's a calendar, the kind you get for Christmas, notecards in a stack that you rip off. It's ripped to today's date, 21 June. Each day is neatly crossed off with red pen. At the end of the month, on the 30th, in Frannie's handwriting, something is written: 6,112 days left. Cathy does the maths quickly and easily. It's the remaining time on Joe's sentence. She flicks to July: 6,081 at the end of that month.

She stares at it, tears filling her eyes. At this evidence, here, of her sister's longing, her sister's guilt, her sister's love. Life will resume, for Frannie, when he's out.

She reaches for the pen that's lying nearby and crosses off today, for Joe, for her sister, for her family.

It's not so long. They can wait.

Acknowledgements

I am unable to stick to a brief, and so, before I write out my acknowledgements, I want to tell a small story.

It was a cloudy, close day in July 2020. I was standing outside the vets' (there is a reason this book is about a vets' and that is probably because it is one of the few places I have been to in 2020!). My retriever, Wendy, had jumped into a pond and taken a few gulps of what I now knew to be poisonous blue-green algae. I was waiting – outside, as per pandemic life – to be told if she would recover, and waiting to see how my book *How to Disappear* had sold. To be honest, I am not ashamed to say that both were of equal importance to me. That is the writer's life: you care so very much.

I kid you not, both pieces of news came at the same time. The vet poked her head around the door and said, 'She's going to be fine!' just as I got the email to say *How to Disappear* had sold 9,000 paperbacks in its first week on sale and was at No. 8 in the UK charts, despite bookshops having only just reopened, despite the pandemic, despite, despite, despite.

I looked up at the white sky, phone in my hand, dog lead in the other, and thought I was so happy I might burst. And so first of all to you, my loyal readers, thank you for buying *How to Disappear* in your many thousands; thank you for making that hard day turn great.

This novel was written in the strangest of circumstances,

set before a pandemic, in one of the worst-hit regions of Italy. I hope you will forgive me for omitting the unpleasant reality in which we currently live, in hope of better times in the future, when we look back on coronavirus and say, 'Thank God that's over.'

First, thanks to my agents Felicity Blunt and Lucy Morris, who pushed and pushed this idea into the structure it is today, and for all their hard work on foreign, film and TV rights, and the astute way they guide my career. It is a privilege to work with two absolute experts.

Secondly to the team at Michael Joseph, especially Maxine Hitchcock, Rebecca Hilsdon, Jen Porter, Olivia Thomas, Donna Poppy, sales and marketing. I say this every time, but I can now say that all five of my books have been bestsellers, and there is hardly a day goes by when I don't think about how lucky I am to call this thing I have done forever my job.

Thanks so much to Becky Hartley for the tour of the vets', plus reading this draft for inconsistencies, fielding countless questions (both about my dog and my book!), meeting up specifically to discuss 'what pets vets have' and 'things only vets notice'. Thanks too to Imran Mahmood for his kind and swift views on courtroom procedure – as a former lawyer, I feel the need to say any errors are mine (and, of course, deliberate. And, indeed, of course no lawyer would accept disclosure less than two weeks before trial, and no practising defence lawyer would agree to piecemeal weekly meetings, but Jason is no ordinary lawyer . . .).

Thanks so much, too, to Luigi Bruno, lawyer of the court of Novara, and to Marcella Compagnoni for describing Italian police procedure, and describing trees and smells and coffee for me, too, in lieu of being able to visit myself (all errors, again, my own!).

Thanks too to my father for reading an early draft of this and feeding back (and for the ingenious suggestion that Joe crash the car to cover up the damage!).

Writing primarily in isolation means I have far fewer experts to thank. Usually, my writing year is peppered with interesting chats, visits to cool places, research trips (oh, to go to Verona . . .). Instead, this is the year I have been most thankful for my friends. Writing is a naturally isolated job anyway, but my friends make it less so. Thanks for the banter, understanding, deep-voice notes, water-cooler gossip and love: Holly Seddon, Lucy Blackburn, Lia Louis, Claire Douglas, Ewa Hiles, The Wades, Becky Hartley and Beth O'Leary. I am my full self with you guys and that is a complete privilege.

Finally, as always, thanks to David. You are Jack in *Everything but the Truth*, you are Reuben in *Anything You Do Say*, you are Marc and Scott in *No Further Questions*, you are Aidan in *How to Disappear* and you are Tom in *That Night*. You are all the heroes.

(He is also Kelly, the male protagonist in my novel that I am writing as we speak, coming 2022. If you did want to preorder that, dear reader, I wouldn't say no.)

Prologue

Jen is glad of the clocks going back tonight. A gained hour, extra time, to be spent doing the ironing she should have done earlier. Jen hates the ironing basket. Eighteen years of motherhood, forty-six years on the planet, and she's not sure she's ever reached the bottom of it.

Now that it is past midnight, it is officially the thirty-first of October. Halloween. Jen is standing on the landing, bare toes in thick carpet, pretending she isn't waiting up for Todd. He's eighteen. He can do *whatever he wants*. It is pure coincidence that Jen is also awake, here, peering out of the window that sits in the exact centre of their house.

She has spent the evening – and some of the night – catching up on the tedious tasks parenthood seems to demand of her. School-trip forms, ordering textbooks. She has interspersed this with a solid five hours of screen time and some googling of *eye floaters – worrying?*

Jen has always come to life at night. When everybody else seems to wind down, she opens up like a flower in the heat. She's even carved a pumpkin, which she sets down now on the windowsill.

She admires its cack-handed smile. Todd won't care, but the neighbours do. The school mums do. A pumpkin, sitting in that picture window, says *excuse me, we have our shit together.*

She hears her husband Kelly's feet on the landing above her and turns to look. It's unusual for him to be up, he the

441

lark and she the nightingale. He emerges from their bedroom on the top floor. His hair is messy, a blue-black in the dimness. He has on not a single piece of clothing, only a watch.

'Jesus,' he says, looking at the pumpkin on the windowsill, but he blows a smile out through the side of his mouth. 'Well, whatever makes you happy . . .' He descends the stairs towards her.

'The neighbours will see you,' Jen says, looking at him. A few of his dark chest hairs have turned white over the past year.

'I don't care,' he says with a grin and, as he turns, that perfect, perfect arse that she's loved for twenty years.

'Todd's not back,' she says.

Kelly checks his watch. 'It's early evening, for him,' he says. 'Whatever,' he adds, as he reaches the top stair.

'His curfew is one.' Jen looks at him.

Kelly just shrugs, then turns away from her.

'The neighbours can now see your arse.'

'They'll think it's one of your pumpkins,' Kelly says, his wit as fast and sharp as the slice of a knife. 'Come to bed? Can't believe Merrilocks is done,' he says with a stretch.

Kelly's been restoring a Victorian tiled floor at a house on Merrilocks Road all week, sending her photographs of the process, the grimy tiles, the mud dissolving, their eventual clean emergence. Jen and Kelly are big texters, always have been, their iMessages a private, detailed archive of their life. They text all day. They text from the living room to the kitchen. They send photos, videos, voice notes, anything. Earlier, he sent her just a video of the rain, slithering down a window. She keeps every single one.

'Sure,' she says. 'In a bit.'

442

She goes downstairs to make a herbal tea. She can never understand how people can go to bed when their children are out somewhere. She'll wait as long as it takes. Both phases of parenthood – the new-born years and the almost-adult ones – bookended by sleep deprivation. Jen drinks two cups of strawberry tea that taste of boiling water. She scrolls idly on her phone, just waiting. Doing nothing except waiting.

Back at the window, at almost two, she stares out into the October mist, wondering how late is so late that she should call.

But there he is, outside on the street, at last. Jen sees him just as Daylight Saving Time kicks in, and her phone switches from 01:59 to 01:00. She can't hide a smile: thanks to the clocks going back, he is deliberately no longer late. That's Todd for you; he finds the linguistic and semantic backflipping of arguing a curfew more important than the reason for it.

There he is, her boy so full of intellect that it has left no room for common sense, loping up the street, coming home. He's skin and bones, doesn't eat enough, consumes science and maths more than food. His knees poke angles in his jeans as he walks, a praying mantis.

But – wait. He isn't alone. He's meeting somebody. Is he? A hooded figure is making its way up the street from the other end. She watches her son and the stranger walking towards each other.

She shouldn't be looking. The lines of parenthood have become blurred in recent years. Bathroom doors now locked, phone screens shielded from view. This interaction is Todd's, as an adult. He doesn't know she can see from up here at her window. She should step back, but she doesn't. The same instinct that makes her wait up for him keeps her here, tethered to the window with her eyes. She places a hot palm on the cold glass, still waiting.

The mist outside is colourless, the trees and pavement black, the air a translucent white. A world in greyscale. Jen knows the last of the leaves clinging on to the trees are an ochre colour, but she can't see them. Their street – the back-end of Crosby, Merseyside – is unlit. Kelly installed a lamp outside their house, a Narnia lamp, and it clicks on as it detects their movement, illuminating the tops of their heads.

Todd has on black jeans, too-white trainers – huge feet – and a dark jacket with fur around the hood. He's reaching towards the other person, who, as he approaches the pavement outside Jen's house, she sees is actually a man; a grown adult, at least forty.

Something about their body language is off. Jen realizes something is about to happen without being able to name what it is; the same way she feels around fireworks and level crossings and cliff edges.

She sets the cup on the windowsill, next to the pumpkin, and takes the stairs two at a time, the striped stair runner rough on her bare feet. She shoves on shoes, then throws on a coat, and pauses for a second with her hand on the front door knob.

What's that? She shakes her head, confused. A feeling that there is more than one of her, of her having been here before, maybe. A gauzy curtain across her mind. *Déjà vu*. She hardly ever experiences it. She blinks, and the feeling is gone, as insubstantial as smoke from a distant fire on the breeze. What was it? Her hand on the brass knob? The lamp outside? No, she can't recall. It's gone now.

As she hurries out, the autumn cold chills her skin immediately. She hurries towards Todd and the man, hoping Kelly is still awake, that he's heard her leave and is coming, too. The thoughts rush through her mind like the clicking of a camera, one after the other after the other. She doesn't act on any of them, doesn't go back for Kelly. All she does is keep moving forwards, out on to the drive, maternal instincts pulling her towards her son with a force that feels as strong as gravity.

By the time she reaches the end of their U-shaped driveway, the man – taller than Todd, and bulkier, too – is shouting Todd's name, and suddenly Todd has the front of this stranger's coat in his grasp, is squaring up to him, his shoulders thrust forwards, their bodies a Yin and Yang sign in the night.

'What're you doing?' she shouts, and that's when she sees the knife.

She rushes towards them. Adrenaline sharpens Jen's vision as she sees it happen. A quick, clean stab. And then, afterwards, everything seems to move in slow motion: the arm pulling back, the clothing resisting then releasing the knife. Two white feathers emerge with the blade, drifting aimlessly in the frozen air.

She stares as black blood begins to spurt, huge amounts of it, way more than she would've thought possible. She must be kneeling down now, because she becomes aware of the little stones of the path cutting round divots into her knees. She cradling him, parting his jacket, feeling the heat of the blood as it dribbles down her hands, between her fingers, and down her wrists. The warm weight in her arms.

She has gone completely cold. She undoes his shirt and looks. His torso begins to flood; the three coin-slot wounds swim in and out of view, it's like trying to see the bottom of a red pond.

'No.' Her voice is thick and wet as she screams.

She looks around her desperately, wanting someone else to take charge.

She lays him on their driveway and leans over him. She blinks, peering carefully. She hopes she's wrong, but she's sure, for just a moment, that he isn't here anymore. His eyes are open and still, no comprehension in them.

The night is completely silent, and after what must be several minutes, she blinks, then looks up at her son, still holding the knife, just gazing down at her, his expression neutral. He drops the knife. It sings as the metal hits the frozen pavement. He wipes a hand across his face, leaving a smear of blood.

Jen stares at the arrangement of his features. Maybe he is regretful, maybe not. She can't tell. It must be the shock, but Jen never could read Todd.

Day Zero

Jen must have slept after they got home from the police station, where Todd was detained. She doesn't feel like she did, but it's now light outside, and time seemed to become elastic, bending and stretching between the hours.

She rolls on to her side. *Say it isn't true.*

She's alone. Kelly's side of the bed is empty. He'll already be up, making calls, she very much hopes. God, he will hate this. Kelly hates any sort of dealing with authority, sat in the reception of the station last night with his hood drawn entirely over his face.

446

Her clothes litter the bedroom floor like she evaporated out of them and disappeared. She steps over them, getting out new jeans and a plain jumper. Their bedroom is filled with warm autumnal light. The floorboards look glossy with it. Last night's mist has vanished without a trace.

Jen scrapes her hair back and ventures out on to the hallway, standing outside Todd's empty room.

Why did he do it? Why did he have a knife on him? Why did he do it outside their house? Who was he, this grown man her son tried to kill? Is he still alive?

Jen stares and stares at the door to her son's bedroom, lost in thought of how she came to raise a murderer.

Teenage rage. Knife crime. Gangs. Antifa. Which is it? Which hand have they been dealt?

She heads downstairs. She can't hear Kelly at all. She glances out of the window on the first floor as she descends their stairs, the window that she stood at only hours ago, while everything changed.

The street bears no stains – the rain must have washed the blood away. The ambulance and police have moved on. Even the police tape has gone.

She raises her eyes upwards, towards the blue autumn skies, then down again. Something is strange about their driveway, and not just the memories of last night. She can't work out what. But it's something.

She hurries downstairs. It smells of last night in here, before anything happened. Food, candles, cooking. She can't even remember what they had – she has a terrible memory, something Todd points out often.

She puts her hands on the kitchen counter and tries to breathe deeply.

She hears a voice, right above her, a deep male register. Kelly. She looks at the ceiling, confused. Where is he? Todd's room? He must be searching it.

'Kell?' she calls out, running back up the stairs. 'We need to get on – I'm going to google for a solic –'

'What?' a voice says. It comes from Todd's room, and is unmistakably his.

Jen takes a step back so massive it makes her stumble at the top of the stairs.

Todd emerges from the confines of his room, wearing a black t-shirt and jogging bottoms. He has clearly just woken, and squints down at her, his pale face the only light in the darkness.

'What?' she says to him. 'How are you here?'

'Huh?' he says. He looks just the same as he did. Not a mark on him. Even in her confusion, Jen is curious. Same navy-blue eyes. Same tousled hair. Same tall, slim frame. But he's committed an unforgivable act. Unforgivable to everyone, except maybe her. But how is he here? How is he home?

'What're you talking about?' he says. 'This is weird, even for you. A Jen out of ten.'

Jen sidesteps the inside joke. Not today. 'Did Dad get you? Are you on bail?'

'On *bail*?' He raises a disdainful eyebrow. It's a new mannerism of his, emerged since he started dating Clio. Jen wonders if it belongs to her. 'I'm about to meet Rory.'

'What?' Jen says in barely a whisper.

For the past few months he's looked different. Slimmer in the body, in the hips, but bloated in the face. The pallor somebody gets who is working too much, eating too many takeaways and drinking no water. None of which she is aware Todd is doing, but who knows? She steps towards him and looks closely at him. 'How did you get home – and what happened?'

'Home from where? Look – we're going for breakfast.'

He regularly goes for breakfast with them, these friends, like he's in an American sitcom. Jen wonders if it irritates her because it was an avenue never available to her.

'I . . .' Jen says, rubbing at her forehead. 'What happened last night?' she says. She looks around her, at the picture window and back at Todd.

He is staring at his phone, at a WhatsApp notification. He swipes on it, then begins typing. After he's finished, he says, 'I played *Call of Duty*,' as though she is a customer who will merely wait to be addressed. She feels a flare of temper.

'*What?*'

'I – what?'

'Stop avoiding it,' she says.

'Avoiding what?' Todd says. His expression twists in bemusement, nose wrinkles up just like when he was a baby.

'Your arrest.'

'My *arrest?*'

Jen can tell when her son is lying – she has had practise at that recently, as almost everything he says seems to be a lie – and he is definitely not lying at the moment. He looks at her with his clear twilight eyes, a question mark inscribed across his features.

'You were outside,' Jen says. She gestures to the mid-landing window. And that's the moment she realizes what the matter is with the scene. It isn't the driveway: it's the window itself. No pumpkin. It's gone.

Todd blinks at her slowly like an animal. He has two tiny scars left over from the worst of his teenage acne. Otherwise, his face is still childlike, pristine in that beautiful peach-fuzz way of the young.

'You were outside,' she says again, tearing her eyes away from the pumpkin-less windowsill that fires anxiety right down her body.

'When?' he says softly.

'I was waiting up for you,' she says, and for once he doesn't roll his eyes. Gone is the teenage attitude of recent times. He must be concerned about her to feel so in control of this conversation. His gaze holds hers.

'I wasn't out,' he says.

'The clocks went back. I was waiting on the landing. I saw you come back and you –'

'Hey?' Todd says loudly.

'What?'

He pauses, maintaining eye contact, exactly the way he did last night when it was him performing impossible tasks, not her. 'The clocks go back tonight.' He doesn't take his eyes off her. Some internal elevator plunges down the centre of Jen's chest. She pushes her hair off her face and heads to the family bathroom at the back of the house, holding up one finger to Todd for just a second.

She is sick into the toilet, the sort of sick she hasn't been in years. Alcohol sickness. Norovirus sickness. Hardly anything comes up, only a sticky yellow stomach acid that sits right at the bottom of the water. She stares and stares. Tries to think.

Todd does not know what she is talking about. That is clear. Even he wouldn't deny this. But why? How?

The pumpkin. The pumpkin is missing. Why does that feel so significant? Where the fuck is her husband?

She sits against the cold shabby tiles. It's forever on their list to renovate, but they never get to it. Kelly's own DIY never gets done.

She gets her phone out of her pocket and stares at it, bringing up the calendar.

It is the thirtieth of October. The clocks do indeed go back tonight, and tomorrow will be Halloween. Jen stares and stares at that date. How can this be? She was mistaken. All day yesterday, she'd thought it was the thirtieth, but it wasn't. It must have been the twenty-ninth. A simple error.

No pumpkin on the windowsill. And Todd in his bedroom, saying he has no idea what's going on. *Not* a simple error.

She navigates to her last text message with Kelly and presses *call*.

He answers warily, but immediately, as he has done for exactly the last six months. Since Nicola Williams. 'Look,' she says, a tiny, sarcastic laugh escaping.

'Baby – what?' She leans into his affection. Her husband, the romantic.

'Where are you?'

'At work,' he says. 'Why?'

'Was Todd arrested last night?'

'What?' She hears him put something heavy down on a hollow-sounding floor. 'For what?'

'No, I'm asking you. *Was* he?'

'No?' Kelly says, sounding utterly baffled.

'But we sat – we sat in the police station. You did your

451

coat up – your hood – right up over your head. The clocks had just gone back, I was . . . I had done the pumpkin.'

'Er,' Kelly says, for once lost for words.

'Wait – where are you?' she says.

'At work . . .'

'But where?'

'Merrilocks Road.'

He said he finished there yesterday. Didn't he? Yes, she's sure he did. He was naked as he said it. She can remember it. She *can*.

She puts her hand to her head. 'I don't know what's going on,' she says. 'What did we do? Last night?' She leans her head back against the wall. 'Did I do the pumpkin?'

'What are you –'

'I think I've had some sort of episode,' she says in barely a whisper. She brings her knees to her chest and stares at them. No impressions where she knelt on the gravel. Not a single speck of dirt on them. Goosebumps erupt up and down her arms.

'We . . .' Kelly says, thrown. 'You cooked a curry. Todd played on his X-Box.'

'No pumpkin carving?'

She hears Kelly shift the phone closer to his mouth. 'I thought you were going to do that tonight. Remember, you said you couldn't be arsed . . .'

'Right,' she says faintly, picturing how perfectly that pumpkin turned out, how he had looked at it.

She stands and stares at herself in the mirror. She looks haggard, but that is nothing new. Thin skin around her eyes, the hallmark of over-forty. A hunted look that she hasn't seen before. More than ever, she wonders what happened to the girl who met Kelly at the pedestrian crossing in 1999.

'Right, I better go,' she says. Kelly tries to interject, but she cuts him off, hangs up the phone. She needs to figure this out, alone, before she gets certified by her husband or son.

She leaves the bathroom and goes down to the kitchen, stopping dead in the hallway. A whole, un-carved pumpkin sits on the side. 'Oh,' Jen says to nobody, a tiny hiccough of a word, a giant syllable of understanding. She approaches the pumpkin as though it is an unexploded bomb and turns it around, but it's whole and firm and cool beneath her finger tips and Jesus Christ last night didn't happen. It didn't fucking happen.

Despite herself, something light moves across Jen's chest. She is a lottery winner, a bullet dodger, a pardoned criminal. It was a dream, a hallucination . . . nothing. No. It must have been a vivid dream.

Todd is upstairs, getting ready. Kelly is finishing the flooring job he actually finished yesterday. And Jen is here, having not carved a pumpkin, but having gone mad instead.

And that's when the thought arrives, fully formed. What if the weapon is in that bag? What if the bullet hasn't been dodged? What if the crime is *going* to happen? What if it was a premonition? The entire lived day, leading up to that horrible moment on the landing?

Jen goes hot and then cold. Exactly the same as she did when she diagnosed herself with epilepsy earlier today. It's probably anxiety. Made up, made up, made up.

Still, she glances up the stairs. Todd's in the shower. She can hear the water.

She grabs the rucksack. Not in eighteen years of

parenting has she gone through his things, but she does today. It's worth it. For her peace of mind or his, she isn't sure.

Front pockets, side pockets. Tuneless shower singing.

There are two folders and a pencil case in his bag, so adorably infantile something unspools in Jen's chest.

The water begins to run. He'll be ages. *Sprucing up.*

The bottom of the bag is lined with the crumbs from a thousand sandwiches before. She'll say she's cleaning it out, if he emerges.

If there is something suspicious in this bag then she is not mad but – but then what? She's psychic? Now that *is* a delusion.

She continues digging. Todd is as messy as she is and screwed up pieces of paper and discarded leaflets cut at the skin on her hands as she frantically digs.

And what's this? Right in the back? A sheath, a leather sheaf. It's as cold and hard as a thigh bone, sitting right there against the back of her son's rucksack. She knows what it will be before she pulls it out.

She breathes deeply, steeling herself, trying to calm down, then pulls at the sheaf, unbuttoning the top and sliding the handle out.

And – inside it . . . a knife. *The* knife.

She stands there, staring at it, at this betrayal in her hand. She hasn't thought what she would do if she found something. There is no way she can just leave it there. She can't take the risk that it was a weird dream, that it was nothing.

She's got to take it. Right?

She wrenches open the under-stairs cupboard. Shoes

and sports equipment crowd out and she fumbles with them, pushing the knife right to the back where it sits like a spectre. She can hear Todd on the stairs. She leans the knife against the back wall and retreats out of the cupboard.

Todd – wet hair, red cheeks, oblivious – picks up his bag. She watches him carefully, to see if he notices the difference, the lightness, but he doesn't seem to.

'I found a knife in Todd's bag,' Jen says, presenting it to her husband the second he arrives home that afternoon.

Kelly stands there in front of her, the knife held across his hands like some archaeological find, inspecting it.

'I didn't ask him about it,' she says. 'I just took it.'

Kelly nods, staring down at it, not saying anything. Jen remembers his heartbroken face from last night – no, from the night that didn't happen – and thinks she sees a milder version of it here, too. Kelly is a lover, not a fighter, one of life's romantics: he said on their first date, when he asked her question after question, that he thought they were going to be together forever.

And he'd been right. They'd made it. The whole way. Twenty years married, seasoned liberally – so liberally – with jokes, sex, laughter. Jen's eyes feel wet as she thinks about it, as she thinks about that fucking email from fucking Nicola Williams.

'It's brand new,' Kelly says, flicking those eyes to her.

'I know.'

'Unused.'

Jen laughs, a hard, unhumorous laugh. 'Right.'

'What?'

'The thing is.' She licks her lips.

'What did you mean earlier. On the phone?' Kelly says, soft Welsh accent spiking the consonants. She has always loved that accent.

'Well. I – I mean. I saw this happen.'

'You saw what happen?' He holds her gaze, waiting.

'I saw Todd stab somebody with this.'

'While you were asleep?'

'I wasn't asleep.'

'What,' he says, the word not lilting upwards, not a question, just a statement of disbelief.

'Yesterday, I carved a pumpkin and then waited up for Todd and he – he knifed someone, on the street.'

'But . . .' Kelly rubs a hand over his chin. 'But you didn't. You didn't do that.'

Jen turns away from him. 'I don't know what I did,' she says, thinking of that smooth, uncut pumpkin, thinking too of the knife. That knife is the only piece of evidence she has that she isn't crazy.

'Look, we'll just ask him about it. When he gets back,' Kelly says. 'And remind him that it's a firearms offence.'

Jen nods, saying nothing. What else can she do? Lock him up? Because of . . . because of what? It didn't happen. She looks at Kelly, whose expression she can't read. It hasn't yet happened.

Kelly's gone to bed, the same as he did yesterday, and Jen's stayed up. She has not carved the pumpkin, didn't want to, didn't want to connect the pumpkin and the murder, as though by not doing one thing it will stop the other.

She makes a different tea to last time, in a different mug. This mug says *Colonel Grumpy* on it, an insult she once levelled at Kelly in a fury that made her incoherent and – according to him – amusing. It's one of their things. Their in-jokes, enshrined forever on mugs. They have tens of them.

Eleven becomes midnight becomes one. The thirtieth ticks over into the thirty-first, just as it did last night. She spends the entire evening on her phone, flicking through celebrity *before and after surgery* photographs.

Three chamomile teabags into the kitchen bin. Three circulations of the living room clock.

Kelly wasn't where he said he was five months ago, the second time in six months that it's happened. He was with a woman called Nicola Williams. Jen knows because it flashed up on his phone while he was in the shower. 'Thanks for today x' it said. Nicola Williams is a depressingly common name, and Kelly has no social media, so Jen can't search his contacts. She is keeping her counsel about it for three reasons: one: because she knows, if he was innocent, that it would destroy him that she asked; two: because, if she confronts him now, he will likely hide further indiscretions before she can find them herself; and finally, three: because it would break her fucking heart if he said he loved someone else.

She bargains with the universe. Maybe not an affair. Let Todd be wayward, stupid about knives, but not a killer. And let this not be extramarital sex. Anything but sex.

Her eyes become heavy at half past one. She thought the adrenaline would carry her through, but it doesn't. She knows it was nothing. A random event that will be consigned to the past. A dream. A bit of confusion. Stress, maybe, her brain's way of escaping her real problems. Now that it's late, and the mug is different, the tea different, she can see that this is ridiculous. This bedtime vigil.

457

Besides, she's got the knife, shoved right into the back of their cupboard. He can't use it. And maybe, maybe, maybe it was something else, she thinks. Some art project. Or just a mistake.

At ten to two, she goes to the middle landing. She can hear Kelly snoring softly above her.

She watches, not blinking, her eyes burning, standing at the window. This time, she has no mug. No pumpkin. This time, she thinks, it will be different. She has her shoes on. She is ready.

01:59 becomes 01:00. 01:01.01:02. She relaxes completely.

Until 01:11. And then he arrives, loping up the street exactly as before, only eleven minutes later.

She runs out on to the drive just as Todd reaches the stranger. He's already got it out, is holding the knife in his right hand, ready.

He reaches the man and draws the blade back, and then it plays out exactly as before. The three stabs, the wound. The blood.

He drops the knife, which strikes a high note on the pavement. She looks at Todd, then at the knife, kneeling down to touch it. It's different. It still has the white plastic tag on the end which she holds in her hand. She stares at it while the death plays out, which Jen is already less affected by than yesterday. The tag says it is an Asda chef's knife. Bought earlier today, she assumes, because she took the first knife. It probably took eleven minutes.

Jen blinks again, and then she is gone. When she wakes up, it isn't day Zero, but Day Minus One. The day before the day before.